Six Crystal Princesses

Six Crystal Princesses

A XANTH NOVEL

Piers Anthony

OPEN ROAD

INTEGRATED MEDIA

NEW YORK

978-1-5040-6690-7

Published in 2022 by Open Road Integrated Media, Inc.
180 Maiden Lane
New York, NY 10038
www.openroadmedia.com

Six Crystal Princesses

Chapter 1

MISSION

Vinia sat beside Prince Ion as he slept, holding his hand. His hair was blond, and so were his eyes when open, in contrast to her dull brown eyes. He was a year younger than she, but a bit larger in body. She loved him, but that was only part of it. She needed to be close to him, because she was hyperallergic, and his ambiance abolished all allergens, so she could, literally, breathe freely only in his presence. Connecting with him had opened much of the cosmos to her, literally. He was a prince and a Magician, while she was nothing, but he loved and valued her. They were perfect for each other and had known it from the first moment they interacted, two years before.

Vinia smiled reminiscently. They had met, and she had learned that he was disabled. There had been an accident that crushed his legs, and he had not been able to use healing elixir to fix them because he was immune to all elixirs, good and bad. But she knew she could fix that, in her fashion, because of her telekinesis. She had put her hands on him and lifted him up, using her magic to make his legs support him. Then she had realized that in her excitement she had committed a social breach, touching a prince when she herself was the commonest of commoners, and tried to apologize. But he, pleased with the ability to stand that she brought him, had kissed her to shut her up. Then he started to demur, feeling that she would not want to associate with someone who couldn't walk, until she kissed him back to shut *him* up. Then they had gazed into each other's eyes, and kissed a third time, mutually impelled—and a little heart had flown up. They were only nine and ten at the time, but the hearts always knew: they were for each other. The others with them had seen the heart and accepted its message. They had been happily together ever since. His family accepted her, especially his sister, Hilda, a princess and Sorceress in her own right, because she truly loved her brother and wanted him to be happy, and Vinia's presence had lifted a burden from her.

But Vinia had a problem. She and Ion formed a tightly knit quartet with Hilda and her boyfriend, Benny. Benny was one of the Animalia, a human/Caprine crossbreed. Benny had known of Vinia, who had visited the planet Animalia as a tourist and stayed because she loved the human/Equine folk, loving horses though she could not get out to ride one because of the allergies. He had brought Ion and Hilda to meet Vinia, and there followed what followed. That was why Vinia liked Benny. He was pleasant and personable and helpful, but it was that giant favor he had done her that won her unending gratitude. Now she had a life!

She looked again at Ion. In perhaps seven years the two of them would be of age, and probably he would marry her, and she would become a princess. But that wasn't what brought her the main joy. It was that he truly needed her, as she needed him; they were a perfect complementary couple. To need and be needed, that was the essence. All else was secondary.

But that was also the problem. Hilda had sewn Benny a thinking cap. That was her talent as a Sorceress; she could sew things with marvelous magic. She had made Ion a little magic carpet, which he had used to travel everywhere. If Hilda sewed a woman a kitchen apron, that person became a phenomenal cook. If she sewed a party dress, the girl who wore it became so sexy as to freak out any man in range.

Benny had tried out the thinking cap, of course. And come privately to Vinia. "My first idea: Hilda could sew Ion a pair of walking socks," he said. "Like walking boots, only these would fit under the boots. They should enable him to walk on his own."

Vinia felt a nasty chill. With such socks, Ion would no longer need her!

"I see you understand," he said. "I haven't mentioned this idea to anyone. I needed to talk to you first."

"Yes. Thank you," she responded, stricken. "Please, I need some time to think about it."

"I will not mention it to anyone else. It is your decision." For Benny was the soul of discretion, and he never betrayed his friends.

Now Vinia was thinking about it. She wanted what was best for Ion, of course, but this might make him better off without her. That could destroy her. If the idea had occurred two years ago, before she had fallen totally in love with him, maybe she could have survived it, but now she knew that without Ion she would not want to live. Her choice was stark: tell him, and lose him and herself, or be silent, carrying the guilt of her secret. It was overwhelming.

Ion woke. "Vinia!" he exclaimed. "You're crying. Did I do something to hurt you?"

"Oh no, no, Ion," she said immediately. "You are blameless."

"I had an awful dream that I lost you. Oh, Vin, I couldn't stand that. I couldn't be happy without you."

She had to tell him. "Hilda could sew you a pair of walking socks, so you could walk on your own. Then you wouldn't need me anymore."

He gazed at her half a moment. "Oh, Vin, put your dear mind at rest. We thought of that long ago and tried it. But the socks had wills of their own, going where they wanted to go regardless what I wanted, and sometimes they tripped, dumping me. We knew early on it was no go." He took a breath. "But more important, do you think I need you only for your telekinesis? I love you! You support me so much more than physically. If I could walk on my own, I would still want to walk with you. The only way we'll ever separate is if you tire of me."

"Oh, no, never!"

"So Hilda sewed me the flying carpet. She had a better template for that, and it was more responsive to my will, and I was quite satisfied with it, until you came on the scene. The socks were more ad hoc, and unruly." He looked at her sharply. "Did you really think that I would dump you if I found a better way to walk?"

Vinia had thought that. She should have known better. Ion was way finer than that. She had judged him unfairly. "I'm so ashamed," she sobbed.

"Yet you told me anyway."

"I had to." Her shame was forming a little cloud around her.

Ion nodded. "Come here," he said, reaching for her.

She joined him, lying on the bed, and cried into his shoulder while he held her close. Gradually she subsided into sleep. Her last thought was how adults seemed to think that children lacked real emotions, such as love. How wrong they were!

In the morning Vinia woke to Ion's kiss. "I will explain to Benny," he said.

"Then we need discuss this no further." Because he was sparing her the embarrassment of her confusion.

They talked with Benny and Hilda. Benny looked like a young human man, but he was only one-third human, two-thirds Caprine, and could change to goat form when he chose. He was adult, but this required some interpretation, because while a human person was considered adult at age eighteen, a goat was adult at age three. Each Caprine year was equivalent to about six human years, at least in youth. Thereafter the ratio diminished, further complicating the comparison. Since he was a crossbreed, his age was a matter of opinion. He looked twenty-four, but chronologically he was six. Crossbreed math was recognized, so he was accepted as adult, but he had existed only a bit more than half as long as Hilda. The others understood this and were mum about it, as there was no point in confusing strangers, and there were times when his being recognized as adult was useful.

All the Animalia were considered animals, without the rights of humans, and all desired to achieve those rights by breeding children who would be more than half human, and thus recognized as human. Benny had been assigned to accompany Hilda on planet Animalia, to assist her in any way she needed, but also perhaps to persuade her to remain there and breed with him when she came of age. Any children of theirs would be two-thirds human. So he was highly personable, handsome as a man, with a white stripe on his brown hair that lent it character. Vinia had once seen a picture of Benny's ancestors, and one was a Toggenburg goat with a similar stripe. He had a neat goatee.

What, then, of his being constantly close to Hilda? Here again his Animalian training and discipline counted. He had the physical capabilities of an adult man, but Benny never treated Hilda with anything but absolute respect. The only time when she was annoyed with him was when she wanted to know what was on the other side of the dread Adult Conspiracy to Keep Interesting Things from Children. He knew but declined to tell her. Her folks knew he honored the Conspiracy, which was why they trusted him.

"So you see," Ion concluded, "your thinking cap is as yet new, and not all its ideas are fully informed. This one was not apt, but the next one may be. We do appreciate your courtesy in telling Vinia privately, so that she could think it through and make her own decision. She decided to tell me." He did not mention the rest of it.

"I see that now," Benny said. "Thank you for clarifying it."

"There is no need to discuss the matter any further," Ion said. That was code for keep your mouth shut, and Benny would honor it. There was a fair amount of silence in their tightly knit quartet.

"Do we have any other business?" Hilda inquired. This was her way of suggesting that they change the subject.

"If I may," Vinia said tentatively.

"Of course you may," Hilda said. "You're our dearest girl. Out with it."

"I have long been curious how your parents met. They seem so happy with each other, with never a hesitation or quarrel. Is there some secret there for the rest of us, when our time comes?"

Hilda smiled. "Hardly. It was sheer complicated chance that brought them together, and even when they were together, they didn't know they were destined for each other, even though they were betrothed as infants."

"How could that be?" Vinia asked in genuine wonder.

"It's a long story. The essence is that they ran afoul of forget whorls left over when the big forget spell on the Gap Chasm dissipated and forgot. Our father, Hilarion, set out looking for his betrothed, but forgot his age and her name, so he seemed to be a generation younger than she and did not recognize her. Ida, our mother, meanwhile set out to see the Good Magician Humfrey. On the way there she got lost, and at one point was captured by a dragon and frozen in a crystal along with half a dozen other princesses. She was rescued by chance and continued her excursion. Then she traveled to Castle Roogna and met her sister, Princess Ivy, only then discovering that she herself was a princess. Then the little moon Ptero came to orbit her head, representing her Sorceress-level talent of the Idea. All the ideas and all the people who had ever existed or might have existed in Xanth were to be found on Ptero and its moons and could be met if a person arranged to adapt and visit. Ida met Prince Hilarion and liked the young man. Then they discovered that he was her age and her betrothed. They kissed and that was it. They have been happy together ever since."

Vinia was perplexed. "I thought that in Xanth men had sons and women had daughters, as indicated by the first letter of their names.

Shouldn't you, Hilda, begin with an I for Ida, and Ion begin with an H for Hilarion?"

Ion laughed. "We guess that this was a trace effect of their original confusion. Somehow the names got mixed up, and it can't be changed. We're satisfied, regardless. Or maybe I am my mother's son, and Hilda is her father's daughter. It seems it can happen, even in Xanth."

"Or at least in our adjacent Kingdom of Adamant," Hilda said.

"Weird," Vinia said, laughing.

"But it still leaves us bored with palace life, with the obsequious servants and set routines that keep us constantly on show as useless royalty," Hilda said. "I miss the kind of adventures we had two years ago, when we got loose on our own. I wish we had a pretext to get out and go on a Quest or something."

Benny put on his thinking cap. A light bulb flashed over his head. "I have an idea," he announced.

Hilda fondly touched his hand. "As if that wasn't brightly evident. What is it?"

"Those other six crystallized princesses—were they rescued?"

"No, only Ida. It was mostly an accident that broke open her crystal."

"Then shouldn't they be rescued too? Aren't they similarly deserving?"

The others shared a three-way glance that soon crystallized into something more tangible. "What *about* those other princesses?" Ion asked. "They shouldn't be frozen in crystals forever."

"Then isn't that your Quest?" Benny asked. "To rescue them from the dragon?"

"Indeed," Hilda agreed, her eyes glowing like crystals themselves.

It seemed to be up to Vinia to bring some common sense into this developing notion. "But would your folk allow it? Dragons are dangerous."

"I've got potions to handle dragons," Ion said.

"And I can sew us fireproof vests," Hilda added.

"But you're *children*."

"As it happens, there is an adult member of our party."

Six eyes turned on Benny. "I'm six years old, chronologically," he reminded them.

"An adult Caprine," Ion said. "There is precedent."

"But it's chancy," Vinia said. "Depending on how they choose to see him."

Hilda nodded. "We need advice."

Benny put the thinking cap back on. There was another flash. "Squid!" he said. "She's traveled a lot as a child, and surely she knows how to handle parents."

Ion reached into a small bag he brought from a pocket. Vinia knew that bag; it was another of Hilda's sewings. It looked small, but it contained everything Ion wanted to put in it, which was a lot. He had extra food supplies in there, and changes of clothing, and folded tents. And his collection of elixirs. He was immune to all elixirs, which meant they couldn't help or hurt him directly, but they affected others. When Vinia had tripped and fallen and scraped her knee, Ion had brought out a vial of healing elixir that mended her knee nicely, when she got out of his range and applied it. But how did this relate to Squid?

Ion found the vial he wanted. "Essence of Squid," he announced. "Who wants to do the honor?"

"I'll do it," Hilda said, taking the vial. She cleared a place in front of her, then poured one drop of essence on the floor. "Invoke," she said.

The drop puffed into vapor, which rose and swirled, forming into a floating cuttlefish with its tentacles spread. Then it put them together, two by two, forming arms and legs. The main mass of it became a body and a head. It stood on the floor, orienting, shaping further into a thirteen-year-old girl with dull brown hair and eyes like Vinia's. She was an animation, but she seemed to be becoming aware of them.

"Hello, Squid," Hilda said. "We are Ion and Hilda, with our friends Vinia and Benny, here in Castle Adamant."

The figure spoke. "I remember. Benny's Caprine. Vinia's telekinetic. Ion's immune to elixirs. Hilda's Xanth's best seamstress."

"That's us," Hilda agreed. "We used a drop of your essence to summon your image for a consultation. We need advice."

A faint man-shaped cloud appeared beside Squid. "It's okay, Chaos," Squid said. "These are friends."

The cloud nodded and faded.

"Demon Chaos is my boyfriend," Squid explained. "He wants to be sure I don't get into trouble."

Vinia nodded inwardly. Word had circulated. Chaos was the strongest of all the Demons, and he loved Squid. The universe would shake, literally, if anything happened to her. But he preferred to stay out of her business, satisfied to observe. He was still learning the intricacies of mortal social life.

"But first tell us where you've been," Hilda said. "The news was that you disappeared for several months, and no one knew where you were. We are curious as bleep." As a child she couldn't say "hell," though she knew the term; the notorious Adult Conspiracy forbade it, along with other pointless restrictions evidently designed to make children feel inferior.

"Readily answered," Squid said. "I was called away to solve a murder mystery. I couldn't decline, because it was my own murder, on another track of Xanth."

"You were murdered!"

"On a different track. There are millions of tracks, and this was the only one where that happened. Still, it wasn't something I could just ignore. So we went, and it was a future track, where I was of age, so I married Larry, who is also Chaos, to lure the murderer back. It worked, and we caught him. Then I made the murderer take over as protagonist until I was ready to forgive him. But no need to bore you with that story. Now it's done, and we're home. And young again, more's the pity. Now what's this advice you need from me?"

It was plain that Hilda wanted to know more about that other track, as did they all, but also plain that Squid had said as much about that as she cared to. She had been of age, and married her boyfriend, so she must have learned all the Conspiracy secrets! But she wouldn't tell those either. How Vinia envied her! "We want to go rescue six princesses from their crystals," Hilda continued. "The way our mother, Princess Ida, was rescued, but there's a dragon in the way. Should we try?"

Squid paused half a moment. Vinia realized that she was communing with Chaos, who could instantly gather the background information she needed. Then she spoke. "That's Dragoman Dragon. He's not a bad sort, as dragons go. He doesn't eat maiden princesses, he collects them. But you will have to meet his terms to rescue the princesses, and that may not be easy. The Quest is worthwhile, but you need to clear it with the Good Magician first."

Ion laughed. "First we have to clear it with our folks. That's the real hurdle."

"We'll put in a word for you." Then Squid's eye happened to connect directly with Vinia's eye. She froze. "Oh, my," she murmured.

Vinia was startled. What did this famous girl care about her? They had met only briefly two years before.

Then Squid broke the connection. She glanced around. "Bye." She dissolved into vapor and faded out.

There was a silence stretching a good moment and a half.

Then Hilda spoke. "Why did she break it off so suddenly?"

"Something occurred to her," Ion said.

"Yes. But what?"

"Aren't you a maiden princess?" Benny asked nervously.

Vinia saw his point. What was to stop the dragon from trying to collect Hilda herself and crystallize her?

"Ion can give me some antidragon elixir," Hilda said. "That should protect me."

She had confidence. Was it justified? Vinia loved Ion, but she also loved Hilda in a sisterly way and didn't want her to get hurt either.

"Still, this may be nervous business," Benny said.

"Squid knows something we don't," Ion said.

It was time to shift the subject slightly. "First things first," Vinia said. "Getting your folks' permission."

"That's Mom," Ion said. "Dad's away on business today."

"Maybe think about it for a day or two?" Benny asked with slight hope. He had suggested the Quest, but Vinia understood his hesitation now that it was turning real. The girl he loved was going to put herself at serious risk. Vinia was not completely easy about it herself, as her ongoing thoughts indicated. Sometimes she wished she could turn off her mind for a while so she could relax.

"Why waste the time?" Hilda asked rhetorically. She headed for the door.

So much for that. They followed her into the hall. Vinia put one arm around Ion and engaged her power, making his feet walk in step with her. It was routine, whenever he walked, but she still loved doing it, and she knew he loved doing it too. It was a pretext for continuing closeness they both valued.

Then Ion looked at her, realization dawning. "You're the protagonist!"

"I'm the what?"

"The main character of the story. The viewpoint person. The one who sees and hears everything, without necessarily affecting it. Squid was the protagonist two years ago: she knows how it is. She recognized you. She has a notion what you're in for."

"What am I in for?" Vinia asked, frightened.

"We don't know. But there are rules. The protagonist always survives to the end of the story. And there always *is* a story, a big one."

"Like maybe rescuing six crystallized princesses?"

"Maybe. It's awesome."

Hilda looked back. "Hey, slowpokes! You trying to sneak in a kiss while we're not looking?"

"Don't tell her!" Vinia said desperately. "Please. I need time to sort this out."

Ion nodded. "You caught us," he called back to his sister. He put his face to Vinia's face, and they kissed. He was covering for her. She loved that about him, among other things: his loyalty to her.

They hurried to catch up.

A palace servitor bowed, his way of inquiring what they wanted.

"Please inform Queen Ida that we are on the way for an audience," Hilda said. No one else could just barge in on the queen, but they were her children.

He faded out.

When they arrived at the audience chamber, Queen Ida was there. Vinia saw her little moon circling her head, just outside her petite gold crown. That would have been an oddity anywhere but here. "Yes, dear; what is your concern?"

Now Hilda deferred to her brother, glancing at him. So Vinia and Ion stepped up to face the queen. "We want to go rescue the six other princesses who were crystallized with you, way back when."

The queen glanced at them, her gaze touching each in turn, and pausing fractionally at Vinia. "Oh, my," Ida murmured.

She knew!

Ion saw that pause, so like Squid's pause, and understood. Vinia knew that Ida herself, a Sorceress in her own right, might have been a protagonist at some time, so was alert for the signals. Vinia averted her gaze.

"I suppose it does get dull for you children, here in the palace," Ida said. "But you should at least travel with an adult."

"Benny's adult," Hilda said promptly.

The queen of course knew all about Benny. Would she accept him in that capacity?

"Perhaps that will do," Ida said.

Now Hilda was suspicious; she knew her mother well. "What, no argument?"

Ida smiled. "Your friend Squid was by, with her adult boyfriend. They seemed to feel that you would be safe enough."

Oh. Because the protagonist would be along, making the safety of the party more likely. Chaos might even have checked an alternate track, a future one, to get an indication.

"Squid said she'd put in a word," Ion said.

"She did. And Chaos left some little bombs for you, just in case. I will give them to you now."

"Bombs?" Hilda asked.

"These are small, invisible, and largely immaterial," Ida said. "Until invoked. Then they generate chaos nearby, for everyone but the detonator. Things go wrong. Confusion abounds. If a dragon were about to bite you, this might cause it to accidentally bite a stink horn instead."

They all laughed. Stink horns were Xanth's worst-smelling plants, absolute disasters to step on, especially indoors or close by. A squashed stink horn made a foul-smelling noise and a hideously filthy stench. That could indeed help protect them and was a nice little gift from the Demon.

Ida held out her hand, as if holding something, though it seemed empty except for a faint glimmer. "They will not be evident on you. They are invoked only by a thought. Do not use them carelessly."

Ion reached out and took the glimmer. It disappeared. Then Vinia did the same. There was a tiny tingle, then it was gone.

They stepped back, and Hilda and Benny took their bombs.

"Now it is time for dinner," Ida said. It was the middle of the day, but dinner was whenever Ida said it should be. Vinia realized she was hungry.

They settled down to a private meal with the queen, catered by the palace staff. The drinks were boot rear, of course, the beverage with a kick in it; all children and some adults liked it. There was a fresh salad with Nine Hundred and Ninety-Nine Island dressing: a rumor hinted that Mundania had found the last island, but who believed that? Square onion soup.

Footsie rolls, which looked like bare feet. Floating baked air potatoes. And pink eye scream for dessert. Dully routine food, but that was palace life.

That afternoon they made their preparations for the journey. Hilda gathered voluminous threads and giant needles and sewed a full-size magic carpet, like Ion's small one, but large enough for all four of them. Vinia assisted in any which way she could, bringing more rolls of basic material and more spools of thread as Hilda needed them. The magic was not in the material, or the thread, or the needles, but in the princess's sewing; the carpet was imbued with the essential magic as she worked. What gradually took shape was the basic carpet, hovering just above the floor, a magic cloth guardrail to prevent accidental stepping off, a canopy, steering bar, reclining deck chairs, and even a private curtained privy consisting of another endless-capacity bag that would hold solid and liquid refuse without apparent weight or odor. They would be able to poop and pee without pausing in their flight.

Vinia was amazed yet again by the sorcery. Hilda could do so much, yet never bragged about it, any more than Ion did about his magic. They just did it as needed and were otherwise normal children.

They boarded the carpet and sat in the chairs, Ion at the steering bar. They took off smoothly, flying up and out an open skylight. It was dusk, and the forested skyline was lovely. They hovered just above the trees.

"We all should practice handling the craft," Ion said. "Just in case there is a disruption." He passed the bar to Vinia. It was not attached to anything.

She was so surprised she almost dropped it. "But, but where do I go?" she asked somewhat plaintively.

"Just sail around, getting the feel of it." Ion closed his eyes as if for a nap.

Vinia took a firm grip and slowly moved the bar. The carpet slowly turned in that direction. She reversed it, and the carpet followed suit. She tilted it slightly back, and the carpet smoothly rose higher. She tilted it the other way, and the carpet descended. She squeezed it, and the carpet accelerated. This was fun!

Soon she passed the bar on to Benny, and he put the carpet through its motions. Then Hilda, who had sewn it but not flown it before. Now they all knew how to do it.

There was a rumble of thunder. In two and a half moments an angry-looking storm cloud headed their way.

Ion took back the wheel and smiled. He steered the carpet straight into the cloud. Lightning jags radiated and thunder crashed all around them, but nothing struck them, not even any spatter of rain. He zoomed it right into the heart of the cloud, and turbulent darkness surrounded them, but there was still no contact.

Ooo, the storm was mad! But it could do nothing. Soon it departed in a huff.

"It's immune to weather," Hilda said. "I sewed in a spell."

They parked the carpet by putting it a continuing circle high above the forest and retired for the night. Ion opened a vial and let out a waft of vapor. "Invisibility elixir," he said. "No one will bother us."

The twins seemed to have thought of everything. But they had traveled before, many times, and knew what they were doing.

Vinia joined Ion on his bed mat, and Benny joined Hilda.

This whole excursion was amazing. "This is so thrilling," Vinia murmured.

Ion kissed her. "I love being with you. The only thing I still wish for—"

"We're too young," she whispered. She had known what all men wanted, even the boys, having taken an orientation course on planet Animalia, which specialized in catering to lusty tourists.

"You could make it happen, the same way you make me walk."

Her telekinesis. She hadn't thought of using it in precisely that manner, but it could be done. She could make a man of him, as it were. "Yes. But no."

"No one need know."

"Pause and consider," Vinia said. "Do you really think your mother would let you go out into the wilderness with a girl who wasn't your sister without taking precautions? Without making sure she knew exactly what you were up to every minute of the day and night? She's the Sorceress of the Idea. Do you think there's any idea you might have that she did not anticipate?"

"Oh, bleep!" he swore.

He was the prince and the Magician, while she was just a nondescript girl. But sometimes she governed their relationship. Vinia suspected that Ion would not care to have it otherwise.

"She's right, you know," Hilda said from the nearby darkness. "Nobody sneaks any ideas past Mom."

Ion sighed. He knew it was true.

Vinia was sure that Hilda and Benny had had a similar dialogue well before this time, with him being the sensible one. Ida did not extend her trust carelessly. No mother did.

Still, the Adult Conspiracy could be a nuisance. If Vinia could have it her own way, with no outside censure, she would do it this instant with Ion, just as Benny would with Hilda. Childhood could be a burden.

In the morning they discussed it briefly and decided to take the scenic route to the Good Magician's Castle. For example, neither Vinia nor Benny had ever seen the famed Gap Chasm. For half a century it had been neglected, being under a forget spell, but when that had finally dissipated, it had become a tourist attraction. The dread Gap Dragon, a descendant of the original one Princess Ivy had pacified, had become almost tame, enjoying the notoriety.

They breakfasted on tomato chips and people crackers, took turns visiting the privy, washing up, dressing, then doused the invisibility spell because it also made the outside realm invisible to them, messing up traveling.

Xanth came into view in all its morning splendor. The sun was glowing behind cloud cover, perhaps doing its own pooping and washing up, girding itself for its arduous climb up into the sky, and the pale mists were sinking into shadows. They angled down to get a better view of the scenery below, the fields and streams and maidens washing in the puddles, then set off north, for the Gap Chasm.

A screech of harpies spotted them and flew in close. "Look at this!" one screeched (of course). "A giant flying carpet! With children on it! Let's have some fun with them!" However, their idea of fun was unlikely to be child's play.

Ion sat at the prow. "Desist, bird brains! This is a private conveyance."

The dirty birds screeched their coarse laughter. The nearest one oriented on the boy, her very gaze filthy. "Private, is it, innocent lad? We'll show you some privates!" She flipped backward to expose her tail section, spreading the feathers. This would have been a violation of the Conspiracy, but harpies did not much honor it, anyway, except in the mocking of it, and bird anatomy hardly counted.

"Second warning," Ion said. "Desist annoying us and go your way in peace."

"Did he say piece?" another harpy screeched. "How's this for a piece?" She thrust her bare bosom forward and inhaled. Vinia had to concede that she had pretty good breasts, exactly the kind that a boy Ion's age should not get to peek at.

"Get back out of range," Ion warned the others. "The privy curtain will shield you."

They crowded into the privy together, to the raucous laughter of the harpies. Vinia was able to see some detail through the curtain. "Look! The kids are hiding!"

"Or pooping!"

"They're party poopers!" The implications were filthier than the words.

Ion uncapped a vial and blew its emerging mist at the harpies. They laughed as the vapor expanded into a faintly roiling cloud. "You think to tease us with a puff of bottled air? We'll give you air!" Several presented their backsides, making rude noises. The thing about harpies was that they were dirty in mind as much as in body. Ion merely waited.

Then they started choking and retching. "Yuck!" one gasped. "What is that odor?"

"Essence of stink horn," Ion answered. He breathed deeply. "Exhilarating, isn't it." He was of course immune to this, as it was a kind of elixir.

The harpies tumbled out of the air, retching uncontrollably. They were amateurs, compared to a stink horn. The lack of the foul sound and hideous color had fooled them into basking in it. They were wise too late.

Even in the protected locale of the privy, Vinia smelled half a whiff. It was the worst stench she had encountered in years. Rotten vomit soaked in parboiled day-old goblin poop after a feast on soiled has beans did not begin to describe it. But she wasn't sorry for the harpies. Ion had warned them.

They flew on, leaving the noxious cloud behind, admiring the colorful fields and forests. The land of Xanth was lovely from this perspective. Ion and Hilda were used to it, but Benny and Vinia gazed down in virginal awe. There were so many intriguing details!

Then a large fire-breathing dragon spied the carpet. Maybe it had seen what happened to the harpies, as it circled them without approaching closely.

"Begone, dragon," Ion commanded.

Instead the dragon oriented and inhaled, readying a blast. Uh-oh. Dragons did not take human directives well. It could toast them from well beyond the range of anything like stink horn stench.

Ion did not seem to be concerned. He reached into his bag and brought out a small glowing ball. He set it on the carpet in front of him. "I call this the mini-nova effect," he explained. "I've been waiting for a chance to use it."

"Nova?" Vinia asked nervously. She was not familiar with the term.

"I traded with an old elf mage: a vial of high-grade youthening elixir for it. I thought it might be useful someday."

That didn't help much. They would just have to see what happened.

"Invoke," Ion said.

The ball abruptly expanded into a sparkling translucent sphere that surrounded the carpet. The dragon saw that and smiled, baring its deadly teeth. It was sure that a thin glassy ball would not withstand a direct fire strike. Then it sent its white-hot spear of fire.

Vinia tried not to flinch as the spear smote the sphere, knowing that Ion knew his business. She saw Benny and Hilda similarly nervously unflinching. She saw it strike.

The sphere flared hugely, making an expanding flame that scorched everything in a wide radius. Vinia could see the dust in the air exploding into ash, and the air itself magically transforming into some other element. The scorch touched the dragon, illuminating it in fire. The dragon was a fire creature, largely immune to heat, but this was clearly of a new order of intensity. Just as the harpies had been no match for stink horn elixir, the dragon was no match for the nova. It fell, its wings burned to crisps, its scales glowing with residual heat. The creature seemed to have survived as it bounced on the ground and wriggled away, trailing ash; it could grow new wings. But it would not bother them again.

In fact, no dragon would try to harass them again. Word would get around. Ion was a Magician, and no one with any sense knowingly messed with magic of that caliber.

Now maybe they had half a notion what a nova was. If this were mini, what would a full-size one be like? Vinia hesitated even to try to imagine that.

Nothing aboard the carpet was affected. The glassy sphere had protected it.

"A nova," Hilda said weakly, obviously as bewildered as Vinia was.

"It's a bit like a black hole, only its force is outward rather than inward," Ion explained. "The protective sphere is roughly analogous to an event horizon."

"Thank you for that clarification," Benny said, similarly confused.

"You're welcome," Ion said. A bit of a hidden smile was hovering in the vicinity.

They flew on without further event, the Xanth horizon unaffected. Soon they came to the famed Gap Chasm.

Benny and Vinia plunged into renewed awe, while the twins watched tolerantly. The Chasm was a phenomenal cleft in the ground, descending a mundane mile or so to a floor overgrown with trees and lesser vegetation. It was obviously a whole separate ecosystem, only tenuously connected to the terrain on either side.

"Let's see the Gap Dragon," Hilda said. "But make us invisible so it's private. We don't want others to know we're on a quest."

"Right," Ion agreed.

"But do let us see out, this time."

"Got it. I have a one-way shield." He fished in his bag and brought out a miniature shield. He set this on the carpet. "Invoke."

The shield expanded, surrounding them. But they could see through it, as they coasted down almost to the ground. Was it really working?

"Let me verify," Benny said. He changed to Caprine form, a handsome buck goat with white patches on his brown fur, then lowered his horny head and leaped off the carpet to the ground. Vinia was a quarter way startled: she knew he could change, and had seen it before, but he had remained in human form while staying at the palace and she had gotten used to his human aspect. All crossbreeds could switch between their ancestral forms; it was their magic.

The buck turned about and gazed back at the carpet for two-thirds of a moment. Then he shook his head. Then he reverted to human form. "I can't see or hear you," he called. "You'll have to throw me a line."

Hilda unwound some thread on a spool, then threw the spool toward Benny while holding on to the end. It landed on the ground before him.

"Thanks," he called as he picked up the spool. Then he followed it as Hilda reeled him in. He passed through the shield. "Ah, there you are," he said, now seeing them. "You are completely invisible from outside. There was just brush."

"No brush-off," Hilda said, the semblance of a smile hovering nearby.

They resumed motion, elevating above tree level. Ion brought out another artifact, this one a little disk with a needle pointing in no special direction. "General purpose compass," he explained. "Gap Dragon." This was evidently another item he had traded for. Potent elixirs could fetch in just about anything.

The needle immediately oriented, pointing a specific direction. They went that way and soon heard a kind of whomping, as if something heavy was being thrown repeatedly on the ground. Then they saw it: a long snakelike dragon with three pairs of legs, at front, middle, and rear. It was a steamer, with wisps of steam rising from its mouth as it breathed. This was the dread Gap Dragon, the scourge of the separate realm of the Gap. It moved by lifting its front end, then its middle, and finally its rear, in the manner of an inchworm but on a larger scale, each section whomping as it landed. It looked inefficient, but the creature was moving right along and could surely catch any prey it went after. Vinia was impressed.

The dragon whomped to a stop. The ferocious head looked their way. How could it see them?

Then it lifted a sign board from somewhere. Words appeared printed on it. HELLO IDA'S OFFSPRING.

Vinia and Benny froze in shock. The dragon knew they were there!

Hilda brought out a section of cloth from her purse. "Hello, Gap Dragon," she said, and the words appeared on the cloth: HELLO, GAP DRAGON. "How did you know we were here?" She dangled the cloth outside the shield.

I SMELLED YOU, HILDA. YOU FORGOT TO MASK YOUR ODORS. WHO ARE YOUR FRIENDS?

Odors! Vinia knew they would be sure to include that next time.

Hilda turned to Ion. "This is cumbersome. We'd better turn visible for the nonce. We can trust him."

"Unvoke," Ion said. There was a faint shimmer as the shield dissipated.

AH, THERE YOU ARE!

They talked. Hilda introduced Benny and Vinia. They learned that Ida's twin sister, Queen Ivy, had given her friend the Gap Dragon the magic talking board so it could communicate with humans when it needed to, and that board had been passed down to its descendants. They also learned that the Gap Dragon did not eat friends. Now Vinia and Benny would be considered friends.

Overall, it was a nice enough visit.

They bid parting to the dragon and floated back into the sky. It was time to brace the Good Magician, who was likely to be more formidable.

Chapter 2

CHALLENGES

They came to the Good Magician's Castle. There was no mistaking it. For one thing there was a plaque at the front gate saying GOOD MAGICIAN'S CASTLE.

They paused there. "Comments?" Ion asked.

Vinia was uneasy. "It's too easy. That's like a path leading to a tangle tree." Because careless folk who followed such a tempting path would get promptly grabbed and eaten by the carnivorous tree.

"I have heard about it," Benny said. "It is said that there are always three Challenges, designed for the particular querents; that is, the folk who query, who come to ask the Good Magician's advice. He doesn't like to be bothered, so he makes is difficult to get in. He always knows who is coming and is prepared."

"But there are four of us," Vinia said. "With different natures and talents. How complicated can he make it?"

"Plenty complicated," Hilda said.

"It just might be that Mother knew we'd never get through the Challenges, so would have to abort our quest," Ion said thoughtfully. "So she wouldn't have to tell us no openly."

"Would she do a thing like that?" Vinia asked, dismayed.

Both twins nodded soberly.

Vinia realized that she still had things to learn about adults. Evidently, they thought it was all right to deceive children, at least if they didn't do it directly. Maybe it was part of the Adult Conspiracy.

"So we may be faced with impossible Challenges," Ion said.

Vinia got an idea. But she hesitated to say it because it might be too stupid.

"I saw the dim bulb over your head," Ion said. "Out with it."

Vinia shook her head. "It's really not worth saying."

"Let us be the judge of that," Hilda said.

"Really, no," Vinia protested, embarrassed. "I'm the stupidest one of the four of us, and the least experienced."

"I'm not sure of that," Benny said. "I had a stupid idea about the walking socks."

"That's because mostly I'm smart enough to keep my mouth shut, so I don't seem as stupid as I am. You would never have known, if that dim bulb hadn't given me away."

"True," Hilda said, bemused. "You are the most modest of us."

"Speak, or I'll kiss you," Ion threatened.

Vinia knew that if he kissed her in this context, her knees would turn to wet noodles and her mouth would start dumping out the contents of her mind like the garbage it was. "Please, no."

"Sometimes what seems stupid is just different," Hilda said.

"But sometimes it's as stupid as it seems."

"That does it," Ion said. "Modesty be bleeped. You have a notion. I'm kissing you."

Vinia was in tears. "Please," she repeated.

"Here is my thought," Hilda said. "The Good Magician has to have seen us coming. He must know what's on our minds. He knows how to block us off. The only way we're going to get past those Challenges is to surprise him. He knows us, but maybe he didn't think to spot research Vinia, who comes across as inconsequential. So the Challenges are not designed for her. She may be the key to our success."

"I think she is," Ion said. "Because—"

"No!" Vinia cried despairingly.

Now Hilda oriented on Ion. "What did you almost say?"

It was his turn to stifle it. "I can't say."

It was Benny who caught on. "Because she's the protagonist!"

"Oh, bleep!" Vinia wailed.

"You're the protagonist," Hilda repeated. "Of course. That *is* the key. The viewpoint character is close to the main characters and always wins through in the end. Even the Good Magician can't stop that."

It was out. "But we can't be sure of that," Vinia protested. "It might make no difference."

"And it might make all the difference," Hilda said.

"So Vinia should be the one to tackle those Challenges," Hilda said. "Because they're not designed to balk her, and as protagonist she'll have a better chance. That was a good idea, not a stupid one."

"But I'm just a minor character. It's not my place to act like a major one."

The others laughed. "I'm going to kiss you," Ion said.

"But I have nothing left to tell you."

"I'm going to kiss you," Ion said more carefully, "because you're a sweet girl and a nice person and I love you."

"And your innocent modesty becomes you," Hilda said. "I'll kiss you too."

"Oh." Vinia blushed an embarrassing shade of purple.

They kissed her, and so did Benny for good measure. The twins were amateurs, but Benny really knew how to do it; Vinia felt the difference. Then they rehearsed her on the nature of the Challenges. There were always three of them, and they were always solvable. The mechanisms were always in the vicinity; they just had to be recognized and applied. That sounded simple, but in practice it wasn't; probably more folk failed the Challenges than solved them. Usually there was not a time limit, so she could keep struggling with a Challenge until she got it right. Persistence was the key.

"Oh, almost forgot," Hilda said. "Personal magic doesn't work in the Challenges. Ion wouldn't be immune; I couldn't sew my way out of mischief. Benny couldn't change form. You won't be able to teleconnect. You will have to depend on your mind and your body to get through."

Her feeble mind and body. Vinia quailed inwardly.

"Another thing I almost forgot," Ion said. "The Good Magician requires a year's Service, or the equivalent, for his Answer. You may be stuck with that."

"I'll do it," Vinia said bravely. "That way the rest of you can go rescue the princesses without having to wait, once I get the Answer for you, if I do."

This time there was a three-way glance careening between Ion, Hilda, and Benny. "She has more generosity than the rest of us combined," Hilda said.

"We are not worthy of her," Benny said. "No wonder she's the protagonist."

"We're not leaving her behind," Ion said. "We can delay the Quest if necessary."

"But I don't want to hold you up," Vinia said, "after you've gone to all this trouble."

This time Ion didn't threaten, he did it: he kissed her so passionately that half a dozen little hearts were flung out, looking surprised by their velocity.

"You are part of this party," Hilda said. "We'll figure something out. We are not leaving you behind, and that's final." It was clear that That was That.

There was one more thing. "I'm allergic to just about everything," Vinia reminded them. "I have to stay close to Ion or I became a mass of itches and hives and can't function at all. I was a recluse until Ion rescued me."

Ion brought out a vial. "Essence of Ion," he said. "A whiff will suppress your symptoms the same way my presence does." He smiled. "I trust you won't dump me, now that you no longer need me."

She opened her mouth, stricken by the awful implication, but no sound came out.

"I'm teasing," he said. "I know you value me for more than my ambiance."

"Of course she does," Hilda said. "You provide her with a soft bed to sleep on."

"And tasty royal meals," Benny said.

They were teasing her too. "And a way to exercise my talent, so it doesn't get stale," Vinia said. They all laughed, though it wasn't that funny.

Then Vinia stepped off the landed carpet, which disappeared behind her, and walked uncertainly toward the castle. A path appeared before her—she was sure it had not been there a moment before—so she followed it. What else was there to do? It surely did not lead to a tangle tree. She felt supremely unqualified for whatever was to come. At least she wasn't sneezing or itching: the mere presence of the vial seemed to be protecting her. Ion could have given her this all along; had he hesitated for the same reason she had hesitated to tell him about the walking socks? Surely not. Yet maybe.

She thought of something else. She tried to move a fallen branch with only her mind. Nothing happened. So that was correct: no personal magic operated here. She really was on her own, as if she were mundane.

Vinia came to a small cottage with a neatly thatched roof and pretty windows. The path led to the front door and expired there. This must be the place. For whatever devious purpose.

She tried the doorknob. It turned, and the door swung inward. She stepped into the house. There was a single room inside, with a small table.

There was a little girl baby on the table. Vinia could tell because there was a cute pink ribbon on her limited hair.

Vinia had had no idea what to expect, but this wasn't it. A baby? She knew next to nothing about babies, and less about caring for them. Why was she here?

Then she realized that this was a Challenge, and not one intended for her. It must be for Hilda, who not so secretly wanted to grow up and have a kid with Benny. She had sewn little outfits, peeking longingly toward the future. So their plan was working; the wrong person was here for the Challenge.

But if Hilda was not yet qualified for such a thing, Vinia was totally out of the picture. She had no idea what should come next.

Then she smelled something. Now she remembered: babies pooped themselves. She had seen mothers handling such events. This one needed cleaning and changing. There was a fresh clean diaper at the end of the table, and a basin with warm water and a sponge.

She had to do what had to be done. There was no one else, thanks to their cunning substitution of her for the real person. She stepped up and put her hands on the soiled diaper, to take it off.

The baby fussed. Vinia put a hand to her head, to try to comfort her.

The baby's hair changed color, from brown to green.

Vinia froze, amazed. Had she misremembered the color? She wasn't sure, but certainly it wasn't green.

But she had a job to do. She took hold of the diaper, loosening its tape to get it off. She pulled it away—and froze again.

The baby's central anatomy wasn't female. It was male.

She looked again at the hair. The pink ribbon was now a blue band. Boy color.

The Challenge was playing tricks on her. Of course. That was its nature.

Well, she could change a boy as readily as a girl. She did know about the difference in central anatomy. She took the sponge and carefully wiped away the poop. Then she took the fresh diaper—and froze a third time.

The baby on the table was now an ogre infant.

Vinia paused for thought. What was really happening here? Why did the baby keep changing? Fortunately, at the moment it was sleeping, so she had time to think.

Then she got it. This was a changing table. A magic one that changed other things than diapers. A pun. She had to prevent it from doing that. Suppose the baby's mother returned, to discover an ogret in place of her baby?

She looked more carefully at the table, as she had not thought to do before. There was an envelope about to fall off it. She caught it and peered closely at it. It seemed to be a discarded mundane artifact. She pressed it, and it opened out into a little screen with printing on it. She read it. MAGIC MARKER. That was all. That was the message? No wonder it had been discarded!

Still, it was marginally better than nothing. She looked at the table again. There was the marker, just lying there as if hoping to be unobserved. Indeed, she had unobserved it, until reading the email.

She picked up the marker. How did this relate to the baby changing table? Was she supposed to use it to mark the table in some manner? That didn't seem sensible.

She peered more closely at the table. There on the side it said, BABY CHANGING TABLE. To be sure: What else would it be? The problem was in the manner it changed the baby.

She got a faint glimmer of an obscure idea. Could changing the table's designation change its nature?

She used the magic marker to write an *S* before the word *TABLE*. The word moved over to make room for her addition. Now it was *STABLE*.

And before her was a stable, with the ogret sleeping on a mound of hay. The words *BABY CHANGING STABLE* were on a support beam.

Well, now. She was making progress. She had invoked the marker and changed the situation. But it wasn't enough. She had found that she could change the table into something else, but that did not revert the male ogret to a female human baby. What possible word modification would do that?

Vinia thought, and considered, and pondered, and cogitated. Slowly, reluctantly, another glimmer occurred. Maybe a different word?

She used the other end of the marker to erase the *S*. Suddenly the table was back, with the sleeping ogret. Then she applied the marker to the word *BABY*. She converted it to *BABYSITTER*.

Nothing happened. A clarification was needed. "I am the babysitter," she announced. "And what I say goes, because this is my Challenge and I am the authority here, until the parents return. It's my job." She put her free hand on the ogret. "And I say this is a human girl baby in a clean diaper."

And it was so.

Then the scene faded, and Vinia was standing on the path just beyond the cottage. She had won the first Challenge!

Vinia walked on. Soon she came to a pool. A little sign beside it said SPRING OF FORBIDDEN LOVE.

Well, this was interesting. Was it a Challenge? She had better understand it before touching it. Well, she had time, so she would use it. She wanted no more errors like changing a baby to an ogret. She sat down and gazed silently at the spring.

She saw a pair of flying bugs come in for a drink. Too bad they couldn't read, or they'd know better. The moment they touched the water, they went into frenzied activity, becoming what she recognized as lovebugs, so absorbed in their activity as to be oblivious of anything else. Well, that was the nature of a love spring. Vinia couldn't see the detail of what they were doing, as the Conspiracy fuzzed it out, but she knew its general gist. They were signaling the stork, or whatever bugs signaled.

But there was something nevertheless odd about it. What was it?

Then a crested kingbird flew in, a male because of his royal crown. And a field mouse, her body in the general shape of a field. Oh-oh; evidently neither of them could read either. They sipped the liquid side by side, as neither was a predator of the other. And abruptly came together is a desperate engagement, madly making love. Vinia still couldn't see the detail, thanks to the Conspiracy, but she saw something else: the brightly colored kingbird had become a dull-colored queenbird, a female, while the mouse became a male, marked by its little beard. Nevertheless, they were going at it in full measure, stirring up a whole cloud of fuzz.

Now, belatedly, Vinia realized the significance of the rest of the sign: it wasn't just a love spring, it was a forbidden love spring. Forbidden because the genders were reversed. What a complication!

She needed to get the bleep away from here. But the brush on either side was ferociously thorny, and the leaves glistened with what was surely poison. She knew without even trying that if she attempted to walk a long way around it, the brush would simply extend, blocking her. This was a Challenge. She could not avoid the spring. She had to handle it. Somehow.

There was the sound of footfalls. An ugly goblin man was coming down the path. She couldn't avoid him, either. He would be after her the moment he saw her, age no inhibition; goblin females were pretty and nice, but the males were brutes. She could escape him only by splashing into the water, and he would pursue her there. Then would come a horror that would give them and the Adult Conspiracy an awful fit.

This was no Challenge for a child! Maybe it was intended for an adult, and she had somehow blundered into it. Or maybe it was intended for Benny, the adult member of their party. In their innocence as children it had not occurred to them that some of the Challenges might be adult.

What was she to do? Her time was running out. The goblin was almost upon her. So much for taking her time to ponder things.

But there had to be an escape. She peered desperately at the pool. This time she saw something. There was a very small wharf or pier at the edge of the spring, just big enough for a person to stand on, and another one on the far side. Why would there be any such things at a (forbidden) love spring? There was no boat in sight to travel between them. This seemed to make no sense.

"Ha!" the goblin said, spying her.

Ah, but it had to make sense of some kind, or it wouldn't be here. The docks wouldn't be here, the pair of them. She had about five seconds, maybe four, maybe three to figure out that sense.

Then an idea shone over Vinia's head, so brightly that she saw the flash. The pair of docks. Pair o' docks. Paradox! The impossible manifesting.

She stepped on the near one, balancing precariously. "Paradox—get me across!" she cried as the goblin reached for her. Naturally it was impossible to get across simply by asking.

Suddenly she was standing on the other dock, across the spring. The goblin, overbalanced by her sudden absence, splashed into the spring. "Yikes!" he, or rather she exclaimed, more annoyed than surprised. Then, spying Vinia across the pool, she set out to swim across and get her anyway. She could grab Vinia by the ankle and haul her in, and she would become a lustful boy.

Vinia leaped off the dock onto the land and fled. And the scene faded. She had somehow navigated the second Challenge!

The path led on to a walled-in garden where several young men and women were on their knees weeding. A forbidding older woman stood by its exit, and a similarly forbidding man was beside her, watching the weeders. Maybe the weeders didn't want to be there, so these were the enforcers. Maybe they were other querents who had tried to pass on through and been caught and put to work. Which would be her own fate if she just walked straight ahead.

But what kept them there? Why didn't they just barge on by the woman?

One weeder started to stand up, rubbing his back. Vinia could see the little lightning jag of pain there. It was hard bending over all the time to grab the weeds.

The guard woman looked at him. A knife flashed from her eye and flew toward him, just missing him.

Then Vinia got it. She was looking daggers! Literally. No one wanted to get stabbed by one of those.

Vinia paused to look about. There were other enclosed gardens to either side, connected by closed doors. One had an odd-looking female horse pacing restlessly back and forth, nibbling on the weeds that had overgrown that location. The other contained several young birds clustered around a statue of a magnet, ignoring the seeds on the ground. Did any of this mean anything? It surely did, because this had to be the third Challenge.

Vinia put her hands to her head as if to squeeze out some competent thought. Ion was smart, and so was Hilda, and Benny had a kind of animal common sense. They might have tackled this setting and figured it out. But Vinia was almost painfully ordinary in mind and body. Her only asset was her telekinesis, which didn't work here in the Good Magician's domain. She had no idea what to make of it all.

But she had to keep trying. She had somehow made it through two Challenges: it would be a shame to mess up on the third. She certainly didn't want to be trapped weeding, menaced by daggers.

She focused on the birds around the big magnet. There had to be a pun there, of some sort. What could it be? They looked like young birds, almost chicks.

The idea flashed. A chick magnet!

So she had the pun. Now all she needed was a use for it, to get her through the Challenge. Still, it was progress.

She looked at the other side. The odd mare became aware of her attention and gazed back at her. She had no idea what species it could be. Not a regular female horse. Not a night mare.

Night mare. This one was too weird for that. Maybe it was a weird mare. What would a weird mare do? Maybe bring disturbing visions to people who were restless sleepers. The night mare couldn't get at them if they didn't properly sleep, so this one filled in. That made sense, didn't it?

Still, what use was it to her? How did it relate to the Challenge? Was it that if she tried to avoid the weeding garden by passing through here, she'd get a nasty vision that would haunt her despite being awake? She didn't want to chance that. No one would.

Vinia looked back at the weeding garden. And saw something else. The mare was starting near the wall, and the girl closest to it had paused in her weeding. A sort of dream balloon was floating just over her head. No, not a dream, because she wasn't asleep, merely drifting mentally. She was picturing the man next to her, who was pretty handsome, standing and stepping up to her, pulling her shirt off to expose her full bosom, bending down to kiss it, the girl not at all averse. A naughty vision. Something she'd rather be doing than pulling weeds, for sure!

Then the man standing beside the dagger woman glanced that way. He saw the vision. He nudged the dagger woman. She glared, sending a dagger right through the vision balloon. It burst, spraying bits of bosom across the yard, where they landed squishily before evaporating. One hit the handsome man on the chest. He looked, eyes widening appreciatively before it faded. He would have liked to share that vision. The girl, fully clothed, hastily focused on pulling her weeds.

So much for letting one's mind drift. The man was the watcher, the sincere sin-seer, cluing the woman in on the weeder's inattention to the job. It seemed to be a mean-spirited but effective system.

Somehow this all had to come together, if only she could figure it out. Chick magnet. Glaring daggers. Weird mare. Naughty visions.

Come together. Well, why not? There would be chaos if those three gardens could be involuntarily integrated. And there, maybe, was the answer.

Vinia entered the mare's garden. The mare oriented on her warily. "Read my mind," Vinia murmured. "I'm here to help you make a barrelful of naughty notions. Just work with me."

Evidently the mare understood. She made no menacing move. Vinia went to the door between gardens and worked the handle, as the mare could not. She slowly pushed the door open partway. "Don't go through yet," she whispered. "Wait until the clamor begins. Then push on through and do your thing. There's a dozen people on the other side, eager for weird dreams."

The mare nodded.

Vinia withdrew and walked quietly to the magnet garden. The closer she got to the magnet, the more it appealed to her. She had not thought of herself as a chick, but maybe she was: a juvenile female. Which was fine: it meshed nicely with her plan. She picked up the magnet, which fortunately was hollow, and carried it to the door between gardens. How she loved the touch of it! She paused to crank open the door, then scrambled through with the magnet. The bird chicks followed her, of course.

She faced the guards. "Behold!" she cried. "See what I have!"

The weeders looked. "Ooo!" the women and girls exclaimed and ran toward the magnet, being attracted because it wasn't limited to a species or age of chick. When the men and boys saw that, they ran after the women, who were now acting quite coquettish. The clamor had begun, signaling the weird mare.

"Hey!" the guard man cried. The guard woman oriented and glared a dagger. It flew to the magnet, crashed into it, and cracked, the pieces dropping to the ground.

Vinia smiled. That was exactly what she had hoped for: a generalized magnet that attracted not only chicks, but metal. Why make a specialized item when a generalized one could more readily be adapted?

Now the weird mare appeared in the garden. Naughty visions started appearing over the heads of the people. Men kissing remarkably cooperative women. Boys peeking under girls' flaring skirts, the girls pretending not to notice. Soon these things started happening in the real life.

A woman in a vision saw a four-legged animal walking toward her on two legs, holding something in its front paws. It was a name badge with her name, JEMIMA. This was a Badge-her! She took the badge and put it on her blouse. She was no longer anonymous. A man saw that and spoke to her: "I wanted to meet you, but I didn't know your name. Hello, Jemima!"

"Oh? I'm happy to answer you, but I don't know *your* name."

Another animal hurried up with a badge. This was a Badge-him with his name badge: JIM. He took it and put it on. He smiled.

A knife flew through the vision, popping its balloon. The vision dissipated into fragments, and the names were lost. The woman and the man looked at each other in real life. "Dam!" they said almost together, using the mundane term for obstructing a river, considered an epithet.

But now there were so many visions that they were overwhelming the dagger lady. Her daggers were flying askew, mostly missing their targets. "Dam!" she echoed. It was worse than that; two-and-a-half-thirds of the visions were so naughty that they were being fogged out by the Conspiracy. But the adults could still see them: indeed, more than one lady was blushing as she headed zestfully for the man under the balloon.

Vinia set down the magnet with its circle of adoring chicks. Some chicks were even admiring the daggers stuck to the magnet. She made her way to the exit and slipped through. She had passed the third Challenge!

There was the entrance to the castle. The gate swung open to reveal an elegant hark-haired older woman. "Welcome, Vinia!" she said. "Do come in."

Vinia hesitated. Was this yet another Challenge? A fake castle to trap her when she thought she was safe?

"No, it's legitimate," the woman said. "I'm Dara Demoness, the Designated Wife of the Month."

This was odd. "The who? The what?"

"I am a small-d demoness." She fuzzed into a dark cloud, then returned to human form, not quite the same as before. For one thing, her hair was light. "The Designated Wife of Good Magician Humfrey. Come in and I'll explain."

She seemed sincere, no pun. Vinia took a flying leap of faith and decided to trust her. She followed Dara into the castle.

Soon they were ensconced in a pleasant living room and Dara was explaining. "The Good Magician did not expect your party to make it through the Challenges, so he and his son and daughter-in-law took the afternoon off, and I am left in charge. I will be handling your case."

"My case?"

"Your Answer. Your Service. But first let me clarify about the Designated Wives. To oversimplify somewhat, when Humfrey lost his wife, he didn't just accept it, he went to Hell to reclaim her. But Hell is a nasty place, so it gave him back all five and a half of the wives he had had over the course of a century or so, preserved after their deaths of old age. They were back in the primes of their lives. That was a problem, because in Xanth a man is supposed to have only one wife at a time. So we take turns, one a month. This month is my turn."

Vinia was having trouble assimilating this. "How many wives?"

"Ah. You have a problem with the half."

"Yes."

"Allow me to list them in order. As a young man Humfrey loved MareAnn, but she knew that marriage was hard on innocence, and she needed her innocence to summon unicorns, so she reluctantly turned him down. You see, her talent was summoning female equines, but she wanted the rare ones, too. I was the next, and he married me as wife number one. But I was foolishly impatient with his mortal limitations and took off. So he married the Maiden Taiwan. When she passed on, he married Rose of Roogna as number three. When she departed, he had hideous trouble keeping track of his old socks, so he married Sofia Mundane, who had no magic but was excellent at tracking and mending socks. She was number four. but she finally got fed up—Humfrey is not the easiest man to get along with—so he married the Gorgon as number five. Would you believe she traveled across Xanth all the way to the castle to ask him a Question, which was 'Will you marry me?' and he made her serve a year's Service to earn her Answer?"

"He *what*?" Vinia asked, unbelieving.

"Humfrey's ways are often confusing to ordinary folk," Dara said. "That actually made sense. She served a year assisting him in the castle, learning all his ways and where every obscure thing was, until she knew better than he did. By the time the year was done, she had a thorough basis to decide whether she really wanted to marry him. Nine out of ten women given that education would get the bleep out of there and find some more amenable man. But she was sure and married him without illusion. And it worked out well enough."

"Oh." It did make a twisted kind of sense.

"She was the one he went to rescue, when she got trapped in Hell." Dara smiled. "He got more than he bargained on."

That seemed to be the case. "But what about the half wife?"

"Ah, yes. MareAnn had aged and gone to Hell in the normal course.

She had discovered that Hell was almost as hard on innocence as marriage, so now she was ready to marry him. He had never stopped loving her, or she him, in over a century. It was a small ceremony, and rather late in their lives, so they considered it half a marriage. That was thirty-two years ago, so he has a half wife of thirty-two years."

Vinia shook her head. "And I thought my life was complicated!" She also suspected that there was a pun lurking, but it probably wasn't worth pursuing.

"Now to business," Dara said. "You seek Humfrey's advice on your Quest to save the six crystallized princesses."

"Well, really it's Ion and Hilda's Quest. I'm just a friend."

Dara laughed. "They are right. You are almost painfully generous and modest." She turned serious. "Understand this, Wivinia: it is your Quest now. You are the protagonist. They are your companions."

"But—"

"It became your Quest when you tackled the Challenges and won through, as they would not have. That was a remarkable ploy that entirely fooled the preset apparatus."

"We did worry that we were supposed to be balked by them."

"Exactly. Ion tends to think in terms of nullifying elixirs, but he couldn't have nullified the Spring of Forbidden Love. You found the alternate route. Hilda thinks in terms of sewing magical items, but sewing would not have restored that baby. Again, you found a different way. Benny thinks in terms of accommodating other folk, but our dagger lady was proof against accommodation. You realized that the opposite was called for: chaos."

"I just sort of blundered through," Vinia confessed. "Maybe I was just lucky."

"And maybe you have a natural feel for what a given situation requires. That may free the princesses instead of messing them up. They are confined for a reason. Incidentally, those Challenge threats were not as real as they may have seemed. Had you fallen into the spring with the goblin, you would not have changed gender and gone into a breeding frenzy, you would merely have lost the Challenge. Similar with the others; your real options were success or failure. The other participants were castle personnel playing their roles." She smiled. "But you did have an effect. Jim and

Jemima have taken an interest in each other, since she managed to show him her bosom in the vision. Men may be slow to pick up hints, but they notice bare flesh immediately."

"I wouldn't know."

"Keep it in mind for when you come of age in the not-too-distant future. Ion loves you for your obliging telekinesis and personality. That's fine as far as it goes. But sex appeal generates prompt compulsion, regardless of a man's intellect or power. Use it judiciously, when."

Confused, Vinia had no response. She blushed instead. Which meant that she did understand, on another level. When the time came to consider marriage, she would remember. There was no sense in leaving such an important thing to chance.

"You may be sure the princesses know it and will use it," Dara said. For a moment her clothing fuzzed out, revealing a phenomenal bare figure. Obviously, she knew how to handle the Good Magician when she needed to.

"The princesses," Vinia said. "We just want to rescue them from the dragon."

"That notion is far too simple and based on simplistic assumptions. First, you assumed the dragon is a mean-spirited animal. That is not the case. Dragoman is doing the princesses a service. Young and impetuous, they were headed for mischief. He put them away until they could find better situations."

"He locked them in crystals!"

"Yes. Timeless, painless storage. He will release them when there are suitable princes for them to marry, as there were none in their time."

"Release them?" Vinia asked, astonished. "He doesn't mean to eat them?"

Dara laughed again. "Of course not! He has refined tastes. He eats nothing but gourmet beefsteak tomatoes ripened by the delicate glow of newly blooming sunflowers. No, his Service is storing the princesses as a community good works, which the Good Magician duly appreciates."

"Good works!"

"It was a deal he made when he was young: a fine estate in exchange for this Service. He has performed it well. Now he is old and ready to retire and enjoy the estate. He needs to be rid of the princesses. That means that each one needs a suitable companion who will see properly to her needs. Princesses tend to be high maintenance."

"A prince for each," Vinia agreed.

"Not necessarily. One is a lesbian."

Oh. "So we will have to search for the right princess for her."

"Perhaps. The point is that it may turn out to be a Challenge that will be beyond the ability of an ordinary hero."

Vinia was beginning to catch on. "And you feel that a party of children would not be able to handle it. So we were to be balked, so that a better hero could be found for that particular mission."

"Something like that," the Demoness agreed. "But then you defeated the Challenges, to our surprise. That complicates the picture."

Vinia was able to translate the sentiment. "You're stuck with it."

"Indeed. I am doing what I can to prepare you for a Challenge that may be worse than the ones you faced here. But there is only so much I *can* do. The rest will be a matter of hope and fate."

Vinia's mind was beginning to take hold, as it had during the Challenges. "Can you tell me more about the princesses? You said they were confined for a reason."

"Indeed. They were endlessly disruptive in their home frames, a burden to themselves and others. There were no happy outcomes to be expected there."

"What's wrong with them?"

"For one thing, they are self-willed. They were refusing to marry the princes their fathers duly selected for them, or indeed, to settle down to support and promote the existing masculine order. Their fathers did not like that."

"They are feminists!"

"In their day there were no feminists, only undisciplined girls."

"That's changed," Vinia said. "Princesses today regard themselves as at least equal to princes. If a prince argues, they flash their panties and freak him out. Even I, as a garden-variety common girl, think of myself as a person with some choices."

"Yes. It is a better climate for them. Even so, it is not necessarily simple. Only one is human."

"Only one! We assumed—"

"As I believe I have indicated, this is not the occasion for assumptions. The others are goblin, elf, centaur, bee, and Demoness."

"Bee! Demoness!"

"You have surely heard of queen bees. They are preceded by princess bees. Their roles are highly defined, and one who balks is not welcomed. They are slated to be confined as lifelong egg layers."

"I can see why this princess rebelled."

"As for the Demoness, that is my friend Demesne, pronounced diMEEN."

"Your friend?"

"We Demons exist longer than you mortals do, generally. I've known her for centuries. She's always had a very fine sense of place. Her name means estate or dominion, or territory controlled by the sovereign. She is destined to control land."

"A suitable prince will have land."

"Which he controls. That won't do for her. So she took herself out of the picture."

Vinia was beginning to appreciate the magnitude of the problem. "It may be hard to find princes they like."

"I'm sure you will come up with something. Meanwhile, Demesne will help you."

"Help me?"

Dara drew an ornate ring from her finger, which Vinia had not noticed before. "This will lead you to her and identify you as a friend of mine."

Friend of a Demoness? That was not a thing Vinia had ever aspired to. "I'm not sure how—"

Dara caught her left hand and set the ring on her middle finger, where it promptly disappeared. "Merely follow the glow."

"Glow?"

"Say her name."

"Demesne?"

The ring was invisible, but there was a glow that was brighter in one direction. That was clear enough.

"You can orient on me similarly by saying my name," Dara said. "I will help you if I can."

"Thank you." Vinia took a shaky breath. "But this is academic, for me.

I have a year's Service to perform. I will give the ring to Hilda, so they can get on with it."

"No. I thought you understood. Keep the ring. The equivalent Service is your Quest to free the princesses."

Vinia paused, assimilating it. "I never claimed to be the brightest flash among fireflies. I did not understand. Thank you."

"No need to thank me. You earned it when you handled the Challenges." She paused. "I almost forgot. There's more to this ring. It belonged, long ago, to a Magician, and it has more than one aspect of magic. It's actually glass."

"Glass?"

"I understand it was formed from the merger of a glass eel with a glass eye, so it is almost invisible, but it sees well. It also brings good luck to the creature or thing it orients on. But this magic, like most magic, is like mundane fire; it can be extremely useful, but also dangerous if misused. So use it only as needed, and do not take it off."

"Why not?"

"Because then the luck tends to reverse, a natural blowback. Like a fire unattended. But that won't happen as long as you wear it."

Vinia focused, relieved. "I will keep the ring on. I'll try first for Demesne."

"She is in a crystal in Dragoman's cave, so orienting on her will guide you to that cave. You will know Dragoman by his tattoo."

"Tattoo?" Vinia didn't like going mono, monosyllabic—whatever the word was for saying single words, but her mind was having trouble keeping up with the concepts.

"He has a tattoo of a shapely human girl on his neck. Usually it is girls who have dragon tattoos, not the reverse, so it's distinctive. Go there, talk to him—he can talk. Explain your mission. If he goes along, your next step will be to locate the princes. Once you have them, and they pass muster, Dragoman will release the princesses and your mission may be accomplished."

Vinia heard the qualification. "May be?"

"Complications are almost inevitable. The princes and princesses will be strangers to each other when they meet. They will need to converse for a time and agree they are compatible. They may or may not be. Or two princes may prefer the same princess, or vice versa. You will have to be ready for spot corrections."

"Oh, my," Vinia said in the same tone both Squid and Queen Ida had used when recognizing Vinia as the protagonist. She was coming to understand the expression better. She had thought the Challenges were done, but she understood now that the worst one lay ahead.

"Exactly," Dara agreed, needing no mind reading to follow her thought. "Now I will signal your companions to rejoin you here. You all deserve a relaxed night before you set out on your Quest."

Relaxed, Vinia thought in the same tone as her one- and two-word responses.

Dara vanished for half an instant, then reappeared. "I told them. They are on their way," she reported. "Look." She gestured to a large picture Vinia had not noticed before. Had it been there?

There in the picture was the magic carpet, cruising toward the foreground. It was a moving picture! The carpet grew steadily larger. Then Vinia realized that it was not a picture but a picture window. The carpet loomed right up to the glass. Then it sailed through it into the room with them. It was an open window.

It landed neatly on the floor. Hilda jumped off and hugged her. "Vinia!" she exclaimed. "You did it! You made it through the Challenges!"

"Most of them," Vinia agreed soberly. There was going to be a lot of explaining to do.

Ion joined her. He hugged her too. "We knew you could do it."

They did? That was more than she herself had known. "Thank you," Vinia said weakly.

"I love reunions," Dara said.

Chapter 3

PRINCESSES

In the morning, after a comfortable night filled with illuminating discussion, they were on their way on the carpet. Dara Demoness had impressed on the others that Vinia was now not merely the protagonist, but the Quest proprietor. She had won the Challenges they would have lost. She was no longer a secondary character, but the primary one, as far as this mission was concerned.

Vinia, embarrassed, had tried to demur, feeling more comfortable as a background character, but all the children accepted it. Just as changing the one to tackle the Challenges had proved to be a winning strategy, they hoped that the same ploy would facilitate the difficult Quest. And if it failed, she would get the blame. But nobody said that.

"But really nothing has changed," Vinia told them. "I'm still a background character in my heart." The others hadn't even bothered to circulate a Look.

Now they sailed over the patchwork quilt that was Xanth, following the flashes of the Demoness's ring. There was a flying dragon on the horizon, and a pair of wyverns, and a griffin, and harpies, and a few birds and insects, but none approached the carpet. Word had indeed gotten around.

The distance was not far, and they had a tailwind, so by early afternoon they reached the mountain where Dragoman's lair lurked and descended. "You will interview the dragon," Ion told Vinia.

"But I'm not qualified to do that! You and Hilda are much better equipped for anything like that."

"Dara informed him we were coming. He will expect the Magician or Sorceress to broach him about the princesses. He will be defensive. You may surprise him, being essentially harmless. We want his cooperation, not his antagonism. We'll be there if you need us."

She was stuck for it. All her life Vinia had deferred to others, and being the protagonist, let alone the Questee, was uncomfortable for her. Yet it had worked to get them into the Good Magician's Castle, so there was a certain perverse logic. She was indeed a harmless type. Maybe if she messed up in this, the others would resume their leading roles and she could relax.

Ion steered the carpet down into the hole in the mountain that was the entrance to the lair. It was unguarded, because no one ever tried to molest a dragon's lair, as a matter of personal health. It was large enough so that they could still fly inside it. They followed it through two and a half twists and three-quarters of a turn.

There was the dragon, large, scarred, and old. "Queen Ida's children, I presume?" His reptilian lips did not move, yet Vinia heard him. She realized that since, as a dragon, he lacked the ability to configure his mouth in the human manner, he must be using limited telepathy to project his thoughts while he made grunting sounds, making it seem as if he were talking verbally. She might not have noticed had she not been so nervous. What she noticed more was the tattoo of the pretty human girl on his neck. She was in a bikini and had the kind of figure Vinia knew she herself would never achieve. This was the right dragon.

Ion nudged her as he parked the carpet. "And their retinue," Vinia said. "Hello, Dragoman. I am Vinia. I will be your companion in dialogue for this session."

Surprised, he oriented on her as a puff of smoke rose from the corner of his mouth. He was evidently a smoker. They were comparatively rare dragons, because smoking was not healthy for any creature. "Hello, Vinia Human," he grunted. Yes, definitely telepathy-assisted.

"These are the Magician Ion and Sorceress Hilda, the son and daughter of Queen Ida, who was once confined in one of your crystals, and Hilda's friend Benny Buck, a Caprine crossbreed." Benny obligingly changed to goat form and back.

"Ida," the dragon said thoughtfully. "I knew her as a princess. I wondered what became of her."

"Princesses mature into queens. She married Prince Hilarion of Adamant, and they now rule that fantasy kingdom."

"I thought I had her safely crystallized. Then one day I discovered the crystal broken and she was gone. I was concerned on her behalf. I am glad to know she survived." He puffed more smoke. "What happened?"

"Mela Merwoman and Okra Ogress were in the vicinity," Vinia said, discovering that it was easier now that she was narrating something she knew about. "They saw her, and Okra sang a sour note that shattered the crystal. They freed her, and Ida went on to discover that she was the twin sister of Princess Ivy, who later became the human queen, or rather, king of Xanth. Ida turned out to have the Sorceress-caliber talent of the Idea, with a moon orbiting her head that contains all the folk ever thought of for Xanth. She is quite well known now, though she has pretty much faded into the anonymity of adulthood and wifehood."

"I am glad to hear it." Dragoman puffed a bit more smoke. It seemed to be a by-product of his thinking. "Mela Merwoman. I believe I have heard of her. Wasn't she the one who made legs, walked on land, and donned panties that freaked out half the countryside?"

"The male half," Vinia agreed. "She was a creature of the sea and didn't realize the power of panties. Once she put on more clothing that stopped."

"Perhaps that was just as well." More smoke. "Enough chitchat. What brings your party here to my lair? Surely you don't mean to attempt to raid my hoard?"

"No raid!" Vinia said, taken aback. "We come in peace."

Dragoman smiled smokily, which was not the most reassuring expression. "Humor. Please state your business here."

Oh. "When Ida departed, she noticed that several other princesses were sealed in crystals," Vinia said. "Her children thought it was past time to rescue them."

The dragon nodded. "Ah, those. Actually they aren't all princesses, merely pretty damsels. Dragons like damsels."

"We noticed," she said, glancing at the tattoo.

"And many damsels like dragons," he said. "So they wear dragon tattoos. It makes them more attractive."

"At any rate, we felt that princesses should not be confined indefinitely, so we are here to free them."

"I do preserve the damsels until there are suitable placements for them. The ordinary beauties are easier to place. Princesses are more difficult, and these particular ones, the last remaining, are a considerable challenge. I certainly would like to get them situated so I can retire."

This was curious. "You make it sound as if it is a duty, rather than pleasure."

Dragoman nodded. "It is indeed a duty. Back in my youth I discovered that I was not interested in smoking living creatures for food; I was essentially a pacifist. That did not fit the dragon mode. So I went to the Good Magician for advice."

"The Good Magician!" Vinia exclaimed. "I did that. I did not actually see him, but his Designated Wife helped me."

"And it seems that advice has now brought us together," Dragoman agreed. A bit of feeling was coming through with the words, and she had the definite impression that he was coming to like her, but not in a threatening way. Maybe it was that in another year or two she would mature into a damsel. "For my Question I asked him to inform me of a beneficial situation that would keep me busy and out of contact with more aggressive dragons. Please understand, I could defend myself, choking and blinding them with smoke, but I didn't like the ridicule. His Answer was really a deal: he would arrange for me to have a fine spacious estate that would support me in the manner I preferred, if, as my Service, I took some of the more difficult maidens out of circulation for a time. It seemed simple enough. He gave me the power to modify my smoke to encapsulate them in crystals that would keep them in suspended animation until there were improved prospects for them. Then I would breathe the nullifying vapor and free them to find their compatible situations. When at last I reached retirement age, I could free the last of the maidens and enjoy my estate in peace."

"You must be near that age now."

"I am indeed. It has been well over a century. Dragons live long, compared to humans and other creatures, but not forever. Now I have only the last six princesses left, and when I free them, my Service is over and my retirement will commence. The princesses, of course, do not age at all while crystallized: they are as young as they were when they arrived. Times have changed, and they should find the present realm more compatible than the ones they left."

"My being sent here is not coincidental," Vinia said, appreciating the revelation. "It is not only to do the princesses a favor, but do you a favor too." Could this Quest turn out to be simpler than she had feared?

"Simple in theory," the dragon agreed. "But not necessarily in practice."

"Oh? What is complicated about it?" she asked warily. She had a notion, from what Dara Demoness had told her.

"The nature of the princesses. They are the last ones for a reason. They are essentially feminists, stemming from times and cultures that did not accept such a concept. Things have liberalized, but I fear not yet sufficiently. Finding suitable princes for them—because for this purpose a princess must be matched with a prince or king—may be a chore even today. That will be your challenge."

Vinia glanced at Ion and Hilda, who had sat in perfect silence. "Our challenge," she said. "We want what is best for them."

"Perhaps it is time for you to interview the princesses directly."

"You will free them already?" Vinia asked, surprised.

"No."

"Um, I may not be the smartest Quester, but—"

"I appreciate that," Dragoman said supportively. "You are a common girl. I will explain in simple terminology. One of the princesses is telepathic. She is a full telepath, not a partial one like me. We have had compatible dialogues. She will connect you to each of the princesses in turn. Their bodies will remain frozen; only their minds will be tweaked, in the manner of a dream. Then you will have the information you need to go forth and find suitable princes for each."

Oh. That was indeed more complicated than she had imagined. "Thank you. How do I contact her?"

"No problem. She is with you now."

Then something changed in Vinia's head. "Hello," a new voice said. "I am the telepath."

"Uh, hello," Vinia answered uncertainly. There was something about the mind that she liked. It was friendly and understanding.

"I am Chloe, a crystal princess. My name means Fresh Blooming."

"Um, I am Vinia. Short for Wivinia, meaning Of the Quiet Life. I am good at keeping quiet."

The presence in her head expanded. "I am a winged centaur." Now there was a picture of an attractive bare-breasted filly centaur with brown fur and long brown hair on her head, but white wings.

"I, uh, am human, brown hair, brown eyes. My talent is telekinesis. That is, I can move things in my vicinity with my mind."

"Have you a mirror? That will let me see you through your eyes. I can't use my own at present."

Vinia fished out her compact mirror and held it before her face so Chloe could see Vinia's reflection.

"Thank you. Now I see you. Our hair and eyes match," Chloe said. "So do our talents, to a degree. We're both tele, kin and path. That's nice."

"Uh, yes." Then Vinia thought of something. "I thought the folk of Xanth either *have* magic or *are* magic. You are a magic creature. I realize that the ability to fly is part of your creature definition, but how can you have telepathy? That's a whole other thing."

"To be sure. But once a species gets thoroughly established, it can develop magic, at least in some individuals. Yet it is somewhat random, but as time passes, there should be more magic showing up in centaurs, elves, ogres, dragons, and others. I, as an early developer of a separate talent, did not fit in well with my peer group. That was part of my problem. The fact that I possessed an independent mind was another."

Oh. "Chloe, you seem like a nice person, and pretty. Why are you here? I mean, surely a smart stallion centaur would like you, mind and all."

Chloe smiled. "All the stallions liked me in my day, royal and common, and some human princes, too. Because I am attractively endowed, physically, a fair-fleshed filly, and easy to ride by the humanoid types because I know the mind of my rider. But I didn't like them, because I could read their minds. All they wanted, really, was one thing. Nothing wrong with that in itself; I like it myself. But it was too narrow for me: I prefer to integrate with the whole person. The purely physical aspect can wait its turn."

That made sense to Vinia. The body was only part of the person. "Yes."

"I see you understand. I am satisfied to remain in stasis until the external situation is appropriate. I hope you are able to find me a suitable stallion."

"I will try," Vinia promised.

"One who won't mind that I can read his mind."

"I will specify that." How did males feel about females reading their minds? Some should be able to accept it. Maybe a telepathic stallion. "Dragoman told me that the two of you have had compatible dialogues."

"We have. He is one male who is more interested in my mind than my body."

They being of completely different species. "While you remained in stasis?"

"Physically, yes. It is like a waking dream for me. He is a limited telepath, mainly to enable his speech, while I am a full telepath, able to read minds, so dialogue is feasible." She paused three-fifths of a moment. "I didn't mean to snoop; I was just orienting so we could talk. But I learned that he really does like maidens of all types. He dreams of being the dragon in a damsel and dragon combo, with the damsel fawning over him. Sort of like girls and horses, really."

"Girls do like horses," Vinia agreed. "I traveled to Animalia because I wanted to see their fine horses. Then my allergies interfered so it didn't work out. But that's a separate story."

"Surely so. Now I will connect you with the next," Chloe said. "I will be here, of course, so it will not be a completely private dialogue, but I will confine myself to the background."

"Yes, that should work," Vinia agreed uncertainly.

There was a shift. "Who is this?" a new voice asked.

Vinia realized from the blankness in the mind that this princess did not understand the situation. "Hello, I am Vinia Human. I have been telepathically connected to you so I can get to know you and find out what kind of a prince you would like me to locate for you to be with when you get uncrystallized."

The other mind absorbed that. "I am still crystallized?"

"Yes. Only your mind has been awakened. Think of it as a dream while you sleep."

"Ah. That makes sense." The mind coalesced, becoming imperious.

"Who are you, please," Vinia said. "I can't see you with my eyes."

"I am Hula Human. It will take some man to accommodate my impulses. The princes I encountered simply didn't measure up. Not smart enough. Not bold enough."

"But if you are a feminist, a dominant man might not measure so much as demand."

"There are feminists and feminists. I don't want a weak-kneed man, I want one who can satisfy me, intellectually and physically. That's a different matter. Dominant is fine; I will match him stroke for stroke, and he'd better like it."

Vinia was having trouble quite understanding that, but the Conspiracy got in the way and stifled her next question. "Uh, okay, I guess."

Hula peered at her. "You are juvenile," she said, catching on.

"Yes."

"So you might have trouble making my case for me. Or any of our cases. Maybe we should speak for ourselves."

"But we have to fetch the princes before the dragon will release any of you."

Hula smiled. "Perhaps we should make holograms."

"Make what?"

"Little moving scenes you can play for the princes, showing what we look like and how we talk. Men can see better than they can think. We can make our own presentations, so you don't get violated as a child."

That made sense to Vinia. She had caught on to more adult business than the Conspiracy realized, but didn't care to advertise it. "But I don't know how to make such a thing."

"Spot research will fix that."

"I will tell the others in our party," Vinia said. "They should be able to research it. Meanwhile I will try to find the smartest and manliest of princes for you."

"See that you do."

Hula faded and a new mind formed.

"Hello," Vinia said. "You are in a dream state, still crystallized. I am Vinia Human, telepathically connected to you to learn what kind of prince you would like to have when you emerge from your crystal." She hoped that would do it without undue confusion. "Please identify yourself."

"A dream state. Ah. I am Goblette Goblin. But I want no prince."

"No prince? But princesses aren't supposed to be with common men." But then she thought of her own relationship with Ion, and Hilda's with Benny. Royals *could* mix with ordinary folk if they so chose and had the gumption to make it stick. "That is, well, usually, unless they decide otherwise."

"I am not usual. I am lesbian. I can intoxicate a man simply by gazing into his eyes, but I don't want him in my bed. Goblin males are such boors! Only the females have any delicacy at all. I want a princess, lesbian or at least amenable."

Oh. Now Vinia remembered. Dara had mentioned that one of the princesses was a ladies' woman. That did make sense. Goblette was certainly right about goblin males. They were uncouth brutes. "I will search for a goblin princess who prefers women."

"Exactly. Of course, she will have to be compatible. Some women can be as bad as men."

"We hope to have each of you make a hologram, so you can make your own cases. You can spell out exactly what you want."

"That will do." Goblette faded out.

Vinia breathed a sigh of relief. It should be possible to find another goblin princess who preferred the niceness of females and wasn't too assertive.

The mind changed again. "We meet at last!" the new princess said. "I am Demesne."

"Demesne! Dara sends her greeting."

"Yes, of course. I recognize her ring. How is she?"

"She is one of the wives of Good Magician Humfrey and seems satisfied."

"*One* of? I remember when she married him. But then she became impatient with his grumpy mortality and took off."

"She finally got bored with the single life," Vinia said. "So later returned to him. But by then he had four and a half other wives, so they had to share."

"Half a wife? There is surely an interesting story there."

"His first love was MareAnn, but she didn't want to sacrifice her innocence."

"I remember. It is a mortal woman's most significant asset. That's when I stepped in, having no innocence to lose."

"But when MareAnn died of old age, she went to Hell, and that was hard on her innocence. So when Hell released all his wives at once, she joined them with a half-sized ceremony. She is the half wife."

"Ah. Now it makes sense."

"They take turns as Designated Wife of the Month. It seems a month is about the limit of their tolerance for the grumpiness of the

Good Magician, so it works well enough. It was Dara's turn when I got there."

"Thank you for that update. Being crystallized got me a bit out of date."

"Dara said you would help me if I needed it. In fact, you already have, because the glow of the ring signaled your direction so we could locate the dragon's lair."

"I felt the signals, but could not respond, being limited. How did you come here? Dragons' lairs are not the usual tourist fare, unless the tourists are suicidal."

"We are on a Quest. Princess Ida was crystallized, but escaped via a fluke, and now her children want to rescue the other princesses."

"Her children?"

"Prince Ion, who is a Magician, immune to all elixirs. Princess Hilda, his twin sister, a Sorceress who can sew the most remarkable magic things. Such as the flying carpet we flew here. They are age eleven."

"Ah. They are descendants of Bink, all of whom are cursed to be Magicians or Sorceresses. But that doesn't explain you."

"Prince Ion suffered an accident and can't use his legs properly, and he is immune to healing elixir. I am ordinary, but my talent is telekinesis. I use it to move his legs for him, so he can walk, at least with me. I am highly allergic, and his ambiance makes me immune to the allergens of the air, so I love being close to him. In fact, I think we're in love."

"That's nice," Demesne said sympathetically.

"The fourth member of our party is Benny Buck, a human-Caprine crossbreed. He is six years old, but adult because that's an adult age for a goat. He's a nice guy. He is Hilda's boyfriend."

"She has an adult boyfriend? A billy goat? Her mother must have something to say about that."

"I think Hilda put her foot down. She can be assertive despite being young."

"Surely so," the Demoness agreed. "I am familiar with the type."

It was time to get back to the subject. "You will want a Demon prince to be your consort?"

"Yes. We Demonesses are versed in being seductive, but it generally takes a male Demon to really satisfy us."

"What was wrong with the males in your day?"

"They wanted to control the land. I need to find a Demon prince who is more interested in power, wealth, or bleep than in land, because I mean to manage the estate."

The Conspiracy gave Vinia a jolt when it bleeped out the word Demesne used. "I'm juvenile. But I think I follow the gist."

Demesne laughed, her body briefly turning smoky. "Gist is foul-tasting stuff."

"We hope to make holograms, so each of you can make your own case to the princes."

"That should be effective. Meanwhile, if you should need my assistance on anything, just speak my name to the ring. I should be able to answer you, now that I know you."

"Thank you. I will."

The mind changed. "Hello," Vinia said, getting better at this. "I am Vinia Human, here to interview you via telepathy provided by Chloe Centaur. You remain crystallized, but this is like a dream state for you. I am not a princess, but there is a prince and a princess in our party. Please identify yourself, as I can't see you until you assume your form in my mind."

"I am Elga Elf," the mind replied. "My name means Tiny Fighter. I am here because none of the garden-variety elf princes interested me beyond the first few minutes."

"All they wanted was one thing. You wanted more."

"Exactly! You understand."

"Actually I don't, because I am only twelve years old. But Chloe clued me in to the nature of men." *And boys*, she thought, remembering how Ion had wanted to sneak in some action. She couldn't blame him, being curious about it herself, but hadn't wanted to get him in trouble with his mother.

"That's it. They are so limited. If I could only find a male, any male, who was truly different, where that was only one of many interests, then it would be another matter. I'm just hoping that the elf princes of my future *are* different, at least to that extent. He wouldn't even have to be my own species of elf."

Vinia remembered that there were many species of elves, light and dark, ranging from small to human size. That broadened the prospects. "We hope to have you princesses make holograms to introduce yourselves to prospective partners. When we find the right ones, we'll bring them here to meet you."

"That seems like a good plan. I will cooperate as well as I am able to."

The mind changed again. This time there was a buzzing sound. That must be the bee princess. "Hello," Vinia said, and introduced herself.

"I am Beetrix," the princess said as her image clarified. She was a healthy blue-and-yellow bee with translucent wings. She was buzzing her wings, but the telepathically enabled scene translated it into words. "My name means She Brings Joy. I'm sure I could have done that, as all the drones were interested in only one thing for their joy."

"Which would have confined you to a lifetime of laying eggs, nothing else," Vinia said.

"You got it. I wanted to fly free, experience the world, enjoy myself. Egg-laying could wait and be intermittent so I could get some variety. Nobody else understood."

Bees did not understand independence, to be sure. "Are you sure you want a drone prince? I understand they hardly have minds at all, just focus on that one thing."

"If an independent one exists, he'll be an outcast like me. That's the one I want, if you can find him."

"All the crystallized princesses are going to make holograms to share their preferences. When you make yours to introduce yourself, make sure you make that clear," Vinia said. "So that he will know you exist."

"I will."

That concluded the interviews. Vinia came out of her trance and looked at the others on the carpet. "I have a lot to tell you." And she did.

"I think you have it," Ion said when Vinia finished. "The next step is to see about recording those interviews."

But Vinia, partly to her own surprise, had a reservation. Something about all this was bothering her.

"Uh-oh," Hilda said. "I have seen that expression before, and that foggy cloud over your head. You have a Doubt."

"I suppose I do," Vinia said apologetically.

"What is it? You're the protagonist; it surely counts."

"I'm not sure. It's just that something about this disturbs me. I don't know what, exactly, just that something's not quite right. Maybe it's just my general background uncertainty."

"And maybe it isn't," Hilda said firmly. "You have more sense than you think you have." She glanced at Ion and Benny, who nodded. So did Dragoman.

But still it didn't coalesce. "I don't know exactly what it is."

"Borrow my thinking cap," Benny said. "It is generally good for one idea at a time. You can tell by the dim flash. Put it on and focus on your Doubt." He held it out.

Vinia wasn't sure that would work, but she was not the type to argue, so she accepted the cap and set it on her head. Then she eyed the little Doubt cloud.

There was a bright triple flash, and the cloud was blasted to fragments of evaporating dark mist. "Oh!" Vinia exclaimed as the cap sailed off her head. Benny quietly recovered it.

"I suspect it worked," Ion murmured. Dragoman's long lip curled in the semblance of a smile, as a puff of his smoke incorporated the last bit of mist.

"Out with it," Hilda said. "All three of it."

Now, at least, things were clear. "The first flash was mixed doubt and idea," Vinia said. "The princesses shouldn't go out to scattered kingdoms, with or without princes. They may not be welcome, any more than they were in the past. We just don't know, so it's a gamble. Maybe they should stay here, not as crystals but alive and active."

"Now wait half an instant," the dragon said. "I am looking forward to a peaceful retirement, not a chronic hassle with awakened imperious princesses. It was bad enough when they were frozen. All too soon they'd be quarreling and getting things all up in a heaval, ruffling my scales. I want them out of my lair."

"Of course," Vinia agreed. "That's the content of the second flash. They would stay here, not in your lair, but on your larger estate. They can form their own feminist kingdom, which the princes can join as consorts, running it themselves in whatever manner they choose. Not in your way at all. You will be like a patron god."

"Patron god! To a bunch of narcissistic girls? Only a Demon could enjoy that, but the damsels might not much like the way he did." Male Demons were known to be grabby, just as female Demons were likely to be seductive.

"That was the rest of that flash," Vinia said. "You may dream of retire-ment alone, but that is unrealistic. You'd very soon be lonely as Hades. No, you don't really want to be alone, after all these centuries with the prin-cesses, even if they are more like dolls than people, in their crystal state. You need some compatible company. You can't deny it."

Dragoman's mouth opened to formulate a denial, but all that came out were thoughtful puffs of smoke. He had gotten accustomed to the pres-ence of the princesses. "I must admit that I have been in touch with Chloe, the telepath. We have chatted at some length on occasion, un-dullifying a quiet evening."

"Precisely. You like girls. That's why you have that girl tattoo. Why you agreed to this Service deal for the estate. It prevented you from being alone, in virtual solitary confinement, all this time, since you don't get along well with your own kind. In your private fancy you really like girls, and want them liking you, hugging you, riding you, kissing your scales, the way damsels in fantasy do with their dragons."

The dragon puffed smoke, unable to deny that, either.

"Well, this is your chance. You let the princesses use your nice estate, and they'll be girlishly grateful forever after."

Now Dragoman had a small objection. "That kingdom they might make—it needs a name. A kingdom is not a kingdom without a signifi-cant moniker."

"That was the third flash," Vinia said. "The name of it will be Thanx, like Xanth backward, pronounced Thanks."

"That will do," the dragon agreed.

"That thinking cap really came through for you," Ion said.

"It really did," Vinia agreed. "But there's still a trace of doubt I can't quite spot."

"Let me check for that," Benny said. He put on the thinking cap. There was a flash. They all looked at him. "Got it," he said. "It's that we can't just decide this for the princesses. They need to discuss this among them-selves, together, since they are the ones most concerned."

"That's it," Vinia agreed. "Can we make a joint dream with them all in it together?"

"And we visitors, too," Hilda said. "We're the ones who will have to follow up, locating the princes for them. It makes a difference whether they plan to go to the princes' home kingdoms, or stay here to form their own."

"I will contact Chloe," Dragoman said. "She will know whether such a large dream is feasible."

After an instant more than a moment, Chloe reappeared in Vinia's mind. "A large joint dream?" she asked.

Vinia explained the problem. Chloe nodded. "I believe I can do it, but it will stretch my mental resource to the limit. I won't be able to participate in the dialogue myself. I'll be too busy keeping everyone else in the picture. You may have noticed that I faded out when enabling your dialogues with the other princesses. This would be more so."

"But it's your decision too. Is there anyone else who thinks as you do, who can speak for you?"

"Demesne, maybe. She's a sensible Demoness."

"Yes. I have a ring to contact her."

"Oh? I didn't see it."

"It's invisible." Vinia looked at her ring finger. "Demesne."

The Demoness's face appeared before her. "Time for my interview?"

"Not exactly. We're going to have a joint dream for a discussion, all the princesses and all the rest of us, too, but Chloe can't participate because she'll be too busy enabling it. Can you speak for her when she needs to answer a question?"

"That depends on the question."

"Whether to make a feminist kingdom here, instead of scattering to the princes' realms."

"Oho! I like that notion."

"But does Chloe like it too?"

"She surely does. She's an independent cuss, like me. Like us all."

"Thank you. You can say that, when you need to."

Demesne faded, and Chloe returned. "I heard," she said. "She's right; I do like the notion."

"Good enough. Now can we make the big dream?"

"Yes, but you waking folk will need to cooperate by focusing to the point of a near trance."

"I will tell the others." Vinia exited her own trance state. "She can do it, but we need to go into trance states to participate."

"On our way," Hilda said. She and Ion sat back and closed their eyes, and Benny followed suit. So did the dragon.

Vinia shut her own eyes, returning to the scene. "On their way," she said.

"Then welcome to Cloud Nine." Chloe faded.

Vinia found herself on a small white cloud with a raised rim so that nothing would roll off it. Beyond it she could see distant mountains. She looked to her other side and saw down to the patchwork of the countryside, similar to the view from the magic carpet. It was floating serenely across the Land of Xanth.

Dragoman was the first to join her there. "She has used this setting before, in our dialogues," he said. "Think of it as like your flying carpet, only softer."

"I think I just did." Vinia pinched an errant tuft of cloud. "You're right: it is softer."

Then, one by one, the other princesses and members of the Quest appeared, ten in all, seated around the cloud in two groups using deck chairs made of cloud foam. The Questers knew about the meeting, but it was new to the princesses. "Uh, I think we need a moderator," Vinia said. "Someone to introduce folk, explain things, and keep order. Maybe you, Demesne?"

The Demoness nodded. "I said I would help where needed. This must be the first occasion." She looked around. "First we need to know one another somewhat. I am Demesne Demoness, with the talent of organization of person or place." She glanced at Vinia. "This is Vinia Human, whom all of you know. Vinia, why did you call this joint meeting?" She knew, of course, but was making it clear to everyone.

"We got an idea," Vinia said. "But the princesses need to discuss it and approve it before it goes any further. It is to make a feminist kingdom here on Dragoman's estate, rather than have you scatter to different kingdoms that may not really be any better for you than our original ones were. To bring the princes in as consorts rather than rulers. To call this kingdom Thanx."

"Thank you, Vinia," Demesne said. "So we have the subject. Now the participants. You all know Dragoman Dragon, of course." She glanced his way. He was coiled on a third area of the cloud. He puffed a ball of smoke in acknowledgment. "He has a vested interest in the welfare of the princesses and won't let us go until he is certain we are where we need to be, with whom we should be."

The others looked at the dragon, recognizing him.

"The children are Prince Ion, a Magician of elixirs," Demesne continued smoothly. Ion nodded. "His twin sister, Hilda, a Sorceress of sewing. There is magic in her craftsmanship. For example, she made the flying carpet that brought them here." Hilda nodded. "And Benny Buck, Hilda's associate." Benny nodded. "They are here because they are the ones actually on the Quest to rescue us. They will have to explain about us to the prospective princes, so they need to know everything they can, including how we look and talk and think. I think they will mainly just be watching our discussion."

The princesses looked at the Questers, evidently not completely certain of their relevance, but did not challenge them.

"And the other princesses. One is Chloe Centaur, who is here in spirit rather than appearance. She is the telepath who is enabling this mutual dream. She looks like this." The Demoness fuzzed into smoke, then formed into the aspect of Chloe, complete with gently waving wings. "Hello, all," she said in Chloe's voice, then fizzed back to Demesne. "Hula Human, who can dance provocatively." Hula nodded as she stood briefly to flex her hips. Vinia saw both Ion and Benny take note, momentarily fascinated; they were evocative hips. "Elga Elf." Nod. "Goblette Goblin, whose talent is to intoxicate a man by gazing into his eyes."

"It's a tease," Goblette said. "And self-defense. My romantic interest is in a princess, not a prince."

"And Beetrix Bee," Demesne concluded. Beetrix buzzed her wings without lifting off the cloud.

"Now the question," Demesne said. "Does anyone have pros or cons about the Kingdom, or rather Queendom of Thanx? Show of hands, please, and I will call on you in turn, to maintain some semblance of order."

All four other princesses raised their hands.

Demesne smiled. "I am glad to see such general interest. Hula?"

"I love the idea. But we can't just take Dragoman's land. What does he think of this?"

"Dragoman?"

The dragon cleared his throat, puffing smoke. "Vinia pointed out to me that I'd be lonely, retiring alone. I would like to have your continuing company, provided it is voluntary."

"Our appreciative company," Demesne said, glancing significantly at the other princesses.

Hula took the hint. She got up and walked to the dragon, her hips swaying. She put her arm around his neck. "If you do this for us, dear dragon, we will do this for you." She kissed a scale.

Dragoman's scales turned pink. He was blushing. Vinia realized that in the real world that might not be possible, but this was a dream scene where special effects were easy.

Goblette walked over. "Me, too, for this scene." She hugged him from the other side, then gazed into his eye and exerted her power. It was of course intoxicating, at least for that side.

Elga joined them. She climbed up on Dragoman's head and kissed an ear. She whispered a sweet nothing. That was apparent by the empty speech balloon that floated up. The balloon itself was heart shaped.

The dragon practically melted. His secret dream was becoming wonderfully real.

"I suspect this will be a daily scene, in the Queendom of Thanx," Demesne said. "Giving thanx should be popular there."

In due course, or maybe slightly overdue, the princesses returned to their places, leaving the dragon in a satisfied slump.

"I think we are agreed that we like the idea of Thanx," Demesne said. "The presentations we record can specify that the princes must come to us, not we to them. That should be an excellent selective device."

The princess bee buzzed. "Yes, Beetrix," the Demoness said.

More buzzing. Then the telepathic translation kicked in. "How will our messages be recorded? We can't transmit dreams."

"Good point," Demesne said. She looked at Dragoman. "Is there anything suitable in your dragon hoard? I know those treasures are not necessarily confined to gems and metals."

"There is," the dragon agreed. "I have half a dozen Dreaming Jewels I saved decades ago in the hope that they might someday be useful. They are extremely rare, being blue rubies." He flicked his tail. "Here they are." Six blue rubies appeared.

Vinia was amazed. They could be brought into this dream? But of course they were evidently the stuff of dreams. As for their color: they had to be rare indeed, as a ruby was red by definition. Anything else was sapphire.

"How do they work?" Demesne asked.

"Simply stand before one, invoke it, and do your presentation. When you are done, say 'Cut,' and it has your scene. Invoking it again thereafter will play the scene as a spot hologram."

"That should do it," the Demoness agreed. "Thanx."

Now Goblette had a comment. "If we are going to have a kingdom, I mean queendom, we should organize it, in case the princes have questions about who's in charge and how it's run. For example, who is to be the queen of it?"

"I hadn't thought of that," Demesne said. "Perhaps we should consider nominations and vote."

"I nominate you," the goblin said. "You have the mind for organizing it."

"Oh, I wasn't thinking of—"

"I second the nomination," Elga said.

"All in favor say aye," Hula said.

All four princesses said, "Aye."

It occurred to Vinia that this could be the good luck Dara's ring was bringing her friend. The ring had oriented on Demesne to bring them here, so she was the target. But it could also just be coincidence.

"But Chloe didn't get to vote," the Demoness protested weakly.

"Majority already carries it," Goblette said. "Would Chloe object?"

"Well, no. But—"

"And the other offices," Hula said. "I believe I could handle Entertainment. I would start with dance classes."

"Chloe should handle Communications," Goblette said. "With her telepathy she can communicate with anyone or any creature. That's important for interkingdom commerce."

"And I can dandle Defense," Beetrix buzzed. "Once I get my hive going. No one with tender flesh will try to raid more than once."

"And I can handle Cuisine," Goblette said. "I'm a wicked cook. Meals are important."

"I know how to keep a castle in order," Elga said. "Elvin design and maintenance are notorious. My job."

Demesne sighed. "It seems we have our assignments."

Was being queen really good luck for her? Vinia wondered. *Or a duty she would have been satisfied without?* It was hard to know.

"Now those presentations," Goblette said. "Who first?"

The Demoness smiled. "You first. You plainly have the initiative for it."

"As you wish." The goblin walked to the dragon's area and picked up a gem. "Maybe we should have a better setting. How about a poolside interview?"

Demesne considered. "Chloe made this dream setting. Maybe she can modify it slightly."

A lovely blue-green pool formed in the center of the cloud, almost dunking Benny. He backed off, smiling. "More bang for the buck," he murmured.

Goblette took her place beside the pool. She set the gem down near it, then stood between the gem and the pool so there would be a poolside background. "Invoke." A spherical flare of light spread out from the ruby to include the goblin.

"I am Princess Goblette Gobliness, a resident of the Queendom of Thanx. I am looking for a suitable princess to join me here and help me run the Cuisine." She continued, neatly summarizing the situation and her place in it. "Cut." The light sphere faded out. She picked up the gem and tucked it in her hair.

The other princesses followed, except for Chloe, who would have to do hers later. It was soon done.

"That's a relief," Hula said. "Let's relax with a nice swim in the pool. I'm sure it is suitably warm and fresh." She doffed her clothes in a single motion and waded into the water. In three-fifths of a moment Goblette joined her, and then Elga. All three had marvelous figures that the bouncing activity did nothing to conceal. They seemed to have forgotten that there were three males watching. Or had they?

Beetrix remained clear, as swimming was not a bee thing, but she seemed to be enjoying the show. Chloe, of course, could not participate directly.

"Oh, bleep, why not?" Demesne asked rhetorically. Her own clothing puffed into smoke, exposing a splendid body, and she sailed up over the pool, coming down in a belly flop that splashed all the spectators. None of them complained.

Then the four engaged in a happy splash battle, while Dragoman, Ion, and Benny watched, raptly. They did not freak out, quite, as one was a dragon and one or two were underage, and anyway there were no panties in view.

Hilda's eye caught Vinia's. Then they got up as one, doffed their own clothes, and leaped into the pool to join the fun. They were younger than the others, but a good splashing party was not to be missed. It was all just a dream anyway, wasn't it? What happened in a dream stayed in the dream, no?

Chapter 4

ELVES

Back in the air, they relaxed. "You girls were naughty," Benny said. "Not that I'm objecting."

"You always say you want to see more of me," Hilda said. "Now you have."

"And Ion saw more of me," Vinia said as she held the guiding bar, it being her turn to steer the carpet. "In his dream."

"Not to mention four grown princesses," Ion said. "They had really nice—"

Both girls glared at him.

"Splashes," he concluded. "In my dream."

They all laughed.

"The dread Adult Conspiracy has trouble policing dreams," Hilda said. "Fortunately dreams are harmless."

"But fun," Benny said, looking at her in a manner that verged on violation.

"I wonder whether in the dream we could have enhanced our bodies to be more, well, mature," Hilda wondered. "Too bad we didn't think of it in time."

"Too bad," Ion agreed. "Maybe next time."

Vinia spoke to her invisible ring. "Castle Roogna, please." Would that bring good luck to the capital?

The ring flashed, showing the direction. She steered the carpet that way as it gained altitude. They were on their way to locate the first prince.

Hilda, peering down into the passing patchwork, spoke. "What is that?"

Ion and Benny joined her. "Something is toasting a butternut tree," Benny said. "The butter is melting into the ground and the leaves are curling."

"That's not nice," Hilda said. "Those trees are harmless, and the butternuts are good on pancakes."

"Maybe we should investigate," Ion said.

Vinia steered the carpet around and down until they came to the tree. It was being enveloped by a fiery cloud and was burning up.

"Hey!" Ion called. "Leave that tree be."

The fire continued. So Ion brought out a vial and loosed a vapor. It expanded and spread, floating toward the tree. When it got there, the fire fizzled out. It was fire retardant.

The fire cloud reacted angrily. It charged the carpet, enveloping it, but couldn't do it or its riders any harm. Then it coalesced and changed form, becoming a fiery human-form female in a flaming gown standing before them. "Who the blazes are you, you puny children, that you dare interfere with me?" she demanded.

"I am Prince Magician Ion, and these are my associates Princess Sorceress Hilda, Vinia Human, and Benny Buck. Who are you?"

"I am Fiera Fire Cloud, evil twin sister of Fracto Rain Cloud. Any fool who messes with me gets burned."

Ion frowned. "Any fool who messes with a Magician gets doused."

Fiera huffed into a raging flame. "Oh, yeah?"

Ion brought out another vial. "Yeah."

Fiera charged, this time reaching the carpet, having become compact enough to pass the protective shield. Vinia tried not to flinch.

Ion uncapped the vial. A cloud of mist emerged. It intercepted Fiera as she moved and clothed her in ice. Her flame-colored hair froze in place, and her gown turned icy, cracked, and fell away, leaving her naked. Vinia saw the boys' eyes widen appreciatively. In this form Fiera did have a figure.

"Why you insolent brat!" she exclaimed, flaming into white heat. "I'll detonate you!"

Ion opened another vial. This time an ice dragon emerged, far larger than the vial. It whipped about and breathed a shivering vapor on Fiera. She was instantly enclosed in a block of ice.

It didn't stop her fury. She exploded like a firecracker, bursting the ice apart. She launched herself at the ice dragon, flinging her arms around its neck, making it sizzle into steam. Then she turned back to Ion.

Who was holding another vial. "I can keep this up as long as you can," he said calmly. As a boy he might appreciate her figure, but as a Magician he was all business. "Until I get annoyed. Then I'll stop playing games and try for better effect." As threats went this was understated, but it was hardly empty.

Fiera started to swell in fury. Then she paused. "You're not afraid of me, are you?" she asked in dawning wonder.

Ion laughed. "Why should I fear a fire spirit? I've got dozens in my vials. They are like elixirs, and I collect elixirs, being immune to them. Now, are you dull witted and need more proof?"

Her transition was sudden. "No, I think I've seen enough. You really are a Magician."

"I really am. Now I suggest you depart, so I can douse this poor innocent tree with healing elixir."

"I'll just burn up other trees, hither and yon. It's what I do. Incidental mischief. You'll never be able to save them all. But you can stop me."

Ion didn't trust this. He glanced at Vinia.

Vinia stepped into the dialogue. "Hello. I am Vinia. Are you bargaining?"

Fiera turned a fiery face on her. "Maybe. He does impress me."

Vinia didn't trust this either. "You offer what for what?"

"I will burn up no more trees, as long as . . ."

"As long as what?"

Fiera turned back to Ion. "As long as you are my boyfriend, Magician. I happen to be short on boyfriends at the moment."

Uh-oh. Probably this moment and any moment. "He's taken," Vinia said.

"By whom?"

This was treacherous ground, but she was stuck for it. "By me."

Fiera nodded. "You're a child. You look to be about twelve. I'm adult, and I don't honor the stupid human Conspiracy. Can you offer him this?" She stood up straight, turning, inhaling, showing off a truly voluptuous nude figure. "I don't have to be burning all the time. I can cool to merely hot." She did a little skip, moving her legs just so. She was hot, all right.

Vinia could see that Ion, no longer in combative Magician mode, was on the verge of freaking out, his eyes reflecting woman-shaped fire. This was no dream. The shape-changing cloud really could offer Ion something special that Vinia herself could not, at least not yet, and she knew he wanted it. Adult naughtiness. What could she do?

Desperate, she glanced at Hilda, knowing she would help if she could. But could she?

"Ion, summon an elemental fire spirit," Hilda said. "A ranking one. Not one of your bottled nonentities."

Responding almost in a trance, Ion fished out a vial and flipped off its cap. Vapor issued forth. There was a peculiar smell. The others waited, but that was all.

Fiera sniffed. "That's a pheromone," she murmured. "But what kind?"

Then another figure appeared, in flaming man form. "I am FireBrand, Brand for short. Who summons me?" an imperious male voice demanded.

"We did," Hilda answered. "We've got a fire fem who is in need of a competent boyfriend. Are you the one?"

"Of course I am," Brand said. "That elixir summons only dominant single handsome males. But is she the one I want?"

Hilda turned to Fiera. "Do your thing again."

Intrigued, Fiera did her turn, inhale, and skip. Vinia was privately jealous; the fire cloud did have the stuff to show off. Of course her form was designed for that effect.

"Answer: affirmative," Brand said. Indeed, he looked hotter than before. What was there about minidances that appealed so strongly to males? Vinia decided to learn that dance for possible future use, when maybe she had the right form for it.

"Then she's yours," Hilda said. "Take her and keep her out of mischief."

"Hey, I haven't agreed," Fiera protested. She glanced at Vinia. "Were *you* just assigned to be the Magician's girlfriend?"

"No," Vinia answered. "It just happened. We liked each other."

"So you did have some choice."

"Yes."

"Isn't that the way it should be for anyone?"

Vinia had to be honest, though it cost her. "Yes." She rather admired the cloud's spunk.

"So we agree on that."

"Yes."

"Enough of this girly chat chat." Brand moved to Fiera, took her in his fiery arms, and kissed her fiery lips. A blazing little heart flew up. So much for her question of agreement or even of choice. Vinia was almost sorry.

The two fire spirits puffed into vapor and faded out.

Vinia seized the initiative, not wanting her boyfriend to suffer an extended afterimage of the fire maiden. He was already halfway freaked out. "Now heal the tree, Ion,"

Ion opened another vial, responding to her voice despite his incapacity. The vapor surrounded the charred butternut tree. Immediately the burned bark sloughed off and little green leaves sprouted. It was healing.

"Good enough," Hilda said.

Now Ion emerged from his near trance. "What just happened?"

"Another dream," Vinia said fondly. Then she guided the carpet up, up, and away, gliding high into the sky.

They reached Castle Roogna, Xanth's human capital, without further event. They had been there before, of course, more than once, but this time it was more important business.

King Ivy greeted them warmly, as always, making sure to include Benny and Vinia. "It's always nice to see my sister's family." She was king, not queen, because of a peculiarity of custom and language that other kingdoms did not share. She and Ida looked similar, except that Ivy did not have a moon orbiting her head. Her magic was Enhancement. "I feel so lucky to have you visit."

A figure of speech? Or was it the ring's luck? Vinia feared she was being concerned over nothing. What did it matter, anyway?

"This time we're on business," Hilda said. "We are rescuing six crystallized princesses of assorted species, but first we need six suitable princes for them."

"Ah, those princesses. Ida spoke of them in passing."

"Yes. She feels they're okay where they are. But we think they deserve more. We met them, in a dream, and like them. Today we need a human prince. Do you know of any who might like to join the small feminist Queendom of Thanx?"

The king's brow arched. "I am not familiar with that queendom."

"It doesn't exist yet," Hilda explained. "But it will once we get the right princes."

Ivy considered. "There are princes, but I fear they would not care to settle for secondary status in a feminist habitat. They're men, you know."

"We know," Hilda said. "It's a problem."

Then Ivy got an idea. "There was a change in the neighboring Shee kingdom last year. The Shee are light elves. It was taken over by a woman, who deposed her father the king. We have gotten along well with the new regime."

"An elf kingdom?" Hilda asked. "We're looking for human."

"There are many varieties of elves, of different colors and sizes. The Shee are so close to human as to be commonly mistaken for us, to their annoyance. Same size, similar features. At any rate, the former king of Shee is now an adviser to his daughter the queen. I would not be surprised if deep down inside he might bear just a bit of resentment for his lowered status. For one thing, his daughter married a bird, so now the bird outranks him in the royal hierarchy. He might be amenable to joining a new kingdom."

"A bird?" Vinia asked, surprised.

"It's a complicated story. He's a very smart, shape-changing bird."

"But a king?" Hilda asked. "Wouldn't he be, well, old for a princess?"

Ivy smiled tolerantly. "Age is less important to a man than to a woman. An older man can be more than satisfied to marry a young woman, especially if she's pretty, and often young women prefer older men, especially if they are smart or powerful. Nothing can be certain until they meet, but we might form a fair estimate. What does your princess look like?"

"We could play her dreaming jewel recording," Vinia said.

They played it, and Hula Human performed her evocative dance, waving her long dark hair about as her ample hips swayed.

"Oh, yes, he'll like her," Ivy said.

"But he doesn't even know her," Vinia protested.

Ivy smiled again in her knowing way. "Men hardly care what is in a woman's mind, just what she looks like. He'll like her. He will agree to almost anything, in exchange for her favor. The only question is whether *she* will like *him*. You must impress on him the need to impress her. That should do it."

It seemed almost too simple. But they had seen how men were captivated by sexy women, and Hula was that. They agreed to give it a try. If it didn't work out, they would resume their search.

They spent the rest of the day relaxing at Castle Roogna, chatting with the resident ghosts and zombies, and next morning they took off for the Kingdom of Shee. They arrived around midday and asked to talk with Queen Birdie. The folk there did seem almost identical to humans. Birds were everywhere, a clearly favored type.

Birdie was gracious. "King Ivy messaged us you were coming. Something about setting up a new feminist kingdom?"

"Queendom," Hilda said, and explained.

"Father might indeed be interested to join a woman of that description," Birdie said. "He hasn't said anything, but I know he's a bit restive about the changed situation here, especially the favored status of the birds. Certainly you should talk to him. I will set up an appointment."

In the afternoon they met with Sherlock, former king of Shee. Like his daughter, he had light blue hair and eyes and seemed completely human. He was in his early forties and looked fit and actually halfway handsome.

"A feminist kingdom?" he asked doubtfully.

"A mixed species queendom. They will call it the Queendom of Thanx," Vinia explained. "It will be small, but surely good for independent women."

"This interests me. After the way I acted as king, I want to support women's efforts to improve their situation."

They played the Princess Hula scene for him. "What a woman!" he said. "And a princess in her own right. She's perfect." Any objections he might have had about the queendom seemed to have vanished. "But would she be interested in me? I am a king only in name, courtesy of my daughter."

"I might be," the figure in the scene said, startling them all. Then they realized that it was an add-on mischievously included, anticipating his likely question.

That settled, they discussed the details. "The princesses will do the choosing," Ion warned. "You will have to impress Princess Hula."

"That comes with the territory," Sherlock agreed. "I have been advising my daughter and have picked up a notion how to play the role." He sighed. "The fact is, I was not a great king. The power went to my head, and I demanded that everything be done only my way. I even imprisoned Birdie to make her accede to the prince I had selected for her to marry, was furious when she escaped, and tried to kill her when she returned. No wonder the people got fed up with me. I had become a rogue king. She has treated me far more generously than I treated her. I am ashamed of my former role, and I mean never to be that way again, regardless of my future power or lack of it."

He seemed sincere. Vinia hoped it lasted. "I wonder," she said. "You are actually an elf?"

"A Shee, a light elf," he agreed. "There are many varieties of elves, as there are of humans. You also have dwarfs and giants and assorted colors."

"One of our princesses is Elga Elf, who stands about knee-high to you and is dusky. She is quite pretty, with long blond hair, but says she has one bad blemish, though we have not seen it."

"She sounds like a fee. Do you have a picture?"

"Better than that. She made her own dreaming jewel presentation, similar to Hula's. We can show it to you."

They played it. "Definitely a fee," Sherlock said. Then as it ended he added, "There's an addendum. It may be important."

"Oh?" Vinia asked. "We saw nothing."

"You are not an elf. Let me touch the jewel."

When he touched it, the recording resumed. "If you see this, you are an elf," Elga said. "You know that each of us fees has one disfiguring flaw. Here is mine." She stripped away her clothing and stood bare. She had a snakelike tail half the length of her body.

Vinia was astonished. "But she splashed in the pool with the others! I never saw a tail."

"Nor did I," Hilda said, also surprised.

"Nor I," Ion said. "I thought her blemish might be a hidden wart on her bottom. Something like that."

"I didn't see it, either," Benny said. "I thought she imagined it."

"Elves are adept at concealment," Sherlock said. "She probably wrapped the tail around her waist and covered it with a flesh-colored belt. For a brief appearance that could have sufficed."

"It sufficed," Vinia agreed.

"But of course we weren't looking at her waist," Benny said. "The rest of her figure was perfect."

"Especially her bare—" Ion started, before Vinia's look cut him off.

"The fee can change forms to a limited degree or turn invisible briefly. She probably did not show you those qualities, either."

"She did not," Vinia agreed. "But we saw her only briefly, in the dream."

"Now you know her secret," Sherlock said. "Do not reveal it elsewhere. That would be unkind."

"We will not," the four agreed.

"We want to help her, not hurt her," Vinia added.

"But will it spoil her for a fee elf prince?" Hilda asked worriedly.

"Not at all. All the fees have deformities. It will confirm her as authentic. That's why she made the addendum. He will have a flaw, too. They just don't care to advertise it to nonelves, understandably."

"They all have snakes' tails?" Vinia asked.

"No, some have ducks' feet. Some have extremely hairy bodies. It varies. But every fee has something."

"Now I am glad we enlisted you as an ally," Ion said. "You are really helping us understand things."

"I am glad of that. I want to make a good impression on the princesses of Thanx. That begins with making a good impression on the four of you."

"Do you happen to know where the fee live?" Vinia asked. She did not mention that Dara's ring could guide them to it, out of simple caution.

"I do. Their kingdom is small, but within range of the Shee. We had distant relations in my day, and amicable ones now that my daughter is in charge. Her birds visit them often. Getting there will be no problem, if you have transportation."

"We do," Hilda said.

"Then I think we are ready to go," Hilda said. "The sooner we collect six princes, the sooner we can complete our mission."

Sherlock shook his head. "I don't want to annoy you, but you are children and you are dealing with adults. There may be problems you don't anticipate. Things tend to be more complicated in practice than they may seem in theory."

Vinia had the nasty feeling that he was making sense.

Hilda smiled. "You can ride beside me and annoy me while we travel."

He nodded. "As you prefer."

They bid farewell to Queen Birdie and boarded the carpet. It was Benny's turn to guide it, so he took his place at the steering bar. Vinia settled near him, as she wasn't certain he had all the details straight yet. Sherlock sat beside Hilda.

"Where to?" Benny asked.

"I will point the direction when we're aloft," Sherlock said.

Vinia had the ring. She would quietly verify it as they traveled.

The carpet took off. "Impressive," Sherlock murmured. "I have not seen a flying carpet quite like this one before, and I have seen a good many."

"It's a custom carpet. Hilda sewed it to our specs," Ion explained. "That's her talent. She sews magic into material."

"And she is a Sorceress," Sherlock said. "I think I had not before fully appreciated the magnitude of it."

"Are you trying to flatter me?" Hilda asked.

He laughed. "I see you are already wary of flatterers. I am, or was, a king; I know exactly how that works. I was completely surrounded by flatterers and was sick of it. But in this case I was genuinely surprised, so the compliment was accidental. However, now a genuine one: your instinct is correct, and you should constantly beware of flattery, as nine-tenths of it is false. Especially when you mature into a queen. The flatterers have their own agenda, and they will find ways to please you, fairly or falsely, so that you will unconsciously support their designs. That is one reason princesses tend to marry princes; they can't fully trust others to be candid."

"Can they trust princes?" Hilda asked.

Sherlock laughed again. "No. A prince is the worst of all, ironically, because he mainly wants to get into her—" He broke off. "My apology. I forgot for the moment that I was talking to a child."

"Get into her what?" Hilda asked.

"My daughter is grown. I have gotten out of practice honoring the Adult Conspiracy. I think you know I can't properly answer you."

But Hilda was determined. "A fire elemental approached my brother, flashing him with her hot figure. It mesmerized him. He would have been in trouble if Vinia and I had not intervened. Ignorance is not bliss. We need to know what we're up against, lest we be hurt by it. We are recruiting princes for princesses. We need to understand what motivates them. What does a prince want to get into?"

Vinia was impressed. Hilda had a case, and she was making it.

Sherlock shook his head. "You are making it difficult."

Vinia interceded. "We understand that a significant part of governance is compromise. Can you compromise on this?"

The man considered. "Perhaps I can rephrase. The word I did not say was 'pants.' In that context it suggests that the prince wants to do something with the princess that the Adult Conspiracy forbids a child to know."

Hilda shook her head. "At this rate of comprehension, I will be an adult before I figure it out."

"Exactly," Sherlock agreed, amused. The others weren't.

It was time to change the subject. "We had four riders," Vinia said. "Now we have five. Where will Sherlock sleep?"

"I will sew an attachment," Hilda said. She got to work.

"An attachment?" Sherlock asked.

"Like an addition to a tent," Hilda explained. "So you have private quarters."

He nodded. "A consideration," the Shee said. "Do you know where the Princess Elga came from?"

"She didn't say," Vinia said.

"There are not many fee tribes in this region. It could be the one we are going to. That could have positive and negative complications."

"Why?"

"If this is her home tribe, they should know her, or of her if she is of a prior generation. There might have been a reason she left."

"She's a feminist."

"That might suffice. The fee are socially orthodox. Princes tend not to like feminism."

Hilda smiled. "Maybe her dreaming jewel presentation will make a difference. It did for you, with Hula."

"It certainly did. We'll just have to see."

In due course they came to the fee area. Sherlock said, "Now their premises are in subterranean crystal caves with secret entrance passages."

"Crystal caves," Vinia said. "And Elga was crystallized."

"Coincidence, I believe. Fortunately I know of one tribe, the Fo. We traded on occasion."

"The Fo?" Vinia asked, perplexed.

"They are one of three tribes we know of in Xanth," Sherlock said. "Fee Fi, Fo, Fum. The fee are small in stature, so don't freely advertise their presence without reason." Then he paused. "Oops. I overlooked a detail."

"Detail?" Hilda asked alertly.

"The fee stand about one-third of our height. Their caves are sized to fit them, not us. We won't be able to enter."

"I think I can take care of that," Ion said. "Accommodation elixir."

"I know of the accommodation spell," Sherlock said. "That enables couples of disparate sizes to, um, interact. There is an elixir?"

"The accommodation spell uses it," Ion said. "I have a collection of useful elixirs, including this one. We will simply shrink the carpet and its immediate environment to fee scale. We will seem to ourselves to be exactly as before; only the environment will seem to triple in size. This would not work in Mundania, because of their odd square/cube law, but this is magic, not science."

"I think I have not before properly appreciated the power of your own magic," Sherlock said. "But of course I have not interacted with many Magicians or Sorcerers of any species."

"The effect will last only an hour, but I can renew it if necessary. That should be enough to make our case."

Vinia knew of accommodation spells that enabled big ogres and miniature imps to interact intimately, but this was new to her. The five of them and the carpet together? She loved and admired Ion, yet hoped that he really did know what he was doing here and wasn't being overconfident.

"One thing to remember," Sherlock said. "Each fee will have a deformity. Do not mention it. Do not even notice it. Just tune it out."

"We'll try," Hilda said. "Does the king have one too?"

"Yes. I understand he has giant ears."

"We can handle that."

"One more thing: it is customary for visitors to bring gifts for the king. I regret I didn't think of it until now. You should have been given more warning."

Hilda looked at her brother. "You have not been using your minicarpet recently. We could give him that, and I could sew you another later on."

"That's fine," Ion agreed. "I prefer Vinia, anyway, no disparagement to the carpet."

Vinia felt a thrill at the compliment, but stayed out of the dialogue.

"But there is a complication," Sherlock said. "Such gifts are not presented outright as such. They are given as if incidentally. It might be awkward to make a magic carpet seem incidental."

"We'll be alert for a pretext," Ion said.

Vinia concluded that Dara's ring had oriented, at least indirectly, on Sherlock, so his considerable usefulness to them was the good luck it fostered. Still, the case was not certain.

Hilda completed her attachment, which looked like a simple square of cloth. She took it to the edge of the carpet and sewed it on. Suddenly it formed into, yes, a new tent compartment. Sherlock's private quarters were ready.

They came to the entrance area. There was a giant acorn tree with a high cluster of spreading branches. "At the top, hidden by foliage, is the entrance to one of the passages to the crystal caves," Sherlock said. "It is time to invoke the accommodation."

Ion brought out a vial as they hovered beside the tree. "Do not be alarmed," he said. "Neither we nor the environment are actually changing. They merely appear to do so. But the effect is persuasive." He uncapped the vial, letting the vapor puff out.

Suddenly the tree expanded to double, then triple its original size. Or were they shrinking equivalently? It was hard to tell.

Benny steered the carpet up, circling the tree. He glided it into gaps in the foliage where the big branches diverged. And there was a hole in the center of the trunk, big enough for them to enter.

"Hang on," Benny said. He had evidently had some prior experience with this type of maneuver. The carpet tilted until it was hovering vertically, not horizontally, above the hole. But all of them remained comfortably in place. It was as if the tree had gone horizontal to match them.

Then they floated down into the hole. There was a faint glow around the edge, marking it as a tunnel. Down, down they went, traversing the length of the tree. Then, evidently belowground, they rounded a curve and flew level again. They were safely on their way to the fee kingdom.

Vinia kept her concern to herself. If this effect was more apparent than real, how could they be flying through a tunnel sized for creatures one-third their height? Yet they did seem to be doing it, and she did not want the effect to end while they were underground. It was better simply to accept it.

Now the walls of the tunnel turned crystalline. They expanded, until they were flying in a lovely subterranean chamber. There was light reflecting back and forth: maybe the fee had a reflective access to the light of the sun above.

They came to a sparkling crystal palace. "This is it," Sherlock said. "I will introduce you to King Finder."

They landed on the carpet parking lot. There was already a stir, and a royal column approached. Leading it was a man with a crown and enormous ears. Obviously the king. At least that made identification easy.

Sherlock stood and stepped off the carpet. "Your Majesty King Finder Fee, I am King Emeritus Sherlock of the adjacent Shee kingdom."

"We remember you," the fee king said. "So the rumor of a change in leadership there is true?"

"My daughter, Birdie, deposed me. But that is incidental: I am now traveling with young human Magician Prince Ion and Sorceress Princess Hilda and their retinue, who have used an accommodation spell for this occasion. They are children. They are on a special mission to fetch suitable princes for six crystallized princesses. We are looking for a prince for Princess Elga, once of your kingdom. Will you be able to help us?"

Finder considered no longer than a third of a moment, which was surely sufficient, considering his size. "Come inside, all of you, and we will discuss this."

Thus readily had Sherlock's introduction smoothed their path. Soon they were comfortable in the palace waiting room, sipping on miniature mugs of boot rear served by pretty fee servant wenches. Each girl had pleasant face and form, but there was an assortment of birds' feet. Some were clawed, some webbed. The floor clacked as they walked on the tiles. But nobody seemed to notice, and soon Vinia did not notice either. That was the protocol.

The girls nevertheless appreciated the courtesy and flirted with Sherlock and Benny. Also with Ion, to Vinia's annoyance. But she reminded herself that within an hour their party would revert to normal size; there was no future with any palace servant, however tempting she might seem at the moment.

Then a handsome manservant with wolf paws flirted with Vinia herself, and she was gratified. Vinia had not used an accommodation spell before and was pleasantly surprised by how natural everything appeared to be. The fee seemed human sized and proportioned, as did their furniture and mugs. She was also impressed by how readily the royalties of different species interacted. It was as though they were all one species, and the servants accepted Sherlock, Ion, and Hilda without question, while treating Benny and Vinia as equals.

"You seem to be more familiar with courtly procedures than I am," Vinia said to the manservant as he was admiring her human hands. "Which I suppose is not surprising."

"We have had some contacts," the man agreed. "And of course there's our interaction with Mundania."

"Mundania!"

"We fees are everywhere. You can tell our presence by official Mundane documents. Wherever they mention monetary fees, we have been involved."

She wasn't sure whether he was joking. Fortunately she didn't have to comment, as the main action was commencing.

King Finder glanced at Ion and Hilda. "I know you are schooling yourselves to ignore our special traits. We appreciate the courtesy. Similarly we will school ourselves to ignore your youth. May I inquire the nature of your magic?"

"I am immune to all elixirs," Ion said. Then he seemed to get an idea. "Indeed, I collect them. Should you need any, I may be able to provide them."

"That is interesting. As it happens, we recently had a plague, and our supply of healing elixir is dangerous low."

Ion produced a special vial shaped like a miniature horn. "This happens, so I carry some minicornucopias. This will supply all you ever need." He smiled. "Pour it carefully." He handed it to Finder.

The king was openly amazed. "All we need?"

"We can demonstrate it now, if you have any folk who have been deprived."

"We do have some beasts of burden who are suffering. We did not feel it expedient to use the last of our supply on them."

"Use this. It will never run out."

Finder spoke to a servant with duck feet. "Bring the tortoise." The servant departed. "We love our animals, and this one has been invaluable. Children ride on him. But the plague struck fee and beasts alike."

Soon the tortoise arrived. It was plain that the creature was suffering. It moved slowly even for its kind, and it limped.

The king lifted the cap on the vial and carefully tilted it over the back of the tortoise. Several drops fell onto the shell.

For a generous moment all was quiet as they watched the tortoise. Then it perked up, obviously feeling better. The shell brightened.

"Is it really healed?" Finder asked.

"Have someone ride it," Ion suggested.

The king glanced at a servant. The man had paws for hands, but evidently knew how to use them. He climbed carefully onto the shell, which was about thigh-high on him, as if expecting the creature to sink down under the weight.

Instead the tortoise stood tall, in its fashion, and commenced a rapid walk across the hall, carrying the man without difficulty.

The king glanced at another servant. That one, also, mounted the tortoise. Still there was no difficulty. Then a third, all there was room for. No problem.

"He really is better," the king said in wonder. "In fact, better than ever."

"He really is," Ion agreed. "Healing elixir is powerful stuff. It may be that he suffered from minor maladies before the plague and is now restored to his full potential."

"And you carry similar vials of other potions?"

"I do."

"You truly are a Magician!"

"Thank you. It is incidental."

More than incidental, Vinia knew. Not only had Ion awed the king with his magic, he had succeeded in giving him a marvelously useful gift. Two for the price of one, as it were. They did not need to give away the little carpet.

They ushered the perky tortoise out of the chamber. It was apparent that all the servants and courtiers were highly impressed. They probably had not before seen Magician-caliber magic publicly displayed. Sherlock looked privately smug: this reflected well on him, too, as he had spoken for the party.

It was time for business. "We know of Princess Elga," King Finder said. "She was a wild one of a prior generation who was not satisfied with our placid existence. She preferred to call herself an elf, which is not inaccurate, as all we fees are a variety of elf. She took off on her own to seek a larger fortune, and we lost track of her. You say she was crystallized?"

Sherlock smiled. "Not in the same manner as here. A dragon caught her and locked her in a crystal for safekeeping along with several other princesses. Now he is ready to release her, provided we can locate and bring in a suitable prince for her."

"She could have had a perfectly suitable prince right here, but she was too independent minded for that. Why should she have changed?"

Sherlock glanced at Hilda. "Perhaps Princess Hilda will agree to show you the presentation Elga recorded."

Hilda was happy to agree. She brought out and activated Elga's gem.

Elga was quite pretty in the holo, and Vinia saw that the king was impressed. She saw him note the tail and nod; she really was a fee. Then Elga said: "If by chance this is being seen by the folk of my home realm, the Fo Fee, let me say that I haven't changed. I mean to join the feminist Queendom of Thanx, where women will rule. But if there is a prince who can tolerate the role of consort, I believe I can satisfy him in other respects." That was a thinly veiled reference to the One Thing the prince would want.

Finder considered. "As it happens, we do have a surplus prince. He is so aggressive that normal princesses can't handle him. He simply wants too much woman. He is not political; I doubt the queendom thing would bother him, provided she is serious about those other respects."

"She is," Sherlock said. Again Vinia appreciated their fortune in enlisting a royal adult: he could refer obliquely to Conspiracy things in a manner that the children could not. Benny could have done it, but it was better coming from a royal person.

The king nodded. "I will summon him forthwith, so that he can see the holo. His name is Furioso."

Soon Prince Furioso was ushered in. His deformity was immediately apparent: he had the wildest red-and-yellow hair Vinia had seen on any human or creature, male or female. It erupted from his head in furious tangles, like a fire freshened by tormenting flurries of wind, and charged turbulently all the way to the floor in the manner of chaotic river rapids, completely undisciplined. Maybe he really was hungry for more than any woman could provide, but it was possible he was forced into a role by that aggressive hair.

Vinia got an idea. "Before he sees Elga," she murmured to Ion, "could we talk with him? We might be able to help him."

"Do it," Ion said, trusting her.

Vinia approached the prince, smiling ingratiatingly. "Please, Prince Furioso, I am Vinia, of the servant class. Could Prince Ion converse with you? He has a small gift for you."

Surprised, the elf glanced at the king. Finder nodded, having had recent experience with Ion's magic. So Furioso accompanied her to Ion. "What's on your mind, Prince?"

"It occurred to Prince Ion that you might have a problem with your hair," Vinia said. "He is a Magician. He has a potent magic conditioner that might help." She knew of it because once she had gotten curse burrs stuck in her hair, and Ion had used the conditioner to drive them efficiently out.

"Nothing helps," Furioso said gruffly. "I can't even iron it flat. It's my curse."

Ion was already fishing out a vial. "Try this."

Furioso took the vial, uncapped it, and poured it dismissively over his head. "Nothing," he repeated.

But his hair was already changing. It undulated like a traveling serpent, smoothing out in a sinuous wave that progressed from his head on down to his feet. The hair was still as long as he was, but now it was completely tame. He had become a fireberry blond, as it were.

There was a murmur of awe from the male and female servants. The visiting Magician had scored again.

"Our visitors are looking for a prince to join a captive princess," King Finder said. "They have a holo she made. I thought you might be interested." Coming from the king, that meant that Furioso had better be interested.

Furioso lifted a hank of his docile hair in his hands. He, too, was impressed by Ion's magic. "I am interested," he said, and he clearly meant it.

Hilda invoked the holo. Furioso watched, fascinated. "I had heard of her, from a prior generation, but had not realized how pretty she was. Is. She seems spirited. Maybe feminists are more robust than ordinary women. Maybe she could accommodate me. I am willing to meet her, without promising any commitment. Will that do?"

"Robust," Hilda said. "Does that mean handling violence?"

"Not at all. The opposite. Plenty of love. I just prefer a lot of woman."

Vinia could see that they were having a problem of Conspiracy censorship.

"As in a large woman?" Hilda asked. "Elga is not that."

"I mean one who can handle a lot of man."

The Conspiracy was not going to let them understand.

Hilda considered. Vinia, knowing her, suspected that Hilda was weighing in her mind how effective a love spell might be, should Elga like Furioso but he not wanting to commit to her. "Why don't you come with us, and meet her, and see how the two of you connect?"

"Good idea," he agreed. "Frankly, just about anything would be better than dawdling here forever, and she seems a lot better than nothing. In fact I like the notion of a spirited princess."

But if Elga were not enough woman for him, what then? Would they be abruptly short a prince? Would that void the whole deal? That worried Vinia, and she know it worried Hilda. But it seemed they would simply have to gamble.

Unless maybe Hilda sewed a pair of magically hot panties for Elga. That would guarantee his interest. But what about Elga's interest? There were invisible clouds of doubt floating here.

Hilda decided. "Come with us, and we'll see. If it doesn't work out, maybe we can figure out something else."

"Agreed."

They turned to face King Finder. "I will go with these folk," Furioso said. "We will see what we will see."

"Excellent," the king said. "Now let's celebrate with a royal feast."

"Time is almost up," Vinia whispered to Hilda. "The accommodation spell."

Hilda nodded. She caught Ion's eye and made a motion as if uncorking a vial, reminding him.

"We regret we can't stay," Ion said. "Our accommodation spell lasts only an hour, and we don't want to risk reverting here in your lovely palace." He hardly needed to say how destructive that could be for all parties.

The king tried to mask a royal shudder. "Excellent point. We are getting along so well I had forgotten. Then we must bid you a fond farewell. But do send word how it works out at the other end."

"We will," Ion agreed. Then the six of them boarded the carpet and took off, Benny at the helm.

Vinia had the impression that this was to an extent an act. They did not want to outstay the spell, true, but it could have been renewed. The king could have hosted a banquet, but probably wanted to get Furioso on his way before he could change his mind. So it was a conspiracy of manners that the royals probably all understood. They really were a class unto themselves.

They zoomed along the tunnel. "This is an impressive carpet," Furioso remarked. "How did you come by it?"

"I sewed it," Hilda said. "That's my magic."

"So you're a Sorceress!"

"Yes."

"You will surely be a lot of woman when you grow up."

Hilda laughed. "I wish I knew exactly what that means!"

"Let it wait. I am satisfied to have joined your party. I understand you made the king a gift like none other, ever."

"We were just following the protocol," Ion said.

"And that you are collecting princes for a feminist kingdom."

"The Queendom of Thanx," Hilda said.

"Do your princesses have any experience organizing a kingdom or queendom?"

"None," Ion said. "They are very female creatures."

"Then you will need the assistance of the princes, all of whom will have been trained for this sort of thing."

Ion and Hilda nodded together. They knew of the distinctions in training for the genders.

"I will be glad to help in whatever manner I am able," Furioso said. The taming of his hair seemed to have tamed his attitude somewhat as well. "I really appreciate what you have done for my hair."

Just so.

They emerged from the tunnel and made the right angle turn up the tree. Then they flowed up into the sky.

Just in time. The spell faded and the outside world seemed to change, becoming smaller. Vinia still marveled at the way appearance overlapped reality. They might not really have been as small as the fee, but they had interacted with the fee court, and brought out a prince.

Vinia looked at Furioso. He was now small, elf size. He had not been part of the spell, and so had not changed.

"Welcome to our size," Ion said.

"Actually the fee can assume human size if we so choose," Furioso said. "But it lasts only for an hour or less, like your accommodation spell. I will demonstrate." And suddenly he expanded to full human size. "But there's no sense expending my magic needlessly," the larger man said. Then he reverted to elf size. "For the right woman I would happily do it, but for traveling it is unnecessary," the elf concluded.

Just so, again.

Chapter 5

LADIES

"Now for the next prince," Hilda said as she started knitting. To her, sewing, knitting, and crocheting were all part of her magic. "Who is he?"

"Or she," Ion said. "We need a goblin princess."

"A lesbian," Hilda agreed. "That may be more of a challenge." She glanced at Furioso. "You wouldn't happen to know of one, would you?" Vinia knew it was a facetious question. Lesbians did not grow on trees, and many of those who existed did not advertise. Unless the luck of the ring really was working.

"Actually, I do," Furioso said, surprisingly. "When I ran out of fee princesses to annoy, I tried dating a gobliness princess. She was close enough to my size to require no adjustment. I liked her. She was nice, and passionate in bed. She had found a bedbug that made into a fine bed for the occasion, complete with fresh sheets." His lips quirked. "I understand that Mundanes don't like bedbugs. Can't think why. Anyway, she might even have been The One. But then she came out."

This was beyond coincidence. The luck was working.

"She left the mound?" Hilda asked as she continued knitting.

Furioso smiled, as did Sherlock and Benny. "This is a Conspiracy thing. Let's see if I can put it pasteurize."

"Past your eyes," Hilda said. "We may be children, but we do pick up on puns. Just say it flat out, and if the Conspiracy doesn't bleep it out, it's okay."

He nodded. "She confessed to being lesbian. It seems that she gave the hetero style her best try, and a very good try it was, but it just didn't work for her, so she told me the truth. It wasn't me, it was her. Her preference for a woman. So it was over, but we remain friends."

"So to be a lesbian is not to hate men," Vinia said. She knew the answer but wanted to verify his take on it.

"Not at all to hate men," he agreed. "She has been very kind to me. She just doesn't want to marry me." He smiled. "She has told me that she wishes she could get hold of a vial of mnemonic plague to spread through her goblin mound. She said it humorously, but I suspect there's a bit of seriousness there."

"What kind of plague?" Vinia asked.

Furioso smiled again. "Mnemonic. It's not a disease, exactly. It messes with memory, or in the case of forgetful folk like the fauns and nymphs, it helps them to remember beyond one day. It can be directed by the person who releases it, limiting it to particular aspects, so that there is not total amnesia. If she spread it among goblins of the mound, they would forget she was lesbian and accept her more readily. But of course such a potion may not even exist." He shrugged. "Too bad she didn't have the talent of omission. Then she could blank out things ranging from the Gap Chasm to awareness of her female preference."

Now Ion, Benny, and Sherlock were paying quiet attention. An incidental dialogue had abruptly turned highly relevant. Ion was especially interested. Maybe he had a vial of that very elixir and was keeping it private. Yet Vinia's instinct sounded a warning background note. This seemed too easy.

"So you can contact her?" Hilda asked. "Is she close?"

"Reasonably close. It was the first goblin tribe I visited."

"What is her name?"

"Georgia. Does it matter?"

"Yes." Hilda glanced at Vinia. "Orient on her."

Vinia spoke to her ring. "Princess Georgia Goblin." The glow formed, indicating the direction. Benny saw it and steered the carpet that way.

"That is the direction of her mound," Furioso said. "You have magic, Vinia?"

So he had picked up her name from her passing introduction. She thought he had not really noticed her, because she wasn't royal. Servants tended to be passed off as items of furniture. "I do, but this is not it."

"That doesn't look like a Promise Ring." He smiled. "No, I can't see invisible things. It showed briefly when you invoked it."

She appreciated the explanation. "Promise Ring?"

"The wearer must follow through on a promise and can't take it off until then."

Vinia smiled. "Almost. It is a magic ring Dara Demoness gave me that enables me to orient on people. I do feel I should not remove it until I have accomplished what I need to and can return it to her."

"I have heard of her. Wife of the human Good Magician?"

"Designated Wife," Vinia agreed, impressed again.

"If I may ask, what is your magic, Vinia?"

He was treating her courteously. Again, the warning note sounded in her mind. Was he assessing her for some hidden purpose? Sometimes princes had errands for servant girls that the Conspiracy blanked out. Vinia had seen it at the court of Adamant. Furioso was an elf only a fraction of her size, but he was a prince, which meant that he ranked above her significantly as a person of note. He could also assume her size, for a while. That could be trouble. But she had to answer. "I am short-range telekinetic."

"I see you are wary of me, Vinia. I assure you I mean you no mischief. I merely like to know whose company I keep."

"She enables me to walk, as I am lame," Ion said. "She is also my girl-friend." There was a background haze of warning in his tone. Not even a prince messed with the girlfriend of a Magician of any age, regardless of her class.

"Ah, so when the two of you walked together to the carpet, it was not mere camaraderie," Furioso said.

"Not," Ion agreed. "On more than one count."

"And Benny is my boyfriend," Hilda said.

"They are an extremely tight-knit foursome," Sherlock said.

"Thank you," Furioso said. "I believe I have it straight now."

Hilda completed the piece she was knitting. "Here is something you may find useful, Furioso." She held it up.

The elf was surprised. "It looks like a small cap. I have never been able to wear one of those. My hair tosses them off."

"Try it."

He accepted the cap and put it on his head. His long hair curled around and slid under the cap, like a thick cord being drawn into a container. There appeared to be far too much hair to fit, yet the length of it slid under the cap and disappeared. In perhaps a moment and a half all of it was gone, and he was left wearing only the cap. "I don't think I understand."

Hilda held up a mirror so that Furioso could see himself. He looked entirely ordinary, with short hair.

Amazed, he lifted the cap off his head. The hair tumbled out, as long as ever.

"It's a magic container," Vinia explained. "The hat will hold all your hair, regardless of its volume."

"This eliminates my deformity," Furioso said, awed as he set the cap back on his head and the hair snaked back into it. "And you knitted it while we talked!"

"It's my talent," Hilda said. "I sew magic into cloth."

"Some Magician-caliber magic is obvious," Benny said. "Like transforming folk into toads or blasting mountains apart. Some is more subtle, like immunity to toxins or sewing material whose magic manifests later. But they are of similar scope."

Furioso nodded. "I mean no offense, but I would never want to have either the young princess or her brother mad at me. I have never seen magic like this."

Both Ion and Hilda nodded. They had made their point. They were friendly, and accommodating, but not to be messed with. Not even by a prince. Ever. Vinia was glad to see it, as it meant the fee would treat them with genuine respect. There would be no mischief here.

Meanwhile Hilda was sewing again. "Your separate quarters," she explained to Furioso.

"It seems that every descendant of the Magician Bink is fated to have Magician-caliber magic," Sherlock said. "They don't necessarily advertise it, but it is there. Thus even two children can undertake a mission that might daunt any ordinary person."

"I have heard that about the descendants," Furioso agreed. "I had not before seen any in action. That is a most distinguished royal line."

"Now let's all get to know each other better," Sherlock said. "To pass the time while traveling."

The others were happy to agree.

"Goblins can be ornery," Vinia said. "Should we take precautions?"

"Once again my friend has the common sense we overlooked," Hilda said. "We have not dealt directly with goblins before. How should we prepare?"

"Protection against outrageous slings and arrows would be wise," Sherlock said. "But since we come asking a favor, perhaps some token gift would be in order for King Gourmand." He smiled. "I understand he likes to eat."

"He does," Furioso said. "Especially rare delicacies, like dragontail soup or invisiBull steak."

Benny laughed. "So common boot rear would not be his style."

"Not," Furioso agreed with a smile.

That gave Vinia an idea. "I have heard there is a rare variant called toot rear. No need to describe its effect."

"He would not appreciate that," Furioso said.

"To serve to someone he privately disliked," Vinia said.

Furioso whistled. "That he would love. He is, shall we say, nasty when balked."

A mean one. It was best to be warned.

Ion reached into his bag and brought out a bottle of boot rear. He took a vial and poured a few drops of its liquid into the bottle. "Potent toot rear," he announced. "I used conversion elixir."

"But just in case," Sherlock said. "You do have some defense against an attack? Just in case they should take something amiss?" Goblins did have a reputation.

"The carpet has an invisible shield," Hilda said. "And other defenses, such as a star flash. That temporarily blinds nearby folk."

"That should suffice," Sherlock said.

"If you are out there," Ion said, "all you have to do is cover your eyes."

Vinia's ring flashed. "Approaching the site," she announced.

They landed beside the goblin mound, which resembled a monstrous anthill. Armed goblins immediately surrounded them, but Vinia knew that they could not damage the carpet or its occupants.

"Lettuce do the honors," Furioso said, standing. Vinia saw that he liked to play with words. He stepped off the carpet. "I am Furioso Fee," he announced. "I have been here at the Scraggle Horde before, dating Georgia."

There was an evil chuckle.

"Yes, I know," he said. "I was the one she first came out to. Now we may take her off your hands. Please ask King Gourmand to join us here."

The goblins burst out laughing. This was a preposterous demand.

Furioso was unfazed. "I gather that the one named O'Clock lived here and departed. When he left the mound, no one knew the time. You seem not to know that it is time for the king to join us here."

The goblins did not seem to be much amused by his cleverness with words. They threw a volley of spears at the carpet. They bounced off the invisible protective shield harmlessly.

Then the goblins brought out a huge battering ram. The ornery beast might indeed butt through the shield.

Furioso covered his eyes. That was the signal. Ion activated the flash. It struck out in all directions, blinding the goblins and the ram where they stood.

"I repeat, ask the king to join us," Furioso said calmly. "The blinding effect will pass in a few minutes."

Now the goblins were ready to listen.

Before long the grossly fat King Gourmand was wheeled out on his portable throne. "Prince Furioso," he said. "My men did not recognize you without your hair."

Oho! That was the detail they had forgotten. Furioso no longer looked the same. "The proprietors of this mission are a royal human Magician and a Sorceress," he explained. "They enabled me to control my hair." He removed his cap and let the long tress unwind.

"Ah." Gourmand reached to the adjacent wheeled rack and lifted out a bottle labeled SUPER RARE WINE. He removed the cap and took a sip, then replaced the cap and bottle on the rack. "What do they want?"

"They would like to take Princess Georgia with them, as they have found a princess of her persuasion."

"Another pervert?"

"A lady goblin who happens to prefer her own gender," Furioso said. "In appreciation for your cooperation in letting her go, they bring a bottle of a rather rare beverage."

"Ah." He was clearly talking the king's language.

Furioso lifted his open hand. Vinia picked up the toot rear bottle and stepped off the carpet.

"Thank you, dear," Furioso said, as he might to the lowliest of servants.

He was playing a role. He took the bottle while Vinia stood meekly in place, playing her role.

"What is it?" Gourmand asked greedily.

"This is a rare variant of the common boot rear drink. It is called toot rear. I thought you might have a use for it, should you have to entertain a visiting dignitary you didn't like but had to be polite to." He paused meaningfully.

Slowly the implication got through to the king. He smiled. "I believe I would have a use for it, on occasion." He took the bottle and set it on the rack at the opposite side to his preferred vintage.

"Now if you care to notify the princess, the proprietors would like to talk with her."

"It pains us to let such a personage go," Gourmand said, taking another sip of his rare wine. "But we do believe in facilitating royal exchanges." He made a signal to his courtiers.

In barely a moment the princess arrived, somewhat disheveled. It had evidently not been by her choice. She was nevertheless beautiful, with a nice figure, shiny black hair, dainty hands and feet, and piercing black irises. Vinia could see why Furioso had liked her; she was everything a man could want, physically.

"My dear," Gourmand said in a patronizing tone, "these kind folk wish to talk with you."

"Well, they can kiss my—"

The king made as if to strike her, and she flinched. She stepped back behind the rack of bottles, steadying herself against it. Vinia recognized the signs; had they not been in public that strike would have landed. "Get your sorry ass over there, slut, before I have it boiled in oil to improve its flavor."

"Trust me," Furioso said quickly, holding up a hank of his hair to be sure she recognized him. "These folk are worth your while."

Georgia hesitated, still supporting herself on the rack. But she did know Furioso, and they were friends. "Okay."

Gourmand smiled as he faced Furioso. "The princess will consider your offer."

Furioso took Georgia's elbow and guided her to the carpet. Vinia followed.

"Good riddance," the king muttered behind them. "Now I can cele-brate with a solid drink."

"Trust me," Furioso repeated to Georgia. "This is infinitely better than your present situation."

"Hell would be better than my present situation," she retorted.

"Hello, Princess Georgia," Hilda said as they boarded the carpet. She remained seated, not from any disrespect, but so she would not stand almost twice the goblin's height. "I am Princess Sorceress Hilda, and this is my brother, Prince Magician Ion."

"Speak your piece," Georgia said shortly. She was clearly in doubt what she was getting into, but firmly maintaining her pride.

"Here is the holo made by Princess Goblette, of another goblin tribe. It is self-explanatory."

The holo animated. Georgia watched it with disdain, then interest, then excitement. "Oh, yes!" she breathed. There were tears in her eyes.

"Have you anything to fetch from your lodgings?" Furioso inquired, knowing that she accepted the offer.

"Nothing worth keeping." Then Georgia flung her arms about him and kissed him. "You were right. You have saved me."

"We are friends," he said, pleased. "I am considering a similar holo offer by the fee princess. That's what this mission is all about."

"We will remain friends." She turned back to Ion and Hilda. "Weigh anchor, or whatever, please. Now. It is time to get out of here."

Meanwhile Vinia was observing something odd. King Gourmand, taking another gulp of rare wine, appeared to be in some kind of discom-fort. In fact he was almost lifting off the ground. "What's wrong with him? He looks as if he tried to steal a book from a lie briery and got stuck by briers in his pants."

"I switched the bottles," Georgia said smugly.

Gourmand had inadvertently guzzled from the toot rear bottle, more than a token sip, and it was violently inflating his gut. Vinia suppressed her mirth for almost half an instant before it burst uproariously out of her.

Then they all were laughing as they caught on. The carpet was already airborne, fortunately. The goblin king had nothing remaining to cuss at, assuming he had the breath for cursing. Georgia had evidently learned about the bottle and had her revenge on the cruel king.

"Now we need another carpet attachment," Vinia said. She suspected she was going to like Georgia Goblin; she had nerve.

"No need," Furioso said. "Georgia can share with me. We understand each other well enough." He glanced at the goblin. "They try to provide some privacy for each prince or princess. I'm sure one can be made for you, too, if you prefer."

"Thanks, no. I am happy to share with you."

Vinia knew that after the toot rear business, they all felt close to Georgia. They would get along.

They talked, getting to know one another. Then it was time to return to business.

"Next prince?" Hilda asked.

"Please, if you list the other princesses for me, perhaps I can help," Georgia said. "I have been looking for other possible residences and may know of one."

"Three remain," Hilda said. "Chloe Winged Centaur, who is telepathic. Beetrix Bee. And Demesne Demoness."

"A Demoness!"

"It seems she was impatient with the males of her species," Vinia said. "They, like most males, really wanted only one thing, while she wanted to be appreciated for more than that."

"That will be a challenge to find," the goblin said. "Perhaps best left to last."

"Perhaps," Vinia agreed.

"But I know of a bee hive with a number of drones. I have learned how to communicate with them. They know that most of them are bound to become surplus. One I was in touch with might be interested in meeting with an isolated bee princess."

Fortune had struck again. Or the ring. "What is his name?"

"Drover."

"Drover Drone," Vinia murmured to the ring. It flashed.

Benny saw and steered the carpet in that direction.

"However," Georgia said, "You will need to haggle, I mean negotiate, with Queen BeeAttitude. She puts a sweet price on everything, even a drone she'd prefer to be rid of."

"What is her problem with Drover?" Vinia asked.

"He's a fine drone. But he suffered an injury of one wing, and now instead of being the hive's faster flier, he's the slowest. He's mortified. He knows he has no chance to catch the new princess in flight, and become the king bee, and the worker bees treat him with contempt."

"Couldn't healing elixir fix that?"

"The queen refuses to spare any for a mere drone, one of dozens. One of the others will do, and then they'll all be surplus."

Vinia saw that it was a tough life for the average bee, especially a non-productive one. "We could fix him," she told Ion. "So he wouldn't be surplus anymore, and no longer be interested in an alternate queen bee."

"Yet if that's his attitude, we might not want him anyway."

"Drover's not that type," Georgia said. "Why not give him a chance?" Ion nodded. "We'll try."

"I have made a study of bees, local and Mundane, since getting to know Drover," Georgia said. "In Mundania, worker bees live for a month, drones live for three months, and queens for three years. But in Xanth, with magic, it's more like one year for workers, a decade for drones, and thirty years for queens. They also approach human intelligence."

"It must be awful in Mundania," Vinia said. "However do they manage, with such short lives?"

"There's a high turnover. There's more: the princess bee in Mundania mates with a dozen or more drones, but only one in Xanth: he becomes her consort. So Drover has a lot on the line. You can't blame him for considering carefully."

Hilda had been listening. "Folks, we'll be entering the hive. For that we'll need three accommodation spells, for size, flight, and speech. You have a notion how it works. We'll have to park the carpet and go in as individuals. Anyone who prefers to stay with the carpet is welcome."

King Sherlock, Prince Furioso, and Princess Georgia looked at one another, then did a mutual shrug. "We're in," Sherlock said. They knew that the regular crew was committed.

They soon approached the hive. It was huge, bulging out of a giant old beer-barrel tree with a cracked trunk. Probably the whole interior was filled not with beer, but honey. Provoked worker bees flew up angrily, more than ready to repel this intrusion. But they were unable to penetrate the carpet's protective shield. That made them angrier.

"Make that four spells," Hilda said as she looked at the angry bees. "We also need one for personal protection. It will make our skins invulnerable to stings. Just in case."

"You have that kind of magic?" Georgia asked, amazed.

"They are Sorceress and Magician," Furioso said. "Do not be deceived by their youth. They have amazing powers."

"Yes. I have not before interacted with that level of magic."

"First elixir," Ion announced, lifting a vial. "Size. Stay where you are: everyone on the carpet will be affected." He opened it, and the vapor puffed out.

Vinia had seen his magic before, but she still was a bit nervous as the mist enveloped her. She breathed it in and moved her arms and legs, making sure it touched every part of her. The others emulated her.

They all shrank to bee size, together with their clothing. The carpet did not. They were standing on a huge expanse of material. This accommodation spell was selective. Vinia noted that all of them were the same bee size, not larger or smaller in the manner of humans and elves or a goblin.

"Amazing," Georgia echoed.

"Actually the carpet has its own protective spell," Hilda said. "So it is excluded from the effect. Our clothing associates with us, so maintains the same proportions."

"Second elixir," Ion said. His bag had shrunk with him, being attached to his clothing. "Flight. We will grow wings, but they are mainly for appearance and to reassure the bees; we will actually fly by the power of our thoughts." He opened the vial.

More vapor emerged. It surrounded them. Vinia saw wings sprout from the backs of the others, through their clothing, and felt the same for herself.

"Try it," Hilda said. "So as to achieve control." She buzzed her wings and lifted a body length off the carpet.

The others tried it, with less initial control. They wound up striking the overhead canopy and falling back on their heads, fortunately not hard. Only Georgia, with more experience with bees, was able to make her first flight controlled. But soon the others got the hang of it. Their wings buzzed automatically when they flew.

"Third elixir," Ion said. "Communication. Again, your minds will govern it. Just talk as you normally would, and don't be concerned how it sounds. The bees will understand us, and we will understand them." He opened the vial.

"Try it," Hilda said after the vapor infused them. There was a buzzing quality to her speech, but it was intelligible.

Vinia spoke, experimentally. "Is this right?" She heard her own buzzing voice, but could make out the words.

"It is," Ion reassured her with his own buzz.

When everyone was satisfied, Ion brought out another vial. "Fourth elixir: protection. No stinger can penetrate your skin." He let out its vapor.

"But don't tease the bees," Hilda warned. "Remember, this is a peaceful mission."

Just as the one to the goblin mound had been, Vinia thought. It was indeed best to be prepared. The mist surrounded her, and she felt her skin crinkle slightly, then relax. That was all. She would have to take its protection on faith.

"Now we visit Queen BeeAttitude," Ion said. "Who wants to do the honors?"

"I can try," Georgia said. "I have been around the hive. They should recognize me, once I introduce myself."

"Take it," Ion agreed.

Vinia saw the goblin hesitate. She had volunteered, but remained uncertain. Vinia knew exactly how that was. She went to join her. "I will be your assistant." The two of them were now the same height.

"Thank you," Georgia buzzed, clearly appreciating the support.

They stepped off the carpet. The bees swarmed down to confront them. "Who the buzz are you?" the troop leader demanded. She was female in the manner of Vinia, her gender clear but undeveloped, yet she was no child. Her fur formed into a uniform, black and yellow, and her stinger was prominent. Her eyes stared at them and her antennae flexed. A warrior.

"I am Georgia Goblin, magically reduced in size for this occasion. I know Drover Drone; we met in the field. You have seen me around the hive. This is Vinia Human, similarly reduced."

There was a stir among the bees. They did recognize Georgia, now that they were adjusting for her reduced stature. She looked like a tiny winged goblin, not a bee, but they had seen her in the field.

"What do you want with us?"

"We speak for a human mission." Georgia indicated the party remaining on the carpet. "We want to take Drover Drone to meet a foreign princess bee, to see if they connect." This was plainly important, because it meant the formation of a new hive.

The warrior bee considered. "This is a matter for the queen."

Obviously so. "Yes. Please conduct us to Queen BeeAttitude."

Vinia waved to the folk on the carpet. Ion, Hilda, and Benny stepped off. Then Sherlock followed. Furioso remained behind, evidently the one chosen to keep an eye on the home base. Again, a matter of being prepared.

"This way," the warrior said. She took off, flying toward the hive.

They took off and followed, single file, first Georgia, then Vinia, then the four others. A bee came to fly beside each of them, not threatening, but close. The hive, too, was being prepared.

They entered the hive. The entrance passage branched, leading to the several activities like the worker barracks, nursery, honey storage, and the queen. Vinia would have had no idea where to go without guidance, assuming she could ever have gotten into the fiercely defended hive.

Soon they came to an antechamber. There was the queen, more than twice the size of a worker, her eyes and antennae restless. Or rather, the front half of her, projecting from a supportive wall. Vinia realized that the rear half was surely busy laying eggs, attended by nursery bees.

"Queen Bee, here is the intruder party," the troop leader said. "They say they want to take Drover Drone to meet a foreign princess."

The cold eyes focused. "Who are you?"

"I am Princess Georgia Goblin, of the neighboring horde. We do not compete with your hive, but our territories overlap. I met Drover Drone in the field and we got to know each other, as you know. These are Princess Hilda Human, and her brother Prince Ion, and their retinue." She introduced Hilda first, because to a bee, the female was obviously the most important.

"What's this about taking Drover Drone?"

Now Hilda spoke. "Several princesses have been sequestered by a dragon, who will release them only if suitable consorts can be provided for them. One of them is Princess Beetrix Bee. It is our mission to locate prince prospects so that the princesses can emerge to form their own queendom."

"A queendom?" She was clearly intrigued. A queen bee was by definition the ultimate feminist.

"Most large folk have kingdoms. They believe that it is time for a queendom. We believe they should be given their chance to show that females can organize and operate a nation just as well as males do."

"Or better," BeeAttitude said. She had attitude, of course.

"Or better," Hilda agreed. "But in the large person realm, this requires proof."

"However, we can't afford to let a valuable drone depart before the Flight of the Princess."

She was ready to bargain. Drover wasn't much valued, because of his wing injury, but this queen was not one to let any opportunity escape.

Hilda hesitated, having assumed it would be just a matter of clearing it with the queen. They had not brought a gift, not knowing how to relate on this level.

Sherlock spoke. "Allow me, please," he said. "I am King Emeritus Sherlock of the Shee Kingdom. I was deposed by my daughter, but I have had a fair amount of experience in governing a country. What seems to be required here is a deal that benefits both parties."

"You talk my language, Shee Drone," BeeAttitude agreed. "What do you offer?"

"What is your interest?"

"Flowers. Our fields are becoming depleted."

"I believe the queendom's proposed territory has some very nice flower fields. But there may be a problem. It is not adjacent to your territory."

The queen sighed with simulated regret. "Too bad. I wish you fortune in finding a suitable drone elsewhere."

Sherlock smiled. He was plainly in his element: hardball bargaining. "There may nevertheless be an avenue." He glanced at Ion. "Is teleportation within your means, Magician?"

Ion considered. "I'm not sure. My elixirs generally operate locally. It's not safe to attempt long-distance transport. There's a square/cube complication that magnifies with size."

"But perhaps at bee scale?"

Ion nodded. "Parallel portals could be set up. It might work."

"What I am thinking of is a connection between this locale and a prime field in Thanx. One that bees could use, going back and forth. That would make the distance negligible. They would simply fly into the near portal and emerge at the far portal to forage, then return with their collected pollen. To them it would seem like an adjacent flower field."

Ion nodded again. "This would be feasible, with some effort."

Sherlock returned his gaze to the queen, who had been paying close attention. "We might be able to make a flower field available for a limited time."

"Why the limit?" the queen demanded.

"When the drone joins the princess, they will form a new hive in that vicinity. It will require a season or two to establish a full complement, but then they will want that field for themselves."

She nodded, tacitly accepting the limit. "What flowers?"

Sherlock looked at Hilda. "I am not conversant with flower species. Can we ascertain what is available there?"

Hilda looked at Vinia. "Can you get in touch? We never got to look at the flowers there."

"I'll try," Vinia said. She spoke to her ring. "Demesne."

In three-tenths of a moment the Demoness responded. "Yes, Vinia."

"What kind of flowers are there in the fields of Thanx? We are making a deal with the bee queen to free a drone."

"One moment. I will check with Chloe."

"She's checking," Vinia reported.

"You have an interesting device," the queen remarked. "Communication?"

"It's a ring that can contact a named person," Vinia explained.

Demesne spoke again. "Chloe checked with Dragoman. He says they have a number of varieties of flowers. It seems he is something of a horticulturist in his free time. He says he planted one rare variety himself. Does the name Heaven-Can-Wait Honeysuckle mean anything to the queen bee?"

Vinia looked at the queen, about to repeat that. But the queen had heard Demesne. She was frozen in place. Alarmed, the workers were buzzing to her.

"Peace," Sherlock said. "She is not harmed, merely rapt. I have heard of that variety. It is considered to be the most special of flowers for pollen, producing honey that transports folk into paroxysms of delight. This is definitely a potent bargaining chip."

The queen recovered. "I believe a deal can be made," she said dreamily.

"It will take some time to set up the dual portals," Ion said.

"It will take some time to arrange for Drover's release," the queen said. Meaning that they would have to deliver on the portal before they got the drone.

"I will set up one portal here. I will need to return to Thanx to place the one there. Otherwise the bees would go there and not be able to come back here. Each portal is essentially one way. Then we should test the pair of them on a bee volunteer to be sure it is safe."

"Drover will volunteer." Meaning that they had better do it right the first time, or they would lose the drone. Oh, yes, she was a hard-tailed bargainer.

Sherlock looked at the queen, nodding. She nodded back. They had a deal.

Next they had to talk with Drover. A worker escorted him into the royal chamber. He was clearly the right one, because one wing hung crooked. He did a double take when he saw Georgia, his antennae goggling.

"Yes, it is me, in your size," she said. "An accommodation spell. I am with a royal human party."

"But why would you come here?"

"They have a bee princess in need of a drone. I recommended you. We have made a deal for your release."

"But why would a bee princess settle for a drone with a damaged wing?"

Georgia glanced at Ion. "We might be able to do something about that."

Ion brought out a vial. "Healing elixir," he said.

"But that's not for me! I'm not a worker."

"This is our own supply," Ion said. "Lend me your wing."

Drover went to stand before him, calling what he thought was a bluff. He turned his back, exposing his wings. Ion sprinkled a drop of elixir on the damaged one. It immediately straightened out.

Drover felt the difference. "Wow!" he buzzed. "It really is the elixir! I am back in perfect form." He flew up in the chamber and around it. He did an airborne flip, then made a perfect landing. "Thank you, visiting prince."

"Now you can catch the hive princess," Georgia said. "But these folk would like you to go to their princess, who will not be at all difficult to catch."

The drone evidently still suspected a catch. "But I don't know her. We might not get along. I do know our own princess. She will make a good queen."

This was the crux. Would he find a pretext to renege, now that his local prospect had been restored? When he had the chance to be the consort of a good familiar queen?

"It seems you have a choice to make," Georgia said.

"My wing for their princess," he agreed. "But it's a gamble. The wrong princess would be a lifelong horror."

He had a reasonable point.

"Perhaps you should view her holo," Hilda said.

If he saw Beetrix and didn't like her, what then?

Drover viewed the holo. They all did, including the queen. Now it was perfectly clear to Vinia as Beetrix presented her case. Every buzz was significant. She was a very fetching bee.

Drover looked stunned. "She will do," he said. "I thought she would be a stupid hag. Why else go to so much trouble to corral a distant drone? I think I was prepared to go there anyway, reluctantly, to honor the implied deal, but now I know that this will be no chore. She's perfect. I will go."

A qualified endorsement. But also not reneging. That would have to do.

"In due course," the queen said. "There are certain arrangements to complete first." Guard bees escorted Drover out of the chamber, cutting off any further dialogue. The queen did not want him reaching their protected carpet.

"I suggest that we draw up a formal mutual assistance treaty," Sherlock said. "So that our deal is made quite clear. Trust but verify."

"Indeed," the queen agreed. "You do understand the basics."

"I wielded power for some time. There are protocols."

"Too bad you're not a drone."

Vinia knew that the essence had been accomplished, regardless of the technical language. Thanx wanted the drone; the drone wanted Beetrix; the queen wanted the Heaven-Can-Wait Honeysuckle flowers for her foragers, at least for a season. The hive would have a marvelous feast in the off-season.

"Are you by any chance familiar with the human game of poker?" Sherlock asked the queen.

Her antennae wavered in a bee smile. "I know of it. But I never bluff."

He nodded. "I'm not surprised. Bluffing is for a weak hand." Then they both laughed. They were complimenting each other. This had been a kind of game, to an extent, though with serious consequences.

"Where do you want the local portal?" Ion asked the queen.

"Right outside the hive." The queen was evidently too canny to allow foreign magic inside the hive.

They exited the hive, and Ion delved into the magic bag to bring out a covered cup. There were several colored rings on it, in the manner of decorations. He drew one ring off. "This operates by forming a circle of transport elixir," Ion explained. "I will dip the ring into the elixir, let it dry for exactly three-quarters of a moment, then set it on a stand. The ambiance of the elixir will affect whatever passes through it. Any bee that flies through the hoop will be transported to the specified destination. In this case, the edge of the field of flowers."

"How do you specify that?" Vinia asked, impressed by the technology of this magic.

"That is where you come in. Put your ring next to the hoop and speak the name of the field. That will orient the portal."

They rehearsed it, to be sure she had it right. Then Ion carefully drew the lid off the cup, so that its dark fluid showed. He dipped the hoop into it, then held it up in the open air for three-quarters of a moment. He glanced at Vinia.

She put her ring finger beside the hoop, almost touching it. "The near edge of the Heaven-Can-Wait Flower Field of Thanx," she said clearly. This was not a person, but it was a specific identity, and the ring could fix on it.

The ring flashed. That was all. But Vinia knew that the critical orientation had occurred. The magic of the ring combined with the magic of the elixir to fashion the one-way bee portal.

Ion covered the cup, preserving the precious elixir, and put it back in the bag. "I will set up the return portal when we are at the flower field. There should be no problem."

Vinia was relieved that it was done. Now they had four of the six they sought. But she feared the worst was yet to come. How were they going to recruit a flying centaur stallion, and then a Demon? Let alone royal ones? Demesne was nice, but a mature male Demon could be quite another matter.

Chapter 6

ISLETS

Back in the air, they faced the next decision. "Which prince?" Benny asked.

"I suspect that the most difficult one will be the Demon, so perhaps best left to last," Sherlock said. "Which leaves the winged centaur."

The others nodded somberly. "Do they even have princes or princesses?" Hilda asked. "We have seen centaur visitors at Adamant, but they never seemed to be royal."

"They aren't, really," Sherlock said. "They believe in equality. So every one of them is royal if they choose to express it that way."

"Yet we have Princess Chloe," Ion pointed out. "Though she never seemed to think of herself as anything other than equal."

"A largely meaningless title, for her," Hilda said. "The other princesses didn't challenge it. What sets her apart is not her station, but her telepathy."

"So are we looking for a telepathic winged centaur stallion?"

Hilda shuddered. "A female telepath seems okay. But the idea of a male telepath peering into my private thoughts alarms me."

"We males want only one thing of our females," Furioso said. "So mind reading makes no real difference. But females have more complicated minds, thus more at risk. So they are naturally wary."

"We are," Georgia said, not questioning his assessment. "I don't like the idea of a considerate female reading my secrets, let alone a thoughtless male focusing on that one thing."

Vinia suspected that she was not joking.

"So no telepath," Sherlock said. "One is more than enough for Thanx."

"Does that mean that any unattached garden-variety disaffected winged centaur stallion will do?" Hilda asked.

They all laughed. But the decision had been made. They would look for such a centaur.

"Next question," Sherlock said. "Where do we find him?"

Hilda looked at Vinia. "Will your ring orient?"

"I need a name."

"And this time we have no name," Ion said. "Do we have a winged centaur village to go to so we can look around?"

"They don't seem to have villages," Sherlock said. "The land-bound centaurs have Centaur Island, but their culture differs. The flying ones are freer spirits. I'm not sure they settle anywhere. I never heard of a winged centaur village."

"There might be one," Benny said. "They might be canny about mentioning it to strangers."

"There might be," Furioso agreed. "Just about any intelligent creature likes to associate on occasion with his own kind."

"Maybe an exercise in logic will help," Georgia said.

"Logic?" Hilda asked.

"A thought experiment. Let's assume that a winged centaur village exists. That no other species knows of it. Where then would it be?"

"Far away," Furioso said. "Maybe not in Xanth proper at all, though it still has to be within its environs."

"Across the water," Benny said.

"Accessible only by air," Sherlock said.

Georgia nodded. "And that would be?"

"An island," Vinia said. "Maybe one of the Sometime Islands."

"I don't think so," Hilda said. "Adamant, where we live, is on a Sometime Island, and we know the area pretty well. We've never seen a flying centaur who wasn't coming directly to visit us."

"And the outside centaurs would be cut off from it much of the time, because of the way the isles fade in and out of Xanth proper," Ion said. "They wouldn't want that."

"So it must be in the normal frame," Georgia said. "Somewhere in the Gulf or the Lantic Sea."

"There's not much in the Gulf," Sherlock said. "I traveled there in my youth. Only the Wet Tortoise Isles, which are low to the ground."

"So by elimination, the Lantic Sea," Georgia said. "I have heard there are many islands there, some of them volcanic."

"Volcanic!" Furioso said. "An old cone would be mainly accessible by air, and a village could be hidden inside."

"So we are looking for a volcanic island," Georgia said.

"But there may be hundreds," Sherlock said. "Scattered across stormy seas."

"Which would take half of forever to check, even by flying carpet," Hilda said. "We need to narrow it down."

"Maybe we need a map," Vinia said. "To study the islands. Do we have one?"

"I can sew one," Hilda said. She got busy with her needlework.

Furious laughed. "We need needles for our needs."

"Can a sewn map work?" Georgia asked. "We need something current and accurate, not a picture."

"You haven't seen her magic," Furioso said. "She's a Sorceress."

Soon the map took shape. It covered the east coast of Xanth and the sea next to it, complete with a number of islands. They were even labeled by name.

"Just the volcanic ones," Ion said.

Hilda pulled out a thread. Most of the islands disappeared. "Got them."

"Now that's impressive," Georgia said.

"There are still too many, too widely scattered," Ion said. "We need to be more selective."

"Maybe remove the active volcanoes," Furioso said. "Can't have a village inside the cone of a live volcano."

Hilda pulled out another thread. More islands disappeared.

"What about inhabited ones?" Hilda asked. "They need to be using an isolated one, with no people there to see them come and go."

Hilda pulled another thread. Now the islands were relatively few, and widely spread.

"Can we have their names?" Georgia asked. "I don't suppose any will be labeled SECRET FLYING CENTAUR VILLAGE, but there might be some hint."

Benny smiled. "If any say CENTAUR TAIL ITCH WEED, we can eliminate those."

Hilda carefully sewed a new thread into the pattern. The names of the islands appeared.

"The more I see of your magic, the more impressed I am," Georgia said.

"I told you she's a Sorceress," Furioso said. "And Ion is a Magician. They can do magic we can hardly imagine."

"True," Georgia breathed. "I see there's one called Thera."

"I have heard of that," Sherlock said. "It was a nasty one, some time back. Worse than Pinotuba."

"Pinotuba?"

"It went ooom-paa! and blew out so much smoke and ash it cooled all Xanth by one degree."

"Oh, *that* one. But it's still alive, isn't it?"

"Yes, still active. So they won't be hiding in *that* cone. At least Thera is now inactive."

"We can check those," Ion said, studying the map. "But it will take several days, because of the travel time between them."

"We can take the time we need," Sherlock said. "There's no deadline, is there?"

"We'll spend hours between each, getting on each other's nerves. We've got to find the right access!"

That started a foolish chain of thought for Vinia. Right access. Thera. The ra could be an abbreviation for right access. The RA. Thera. "We should try Thera first."

Ion glanced at her. "You have a reason?"

"Yes, but it's too foolish to mention."

"We have seen her foolishness before," Hilda said.

Ion nodded. "Right. Thera it is."

"Thera," Vinia said to the ring. They had the map, so could find it regardless, but she wanted to verify that it could orient on a place name as well as a person name. It flashed a direction, matching the map direction.

They flew across the sea, which was dull compared to the land because it was all the same, just level water.

"Uh-oh," Benny said, gazing ahead as he steered the carpet.

Vinia looked. Clouds were swirling villainously. A storm was brewing.

"How well can this craft handle inclement weather?" Sherlock asked Ion.

"Well enough. Neither rain nor hail can penetrate the shield, and it will deflect lightning, but the winds can buffet it. We can ride it out."

"I get seasick," Georgia said. "I was on a boat once, and when the waves got rocky, I vomited."

"Me too," Furioso said. "I am a land creature, when it comes to a storm."

"Can we go around or over it?" Hilda asked Benny.

"I don't think so. It is spreading out pretty wide, and reaching high. There can be turbulence above a storm too. It may be better to wait it out."

"Right when we are on the verge of recruiting a winged centaur stallion," Ion said, annoyed.

Outlying winds pushed against the shield, sending the carpet rocking. Both the goblin and the elf looked uncomfortable.

Vinia got an idea. "Could we go under it?"

"Like a boat on the water?" Benny asked. "That would really be rocky."

"No, I mean under it. Under the water."

The others looked at her. "She's doing it again," Hilda said. "Coming up with a weird idea that maybe makes sense. Can the shield handle the pressure of surrounding seawater?"

"Yes," Ion said. "But if we stayed under too long, I would need to vent a vial of oxygen."

The others did not understand his concern, so ignored it.

Hilda peered at the storm ahead. It looked increasingly formidable and seemed to be developing a circular pattern.

"This is what the Mundanes refer to as a hurricane," Sherlock said. "They do frequent this region in summer."

"A hurry cane?" Furioso asked

"Not exactly. A hurricane is a huge storm in the shape of a giant circle, which can last for a week or more. Not something we want to be in."

"Thank Q for that clarification."

"Then down under it is," Benny said, and he put the carpet into a dive. It plunged toward the surface of the sea and did not level off: instead it splashed out a great sheet of water to either side.

Vinia was not the only one who flinched, though she knew they were safe.

The carpet sank under the sea. They saw the water rising around the shield, higher and higher, as if they were in a giant bowl. Then it closed over the top, and it was more like a giant bubble.

And the rocking they had been increasingly experiencing stopped. The ocean down under was calm. Vinia looked up through the top and saw the surface of the sea being lashed by the storm, but there was no echo of it here below.

"Well, now," Furioso said. "I like this calmness."

"Me too," Georgia agreed.

"And there are fish," Sherlock said.

They looked. Fish of assorted sizes were peering through the shield, as though the carpet with its riders were oddities in a tank. Then a giant turtle swam up.

And a water dragon. It looked hungrily at the people and licked its formidable chops. But when it tried to take a bite of the shield, miniature lightning jags radiated, shocking it in the teeth. The dragon hastily retreated.

The carpet accelerated, forging through the water. At first the fish tried to keep up with it, as if it were a racing game, but they soon fell behind. They were making good progress. Vinia was impressed yet again with the magic of Ion and Hilda, who had worked together to make this vehicle work.

In due course Benny aimed the craft back upward. Either they had passed the storm, or it had blown on past them, or a combination of the two. The surface of the sea was now almost calm.

"May I say that I am impressed by your magic, too, Magician," Georgia said to Ion. "It is simply amazing. I never even imagined anything quite like this."

Ion, caught off guard by the compliment, was silent. Vinia stepped in, as she was used to doing. "He appreciates your appreciation, Georgia. But he doesn't brag about his magic. He just does what is necessary."

"It is beyond bragging," the goblin said. "I am awed."

Vinia knew that Ion was deeply pleased.

They slid along the surface, as Benny looked around, then lifted into the air.

"Land ho!" Sherlock said.

And there it was: an islet consisting mainly of a huge volcanic cone. They had found Thera. But was it the secret home of the winged centaurs? This was after all just her guess based on a passing mental exercise. Her luck was bound to fall flat some time.

Hilda looked at Vinia, picking up her doubt. "Unless the luck of the ring goes with you as well as the ones you name to it. You are after all closely associated with it."

"I never thought of that," Vinia said. "I suppose it could have an ambiance, just as Ion does."

"Make sure not to lose it."

Oh yes! She really needed the ring.

"Uh-oh," Benny repeated.

They looked. "That volcano's alive," Hilda said, surprised. "Yet it can't be; my map now shows only the quiescent ones."

Still, there was a bright rim of lava at the top of the cone, just about to overflow, and fiery smoke was roiling into the sky above it. The volcano certainly looked active.

"Illusion!" Sherlock said. "Oldest trick in the book. Which means that this must be the place. Why clothe a deserted islet with illusion unless it has something to hide? That's a giveaway."

Vinia hoped so. She still didn't trust her guess, and wasn't sure about the luck, but they did need to find the winged centaurs.

"But centaurs don't like to use magic," Hilda said.

Sherlock laughed. "That's a popular confusion. They don't like to *be* magic, except to the extent it facilitates their flying, but they will *use* it as convenient. So the telepathic princess you mentioned must have been an outcast. That would explain her separation from her kind. The winged ones are, however, more liberal in this respect than the land-bound ones."

"She never said, in her holo. I mean, she says she's telepathic, but not a word about how other centaurs might have reacted to it."

"It could be a sensitive issue." Sherlock eyed the fiery top of the mountain. "Meanwhile we have to decide whether we are certain enough that it *is* illusion to fly through it. Is the shield strong enough to resist real volcano heat?"

"Yes, for a few minutes at least," Ion said. "It is designed to withstand dragon fire, which usually comes in brief bursts. We can fly quickly through it." He looked around. "Are we game to try?"

"If you say your magic can handle real heat, then I'm game," Georgia said.

"Ditto," Furioso agreed.

"One other thing," Sherlock said. "Assuming it is illusion, and that beyond it, inside the cone, there is a winged centaur community, they may not welcome our invasion. Do we have a protocol to establish a dialogue?"

"Maybe say 'Please, we need your help'?" Vinia suggested. "Or is that too stupid?"

A glance went around, turning positive. The others were catching on to her supposed stupidity. "That seems apt," Sherlock said.

"Now we brave the fiery illusion," Benny said.

The carpet zoomed toward the fearsome summit. Vinia couldn't help herself; she closed her eyes as they plunged into the smoke.

"I'm nervous too," Georgia said beside her.

That helped.

"We're through!" Benny announced. Obviously he hadn't shut his eyes.

Vinia looked. There was no incipient eruption. They were now flying across the giant empty caldera, the basin of the center of the extinct volcano. Tucked into one wall of it was a big building like a stall. That had to be the home of the centaurs. Vinia noticed that a wisp of steam was curling up from the other side, which suggested that even after centuries there remained some heat.

Ion took her hand and squeezed it. "I'm the Magician, but sometimes I suspect you have equivalent magic."

"Oh, no, not me!" she said, embarrassed. "It's just the ring."

"And who was lucky enough to get the ring?"

A winged centaur flew up from the stall to intercept them, the final confirmation of their success. He was a handsome stallion with blue-brown fur on his flank and head, and muscular arms. He was naked except for a sheaf of arrows on his back, and a long bow in his left hand. He would of course be a dead shot with that bow; all centaurs were. He pointed to a corner of the stall roof where they should land.

Benny nodded and guided the carpet there. They made a soft landing. "Go talk to him," Ion told Vinia.

"Me? But I'm not the leader!"

He merely looked at her. Oh, yes; she was the protagonist. She turned around and went.

Vinia stepped off the carpet and approached the stallion, who had landed the same time they did. He had hung his bow across the sheath on his back, evidently not considering her to be a threat. He was even more imposing up close, his human portion standing considerably taller than she did. She saw that his eyes matched his hair. "Please, we need your help," she said.

"Obviously, or you would not have come to Grand Centaur Station," he replied. His voice was vibrant. "You have considerable magic, to locate us and penetrate our defensive illusion. That suggests your concern is important. Now let's introduce ourselves. I am Cedar Centaur, Officer of the Day. It is my job to handle whatever occurs at this time."

"I am Vinia, a human child." When he did not respond, she lurched on. "Prince Magician Ion and Princess Sorceress Hilda are on a Quest to free six crystallized princesses. One of them is a winged centaur filly."

Now he spoke. "Queen Ida's children. You would be the one who assists Ion in walking, with your telekinesis. Hilda would have sewn the carpet."

"You know!" Vinia said, surprised.

Cedar smiled. "We centaurs have encyclopedic information, and the descendants of Bink Human are known, as are all those with Magician-caliber magic. When you named them I was able to orient. You mentioned a filly. What is her name?"

"Chloe." This was easier than she had feared. So far.

"Chloe," he repeated, orienting. "She disappeared a century ago. She was telepathic."

"Yes. She got crystallized by Dragoman Dragon. Now he will release her if we can find a suitable stallion for her."

Cedar frowned handsomely. "That may be a problem. We centaurs are not partial to personal magic in our species. It does happen on rare occasion, but we do not consider it an asset."

"Yes. We hoped you would know of someone suitable. Someone who doesn't mind her telepathy. We have reached four princes, or the equivalents, so far, and have only this one princess and one other to go."

"What is the one other?"

"Demesne Demoness."

He oriented again. "Our records indicate that she is a lovely, talented, personable person, the friend of the Good Magician's wife Dara Demoness, who disappeared some time ago." He glanced at Vinia's hand. "Dara—whose signet ring you wear."

Oh, he was fearsomely smart! And observant, considering that the ring was invisible. "She lent it to me, to help with the Quest."

"Which implies the support of the Good Magician. This is not something we can afford to ignore."

"You will help us?" Vinia asked, too eagerly.

"Perhaps. I will convene an assembly of celibate centaurs. You can provide more specific information on her?"

"She made a holo recording to present her case. We can play it for you."

"That will do." He glanced at the carpet. "Inform your party that they may emerge to witness our consideration. I will summon the bachelors now, and they will decide which, if any, will do." He put his hands together, forming a cup, and blew a flutelike note.

Vinia returned to the carpet. "He is Cedar. He knows who we are. He is calling the single centaurs. They will decide. We can come out to watch."

"Good work," Hilda said.

They trekked out, leaving only Benny to mind the carpet.

The bachelors were already arriving. All of them were handsome. So why didn't they have fillies? Was there something about them?

"We centaurs take time to decide on mates," Cedar said, answering Vinia's mental question, which was surely a common one. "As do the fillies. Love at first site is rare."

"Site?"

He smiled. "So you are paying attention. Sight, of course."

Six stallions lined up before Cedar. "Before us are human Prince Magician Ion and Princess Sorceress Hilda, together with their retinue," he told the centaurs. Vinia saw them doing the orientation. "They wish to locate a stallion for the filly Chloe, who was crystallized by Dragoman but now will be freed if an amenable stallion becomes amenable." He glanced at Hilda. "You may play the holo, Sorceress."

Hilda played it. They all watched Chloe make her case. But Vinia could see that her telepathy was not playing well for this audience.

"Volunteers?" Cedar asked.

The six centaurs were silent.

Vinia opened her mouth to protest. But Hilda's glance shut her up.

"Since none of you care to join the telepathic filly in their new Queendom of Thanx," Cedar said, "as Officer of the Day I am required to handle this matter myself. We cannot afford to balk a project of this progressive nature, tacitly supported by the Good Magician. Nor can we ignore our own crisis. The two may converge. Therefore I will undertake the chore." He glanced at one of the stallions. "Cedric, you are now OD."

That would be the abbreviation of Officer of the Day.

The designated stallion stepped forward and turned to face the others. "Return to your stalls," he directed. The others took off and departed. Then, to Cedar: "I will register your departure."

"Appreciation," Cedar said. "Perhaps in due course I will contact GCS as a representative of Thanx."

That would be the abbreviation of Grand Centaur Station. The centaurs were certainly efficient. But Vinia wondered whether there was any love or romance in their culture. How could Cedar summarily undertake to join Chloe when he didn't even like the idea of her telepathy? Was duty that important to him? What would Chloe think of that attitude?

Cedric spread his wings and ascended into the sky, doing a spot survey in case there were any other intrusions. Vinia doubted that there would be any others. Their own intrusion had been chancy enough.

Meanwhile, Cedar approached the carpet. "You will need to sew another amendment, Princess," he said. He clearly understood the nature of her magic.

Hilda was already busy sewing a patch.

Soon they took off again, with Cedar aboard. "You mentioned a crisis," Ion said alertly to the stallion. "Is this something we should know about?"

"Yes, Prince. It is that Thera has been dormant for the past several centuries, but is now about to come alive again. We have investigated the signs, such as new steam vents and rising of the caldera floor. Magma is accumulating. Pressure is building. The process is slow but sure. We shall have to establish a new base within the decade."

"And Thanx might do!" Hilda said.

"This is my thought," the centaur agreed. "While the notion of a telepathic mate does not appeal to me, it may be a necessary sacrifice for my species."

So it was not lack of romance so much as an overwhelming need. Cedar had to do what was required for the sake of the welfare of the winged centaurs. Vinia could respect that.

They talked as Benny guided the carpet up out of the cone and through the illusion and out to sea. Cedar relaxed, now that the decision had been made, and turned out to be a fairly affable guy, with an extraordinary amount of background knowledge. He should be okay in Thanx, assuming that side of it worked out.

Vinia hoped that was not too big an assumption. Their Quest was by no means certain of success.

"Next prince," Hilda said. "The Demon."

"Do you have a particular one in mind?" Cedar asked.

"No. We're not even sure how to proceed. Demons are a whole other challenge."

"They are indeed. The Demons originated in Hades, which is probably not where you wish to go for information."

"Maybe Dara will have a suggestion," Vinia said.

"May I offer an alternative?" Cedar said.

Was the luck of the ring kicking in? "What is it?" Vinia asked.

"Go to the main source of Demon information this side of Hades. That is Demon Professor Grossclout, who has taught at the University of Magic for the past century or so. He knows more about small-d demons than anyone else. He would surely know of a suitable one."

"Grossclout!" Hilda said. "The notorious curmudgeon who terrorizes whole classes of Demons at a time. Why would he ever bother with us?"

"He is said to have a soft spot for children. He doesn't terrorize them."

"And we're children," Hilda said. "At least he wouldn't blast us beyond the moon."

"But we have no idea where he is," Ion said. "And being a Demon, he may not remain in any one place long enough for us to catch up with him."

"He is currently visiting the Islet of Longer Hands to give a lecture on diabolics. You should be able to catch him there today."

"Then we'd better do it," Hilda said. "Vinia?"

"Grossclout," Vinia said to the ring. It flashed a direction. Benny aimed the carpet that way.

"I have not heard of that islet," Sherlock said.

"It moves about," Cedar explained. "There's an equivalent one in Mundania called the Islet of Langerhans, which relates to diabetics."

Sherlock groaned. "Longer Hands, Langerhans. Diabolics, diabetics. Xanth is mostly made of puns, but this is almost insufferable."

"No worse than Grossclout himself, who is a parody of a fearsome Mundane professor said to have required his students to chase paper."

"Demons are mischief," Ion said. "Fortunately the worst we have encountered is a passing scene with Metria."

"Don't say her name!" Hilda warned him sharply.

"Who?" Cedar asked.

"Metria Demoness," Vinia said helpfully, then covered her mouth.

A small black cloud appeared before them. "Did I hear my epithet?"

"Too late," Ion groaned. "I wasn't thinking."

"Me neither," Vinia said ruefully.

"Epithet?" Cedar asked. "A talking cloud?"

The cloud expanded, projecting four or five extensions. "Defamation, calumny, denomination, identification, appellation, designation—"

"Name?"

"Whatever," it answered crossly as the extensions formed into arms, legs, and head. "Who the bleep are you?"

"Cedar Centaur. And I gather you are the nefarious Metria Demoness."

The figure shaped into a smoky woman clad in a taut little skirt and a halter that was a size and a half too small for its content. "The same." She looked around. "This looks like a magic flying carpet with a mixed cargo of princes and children. There must be something interesting happening here."

"Nothing interesting," Hilda said desperately. "Boring as bleep."

"Hilda. And Ion," Metria said, recognizing them. "Sorceress and Magician. Are you involved in something your folks shouldn't know about? That's bound to be interesting."

Hilda sighed. "Might as well tell her. She'll never stop pestering us otherwise."

"Tell me what?" the Demoness asked attentively.

"That we're on a Quest," Ion said, accepting the inevitable.

"Aha! I knew there was something interesting going on. Here you are with your helpers on a giant flying carpet with a canopy and shield, along with an old Shee elf, a wild fee elf, a lesbian gobliness, and a handsome winged centaur, heading for who knows where. But what kind of Quest would assemble such a menagerie? It is to wonder."

"How did you know?" Georgia asked, annoyed. "That I am lesbian?"

"By the way you looked at my clothing."

"I looked the same way the men did."

"Exactly."

While Vinia and Hilda had frowned at the minihalter, half in irritation at the bad fit, half in envy for the generosity of the content, the men had looked with pleased interest. The Demoness knew exactly what responses she was trying for, and getting the right one from a woman was a live giveaway.

"You're a pretty sharp cookie, Demoness," Sherlock said.

"Thank you, dull elf."

"I'm Sherlock, King Emeritus of a local Shee kingdom. I have encountered Demonesses before, usually in passing, sometimes in bed, but have been more impressed with their bodies than their minds. You are evidently different."

"What's wrong with my body?" Metria demanded, inhaling so that the halter started to rip.

"Nothing. It's your mind that differs. You seem to have a speech impediment, but acute observation. That makes you interesting."

What was he up to? Vinia had seen enough of Sherlock to know that he was not flirting with the Demoness, at least not with seduction as the object. He had something in mind, and it wasn't her clothing.

"What about my mind?" Metria asked, intrigued. Yes, he had gotten her flighty attention.

"You plainly have more potential than you are using, so that you are not all that you could be."

Vinia saw that Ion was paying attention too, as were the others, especially Georgia. Sherlock was smart and knowledgeable, probably more so than Metria, but he wanted something from her. He was not so subtly flattering her. Why?

"What potential?"

"That requires some explaining. There is a contextual background."

She was hooked. "So explain, elf." He had actually gotten her interested in something technical. But what was he trying to do?

"I was an arrogant king, not suffering any back talk from anyone, including my daughter and heir. I had power and I wielded it relentlessly. That was effective; my kingdom prospered. But the fact that I listened to no one else meant that I was slowly going wrong, without correction. That was ultimately mischief. I lost my position when there was an insurrection by my alienated people that put my daughter in power. Only when I lost power did I come to understand and appreciate the other side of things. My daughter treated me far more tolerantly than I had treated her, and she was that way with everyone. She listened to contrary opinions and took advice. Not only was she more popular than I had been, she is in no danger of another insurrection. And the kingdom is prospering better than it did in my day. That was a significant lesson that I will keep in mind for the rest of my life. There really is merit in doing the right thing. The decent thing. In helping others rather than oneself. It may not be apparent at first, but in time it becomes a powerful tide. I have no power now, so it may be academic, but if by some fluke I should ever regain power, I would be a better ruler by far than I was before."

Metria's interest was starting to flag. "What has this to do with me?"

"Everything. You are much the way I was, proceeding with your projects without concern for the welfare or opinions of others. That leads to negative reactions, as you have seen by the way Ion and Hilda evidently view you. They want to be rid of you, which makes it difficult for you to discover, let alone participate in anything interesting. My guess is that this is typical of your other contacts."

"So what?"

"Ultimately it is a person's own judgment of his own character that counts, rather than the satisfactions of the moment. When a person assesses himself, what does he prefer to see, a string of annoyances and exclusions, or folk who welcome and appreciate his presence? Were you to tune in on their interests the way you did on Georgia Goblin's, for example, you could be phenomenally more popular than you are now. You could so readily change your reputation for the better and become a model others seek to emulate."

"Bleep," Metria swore. "I fear you are making sense. I *am* tired of being unpopular."

"As was I," Sherlock agreed.

"But what can I do? I am the way I am. I seek interesting things, and they don't hold my interest long."

Sherlock angled his head persuasively. "How are you at dealing with Demons?"

She laughed. "I *am* a Demon. Didn't you notice?" Her halter fogged out, leaving only trace wisps to cover parts of her bared bosom.

"We are hoping to talk with Demon Grossclout. Do you know of him?"

"Do I ever! I used to take his classes in magic at the U. I had no interest in the subject, but enjoyed teasing him by wearing a short skirt over polka-dot panties with no cloth inside the dots. Then I'd cross my legs so the dots showed. He never admitted it, but I know that drove him crazy, because he always had an eye for the ladies. Too bad he knew I wasn't a lady."

"You know Grossclout! Then you can surely help us talk with him, if you care to."

"Why would I care to? He's a crusty old bore."

"Because we need his help to recruit a suitable Demon prince for a Demon princess, so that six princesses can be released from their crystal prison."

She considered. "Now that's interesting, all right. What are those princesses going to do?"

"They hope to form the feminist Queendom of Thanx."

"A feminist queendom! That's fascinating. I'm all for it."

"Help us talk with Grossclout, and you'll be helping the queendom to come into existence."

At last Vinia made the connection. A Demoness to facilitate their dialogue with a Demon. Metria could indeed do that, if she chose to.

"So that's it. You want me to get Grossclout's attention for you."

"That's it. You might be able to accomplish what we can't."

"Why should I bother?"

"Because it would be a decent thing to do."

Metria paused, processing a new concept. "A decent thing. You prospered, at least intellectually, by becoming halfway decent. I might be less bored if I were decent. Still, it would be a chore, because he banned me from his classes."

"He is about to give a lecture on diabolics at the Islet of Longer Hands. We hope to catch him there."

Still she hesitated. "I don't know. Who is the crystal princess?"

"Demesne," Vinia said.

"Demesne! I know her. She was the top student in class. She always paid the closest attention to what he was saying. He thought it was because she was interested in the subject, but actually it was because she had a crush on him. A gnarly old codger like that! She finally left, knowing it was hopeless. Too bad, because I know the signs: he found her interesting. If she had had my expertise, she'd have soon seduced him."

Demesne had had a crush on Grossclout? That was news. That might explain why she had gone out on her own and gotten crystallized.

"He found her interesting?" Sherlock repeated. "She might have had a chance with him after all, had she but persevered."

"She sure might. He was turned on by her attention in class, and her smarts, but her body wasn't half bad either."

Since Demons could assume any form they wanted, Vinia thought, most of them did have good bodies. But they tended to stick to their most familiar forms, so could usually be recognized.

"I have a wicked idea," Sherlock said.

"I like wicked," Metria said.

"Suppose we go and try to talk with him, but he won't give us the time of the minute, let alone the time of day. Then you assume her form and smile at him. Would that get his attention?"

Metria nodded. "You're right. It would. That's wicked. I love it."

"And in the larger context, it would be a decent thing. We know that you have no personal interest in him, but you would be helping us to make the case for him getting together with the real thing."

"Wicked and decent together," Metria agreed. "A weird juxtaposition. How can I resist?"

"Then remain here with us and accompany us when we intercept Grossclout. Maybe conceal your identity, for now, so that he doesn't recognize you."

"That's easy. I'll just take a nap while you travel." The Demoness dissipated into smoke. It formed into a pretty little starflower, which landed on Sherlock's jacket as a decoration. It twinkled twice, then went still. She was napping.

"I believe we are ready to address Demon Grossclout," Sherlock said.

"We certainly are," Hilda agreed. "You were amazing."

"Merely doing my bit to facilitate the cause." But he was clearly pleased by his success. Vinia realized that he was already committed to the formation and success of Thanx.

They followed the direction indicated by the ring and soon arrived at a small island in the shape of a very long-fingered hand. "Invisible," Hilda told Ion, and he opened a vial. Nothing seemed to change, but Vinia knew they now could not be seen or heard from outside.

The ring flashed in changing directions, meaning that the subject was close and moving. This was the place.

"Metria," Hilda said. "We're here."

The starflower blinked, then puffed into smoke, which in turn formed into Metria in sexy dishabille. Nobody protested, for different reasons. "Did I hear my repute?"

"We don't have time for that rigmarole. Grossclout is near."

Indeed, a Demon was walking along the walk below, evidently departing a lecture hall by a private exit, as he was alone.

"That must be him," Cedar said. "But why is he walking, when he could simply pop over to wherever he is going?"

"Mainly courtesy," Hilda said. "The students here will be mostly physical, accustomed to physical professors, so he doesn't rub his nature in their faces, even when taking a private route. Walking short distances probably saves him energy, too."

"You seem remarkably knowledgeable." He didn't add "For a child."

"I'm a princess. Proper decorum when entertaining guests has been drilled into me. It's one reason I prefer to get out on my own, with people I can be informal with."

"Right on," Furioso agreed.

"Who goes to meet him?" Vinia asked.

"You try first," Hilda said. "Maybe your luck will hold. Take Metria with you."

"I'll be invisible," the Demoness said. "At first." She faded out.

Vinia had sort of known she would be on the spot. It was expected of protagonists. She would just have to muddle through, as usual. "Um, should I take the holo?"

Hilda handed it to her.

The carpet dived to the walk ahead of Grossclout. Vinia stepped off, becoming visible. "Hello, sir," she said politely.

The Demon paused. He was indeed formidable, with gnarled horns, a swishing tail, and a natural glower that seemed somewhat larger than his face. "Are you a late student? I don't recognize you."

"No, sir. I am Vinia, on a separate mission. I have come to ask you—"

Grossclout vanished in a puff of smoke, reappearing beyond her on the walk. So much for the direct approach. He didn't mess with strangers.

"Time for the first team," Metria said in her ear. "I'll take you there." She put her hands on Vinia's elbows and lifted her. There was a wrenching, and suddenly they were on the path ahead of Grossclout.

This time Metria was visible beside her, in the exact form of Demesne.

Grossclout huffed, about to pop past again, but froze, staring. Obviously he recognized her. "Where have you been?" he demanded gruffly.

"This is not really Demesne," Vinia said. "Merely her image. Please, I come on her behalf."

And this time he remained in place. "How so?"

"Let me play her holo for you. That explains everything."

"Play it."

Vinia activated the holo as Metria faded out. Demesne made her case for connecting with an amenable Demon prince, and the holo ended.

Now Grossclout gave Vinia his direct and formidable attention. She tried not to quail. "Did she know you would come to me?"

"No. We didn't know. I think she expects a younger prince."

"Age is immaterial to a Demon. We are all ageless as we are crafted in Hades, then choose our appearance and manner. I think I require your opinion."

"Sir, I am just an incidental child. My opinion is irrelevant."

"A child who wears Dara's ring. The protagonist of this story. Who has uncanny finesse in handling unusual situations. Hardly incidental."

Taken severely aback, Vinia oriented on one thing. "You see the ring?"

"I see it, child. I gave it to Dara a century ago to facilitate her training of the Good Magician Humfrey. She did accomplish that."

"But she said it belonged originally to a Magician."

He merely looked at her. She realized that Grossclout was the Magician. She had put her foot in it.

"You know nothing," he said.

She might as well be a student in his class, who had not done her homework. "Yes, sir."

"A true innocent. The rarest of creatures."

He had her nailed to the wall. "Yes, sir," she agreed, ashamed.

"Which means you have no preconceptions to interfere with your intellectual development. I like that."

He liked her ignorance? Vinia had no idea how to respond.

"In contrast to that vulgar insult to the species, Metria."

So he saw Metria. He didn't miss a trick.

"Hey, I'm reforming," Metria protested as she appeared. "I'm trying to do something decent for a change."

"Anything would be more decent than those stuffed polka-dot panties you insisted on flashing in class."

"I mean like putting you on to Demesne, who had a crush on you."

He seemed taken aback. "If she had one then, she has it now. Demons don't change their biases. It was nevertheless a pleasure teaching her. She was a sensible lass and an apt learner."

"That's my thought," Metria said. "She is all the things that I am not. So why don't you follow up on her? You're about ready to retire anyway."

Grossclout shook his head, bemused. "Out of the mouths of babies and sluts."

Vinia wished she had half an inkling how this was going. Was he interested in Demesne, or was he utterly disgusted?

"Your opinion, Vinia," Grossclout asked. "Would Demesne be interested in my company today?"

Would she? "I don't know. She's about to be queen of the feminist Queendom of Thanx."

"Perhaps we should talk. Contact her."

Maybe that was best. "Demesne," Vinia said to the ring. The name had been in play before, but this time it was for contact.

"Yes, Vinia," the Demoness answered after a moment.

"I-I have Demon Professor Grossclout here."

"Grossclout!" Demesne sounded like a trapped schoolgirl. That was surprising, considering her prior competence.

He spoke. "It has been suggested that I retire and join you in your forming Queendom of Thanx."

"Join me! You?"

"As your consort. Does that interest you?"

"My consort!" Demesne echoed faintly, a dawning blush coloring her voice. "I never dreamed—"

"Demons don't dream."

She rallied. "Some do. I do. I'm dreaming now, technically. But still—"

Grossclout looked impatiently at Vinia. "You, innocent. Should I go there?"

Vinia desperately focused. The Demoness wanted a prince. Grossclout was more than qualified. Demesne had crushed on him before, but thought he was beyond her reach. Now he was within reach, but she hardly believed it. Just as Vinia herself had discovered Prince Magician Ion to be within her reach, amazingly. And there was the answer. "Yes!"

Neither party protested.

"Then I will join her at the concourse of suitors. Inform your companions." He vanished.

"Oh!" Demesne said happily and clicked off.

"Well, now," Metria said. "I think I helped."

"You certainly did!" Vinia agreed and hugged her. "You did the decent thing."

"I did, didn't I," Metria agreed, pleased. "Sherlock's right. It does feel good."

It was time to return to the carpet with the good news. Their Quest was now complete.

Yet Vinia still had a faint nagging doubt. Was this too easy?

Chapter 7

NO THANX

It was predawn, the landscape just beginning to fight off the gloom of night. They had been napping during the dark flight. Metria had stayed with them awhile, then departed, satisfied that she had done her bit of good, still digesting the implications. It was time for them to start stirring.

The carpet approached the entrance to the cave that housed Dragoman's lair. They were almost there, their mission complete. Then Vinia thought of something. "Um—"

Hilda laughed. "Out with it, girl. If confidence were visible, you'd be invisible. Yet you're the protagonist. Everything connected to you is important."

"Fate must love shy folk," Ion said. "Just as I do."

They were teasing her. She liked it. "It's that we've had a several days' long flight, and while I know the potty capacity is limitless, the stuff is in there. If it got accidentally kicked over—"

"There'd be a mountain of bleep in a confined space, a stench to rival a stink horn," Furioso said, laughing. "And you're right. We should empty it before we go inside any caves, just to be safe."

"I'll do it," Vinia said.

"With four virile princes aboard? You'll need help digging the hole, which must be big enough to hold it all. In fact, we can do it, so that you need not soil your ladylike hands." He glanced at the two other princes, who nodded. Ion didn't count, for this.

"But royals aren't supposed to do menial work," she protested.

"Neither are ladies."

"I'm not a lady! I'm a servant girl."

"A tourist who joined our party," Hilda said. "A different thing."

"Shall we hold a vote?" Furioso asked rhetorically. "All in favor of Vinia being considered a lady say aye."

"Aye!" the others said together, all seven of them.

Vinia wasn't sure how much of this was teasing, or how to react.

It was Georgia who came to her rescue. "Technically you're servant class, as is everyone who is not royal, but we have all come to know you and respect you and to us, you're a lady. We regard you as equal to us, regardless of societal standards. If you have work to do, we want to help you." She glanced at Sherlock and Cedar, who nodded. "So we'll do it together."

Vinia was unable to argue with that.

Benny brought the carpet to land on the level ground outside the cave. Cedar heaved himself to his four feet and went to pick up the potty. He carried it off the carpet. Sherlock went to the cloth tool bag Hilda had sewn, opened it, and drew out a spade his size. Then another, Furioso's size. The two followed the centaur to the outside. Vinia had to hurry to catch up. Georgia came with her. They walked across the deeply shadowed terrain, passing plants and minipools of water.

Cedar stopped at a sandy spot. "This should do."

Sherlock and Furioso went to work with a will, digging a hole in the sand. Soon they had a fair-sized pit, a black hole because of the morning gloom. Vinia realized that the spades were magic, excavating many times the amount normal spades would have. The twins would not have stored garden-variety tools.

"That should do," Cedar said. He lifted the potty out over the rim and turned it over. Slop poured out, like a giant sewer hose turned on, splashing messily into the depth. The smell came with it. The brown stream kept coming, filling the pit until it threatened to flood. Furioso had to leap back to avoid being splashed, dropping his spade. It was amazing how much had been put into that potty in a short time. Unless maybe this was not the first time it had been used.

Fortunately, the potty emptied just before the pit overflowed. Maybe the spades had known. Sherlock started spading loose dirt over, to bury the slop.

Vinia went to the small spade and picked it up, determined to do her part. And felt her hands hurting. She had run afoul of stinging nettles. She dropped the spade.

"Oh, get them off you quickly, before they dig in," Georgia said. She used her own hands to dip water from a nearby pool and poured it over Vinia's hands, washing off the nettles. That helped.

But the stinging continued in one place. The nettles had gotten under the ring. Vinia had to yank it off so that she could plunge her hand into the pool, clearing the remaining nettles. In about one and a half moments the pain faded. The nettles had not had time to dig in.

Meanwhile Furioso had recovered his spade and gone back to work on the pit filling. Soon he and Sherlock had the ground modestly mounded, covering the slop. The odor was reluctantly thinning. They were done.

The five of them returned to the carpet. It lifted and glided into the cave.

"Oh!" Vinia said.

"What is it?" Georgia asked.

"I lost the ring! I was distracted by the nettles, and it must have dropped to the ground or into the pool."

"I don't think the carpet can turn around here in the tunnel," Georgia said. "But it's still too dark to find it readily. We can return for it when there is full daylight. It should be right there."

"I hope so," Vinia said weakly. She felt somehow naked without the ring. It had zeroed in on key people and had brought good luck. Now there could be a backlash.

"You're back!" It was Chloe, the telepath, speaking to Vinia in her head. "Did things work out well?"

"We have the princes!" Vinia replied. "Four of them here—well, one's a princess—and two to come."

"That's wonderful. We can't wait to meet them. I will tell Dragoman."

They landed in the main cave, before the dragon. They filed off the carpet.

"Chloe says you got the princes," Dragoman said, aloud, with his buttressing telepathy.

"Yes. With two to come."

"*One* to come," Demon Grossclout said, appearing beside them, glower and all.

"Grossclout!" Dragoman said, amazed. "Don't you have Demon classes to teach? Terrorizing the novices?"

"I am retiring, to be with Demesne, if she'll have me." He glanced at Vinia's bare finger and frowned without comment. He knew the qualities of the ring. Vinia felt guilty for losing it.

"I will see to the last of the princes now, to make the roster complete," Ion said. "I must set up the local portal."

Vinia joined him, as she had to for more than one reason, and they walked to a side exit and out to the flower fields, while Hilda handled the remaining introductions.

It did not take long. Ion set the portal up on a little stand, like a flat picture. And Vinia suffered another horrible qualm. "The ring! I'm not wearing it."

"I know. But in this case, we don't need it, fortunately. The local portal can orient on the distant one, being within its orientation field."

"Oh," she said, relieved, though she hardly understood what he said.

Ion brought out the cup with the elixir, dipped another ring, spoke the necessary words, then poked his finger through, making a beckoning gesture to the bees beyond. It was weird, seeing his finger disappear, but Vinia knew it was routine. Soon a solitary bee buzzed through, Drover Drone. "Hello, Ion!" he buzzed. "Hello, Vinia." The effect of the communication elixir remained; they understood him perfectly.

"Tell Queen BeeAttitude that the return connection has been established," Ion said.

"Forthwith." Drover flew back through the portal. In barely two and a half moments he emerged again. Evidently the queen had been in close touch, eager to verify the portal and the precious flowers beyond. "Get clear."

They stood back as a line of worker bees zoomed through, like miniature bombers in a Mundane formation. They headed immediately for the Honeysuckles, orienting by smell. That was the rest of the verification: the invaluable flowers.

"We're done here," Ion said with satisfaction. "Drover, it is time for you to meet your princess."

"I am all aflutter," the drone buzzed. "Where is she?"

"We're going there now. She will be one of six princesses of different species. We still need to verify that all of you are compatible matches."

"You may perch on my head, if you wish," Vinia said, suspecting Drover would be uncomfortable flying through the tunnels.

"Thank you, lady." He flew across to land neatly on her hair.

There it was again. She was considered a lady. Vinia couldn't help feeling pleased, though she knew nothing had really changed.

They returned to the cave. "Ah. The roster is complete," Dragoman said. "Line up before the crystals, and I will release the princesses." He glanced at Vinia. "Line up with them, lady, so the drone does not have to sit on the floor at risk of getting stepped on. I'm pretty sure Beetrix will not confuse you for Drover." There was a murmur of laughter. It was a fair tension reliever.

They went to the crystal chamber. There were the six crystals, like giant gems. Vinia helped Ion to a chair by the side so that he could sit in comfort to witness the proceedings. Hilda stood beside him. She had his little flying carpet, if he needed to move around while Vinia was helping the bees.

The princes and Georgia lined up, and Vinia went to stand beside the goblin. "Hello again, Drover," Georgia said. "I hope we both get what we came for."

"Amen," the drone buzzed, the wind from his wings blowing Vinia's hair.

"Ready, Chloe?" Dragoman asked.

"We are all more than ready," the centaur filly replied in an all-person broadcast, mentally flicking her tail. "This is a phenomenal occasion."

The dragon breathed out a plume of white smoke. It suffused the cave, surrounding the crystals, smelling faintly of menthol. The crystals evaporated, dissolving into the smoke, which coursed on up through a vent in the ceiling. In almost a moment the six princesses stood there in their beauty, or rather five princesses standing and one buzzing in place.

They gazed jointly at the princes and Georgia. The princes and Georgia gazed at the princesses. A little heart flew up. Scintillating lines extended from it to the two who had first connected. Elga Elf and Cedar Centaur.

What?

Vinia saw that she was hardly alone in her confusion. What was happening here? Those two were not supposed to be a couple.

Cedar stepped forward and extended a hand to Elga. She accepted it, then sat on it. She was a scant two feet tall; his human portion was a generous six feet, and of course there was a lot more of him behind. She was like a doll on his hand, but both seemed perfectly at ease with the situation.

Love was blinding them to the anomaly of it. He lifted her up and brought her to his face. They kissed, and another little heart flew up, confirming the diagnosis.

The hearts never lied. The elf and the centaur were in instant and permanent love. But how could this be? They were grossly mismatched, their species not even close to each other.

"We will require an accommodation spell to do much more, my love," Elga murmured. It was apparent that she did want to do it, whatever it was.

"Prince Ion has one," Vinia said before her brain caught up with her mouth.

"Thank you," Cedar said. He walked across to Ion, who wordlessly handed them a vial. Elga took it, holding it carefully. This was what made it possible as well as desirable. They trotted on out of the chamber, seeking suitable privacy for business that had become abruptly urgent.

Another heart appeared. This one connected Sherlock and Hula. "That's an immense relief," he said as he went to her. They kissed but did not depart. They were technically elf and human, but close enough to have no problem.

"I love you," Hula said. "But I want more."

Oops. So there *was* a problem.

"Understood. I am happy to have the share of you I can manage. I look forward to watching you dance, and of course we will converse."

"We will dance and converse," she agreed.

Which seemed like an odd kind of connection, Vinia thought. But if they were satisfied, it would do. Problem solved.

"I understand you have been a king," Hula said. "That means you have had a lot of experience and possess competent background knowledge. In sum, a mind."

"I do."

"I want that, too."

A third heart appeared. This one connected Drover and Beetrix. There was a general relief as she flew across to join him on Vinia's hair. Another proper match.

"Let's go fly among the flowers," Beetrix buzzed.

"We'll do more than fly," he buzzed back.

"First you must catch me." She flew off, going for the smoke exit, her path a flirtatious curve, and he followed. Their nuptials would be in midair. To others such a liaison might only feel like flying: with them it was literal.

Then a fourth heart, connecting Grossclout and Demesne. Their long-stifled interest in each other was finally working out, since he was no longer the professor and she no longer the student. She was to be the Queen of Thanx, and he her consort. That was a new and surely challenging relationship. They came together and kissed, then stood, concerned about the remaining matches.

A fifth heart connected Goblette with Georgia. They kissed. They were a couple. Vinia knew that both were vastly relieved, after the disapproval they had experienced by other goblins. They understood each other.

That left Furioso Fee and Chloe Centaur. "I mean absolutely no dis-respect, filly, but my inclination is not for you or your telepathy," he said.

"Ditto here," she agreed. "It seems we both have been jilted."

"But there needs to be a sixth couple, or the terms of the deal have not been met."

Then both looked at Vinia. Uh-oh. She was expected to come up with an amazing solution to an insoluble problem. Because she was the pro-tagonist, and the one with the lucky ring.

The ring! In the rush of events she had lost track of that problem. She no longer wore it, and the bad luck had struck. It was her fault.

"No, it's not your fault," Chloe said, reading her mind. "Merely an awk-ward coincidence."

"Then whose fault is it?" Vinia retorted. "San Andrea's?" She was refer-ring to a notorious Mundane artifact that took the blame for enormous mischief. Whole buildings were said to shake when it was active.

"Sometimes things just happen. We must not allow them to overcome us. There will be an answer."

Which Vinia was somehow obliged to provide. She had lost the ring; she had to make up for its damage.

She looked wildly around. The others were looking at her. Grossclout was locked into a fixed glower. No inspiration there.

Benny lifted his hand. She looked at him. He tossed her his thinking cap.

Well, why not? If there were an answer, that might be the way to catch it, like a bee in midair.

Vinia put the cap on. And the idea exploded in her head, followed by another. She ripped the cap off before any more could strike and tossed it back to Benny.

"Furioso," she said. "Your problem has been that no elf has been woman enough for you, physically or emotionally." Yet again she wished she knew exactly what the details were.

"True."

"And Hula's problem is that no one man is enough for her. She's a lot more woman than a fee or an elf."

"True," he said, eyeing Hula. She eyed him back.

"You can assume human size when you choose, for an hour or so. How much can you do in an hour?"

"Plenty," he said, licking his lips.

"A half share of her for an hour . . ." She let it trail off, because she didn't know what was supposed to fill that ellipsis but was sure *he* knew.

"Well, now," he said, looking again at Hula. She waggled a hip at him. She knew the ellipsis content, too. "My initial interest is mostly physical rather than mental."

"As it happens, I have the mental aspect covered." She glanced side-long at Sherlock, who smiled. It was acceptance he wanted as much as romance. He could have both, with even half of her.

Furioso joined her, assuming human size. "Then let's put it to the test."

"I will certainly test you," Hula agreed.

The three of them exited the chamber together. One more match had been accomplished.

"Which leaves one winged monster," Chloe said.

Vinia delved into the second idea the cap had given her. "There is another winged monster who knows you and respects you and I think would really like to be with you, but who suppressed the desire in that manner Demon Grossclout did when he taught at the University of Magic, because it did not seem appropriate. Your telepathy is no deterrent: he has his own more limited version. You can verify that now." Vinia looked at Dragoman.

Chloe looked at the dragon, reading his mind. "It's true," she said, surprised. "He wants more than just the appreciation and friendship of princesses. We have been mentally compatible all along. In fact, we have known each other mentally for years and are friends. As for the physical,

an accommodation spell will more than suffice. And of course, now we
can fly together." She did not even need to ask the dragon whether he
agreed: she knew his mind. Vinia wondered whether winged monsters, a
category that included even the most petite flying elves, did anything in
the air similar to what the princess and drone bees did, whatever it was.
Oh, the Conspiracy peeved her!

"Of course, we do," Chloe said in her mind. "Except for those with a
fear of flying." She laughed mentally.

Vinia was yet again desperate to grow up and find out what it was all
about.

An hour passed, while those remaining in the cave snacked on people
crackers and extra dull charcoal cheese. Vinia wanted to go out to search
for the ring, but first she needed to unwind after the effort to match the
mismatched princesses. Also, Queen Demesne had something on her
mind, so when the departed couples returned there was an informal strategy meeting. "I know that all of you want to get busy with your roles,"
she said. "Goblette and Georgia will be establishing the schedule for the
several daily meals so the rest of us don't go hungry. Hula will be organizing the queendom entertainment so we can relax when we have time. Elga
and Cedar will be setting up a pavilion we can use as a temporary official
palace, so as not to intrude on Dragoman's lair anymore, and putting the
grounds in order. Chloe will be establishing formal relations with established kingdoms and monarchs, such as the human King Ivy and the Shee
Queen Birdie. But I feel that we need to establish at least token diplomatic
relations with the neighboring tribes as soon as possible, so they don't
mistake our new activity as hostile. There is no call to distract Chloe from
her business; I can handle the purely local details myself."

"A sensible suggestion," Grossclout agreed. "Folk are ever prone to
misunderstand what they don't understand."

"Thank you," Demesne said, flattered by his approval, her dress momentarily thinning in a manner Vinia was sure wasn't meant to be teasing, but
of course was. It would take Demesne time to get past her old awe of him
as the professor. It would also take him time to get used to admiring her
openly, instead of trying to mask the way his eyeballs expanded when her
blouse accidentally fogged or she crossed her bare legs.

"Who are the neighbors?" Cedar asked.

"There are six kingdoms or the equivalent," Dragoman said. He, like the others, seemed singularly relaxed, after his first flight with Chloe; obviously there was no fear of flying there. "Human, goblin, ogre, troll, gnome, and dragon. They quarrel sporadically with one another, but I have gotten along because my crystals were never any threat to them."

"May that continue," Demesne said.

"Any of those species can be ugly when the fickle finger of fate gooses them the wrong way," Cedar said. "But perhaps if we make formal peace with one of them, the others will follow that lead."

"But which one?" Elga asked. She was now perched possessively on his broad back. Vinia wondered yet again what the accommodation spell had enabled them to do, as it had certainly mellowed them.

"May I suggest human?" Sherlock asked. "Most of us have some human component, which may aid understanding."

Demesne looked around, seeing agreement. "Human it is."

"They are the Hoo-Hah Humans," Dragoman said. "Given mostly to wine, women, and song. Whoever approaches them should be fair of feature, so as not to arouse their foolish rivalry, but ready to defend herself from grabby hands."

"That would be me," Demesne said.

"Then I will join you," Grossclout said. "Invisible, if you prefer."

"Perhaps that would be best. It is not that I object at all to your presence, dear. It is that your inherent glower might give them the wrong impression."

"Point taken," he agreed, and he faded out.

She had called him dear, and he hadn't glared. She was well on the way to taming him.

"Next item," the Demoness said. "I will need a retinue, to appear properly queenly. Any volunteers?"

"Us," Goblette said, holding Georgia's hand. "We can be fair featured, when we try." There was general laughter; they were both quite pretty girls.

"You should come bearing a gift," Sherlock said. "A token will do. It's the gesture that counts."

Vinia remembered the goblin king running afoul of the gift. She suppressed a naughty smile. Was he still up in the air?

"What would a wining, womanizing, singing king like?" Demesne asked. Vinia had to smile at how close one word came to "whining."

"Perfume for his queen. The kind that generates powerful potency when he sniffs it."

So there was a selfish motive when a king gave a queen something, Vinia thought. But Sherlock was probably correct.

"I have an elixir," Ion said.

"So you can join the party," Demesne said.

That meant Vinia would also be along. Somehow, she had known she would. It came with being the protagonist.

"Do we need to make an appointment?" Goblette asked.

"They are so informal they don't make appointments," Dragoman said. "Just go and ask to see the king and hope for the best. He's probably partying."

So they went, walking: the six of them, Demons, goblins, and humans, ready to depart quickly if there should be danger. There was unlikely to be any threat to the Demons, but they would not vacate while their friends were in trouble.

They passed the flower fields, where the visiting bees were busily harvesting Heaven-Can-Wait pollen, and came to a barren, rocky field beyond, strewn with litter. Obviously, the Hoo-Hah had no special pride of property. They heard the faint sound of music and followed it to a hill overgrown with grapevines, where workers were harvesting the grapes. None paid them any attention.

There was a desultory path winding up the hill, lined with kitchen trash. They followed it up to a castle, which had an outer and inner wall, in lieu of a moat. It was not impressive: the walls were in ill repair. Vinia realized that the well-kept buildings of the Kingdoms of Adamant, Xanth, and Shee were not necessarily typical of the hinterlands.

They came to the front gate. It wasn't even guarded. They walked on in, collared the first person they saw inside, and asked to see the king. "That way," the person said, pointing.

They went that way and came to a hall where music was playing and scantily clad girls were dancing. Vinia had never understood why men liked women who were not completely dressed, but obviously they did.

Servants were carrying jugs of wine in and out. No one paid any attention to the intruders.

"Are we sure this is worthwhile?" Vinia asked.

"All we can do is make the effort," Demesne said, frowning. As neighbors went, this was not promising.

They spotted the king, because he was the one with a crown and royal robe. He was trying to dance with a pretty girl but was too drunk to do more than stagger and clumsily paw her torso. The girl's face was set in a fixed smile. She was evidently used to this.

"Idea," Grossclout said. He remained invisible. "Do you have a sobriety elixir, Ion?"

Ion brought out a vial. He took it to the dancing couple and opened it. Vapor emerged and wafted to the king, who suddenly stood up straight, spying them. "What the bleep is this?" he demanded.

"I am Queen Demesne of the Queendom of Thanx, next door to Hoo-Hah."

"Never heard of it."

"We formed it this morning. It is feminist, governed by women of several different persuasions."

He peered at her as if trying to see through her clothing. "You're a Demoness!"

"I am. But Thanx is not a Demon domain. I merely happen to be the present queen. It is open to all who wish to become citizens, whatever their nature."

Vinia saw that the servants and dancing girls were paying attention. This interested them. Especially the girl the king had been trying to dance with, who now stood sedately behind him as she adjusted her mussed halter and skirt.

"Governed by women?"

Demesne nodded. "Yes. But we plan to be fair to all citizens, male and female. In fact, we hope to become a model state, a pleasant residence for everyone. We hope to have amicable relations with our neighbor states, yours included."

The king seemed to be having difficulty assimilating this despite his sobriety. "Women rule it?"

Demesne smiled tolerantly. She had a very nice smile. "Indeed."

He scowled. "Feminist."

"Yes. We feel it is time for women to have a say in things."

Vinia saw the girl nod. She liked what she was hearing.

The king exploded. "Apostasy! It must be extirpated immediately!"

This was not a positive direction. Demesne's mouth twitched almost imperceptibly. Then she carried on. "And to initiate good relations we have brought a small gift for you." She glanced at Ion, so Ion and Vinia stepped up to join them. "A seductive perfume for your wife."

The girl winced. Vinia could guess why: she wished the king would pay more attention to his wife and leave the dancing girls alone. Such a potion would not necessarily accomplish that.

"Seductive?" At least the distraction was working.

Ion held forth a vial. "One whiff and she's yours." Ion, of course, could not define it further, because of the Conspiracy, but the veiled reference more than sufficed for the king. "Dulcie," he said, looking at the girl. He was no longer drunk, but that did not alter his underlying nature.

"I'll fetch your wife immediately," the girl said and hastily departed.

"Hey, that's not what I—" But she was already gone. Vinia suspected that Dulcie had deliberately misunderstood, so as not to get doused with the elixir herself, even on a test basis. The king could hardly object publicly to his wife being summoned for a gift for her, however much it might annoy him.

"I'm sure your wife will love it," Demesne said.

The king's frustrated eye fell on her. An idea occurred to him. There was of course no question of its nature. "How about—"

"My consort might object," Demesne said.

Grossclout faded into view beside her. He let out a token glower.

The king stepped back as if burned. There was no mistaking the intimidation of that glower. Grossclout was the Magician of Intimidation. Then the king's roving eye fell on the two pretty goblin princesses. They were not human, but human men appreciated goblin girls almost as much as they did human ones. A goblin girl could freak out a human man by flashing her panties with no effort at all. "Maybe two small ones would be better than one full-sized one."

"We're lesbians," Georgia said as Goblette nodded agreement.

The king was undeterred. "That simply means you're passing the time until you can find a real man. Let's douse you with the potion and see what happens."

This was mischief. The girls did not want to make an ugly scene that could mess up the diplomatic mission, such as it was, but neither did they want to get into it with this crude king. Flashing their panties would be an act of war in this situation. His version of lesbianism was the standard male one, Vinia knew, because the average man simply could not conceive of any woman not wanting any man. And she realized that this was more bad luck striking, in the absence of the ring. So it was her fault, again. She had to do something to stave it off until the wife arrived.

But what? She saw that this had attracted the attention of the rest of the room. The music had even faded out, and the dancing girls had paused in place, listening.

Then she thought of Benny's thinking cap. If only she had it now! But maybe there was a way. She imagined it landing on her head.

And she got an idea. It was a naughty one, but what choice did she have?

She used her telekinesis to make the royal robe goose the king. He was within her range and facing away from her as he leered at the goblins. His fat behind was a perfect target. The robe convoluted as if a giant hand were grabbing it. It flexed powerfully inward.

"OoOoo!" the king howled, leaping into the air with surprising agility.

"Oh, dear!" Vinia exclaimed innocently. "I fear that invisible wild goose must have followed us inside." Wild geese were notorious for just such rascality, and remarkably common when parties got chaotic. Normally their taste was just for the ladies, however.

Demesne was quick on the uptake. "It must have," she agreed, stifling a laugh. "We must shoo it out before it scores on anyone else." She made shooing motions. The other members of their party quickly joined in. Then so did the dancing girls, though some of them seemed to be in a remarkably good humor about the intrusion.

At this point Dulcie and the wife arrived. "What is going on?" the lady demanded. She was a forbidding woman, but shapely, in the manner of a trophy wife, surely by no coincidence.

The king seemed suspicious. Vinia knew that his courtesans would soon learn about the nature of Vinia's talent. They had to get out of here before the girls told the king.

"We have a gift for you," Vinia said to the wife. "Perfume."

Wife's interest was immediate. Acquisition was in her nature. "Oh? Let's have it."

"Here," Ion said. He opened the vial and the vapor wafted out and clouded around both the wife and Dulcie.

The king's wife sniffed. "Delicious." It did not affect women the same way as the men.

"Well now!" the king said as a waft drifted across to tickle his nose.

"Uh-oh," Dulcie said, evidently recognizing the odor. She tried to back away, but the wife grabbed her arm.

"What is it?" the wife demanded distrustfully.

"Potency elixir!"

"Oh, bleep! We don't need that around here. We've got more than enough."

Dulcie nodded. So did several of the dancing girls.

Then the king charged them. They fled together, but he pursued, his hands reaching eagerly forward for any flesh they could capture. In three scrambled moments all three were out of the hall. Vinia suspected that there would be quite a scene, once the king caught up to them.

"Let us depart," Demesne said with as straight a face as she could manage. "I believe we are done here." She glanced around at the audience that had formed. "We bid you farewell, kind folk, and thank you for your courtesy. Visit Thanx anytime."

They walked sedately out of the hall. No one tried to stop them. Something was brewing among the servants and dancing girls, and finally it burst out uncontrollably: laughter.

"I am not certain exactly how well that went," Grossclout remarked. He was trying to maintain his glower, but it was eroding.

"You naughty girl," Demesne said fondly to Vinia. Then the laughter caught up and overwhelmed them, too.

"I fear I caught a whiff of that elixir," Grossclout said to Demesne as they subsided.

"A likely story," she retorted, not at all annoyed. Then the two of them vanished in a heart-shaped cloud of smoke. It was apparent that their relationship was working out well.

The other four of them returned to the lair. "There was a problem," Ion said.

"We gathered that," Chloe Centaur said severely. She was now the Minister of Communications. "Hoo-Hah just declared war on Thanx, and it seems the other surrounding kingdoms are following suit. They plan to invade and destroy us tomorrow."

That made them pause. This was an extremely serious complication. Then the four of them burst out laughing again.

"Oh, I see," Chloe said, reading their minds. She tried to hold it in, but the laugh tore out her too.

"What the bleep happened?" Dragoman demanded. "War is a most serious business, especially when it threatens one's home turf."

"The king of Hoo-Hah was about to go after Goblette and Georgia, and Vinia goosed him telekinetically so they could get away. Then Ion's potency elixir doused both the king's wife and his girlfriend, together."

"Together!" Furioso said, amused. "That's not normal protocol."

"No wonder Hoo-Hah declared war!" Sherlock said.

"The king's hatred of feminism might have had something to do with it," Georgia said with a straight face.

"He doesn't seem to much like the idea of women making their own decisions," Goblette agreed. Both tittered.

"But now we have a rather serious situation to handle," Chloe said. "Ah, here come Grossclout and Demesne now."

The two appeared. Grossclout looked a bit odd without his glower. Evidently their private session had been hard on it. "We may have doomed Thanx, but it was almost worth it," Demesne said, reforming her mussed robe. "That is one rude, crude neighbor."

"But why did things go so drastically and suddenly wrong?" Cedar Centaur asked.

"I lost the ring," Vinia said, ashamed. "It was charmed for good luck, but there's a blowback effect when it's gone."

"Then we'd better find it in a hurry," Elga said.

"Good advice," Grossclout agreed. "I did not make the ring, but know it is a singularly powerful talisman, for good or ill."

They headed out as a group. It was now full daylight, but the region was larger than it had seemed in the predawn dusk, and the search seemed impossible. The little pool was a mass of mud; something must have dragged through it.

"I have a magnifying glass," Hilda said, bringing out a round one on a handle. "I use one aspect of it for my needlework. It should help."

Vinia wasn't sure of that, but kept her mouth shut as Hilda went to the area of the pool where the ring had disappeared.

"I am not clear how this will help locate something lost in muck," Sherlock said.

"This way," Hilda explained. "The ring was formed from a glass eel and a glass eye, magically merged. The other aspect of my glass magnifies glass. Ah, there!" For something had appeared in the mud: a doughnut-size shape. She took it and rinsed it off. It looked exactly like the lost ring, only ten times the size.

"It is now a torus," Ion said.

"But I can't wear this," Vinia said. "It's more like an anklet than a finger ring."

Hilda turned the magnifying class over and looked through it at the torus, which immediately reverted to ring size. Oh. Of course, it mattered which way you used a magnifying glass. Vinia put it back on her finger, where it fit perfectly. "The bad luck should be over," she said. In the background of her mind she was surprised by how much Hilda had known about the ring. She saw that Grossclout was surprised, too. Hilda evidently appreciated jewelry.

"It is enough," Demesne said, as they returned to the lair. "Now all we have to do is figure out how to handle an invasion by all our neighbors. If we don't stop it, by the end of tomorrow there'll be no Thanx."

"No Thanx," Grossclout echoed, with a brief lessening of his glower.

She was not amused. "What are we going to do?"

"If I had my hive at full strength," Beetrix buzzed, "We could sting them so bad they'd never bother us again." She and Drover had come in for the meeting. "But that won't happen until next year."

"We do have a mutual defense pact with your home hive, Drover," Demesne said. "Would they be willing to help tomorrow?"

"Yes!" the drone buzzed. "But I know Queen BeeAttitude. She will allocate only enough warriors to protect the Heaven-Can-Wait Honeysuckle field."

"Well, that's progress," Demesne agreed. "But we have five or six more sectors to defend." She glanced at Sherlock. "You must have handled a war or two in your day. What do you recommend?"

"You will need allies," Sherlock said. "Savage ones, I think."

"And how can we win allies, when as yet we have very few resources and less experience?"

"This is a challenge," he agreed. "Conventional ones will not do, as they may take years to cultivate. We need instant ones, and probably highly unusual ones."

"You have something in mind," Chloe said.

"Yes. Consider nickelpedes."

"Nickelpedes! They are a scourge no one can tolerate!"

"Precisely. They could mount a very good defense against any aggressive neighbors. The key is how to recruit them."

"But they're not even intelligent."

"They have the hive mentality." Sherlock glanced at the bees. "As do bees, and they do well enough, especially in the presence of those with human intelligence. There will likely be a queen nickelpede who will have enough of a mind to dicker. The question is, what would she want from us?"

"Recognition," Drover said. "Of their merit as a species, and her femininity. The Queendom of Thanx can offer both."

Sherlock nodded. "I believe it can. We need to make a pact, a mutual assistance treaty, as we did with the bees. They come here and drive off the invaders, then they can stay, and the Thanx citizens will welcome them as long as they never attack a citizen. They attack no citizens, and no citizens attack them. Maybe folk can even carry them from one place to another, to forage or just to see the sights. They have never in all the history of Xanth had treatment like that, and I suspect they would find it highly addictive."

That concept circulated, and it started to make sense. The nickelpedes might indeed have a longing to be accepted as citizens, rather than vermin. It was certainly worth a try.

"What others?" Demesne asked. "Ideas?"

"Salamanders," Benny suggested. "They can set fire to anything except their own ashes or the ground they walk on. They could give invaders such hotfoots as they would never return. But they don't have to burn; otherwise, they would not be able to go anywhere without going up in smoke, literally. But they could heat a house in winter, without burning it, if they wanted to."

"And they might want to, if they were given acceptance and a province of their own, here in Thanx," Goblette said.

"Ghosts," Furioso said. "They don't *have* to spook everyone they see. We could offer them freshly built haunted houses, and our children could visit them to see spook shows. Maybe some could live in our homes, the way the ghosts do in Castle Roogna. I understand that a ghost can be pretty friendly, when given a chance."

Hula eyed him. "*How* friendly?"

He laughed. "They can firm up parts of their bodies so they can howl, and maybe other parts too. But a lady ghost wouldn't try to be seductive as long as she saw you lying between Sherlock and me."

Hula nodded, satisfied. She could keep them both busy. There would be too little left over for any ghost to seduce.

"Sirens," Georgia said. "The invaders are likely to be male, and they'd lure any males to their doom."

"But who would recruit sirens?" Demesne asked. "Not any of the princes, and I should think the princesses would be wary of them, too, albeit for different reasons."

"A girl child, a nonprincess," Georgia said. "She'd be largely immune."

And of course, that meant Vinia. "I'll do it," she said with resignation.

"You are entirely too obliging," Demesne said. "If you're not careful, you will wind up recruiting them all, from nickelpedes to ghosts."

Vinia laughed. "But you need them all today, simultaneously recruited, and I would have to be in five or six places at once."

"We can't do it," Hula said. "We have our other chores to do."

"You do," Demesne agreed.

"Actually," Ion said, "I have a split personality elixir. You *could* be everywhere at the same time, using different hosts."

"I was joking." But even as Vinia spoke, she saw the joke wearing thin. The idea had taken hold: they were all considering it. She knew already that she was bound to be stuck for it. She always was. Princes and princesses were not much for menial tasks, and certainly not for messing with nickelpedes or sirens, and they were going to be quite busy with their roles in the queendom. They really did have more than enough to occupy them, getting the new order started. "But I suppose I can do it."

They were satisfied not to argue with her. She was indeed stuck for it.

"The ring should facilitate your effort," Grossclout said. "And facilitate your mission. You are better equipped for this than you may suppose."

"I'd better be," Vinia said. Because she felt staggeringly incompetent.

"I've seen that look before," Hilda said. "Your self-no-confidence vote. You will need someone to protect you and encourage you, so that you can do what you must do. I don't think I am qualified to help you in this, and neither is Ion. Is there anyone else?"

"I believe I am free," Grossclout said. "I should absent myself so that Demesne can go about her business undistracted."

"Grossclout!" Vinia repeated, horrified.

Demesne laughed. "Two things, my dear. First, he really can protect you from unexpected threats. Second, he is capable of being social, even vaguely friendly, when he tries. He will be on your side, not against you. That counts. Give him a chance."

"A chance," Vinia agreed faintly.

Chapter 8

SIRENS ETC.

"Why don't you two go out and get started," Demesne suggested. "while we organize the queendom here?"

Vinia froze, having no idea what to do. It was as if she had just been given a construction pencil to clean after it had written dirty words. She was afraid she would mess up badly and wind up solidly dirty and smelling like a stink horn with nothing accomplished. She had been lucky so far, but luck was a treacherous ally, as her temporary loss of Dara's ring had demonstrated.

"This way," Grossclout said surprisingly softly, taking her by the elbow and moving her to an unfamiliar exit.

In a few moments—she wasn't sure how many, being lost in her confusion—they were standing beside a lovely pool. A mountain stream coursed from a convenient mountain and plunged gladly into the pool. But there seemed to be no exit stream. "Where does the water go?" Vinia asked, focusing on this minor detail rather than the major question of how to accomplish what was barely possible. Of how to work with a Demon who frightened her even when he was being nice. Of how the bleepity bleep had she managed to get herself into this nice mess. She was staring at her reflection in the pool, realizing that at the moment it was mental as well as physical: her mind was churning despite the serenity of her appearance. Could she use the pool to wash off the dirt left by her mental construction pencil? Probably not, alas.

"This is Whirl Pool Pond," the Demon explained. "Every hour or so when the water level gets high, it whirls itself down into the unknown depth. It is one of the better features of the dragon's domain."

"The unknown depth? I think I'm already there," Vinia said. Then she burst into tears. Which struck her as an ultimate foolishness, especially in the present company, but she did it anyway. She might be the protagonist, for whatever little that was worth, but she was not a bold princess or a powerful Sorceress; she was a mere ordinary reasonably ignorant girl child, subject to getting overwhelmed on short notice. She was ashamed of herself.

Then Grossclout did something weird. He hugged her comfortingly. The amazing thing was that it worked: she felt better. In fact she felt downright self-assured. How could that be?

"Prince Ion gave me some reverse elixir," the Demon explained without requiring the question. "I am the Magician of Intimidation. The elixir makes me a temporary Magician of Encouragement." Indeed, he seemed like a kindly grandfather radiating approval and calmness. Even his gnarled horns appeared friendly as he let her go.

"I am amazed," Vinia said confidently. "But I'm not crazy. I know that this job is beyond my capability. Fake courage is not enough."

"You are a sensible girl. That is the prime reason Demesne wanted you for this mission. She knew you could accomplish what another person might not."

"Me? But—" Then the confidence caught up with her again. "I suppose that's true. I have succeeded elsewhere, to my surprise. But it's still a formidable challenge."

"That is why I am along. I am capable of providing the elements you require to function efficiently, and efficiency is at a premium at this time."

Elements were starting to coalesce. "I was selected, and so were you?"

"Correct. The others were privately advised." He smiled, and the expression seemed pleasant. "They did not desert you, Vinia. They understood that you were the proper one for this vital task."

She shook her head. "I hope they weren't mistaken. I still have little if any idea how to proceed."

"Fortunately, I do. Ion provided me the split personality elixir. When you inhale that, your host body will remain here, inert, so as not to get into mischief, while your several partial selves will depart for the domains of the six prospective allies."

"I don't even know where those allies are."

"Sorceress Hilda provided us a map." The professor brought it out and spread it before her. "Each self will touch a spot on the map and be astrally transported there to occupy a compatible host who has been advised that you are coming and will cooperate to the best of her ability. Then you will approach the leader of that tribe and make our case."

"But how will the allies get here, assuming they decide to come?"

"You will guide them. You wear the ring. You will always be able to return to it. You will show them the way."

"But they aren't astral. They can't just zip to a new host."

"I will bring one of Ion's miniportals to each site where necessary. That will suffice for all but one of the groups, they being small of stature, like the nickelpedes, or diffuse, like the ghosts. The one exception is the sirens. They are physical and of human size. They will also have to travel by water, to this pool, which will suit their nature."

Vinia stared at the pool. "They will want a whirlpool?" She knew that sirens were mermaids with special voices.

"Yes. It represents no threat to them and is suitable for drowning and disposing of unruly mortal men."

"But—"

"Your host will explain their lifestyle to you."

"My host." She was still assimilating the notion of being a spiritual visitor to another person's body. "Who is that?"

"Signal Siren. She took one of my classes recently, so I contacted her, and she is amenable. She is expecting you."

So he knew a siren. "She didn't sing and try to lure you to your doom?"

"That would have spoiled the class. In any event I would not have succumbed, despite her prettiness, having encountered many varieties of dangerous females such as gorgons and basilisks, not to mention Demonesses."

"Like Metria and her polka-dot panties?"

"With the missing material," he agreed reminiscently. "But she was merely mischievous. She did have nice thighs, though perhaps too much displayed."

They were drifting from the subject. "Why was a siren in your class?"

"She wanted to learn incidental magic, such as air flotation, so that she wouldn't have to use a spell to get around on land. She was a good student and did learn. But that was mainly a pretext. Her tribe was in trouble, needing a new home. They had annoyed the local king by dooming too many of his warriors, and he made ready to besiege their lake with female warriors. I said I would do what I could."

"You taught her the magic but also agreed to help her tribe?"

He smiled. "She bribed me. She was quite up front about it, and she had a very nice front. Tit for tat."

Vinia was curious. She had a notion what a woman's tit was and could maybe guess about the man's tat, if the Conspiracy allowed it. "What could a pretty mermaid have that a powerful Demon might want?"

"The Adult Conspiracy prevents me from answering."

So she had not gotten around it. Bleep. "I'm sick of the Conspiracy!"

"Patience, child. It protects your invaluable innocence."

"I'm sick of being innocent!"

"Yet you will sincerely regret losing it, in due course."

Vinia doubted that, but she knew it was pointless to argue the case. "So this is the place you found for them?"

"Yes. It is ideal, being mutually beneficial. They will protect Thanx from any hostile soldiers who attempt to pass this way, and we will provide them a nice pond and compatible company."

"Company? You mean ladies?"

"And men. They don't drown well-behaved men, only those who seek to brutalize them."

That reminded her of something else. "Why would a land man want to be with a woman with the tail of a fish?"

"Their upper sections are appealingly human, as Signal demonstrated, and there are men who like a piece of tail. Again, you will understand in due course."

"Bleep."

He laughed. "Are you ready for the split personality elixir?"

"I had better be. We have wasted too much time talking."

Grossclout brought out the vial of elixir. "Breathe this. The effect will last several hours, during which you will accomplish your mission. Focus on one facet at a time. The visits will be simultaneous, but your focus will enable you to experience them as consecutive. It is a mental exercise. Meanwhile I will pop into whatever section where you need me. Are you ready?"

"I hope so."

He opened the vial. Vapor emerged. Vinia breathed it.

Suddenly she fragmented. There were six of her, jostling for attention. It was confusing.

"Focus," Grossclout said.

Oh, yes, that. She focused on the one visiting the sirens. The others faded into background noise.

The Demon held up Hilda's map. It was of the whole of Xanth, with the six allies marked. The closest to Thanx was the sirens. Vinia reached out her spectral hand and touched that spot.

Then she was there. She felt the different body, in the water, with the fish tail. *Hello.*

"Uh, hello," Vinia said, knowing it was just a thought, but it was easier if she phrased it as speech. "I'm Vinia."

The other responded similarly. "I'm Signal."

"I am here about Thanx."

"Yes. Grossclout told me. We will swim to see our queen now."

They swam. The mermaid used her hands in the breaststroke, guiding her course, but it was her powerful tail that propelled her forward. Vinia borrowed her eyes to see her body. Signal did indeed have an impressive front. She must have been selected for it, to go to the class and impress Grossclout. Evidently that had worked.

"Yes, it worked," Signal said. "He was just as impressive as a lover as he was in class. It really was no burden. In fact—" She broke off. "But you are underage. I can't go into detail."

"Bleep." Her thoughts were not private, but that area remained a mystery.

Signal laughed, which made her front even more impressive. "You'll get there in due course. I promise. You will be lovely: I can tell already, by your mental image of your own body. You think it's not much, but the architecture is there. You will make some man very happy."

"Prince Magician Ion," she said. "I am his girlfriend."

"A prince and a Magician! You are fortunate indeed. But how did you get his attention while still a child?"

"He is lame. I have telekinesis I use to enable him to walk." She thought briefly about the situation there, so Signal could pick up on it.

"That does make sense," Signal agreed. "You are fortunate. But so is he, to have you. Ah, here we are approaching Queen Siesta."

Siesta was an older mermaid, but she too had an impressive front. Her hair trailed down to her waist, voluminous despite being wet, just as Signal's did. She swam in place, her upper section above the surface of the water. "Yes?"

Vinia used Signal's mouth to speak. "Hello, I am Vinia, a land-bound human child, visiting Signal astrally. I come from the new Queendom of Thanx to offer you a nice pond with a central whirlpool. We ask only that you do not drown our men and help protect us from invading men. We will be invaded tomorrow, and the pond is next to the ogre kingdom."

"We can handle ogres," Siesta said. "They freak out much as human males do. Normally we don't even have to show panties, which is just as well because we prefer not to wear them. Our upper sections are sufficient."

"Then will you come?"

"Yes."

Was this too easy? Vinia was developing a deep distrust of easiness. "Don't you want to negotiate terms?"

"No need. The professor was here. We know him of old. He's a tough old codger, but he means exactly what he says." The queen smiled, revealing her pointed teeth. "We understand that he is being tamed by a smart Demoness."

"Queen Demesne," Vinia agreed. "She was once a student in his class. They impressed each other. Now they are making something of it."

"I dare say. A Demoness can put a mortal female to shame, when she tries. Even a siren." She frowned, irritated by the notion. "Now I understand that Thanx is not far from here, but the river channels are dry. That is a problem."

Grossclout, Vinia thought.

He appeared beside them, standing chest deep in the water. "Nice to see you again, Signal," he said, eyeing her bosom. He turned to the queen. "And you are Siesta. I am pleased to make your acquaintance."

The queen inhaled impressively. "Likewise, I'm sure. Signal reports that you are as good in bed as in the classroom."

"She perhaps exaggerates. Intimidation is not as effective in bed as in class."

"We understand that you ran off with a student."

"Demesne," he agreed.

"Too bad. We sirens could have given you something to think about."

"Surely so." Vinia realized that Grossclout was avoiding any argument with Siesta. He wanted her cooperation.

"Now how do you propose to transport us from here to there, with the river channels between us dry?"

"In this manner." Grossclout faced the nearest dry channel. A cloud hung above it, watching the proceedings. Folk seldom realized how much clouds saw of their doings. The Demon inhaled and fired off a phenomenal glower. The cloud, caught by surprise, was so frightened that it wet its pants. Since it had no pants, the water coursed down in a sheet. In two and a half moments the cloud was a mere wisp of fog, but the channel was flooded.

"That will do," Siesta said approvingly. She put two fingers to her mouth and whistled piercingly. There was the sound of splashing as the other mermaids converged. "Follow the channels," she called. "The professor is intimidating the clouds." Then she swam up to Grossclout and planted a close-up buxom kiss on his face before plunging toward the newly filled channel. His hands came up defensively, but all they got was copious handfuls of bare bosom.

"I knew she was going to do that," Grossclout murmured, satisfied.

"And you stood still for it," Signal said. "So stay in place just a bit longer, Prof." She swam up and planted her own buxom kiss, knocking back his hands with her own bosom.

Vinia, along for the ride, was amazed. It was is if she herself were kissing him and arranging to collide her bountiful front with his hands. The contact delivered a jolt of naughty pleasure. She realized that the touching was not coincidental by either party: the art was making it seem so. If this was what adulthood offered, she wanted it. Once she had breasts to flaunt.

"Maturity does offer that fun, in part," Signal said as she swam on, following the queen toward the flooded channel. "It's a kind of heavy flirting. Of course, it helps that we were once lovers."

Vinia looked back to see that the other sirens were doing the same thing as they passed the professor. It was a kind of game. There were a dozen sirens in addition to the queen.

"But don't you have things to pack?" she asked. "Preparations to make?"

"No. All we need is water and motive."

They swam to the end of the channel. The water was draining away, threatening to strand them in the channel. But the Demon appeared before them. He aimed another glower at a cloud and terrorized it into letting loose all its water so that only meager mist remained. He truly was the Magician of Intimidation.

"But those of us who know him well enough can handle it," Signal said, picking up again on her thought. "He's a softie when you get beyond the glare. He really helped me."

"But you bribed him."

"Before that."

Vinia's insatiable curiosity got the better of her, as usual. "How?"

"One day in class a mean human classmate played a cruel joke on me. I think he wanted to make me let him handle, you know, my superstructure. We water creatures don't wear clothing. I had as usual unpacked myself and my water bucket from the flying chair I used to travel overland. He grabbed the empty chair, which was turned off, and I was stuck in my class seat, unable to move from it. My tail, you know; it's useless on dry land. I was distraught. Grossclout merely said curtly 'Use your magic, nymph.' 'But if I do that—' I protested. 'Cover your ears,' he told the class. They did, and then I sang. That caught the joker, who couldn't cover his ears because he was carrying the heavy chair. He came back in the class, up to my bucket of water for my tail, dropped the chairs, and plunged his face into the bucket almost before I could whip my tail out. I stopped singing before he drowned, of course, but it was effective in halting other such jokes. Grossclout merely nodded. He had shown me how my original magic could protect me even here."

Vinia appreciated that. She had not thought much before about the problems a mermaid might have on land.

"By the time I finished the course, I knew how to make a flotation spell myself, so I would not have to rent a flying chair. But I still appreciated how Grossclout had helped me. That encouraged me to seduce him, per my mission, once I was no longer a student. He refused to mess that way with students." She smiled. "But I had made sure he noticed my upper torso. I almost got dizzy from all the deep breathing."

That was confirmation of the Demon's ethics. He was interested, but never made a move on Signal in class. Vinia was glad to have it, because otherwise her developing respect for him would have suffered.

They proceeded in this manner, flooding channel after channel, leaving emptied clouds behind, until at last they came to Thanx. A final glare flood brought them to the pool.

The mermaids splashed into it, delighted. The surplus water caused the whirlpool to start in the center of the pond, sucking the water down and away to neverland. They liked this ever better. They swam to it and into it, able to avoid getting sucked down themselves. "Glorious!" Siesta exclaimed, hugging Grossclout so closely that her body flattened against him. "This is perfect!" She kissed him, then went to disport herself with the others.

"Come swim with us, Professor!" one called.

Grossclout, hardly reluctant, popped over to join them. He now had a woman of his own, but this was passing entertainment. Demesne would surely understand. "Oh, I must get in on that," Signal said. "Hang on, Vinia." She swam to the whirlpool, and in moments there were fourteen mermaids swimming half out of the swirling water around the Demon. Vinia was reminded of the splashing party she and Hilda had joined on Cloud Nine. Girls just had to be girls.

But she couldn't dawdle on that. There were five other spot missions in progress. She focused on the nickelpedes. "Do I have a host?" she asked Grossclout via the ring.

"Nimbus," he said as he ducked a buxom flying tackle by a mermaid. Vinia realized that in all this melee the sirens had never uttered a note of song. They were honoring the truce with Thanx, beginning with the professor. She had heard part of the melody in the background as Signal reviewed the bucket incident, and appreciated its power, even though she was a female child, who should be largely immune. These laughing girls really were deadly predators when they sang. "Touch the map."

Oh. "Map," Vinia said to the ring, and the scroll appeared in the air before her. She poked her finger at the spot marked NICKELPEDES.

Vinia was low to the ground, foraging for seeds and bugs. They were okay, but her abiding hunger was for meat. She had about fifty small legs, several eye stalks, and of course her formidable mouth for gouging out nickel-size chunks of flesh. Now it was chewing on a dirty plant stem tasting of week-old rubbish. Vinia could appreciate already why the nickelpedes wanted more.

"Hello," Vinia said tentatively.

The creature paused. "Oh, you must be the visitor." She spoke by clicking her mandibles, but her mind made it clear as speech.

"Yes. I am Vinia Human from Thanx. The Demon professor sent me."

"He said you'd be just a spirit, hardly more than a thought."

"I am an astral copy, one of six."

"And I am Nimbus Nickelpede. Now that you're here, I will take you to see Queen Nitro."

The creature set her multiple legs in motion and propelled herself forward at a fast clip, probably several feet an hour. The local stems whizzed by, what would be small plants to Vinia's normal body seeming more like a forest here.

They encountered a smaller creature crossing their path. It had a hundred legs. Vinia was alarmed, but Nimbus reassured her. "A centipede. Harmless to us. If it tries anything, I'll eat it."

The centipede got hastily out of their way and they resumed speed. Soon they came to a smaller, silver-colored creature. "Dime-i-pede," Nimbus said. It too was no trouble, though it clearly did not fear the nickelpede. Maybe its silver was invulnerable to the nickel's bite.

But then they came to a larger creature. It swung its head around to orient on them, teeth gnashing dangerously. Now it was Nimbus who backed off. "Quarterpede," she explained. "They're worth five of us and know it." She found an alternate route.

"But at least you avoided it," Vinia said.

"This one, this time. But a swarm of them is moving in, and we're running low on places to retreat."

Vinia was coming to appreciate their problem. There was no way a nickelpede could stand up to a massive quarterpede.

They reached the rotten stump that served as the swarm headquarters. "I have the visitor the professor promised," Nimbus clicked to the others.

"Nitro is waiting impatiently," a guard clicked. "She's about ready to explode. Quarterpedes raided our choicest foraging patch today. We offered no resistance: we couldn't afford to lose five of us for every one of them."

"At least they weren't dollarpedes," Nimbus clicked.

"Not yet," the guard agreed with a shudder.

They reached the queen. "Hello, Queen Nitro," Vinia clicked. "I am Vinia Human, from the Queendom of Thanx, visiting astrally. We can offer you a safe patch, if you will help defend us from our enemies tomorrow."

"We can't stop the quarterpedes," Nitro said, exasperated.

"For us, in that sector, it's goblins."

"Goblins are easy," Nitro said. "And tasty."

"Then come to Thanx. We have a portal."

"What else?"

Else? Oh, she expected hard bargaining. "In Thanx you must attack no citizens, however tasty they may be. No citizen will attack you. Permanent truce. You will attack only those who attack the queendom."

"Goblins."

"Yes, tomorrow. But we have at present two goblin princesses who are citizens."

"They are the tastiest of all! There is no more delicate flesh."

"Nevertheless, they must be spared." There was the hard bargain.

"Agreed," Nitro clicked reluctantly.

"Grossclout," Vinia said to the ring.

"Present," the Demon agreed, appearing. Vinia realized that probably Metria Demoness could appear fully formed, instead of going through her act as a cloud, if she wanted to. "I greet you, Nitro. I told you I could arrange a deal for you."

"But you are denying us the goblin princesses."

"I never promised you any princesses. They are reserved mostly for the princes."

Nitro swelled up, ready to explode. Then there was a roar from upwind. "The quarterpedes are charging!" Nimbus clicked, terrified.

"I will back them off while you take the portal to Thanx," Grossclout said, setting down a portal. "Line up. Start going through."

The queen hesitated. The Demon started warming up a glare. Nitro decided to yield the point. She led her minions toward the portal as Grossclout turned his now fully potent glare on the charging quarterpedes.

Caught by surprise, they stumbled and crashed into one another, making a mess of their charge. They tried to reorganize, but the Demon glared at their leaders, who fell on their backs, their feet wiggling helplessly in the air.

The nickelpedes ran on through the portal in a straight line, disappearing at a swift rate. By the time the quarterpedes managed to get there, the last nickelpede was gone. Except for Nimbus. So they converged on her, cutting her off from the portal. Vinia suffered an ugly jolt of fright. "Grossclout!" she clicked desperately.

The Demon popped across, picked her up, and deposited her before the portal. He could indeed protect her. They scuttled through. Suddenly they were in Thanx.

There was Chloe Centaur with Dragoman. The nickelpedes were climbing all over them. Oh, no!

Grossclout appeared beside her. "Be at ease, girl. There's a truce, remember? The nickels are being welcomed to the queendom with joy rides on dragon or winged centaur. They are loving it. They have never been airborne before."

And Chloe was telepathic, so was in perfect communication with the new arrivals. Vinia relaxed, chiding herself for her momentary foolishness. Then she and Nimbus raced to get aboard Chloe.

Chloe and Dragoman took off, flying above the field and forest, giving the clinging nickelpedes the rarest view of their lives: the sight of the landscape of Xanth as seen from above. Their chittering was rapturous.

There is more, Chloe thought to them all. *You will be welcome in any Thanx house, to prey on any vermin there, like rats or roaches. Citizens will carry you anywhere you wish to go. The benefits are mutual. This is what the truce means, here in the Queendom of Thanx.*

"This is Bug Heaven," Queen Nitro chittered.

But tomorrow, the invading goblins. Except for our two goblin princesses.

"Those goblins will wish they never even thought of invading!" But then Nitro had a second thought. "Won't the princesses be mad about what we do to their kinsmen?"

No. They know that the goblin soldiers would gang-rape them if they got the chance. They are from a different tribe.

"We don't like rape. Gouging out nickels is all in good fun, but rape is nasty."

Just so. It seemed that it was working out.

"I must leave you now," Vinia said to Nimbus. "I have other allies to recruit." It was more complicated than that, but it would do.

"I hardly know you, but I like your mind," the nickelpede replied. "Can we meet again some time, maybe physically?" She smiled mentally. "I will promise not to gouge."

Vinia realized that she liked Nimbus back. She had never dreamed that she would ever become friends with a nickelpede, but she was getting rapidly educated. "Why not? I am making friends in the course of this mission. Maybe we can all get together, once the queendom is secure and things settle down to relative dullness. But how will I know you, when I'm not *in* you, as it were?"

"I will don a swatch of ribbon."

"I will look for it. I will wear one, too, so you know me from the other humans." Because to a nickelpede all humans would look alike.

"I will see you then."

Vinia focused on the next ally. This was the salamanders. She touched the map.

She found herself in another low-to-the-ground host body. This one had only four legs; could they be enough? Her skin was bright red. She seemed to be tending a garden; the odor of the flowers was appealing.

"Hello," Vinia said. "I'm Vinia Human."

"Ah, the visiting spirit. The Demon said you would be arriving soon. I am Sali Salamander, and this is my section of our communal garden, such as it is."

"There is a problem?"

Sali pushed some ash from nearby to the base of the nearest stem. "This area is largely burned out. After a few years, the ashes lack the nutrition of a fresh burning. So we have to move to find new ground to process. Our flowers need it, or their bouquet suffers."

Vinia looked at the small brown blossoms on the plant. They did seem slightly malnourished. That perhaps explained why the salamanders needed to move. She had never thought of them as gardeners; quite the opposite. "What kind of flower is it?"

"*Stinkus hornibus*, popularly known as stink horn. It is our specialty."

"Stink horn!" Vinia repeated, astonished. "But that's the worst-smelling stench of all!"

"Perhaps to large creatures who like to trample innocent pods. The fragrance is refined to repel them, so they don't do it again. We don't like to have our gardens trampled."

It was beginning to make sense. A bad smell could indeed cause a ham-footed monster of any size to back off. "I am here to proffer an offer by the new Queendom of Thanx. Fresh fertile unburned land in exchange for protection from the trolls who will invade tomorrow."

"We don't much like trolls. They have big careless feet. We give them hotfoots, and if that is not effective, we burn them out."

"We would ask that you restrict your burning to your territory. We are nervous about uncontrolled fire, and salamander fire is notoriously difficult to extinguish."

"It's impossible to put out, except by spreading its own ashes on it," Sali said proudly. "But we can direct it so that it doesn't stray beyond our area. There's no sense wasting perfectly good fire on regions that are not right for gardening."

"Um, yes. At any rate, if your queen is interested, I would like to talk to her."

Sali spread some more nutritive ash. "She's interested. We all are." She held up a chunk of burnt residue. "This is a largely inferior fragment," she said, frowning. "New territory would provide much finer pieces of ash."

There was something about the way she said it that hinted that there was some risqué humor, but the Conspiracy prevented Vinia from figuring it out. Bleep the Conspiracy!

"Then if you will take me to your leader . . ."

"Queen Sapphire." Sali tamped down the ash. "I believe I am done here for now. We'll go see her."

"Are you a matriarchy?" Vinia asked as they walked.

"Not at all. We merely separate the genders so we can get more work done. Otherwise there tends to be distractive flirtation, even outside of mating season. The boys are trying to get precommitments from the girls, and the girls are trying to secure the highest placements among the males. We all want the hottest collisions. Then when mating season comes, whomp! Each one can make out with up to five opposites in the first few minutes. What a wild party! The flames are ferocious. So King Saber runs the male division, and Queen Sapphire the female division. When we congregate for mass mating, Saber and Sapphire have to do it first." She tittered. "Though they really don't like each other much. But it's the protocol. They must act like blistering old flames. After that is more like a free-for-all, and we don't have to pretend to be baking in passion."

Vinia realized that Sali didn't realize that she was underage. Vinia kept her mind shut on that score, though she was understanding only tantalizing fragments. It was as if she were getting the ashes instead of the flames.

They came to a fort made of tamped ashes. There was the hot queen on an upper section, watching over the salamanders as they tended their sections of the garden.

"Sapphire, I bring the human delegate," Sali called. It was a sort of whistle, but Vinia understood it as speech. "The one the Demon promised."

"Good enough," the queen said. "Where is this region? Has it been burned over recently?"

"Hello, Queen Sapphire," Vinia said through Sali's mouth. "I am Vinia Human, representing the large-creature Queendom of Thanx. I don't think it has been burned; it is protected by a dragon who is a smoker, not a fire breather."

"That seems promising," Sapphire agreed. "However, we need to be sure we would be welcomed there."

"We need you to stop the trolls from invading tomorrow. Do that and you will be welcome."

The queen smiled in her fashion. "We can handle trolls. They don't much like hotfoots."

"All you need to promise is that you won't burn anywhere outside your selected section," Vinia said. "The sirens have promised not to drown any citizens of Thanx, and the nickelpedes won't gouge any citizen either. It is part of the truce."

"You have sirens and nickelpedes going there?"

"Yes, and we are negotiating with ghosts, snails, and love/hate bugs. We want everyone to get along and live in peace with one another. Females will govern Thanx: it's a feminist queendom. The male kingdoms seem not to like that, but those who have felt oppressed by males should like it there."

"This interests me," Sapphire said.

"We believe any females of any species will be comfortable there," Vinia said. "As long as they treat each other with courtesy."

There was a rumble of thunder. They looked around. Three nasty little clouds were floating toward them, darkening as they went.

"Oh, waterlogs!" the queen swore. "We can burn anything, including water, but a storm is mostly air and vapor, hard to focus on. We're going to get horribly doused. That will mess up our transplanting of horn seeds. We need more time."

"Maybe not," Vinia said. "I know someone who can help, if she chooses to." She focused on the copy of the ring that had flaked off the original, along with her mind. The astral spirit of the ring. "Fiera," she said. Would it work? The original ring would, but this was only part of it.

An answer came. "Who's calling?"

It did work! But would the fire cloud cooperate? "This is Vinia Human," she said. "We met when Prince Ion summoned the fire spirit Brand for you. We had a brief dialogue about choice. Do you remember?" Because Fiera might not.

"I remember. What's this about?"

Or might not care if she did remember. "I am helping a band of salamanders move to the Queendom of Thanx, where feminists rule."

"Feminists?"

"They believe that females should have more choices, and not be subservient to males."

"Now that's interesting."

But was it interesting enough? "But some nasty little male storm clouds are threatening to douse us. Will you help?"

"Maybe. What's in it for me?"

"Maybe you could come to Thanx, too, along with the salamanders. I think you would like it there, with all the independent females. But you would have to promise not to burn anything outside the assigned fire zone."

"Aww." But the cloud was intrigued.

"Please come. If you back off the stormlets, I think you will be welcomed to Thanx. This wouldn't interfere with your relationship with Fire-Brand; it would just give you a home base of your own. You might like the feminists."

"A kingdom of feminists," Fiera said, intrigued again. "I might indeed."

"Queendom." Did the terminology really matter?

"On my way." The scintillating cloud appeared before them. "Where are you?"

Oh. Vinia was not in the body the cloud had seen before. "I am here, astrally visiting with a salamander. We encountered these nasty little clouds over there."

Fiera extended a burning vapor tendril with an embedded eyeball and looked. "Oho! I have seen these brats before. I'll whip their soggy little bottoms." She floated off to intercept the ministorms.

They watched as Fiera flashed a display of fiery lightning. When the stormlets did not back off, being determinedly bad boys, she formed a jagged fire bolt and fired it into the nearest cloudlet. The bolt struck it dead center, and the heat made the cloud explode into fragments of singed vapor. The other two cloudlets hastily retreated, knowing they were overmatched.

"I think we're going to get along," Sapphire said approvingly.

Wonderful! "Grossclout," Vinia said.

The Demon appeared. "Good thinking, girl," he said. "I will clear it with HQ. Meanwhile you get them started crossing over." He set down a portal and vanished.

"Go through this," Vinia told the queen. "It leads to your section of Thanx."

The salamanders quickly gathered a number of the smaller plants, together with mature horns, and hauled them to the portal. Then they started going through themselves.

"What about me?" Fiera asked.

"Go on through," Vinia said. "Squeeze yourself into a tube of vapor and dive in. You will find yourself in Thanx."

"Thanx," Fiera repeated. Vinia wasn't sure whether this was appreciation or a question about the destination. The cloud wrapped into a rope-shaped column and threaded down into the portal.

Then Vinia and Sali went through. They were in Thanx, and Demesne was there to welcome them. She had assumed the form of a large burning salamander, and they were paying close attention.

Vinia looked about and saw that Fiera was hovering a moderate distance apart. She was not a salamander, despite sharing their fiery nature, and perhaps felt unwelcome. She needed reassurance. "Is it okay if I talk with her?" she asked Sali.

"By all means. I saw how she helped us. I'll pipe down and stay out of your way."

"Thank you." Vinia focused. "Fiera," she said to the ring.

"Ah, there you are." The cloud floated over. "You were lost amid the salamanders."

"I know Grossclout cleared it with the queen, so you are welcome here," Vinia said. "I just wanted to reassure you personally."

"Thank you," Fiera said. "I wanted to talk with you anyway. That's why I answered your call."

"You mean you weren't being nice?"

"Nice? How can I be nice? I'm the evil twin sister, remember?"

Fracto's twin. "We were on opposite sides, I guess, but you seemed sensible to me. You felt females should have rights."

"I do. But I have no friends."

"No friends? What about FireBrand?"

"He's my boyfriend. That's different. He is satisfied with just one thing, and if I give him that, he is not interested in my mind at all. It's all physical. Which is fine; I like a fiery fling too. But I'm still lonely for a companion I can talk to. Share feelings with. Someone like you."

"But I'm a nothing girl! A child."

"You're a caring person. That's relatively rare. When you called, I remembered. So I came."

"You came," Vinia agreed. "You helped."

"The truth is I wouldn't have come just to help. Helping is not evil. I wanted to be with you."

She wants a friend, Sali thought.

Vinia realized that another avenue was opening before her. She had become friends with a siren, a nickelpede, and a salamander. Why not a fire cloud? What counted was the person, not the form.

"Yes, I'll be your friend," Vinia told Fiera.

The cloud brightened, radiating wisps of orange vapor. "Oh, thank you!" She floated away.

"You're nice," Sali said, somewhat surprised.

Chapter 9

GHOSTS, ETC.

Vinia moved on to her next host: a ghost. She wasn't certain about this, but then she had not been certain of the other hosts, before she got to know them. Still, they had all been living creatures, while ghosts were, well, not exactly alive.

She found herself in a nebulous region. It was somewhere, but where? Something was there, but what? "Hello?" she inquired uncertainly.

The weird space answered. "Oh, you must be the recruiter! Ghrossclout told me you were coming. I'm Ghorgeous Ghost. It's my nickname from when I was alive. You know, Gorgeous." She evidently omitted the *H* with an effort.

"I'm Vinia Human, in astral form," she answered, relieved.

"Hello, Vhinia."

"Uh, yes." Then, because she remained uncertain, Vinia passed the intangible ball to the other. "How did the professor get to know you, to set this up?"

"We are in a haunted house in what you call Mhundania. But—"

"Mundania!" No wonder the environment seemed strange. "But there's no magic there!"

The ghost made a hollow laugh. "Two things. One is that there is some magic in Mhundania. It's just that the locals don't believe it. They see things like the rhainbow, which can be seen from only one side, and try to make up reasons for that impossibility. They see the magic of perspective, where the more distant things move to keep up with a traveler while the close things don't, and think it's an illusion, instead of the plain fact that the more distant things can't be stopped from moving, so take advantage of that. Mhundanes simply refuse to believe what they see, the more fools they. I know how they are in denial about magic, because I was one of them, in life. The other reason is that ghosts are not magic; we are chained spirits."

That made sense, maybe. "Oh. Sorry I interrupted you. What were you saying?"

The ghost picked up exactly where she had broken off. "But our haunted house is about to be demolished. We are desperate, because we are chained to our place of death, and if the house goes, we will be caught haunting thin air. What a ghastly fate! So I went to take the professor's class, to learn what to do."

Vinia was bemused by the use of words that actually had an *H* in the second spot, like *Ghastly* and *What*. There were surely others. But she had another question. "If you are chained there in Mundania, how did you take Grossclout's class?"

Ghorgeous made the ghost of a smile. "We are bound, but we can move about. It's like elastic: it can be stretched, but the farther it lengthens, the tighter it becomes. So I put all my effort into reaching the classroom, and when the Demon entered I called 'Please! I want to take your class!' And he used a spell that weakened the bond and enabled me to be somewhat free. Of course, I had to bribe him. Fortunately, I died at the height of my beauty, at age twenty-one, so I had the wherewithal. That's why I was chosen to make the effort."

"Of course," Vinia agreed, remembering Signal Siren. The Demon professor liked pretty girls. If only she knew *how* they bribed men! "But don't you have to be, well, physical to do that sort of thing?"

"I practiced making key parts touchable, beforehand. Lips, bosom, bottom. It requires strong focus but can be done for a few minutes at a time. It was enough."

What was so magic about those particular parts? But Vinia knew she was as usual doomed not to know until she grew up and joined the Adult Conspiracy, which was too late. "I'm not sure how I can help you. I'm just a garden-variety girl child with the talent of telekinesis, which I think wouldn't work on a ghost. Certainly, I don't have magic to free chained ghosts."

"Still, you may be able to. Ghrossclout believes you have a special talent for solving intractable problems. Also, you represent the Queendom of Thanx, whose approval we need if we are to move into its ramshackle house."

"For that you need Queen Demesne."

"But if you should ask her?"

Vinia pondered that. "Maybe she would." Then she remembered. "In fact I'm sure she would, because they need a defense against the invading dragons. They can fly, so ground-bound folk can't stop them."

"We can float, which is similar to flying. I believe we could stop them, if they are at all spookable. We'll certainly try." Ghorgeous shrugged intangibly. "But come meet my housemates, so you know more about our situation."

"But I still don't know how I can do anything," Vinia protested. "You need magic to get unbound."

"Not exactly. What we need is to solve the riddle of my murder, and gain justice, so that that unfinished business will no longer anchor us here."

"I don't know a thing about murder mysteries."

"Yet the Demon thinks you may find an avenue. He suspects you have a talent for finding avenues."

Vinia sighed inwardly. Others had such beliefs in her, but she had just been lucky, and luck was not her magic, even if some magic worked in Mundania. But what could she do except try? "Tell me about your murder."

"We don't know it was murder, but Ghrossclout thinks so, and if it was an accident, we should not be bound here. What happened was that the night before I was to marry my sweetheart, a car was left running in the garage, and the house was closed up because it was a cold night, and the carbon monoxide wiped out all twelve of us."

"Twelve? Carbon paper?"

Ghorgeous laughed again. "Carbon monoxide. It's a poisonous gas. We were having a girl party, a bunch of my friends and me, and my parents were sleeping upstairs, so the house was full. Someone must have forgotten to turn off the motor, and the fumes spread into the house. It seemed like a horrible accident."

Vinia labored to dissipate her confusion. "I thought a car was a vehicle."

"It is. But its internal combustion motor generates lethal fumes, if confined to a limited space. A car should be parked in a garage, not run there for hours."

Vinia questioned her further and began to get one of her foolish notions. A car, in this respect, was like a fire-breathing dragon. Outside it could be escaped, but if it caught a person in a confined space it could fry him. "I think we need to look at that car."

"Oh, the living folk hauled it away."

"I mean when it was parked and left running. Is there any way to go back in time and see it?"

"Time travel? Not in Mhundania!"

Vinia strained her limited intellect. "In Xanth we hear stories about Mundania. Maybe not all of them are true. One is that they have a way to record events in places, like buildings, that can be looked at later."

"Oh, videotapes. We do have those. But not here." Then she paused, considering. "Then again, now I remember there might have been one. An automatic camera triggered by motion. Those tapes are saved by the police for a decade, then wiped."

"How long ago did you die."

"Nine and a half years ago. I haven't aged a day since, since ghosts don't age. That's why I still look twenty-one. But—" She paused again. "Oh my ghod! That tape could still be there!"

"Can we see it? I've got a hunch there might be something on it."

"Ghosts really can't handle physical equipment like that. We couldn't play it; for that you need a living person."

"Is there a living person you could contact, who might do it?"

Ghorgeous was getting excited. "My brother Gheorge. He was off at the bachelor party that night. He was mad as anything about the way we died, but he couldn't do anything about it. He was going to be best man at the wedding."

"Can you contact him now?"

"Oh, yes. We were very close. We fought, of course, but we loved each other. Sometimes I visit him, and he knows it's me, though others say he is just imagining it." Her lovely lips quirked. "They don't believe in ghosts."

Vinia knew that many Mundanes were in denial about ghosts, as they were about the way their world was overheating, likely to make them all ghosts sooner than they liked. "Can you visit him now?"

"Why not." Ghorgeous zoomed through a wall and to a nearby house. She went inside. There was a man of about thirty-two reading a book.

Ghorgeous phased into his head. *Gheorge!* she thought.

George looked up. "Is that you, Gorgeous?"

"Yhes! I have an idea. The motion-triggered automatic camera tape the night of the murder. Can you get it and play it?"

George's jaw dropped. "I never thought of that! You're a genius, sis!"

"Nho, it's Vhinia who thought of it."

"Who?"

Vinia was there in his head along with Ghorgeous. "Hello, George. I'm Vinia, from the magic land of Xanth, visiting your sister. I'm not a ghost, just a temporary spirit. It's a confusing story. Can you help?"

"Hello, Vinia! I'll bet it's confusing! Yes, I think I can get a copy of that tape."

Before long George did just that, talking persuasively to the police, who quickly understood his logic. They wanted to solve the murder too. It was what they called a dead case, maybe because it related to ghosts. They located the key tape and he viewed it, with Ghorgeous and Vinia watching over his shoulder.

The tape showed Gorgeous and her lady friends driving into the garage, parking the car, turning off its motor, and going into the house as the garage door rolled magically down to close it in. Then it showed a man sneaking in.

"Who is that?" Vinia asked.

"That's Rupert!" Gorgeous exclaimed. "I dated him twice and broke it off. He got too serious, too fast, and I didn't trust him."

"I've seen that man before, somewhere," George said.

Gorgeous extended a vaporous finger into his head.

"Rupert!" George exclaimed. "Now I remember. A creep who just wanted to get into my sister's pants. She told him to get lost, and I amended it with a gentle warning." He lifted one fist. "He got the message."

The tape showed Rupert using a tool to do something to the car. The motor started up. "He hot-wired the car!" George exclaimed. "He must have figured that if he couldn't have her, nobody else could, so he killed her."

"Give us the details on this Rupert; somehow this tape got overlooked in the original investigation," the police detective said.

George did. Soon they had looked Rupert up and knew where he currently lived. "Thanks. We'll take it from here."

"I feel it!" Gorgeous said. "We solved our murder. We're free!" She mentally kissed her brother. Then they returned to the house.

"What did you do?" a ghost friend asked. "We feel the release."

Gorgeous quickly explained, giving Vinia full credit for the idea. "Now let's go to Xanth, and Thanx," she concluded. "We have some heavy haunting to do."

The others were happy to agree.

"But how do we get there?" Ghorgeous asked. "We've never been there. Indeed, in life we did not believe it existed."

"I have a way," Vinia said. "Follow me." Then she reconsidered. "Um, can you hold hands or something, so we can all go together? I don't want anyone to get lost. Remember, we're no longer anchored."

The ghosts extended vaporous tendrils that connected to Ghorgeous.

"Map," Vinia said to the ring. It appeared. She reached out with Ghorgeous's hand and touched the section marked THANX.

And they were there, clustered before the run-down house. "OooOoo!" the ghosts oooOoooed, delighted. This was perfect for them.

Grossclout appeared, frowning. "I see you got here, spooks. It's about time."

Ghorgeous floated up and kissed him, firming her lips for the occasion. "I'm glad to see you, too, Professor Ghrumble. And thank you." She firmed up her bottom for his grope. Vinia felt it too, being part of the ghost now and wondered yet again what was supposed to be so compelling about such handling. Why should anyone care about kneading a buttock? It was mainly for sitting on. Then the ghost floated on to the house, along with the others. They were eager to start shaping it into a scary scene.

"I need to move on," Vinia said. "There are two more contingents to recruit."

"And thank *you* so much, Vhinia, for all you have done for us. I hope we can remain in touch, and be friends, though I know we are of rather different types."

There it was again: Vinia had never dreamed of being friends with a ghost, but she did like Ghorgeous. "Yes, I would like that. I may not be staying here in Thanx, after this mission, but I hope to visit."

"I can visit you, wherever you may be, now that we are free. Just use your ring to contact me, and I will come to you."

"Oh, I wouldn't want to bother you."

"Being with you will be my pleasure, not bother. Farewell for now, living friend." Ghorgeous mentally kissed her. Vinia was surprised by how well she liked it.

Vinia detached, as her job here was done. She resumed solid form and returned to Grossclout. "Good job," he said gruffly.

Vinia was so amazed and flustered at the unexpected compliment that she almost wet her pants. Fortunately, she was not completely solid, so there was no damage. "I just did what I had to do."

"Exactly. Now the next."

She realized that Demesne must have advised him to encourage her on occasion, so he had grudgingly done it. Still, she was pleased. "Map," she said to the ring.

The map appeared. Vinia touched the section marked SNAILS.

And she was there, in the host body of a snail, complete with a spiral shell. The snail was perched on the stem of a tall plant waving gently in the breeze. But she was getting used to this type of shift in perspective. "Hello. I am Vinia. Professor Grossclout sent me."

"Oh, you're the one! He must have found us a field."

"Field?"

"A field of florescent fennel to graze on."

Oh. "I haven't seen it myself, but if the professor says it's there, it's there. He's as good as his taciturn word."

The snail laughed, internally. "I gather you have interacted with the Demon. Hello. I am Snazzy Snail, one of the stickiest mollusks."

Vinia gathered from the context that this as a good thing. "Yes." That was technically an agreement that she knew the Demon professor but could be taken as approval of stickiness.

"The professor said you would need some background on us, so you could handle your mission properly."

"Yes. I am not a snail, and I don't really know snail ways, except that they may be rather, well, dilatory. I should be able to guide you better it you acquaint me with your history and need."

"We do have time to converse, because it will take a while to join the group. I am setting off at my briskest pace, but you may find it slow."

Her briskest pace? Vinia had not been aware that the snail was moving at all. But she saw now that Snazzy was making a slow turn to loop about and travel down the stem toward the ground. "Yes."

"You will want to know why we need to move, since we snails can survive just about anywhere on land or underwater. We don't breathe the way fish or mammals do."

"Yes." It was amazing how much that single word could suggest. If Snazzy thought it was relevant, Vinia did want to hear it.

The snail completed her U-turn and started down the stem at what might be a dizzying velocity for her kind, but as slow as the shadow on a sundial for humankind. Whatever could snails do to stop an invasion by speedy gnomes? Vinia hesitated to ask. "We are a very special variety of snail. We feed exclusively on florescent fennel. We have powers that most other snails lack."

That might be interesting. "Powers?"

"We can project moods to creatures we are close to. For example, I helped Professor Grossclout. That's why he's helping us now."

She couldn't mean doing the sort of thing that Signal Siren or Ghorgeous Ghost had done. She was tiny compared to them, and, well, she was a snail.

"I am not clear how you helped Grossclout, or how you even encountered him, or why. Maybe if you could provide me more background?"

"Certainly. We have been happy for millennia, feeding on our special patch of fennel. In return we help protect it from marauders. Our feeding is relatively slight, while others might gobble up the whole field in days. But now something unforecast is occurring, and we are desperate. The sea is advancing and soon will swamp the field."

"But you can survive in water, can't you?"

"Yes, but the fennel can't. It needs air for its flowers and spores. If it gets flooded, it will die, and we will die with it, because we can't eat anything else. We are bound to it."

"Now I appreciate your problem. The sea must be stopped. But why is it intruding, after so long a time?"

"The professor explained it to me. He knows all about every kind of magic, including the science magic of the outer reaches. You see, we live in what you call Mundania."

"I know of it. In fact, I just interacted with a ghost there."

"One of the barbarian species has gotten out of control," Snazzy continued. "It is burning so much fossil fuel that it pollutes the air and makes it warm up. That warms the water, which magically expands when heated, and it is flooding the lowland plains like ours. Dry land is disappearing, and so are all manner of species of creature."

Vinia realized that the barbarians were the humans of that bleak region. Like herself, only phenomenally ignorant and selfish. She hadn't realized that the warming was caused by the humans themselves. "But don't the barbarians see what is happening? Why don't they stop the burning?"

"They do see it, but they don't care, so they keep right on doing it. They will continue until their land becomes unlivable for them, and then they will die out."

"But this is crazy! They are committing suicide."

"Yes. But that's tomorrow, meaning the future. All they care about is today."

Vinia shook her head. That didn't work, because she was not in her own body, and the snail didn't really have a head. "The professor knows about it? Why doesn't *he* do something?"

"He says Mundania is better off without them, so he's letting nature take its course. Things should improve thereafter."

Maybe he was right. Anyone who knew that his present course meant doom, yet refused to change it, surely deserved that doom. The problem was that this also meant doom for other species who didn't deserve it, like the snails. That bothered Vinia. For one thing, how would Mundane letters ever get delivered without snails?

Well, that was a problem for others to ponder. "How did you manage to notify the professor?"

"That was the magic of coincidence, which it appears works well beyond Xanth. It seems that there was a siren, a kind of mermaid with a good voice, who wanted to visit with her distant relatives in Mundania, to try to persuade them to leave before they, too, got washed out. But all she found were dugongs. She came and sat on a rock at the shore near our field, admiring the different colors of the fennel while she pondered. It happened that I was feeding on a fennel beside that rock. A lock of her hair dropped down and stuck to me. Before I realized, she plunged back into the sea on the other side of the rock and swam away, and I was hauled along before I could unstick the hair. I didn't want to let go in the middle of the sea, because it would take me an awful long time to make my way back to the fennel field, so I made the best of it, hanging on to her hair, hoping she would return to the field soon. But she didn't; instead she swam to join the professor. It seemed they were having a tryst, and he had brought her to Mundania as a favor so she could check on her relatives. Then the tryst got hot and heavy, and they were whipping fiercely about, and I wound up stuck on *his* head. So as soon as their siege of activity was over, I used my power to send him a peaceful mood and a thought, and that's how we came to know each other."

"You sent him a peaceful mood?" Vinia repeated, bemused.

"Yes. It was an effort, because his mind was violent, but I bore down and accomplished it. Unused to it, he promptly slept, using the mermaid's bosom for a pillow. She seemed glad for the respite."

Vinia suspected that the pillow had something to do with his peaceful mood. She had heard of grown women putting men to sleep that way. When she was grown, and had equivalent pillows, she meant to try it on Ion: it could be a useful ploy. "What was the thought you sent?"

"My identity, and our problem with the rising water. I sent it into his dream. It is possible to accomplish a lot in a dream, because folk more readily accept what they encounter there."

Vinia remembered the pool splash party the girls had had on Cloud Nine, which was a kind of dream. "Yes."

"Once he was aware of me," Snazzy continued, "we made a deal. Several nights of his peaceful sleep in exchange for his trying to help us save our field. So I stayed with him awhile, before he returned me to my field. He said he would send someone to help, once he was able to put it together. And here you are."

"Here I am," Vinia agreed. "I do know of a place where you and your tribe could live."

"You do?"

"But you will need to earn your keep. It is an area about to be overrun by gnomes. They have to be stopped."

"Oh, we can do that. Gnomes are easy. It's the implacable sea that's hard."

"You can stop them? How? They move so much faster than you do, and are so much larger, and they can forge right through deep ground."

"We can stick them. You'll see."

Vinia remained deeply uncertain, but she had to trust Grossclout's judgment. If he thought the snails could stop the gnomes, maybe they could. "But there are details to work out. Such as the fact that you can't just transfer to a new field; there is no such field in Xanth, as far as I know. We'll have to move your present field there. I don't know how to do that."

"Maybe Snafu will know."

"Who?"

"Our queen. Her name translates to Situation Normal, All Fixed Up. She's good at solving insoluble problems."

Now Vinia remembered a similar acronym, though she wasn't sure it quite matched. No matter; if it meant the queen could solve the problem, it would do.

They continued to race along at a snail's pace. Vinia decided to use the time to get more information, in case it should be useful. "Do snails have any social life?"

"Why certainly. We are very social creatures. Only . . ." She trailed off into an ellipsis that did not seem to be related to signaling a stork, at least not directly. If snails even used storks.

"Only what?" Vinia asked, genuinely curious.

"Oh, you'd be bored with my problems."

"Maybe not. Remember, I'm a completely different species. It's all new to me."

"So you are," the snail agreed thoughtfully. "It's that I have the prettiest shell, and it attracts the males. I don't want them, at least not yet, but they come anyway. I must encase myself in supersticky slime to keep them off me. But my appeal makes the other females jealous, and they exclude me from social events like gossip parties. I really don't have any friends. That's why I graze at the edge of the field. I wish I had some girlfriends."

Vinia got an idea flash. "I wonder."

"I saw that flash. Remember, you are in my mind. What are you thinking?"

"It's that I have some unusual female friends that I made while on this special mission. They are adults, while I am a child, but we really like and respect one another. You might join that group. I think you would like them."

"You're not talking about snails?"

"Not snails," Vinia agreed. "They are Signal Siren, Nimbus Nickelpede, Sali Salamander, and Ghorgeous Ghost. They don't know each other yet, but we plan to get together after the mission, and I think it will be a great group. They have nothing in common except that they are young females, and should relate, because males seem to be, well, sometimes similarly obnoxious, at least where pretty girls are concerned. You can be part of it if you want to. They will all be at Thanx, so could meet physically, with a translation spell. Or maybe astrally, as I am now with you."

"This intrigues me," Snazzy agreed. "But I'm not sure how well I could relate to, well, for example, a ghost. Aren't they dead?"

"They are dead physically but can be very much alive as spirits. I can introduce you to one now, if you'd like."

"This makes me shiver, which is odd because snails don't shiver. Are you sure it is safe?"

"Oh yes. I know this one. She's nice."

"Then bring her on." Snazzy braced herself for the impact, which was also odd, because snails didn't brace. Then Vinia realized that it was her influence, because she could shiver and brace.

Vinia focused on the ring. "Ghorgeous."

And the ghost was there. "What, are you in trouble already, Vin? I got your call." She looked around. "Exactly where are we? We seem to be standing still on dirt."

"We are sharing the host body of Snazzy Snail as we race along. Snazzy, this is Ghorgeous Ghost."

"You are beautiful," Snazzy said, surprised. "So diaphanous."

"So are you. What a lovely shell."

Vinia knew already that it would work out. Soon they were in a pleasant three-way dialogue, agreeing that males could be problematical and females difficult, whatever the species. Then the ghost departed, as she had haunting to do, and the snail was reassured. She could indeed relate to a ghost. They would get together again in due course.

They were coming up to the stalk where Queen Snafu resided. There was a quick introduction, followed by Vinia's summary of the situation.

Now Snafu focused. "Your boyfriend is a Magician? With many elixirs? And his sister is a Sorceress, who can sew magic into her cloth?"

"Yes, and yes," Vinia agreed. Had she mentioned Ion and Hilda? She didn't think so. That meant that the queen had her own sources of information. Maybe Snazzy had mentioned Grossclout, and Snafu had done some spot research. But how did this background information relate to the present problem? "But this is Mundania, where such magic doesn't work."

"Pshaw! Magic works here, for those who believe in it. Mundane mammals don't. We mollusks do. We are not limited the way they are. You are magically here, after all."

She seemed to have a point. "Still, I'm not sure how such magic relates."

"Could Hilda sew a flying carpet big enough to support the field of fennel?"

"I suppose she could," Vinia said. "But it would take her a lot of time and a great deal of yarn."

"I understand she has a bag of yarn that can't run out. Ion has a time contraction elixir?"

"I believe he does. But—"

"And he has an accommodation elixir?"

"Yes, but—" Then it registered. "Apply time contraction so Hilda can take the time she needs to sew the giant carpet. Put the field on the carpet. Use the accommodation elixir to make it fit through the portal to Thanx."

"Smart girl."

"This is genius!" Snazzy exclaimed.

The queen made a mental smile. "Elementary, my dear."

"I will contact Ion and Hilda," Vinia said. But she still wondered how the tiny snails could stop the gnomes. She decided to keep her mind shut.

After that things moved rapidly along, albeit at a snail's pace. Vinia used the ring to get in touch with Ion and Hilda, and surprisingly quickly they were there in snail size with an enormous rolled carpet. Hilda and Snafu conversed with the help of a translation spell, and it was clear from the outset that they each admired the other's magic and intelligence. Vinia would have liked to pick up on more of their dialogue, but Ion corralled her for some kisses. That was weird because she was only one-sixth of her normal physical self, and she was now in the host body of a snail, but it was still fun. Maybe there was more to kisses than just the touching of lips.

Ion used some sort of elixir to enable the carpet to slide under the field of fennel. Hilda made the carpet slowly lift, and they all boarded the now flying field. Ion opened the accommodation elixir, they became smaller yet, and flew into the portal. Suddenly they were in Xanth, and in Thanx, at the designated plain for the field. Grossclout and Demesne were there to welcome them, and there were more introductions. Ion released the accommodation spell and the field expanded and unrolled. The fennel flashed its colorful florescence, making the field lovely. The snails were delighted that no rising sea was threatening to flood it out. This mission, too, was a success.

"One to go," Demon Grossclout said as Vinia detached, as if it were a routine class exercise.

Vinia was finding this mission surprisingly fulfilling, but she would be glad when it was finally accomplished. "Map," she said. It appeared, and she reached out to touch the last spot: LOVEBUGS.

"Halt," Grossclout said quietly beside her.

Vinia jumped. "Oh!"

"There is a complication. We must rescue two swarms."

"Two?" she asked blankly.

"Spot biology lesson. These bugs come in two varieties, the female lovebugs, and the male hatebugs. When they bite animals of either gender, they either love or hate, or both if a bug of each type bites the same creature. They are therefore not popular with other creatures, and in many areas are extirpated on sight. Caution is advised."

"I could be ex, extir, um, killed?"

"Ion provided a spell of invulnerability that should cover you and your hosts for the duration."

Vinia's mind was spinning. "Hosts? Plural?"

The Demon frowned. "It seems that you are not the brightest wick on the candelabra."

"I am not," she agreed, flustered. "Hosts?"

"One lovebug, one hatebug."

"One of each," she agreed. "But how can I—?"

"You must fission this identity. Because this was not in the original program, you will be the same person, half in one host, half in the other host. The two will be in mental contact with each other, perhaps confusingly. You will need to focus."

"Focus," Vinia said. Then her forgotten hand sank down and touched the map. Oh, no! She wasn't ready.

She was there in a white bug, flying through the air. And in another bug, a black one, perching on a twig in a completely different location. "Hello. I am Vinia Human, sent by Professor Grossclout," she said automatically, in dual mental voices.

"Oh, the professor told me you would come," the white bug replied. "I am Lorna Lovebug. We got blown by a terrible storm and now are stranded on an isolated island. We can't fly far enough across the sea to save ourselves."

"What are you doing in my mind, intruder?" the black bug demanded.

Focus. Vinia shut down her black awareness and focused on the white one. "Yes. We will talk in a moment. Right now, I have to answer another line."

"Okay," White agreed amicably. She was female and amenable.

Vinia switched focus to the black bug. "I am here to help you. Do you want it or not?"

"Not. Get out." She was male and hostile in this host.

Oops. Vinia marshaled whatever nerve she could manage, knowing that this one had to be recruited also. "No. You must be in trouble or I wouldn't be here. Now tell me what trouble you are in." Something else was bothering her in the background.

"Very well. I will tell you. Then you can get out."

"I am listening. Start with your name."

"Why the hoo-hah should I give you my name?"

Vinia thought as rapidly as she could arrange for in her flustered circumstance. "The human Kingdom of Hoo-Hah has nothing to do with this."

It worked. The bug was taken aback. "Delete that name. The question remains."

But the pause had given Vinia time to think of a reason. "Because I won't be banished by an anonymous bug. Anonymity has no power over me."

That aggressive tone seemed to get through. "I am Hayes Hatebug. Our swarm was chasing a flock of rabbits so we could sting them into mayhem, but when we caught up to them, they transformed into Demons and dissipated. It was their joke on us. But they had mischievously led us so far astray that now we have no idea where we are. We are hopelessly lost and will soon perish if we don't find our way back before the gnat-catchers come. Now go."

And in the brief interim Vinia had figured out what else was bothering her. She had recognized Hayes as "she." She had thought it was a mental typo, "She was male." But it wasn't. This was a female masquerading as male. Why?

She tackled it tail on. "Hayes, you are female. Why the subterfuge?"

"Oh, bleep!" the hatebug exclaimed, near tears. "You know."

Vinia morphed into support mode. "I said I was here to help you, and I am. But you must be candid with me. Why are you pretending to be male?"

Her secret exposed, Hayes collapsed into her real nature, which was gentle. "I-I am a female who prefers females."

"A lesbian," Vinia agreed. "I have a lesbian friend, in another species. She's a good person. Maybe you are too." The logic was strained, as species and romantic orientation were rather different qualities, but she needed to work with the bug, not against her.

"The other bugs don't understand my orientation. I knew I would be driven out of the swarm if they found out. So I dipped myself in black powder, practiced my hate, and managed to fake being male well enough so I could join a male swarm. The males all focus on what they'd like to do with females. Lovebugs and hatebugs, we are all the same species, really. So I join them in wanting to catch a female, to breed with her, and they don't suspect. If they ever did catch on, I'd soon be raped to death. Please, please don't tell!"

"I won't tell," Vinia promised. "Maybe I can help you in that, too, as well as saving your swarm."

"Oh, thank you!"

Then Vinia got another notion. Grossclout had to have known of this complication, because he knew just about everything. Why had he sent her here? There had to be a reason, and she was getting a suspicion what it was. "I am only half here. My other half is with a female swarm. Hold on while I consult with her." She changed her focus.

Now she was back with Lorna. "How did you get in touch with the Demon professor? Did you take his class in magic?"

"No, it was more prosaic. I was just emerging from the ground when—"

"The ground?" Vinia asked, surprised. "But you are a flying creature."

"Most of our lives are spent developing and maturing in the ground. Only when we are ready to mate do we emerge as winged bugs. We don't eat, being in our terminal form. Then we find our opposite gender, mate, and die."

"That must be awful!"

"I agree. But I am stuck with my nature." She shrugged the length of her body. "But you asked how I met the professor. He had used his formidable mental powers to zero in on a spare webcam that it seemed he needed for his class and found one that must have fallen from its web. It looked like a disk with an off-center handle. I don't know how it worked, but understand it enables folk to communicate with each other at a long distance. But this one was dirty, and he wanted it clean before he took it to the class. Then he spied me emerging and asked me: 'Lovebug, I need a lake or a river, or at least a pond with clean water. Is there any near here?' And I answered that I was familiar with this ground, having spent all my youthful life in it, and knew of a local underground river. Would that do? He agreed that it would, so I led him to the rock that marked the location of the river, and he popped down below with the webcam."

"I would have thought that he could have simply wiped it off with Demon smoke," Vinia said.

"I think he didn't want to get his own substance dirty. Anyway, he soon popped up again, and the cam was clean. "I will return the favor you have done me in double measure," he said. "Speak my name when you need it, and I will respond in due course." Then he dissipated into smoke and was gone." Lorna shrugged again. "I thought no more of it, until my swarm got blown away. Then I tried it, and in due course you appeared."

So the professor had cunningly used the need of Thanx to return a favor to the lovebugs. Except that he had said in double measure. What was the other half of it?

"I need to know: which do you prefer to be with, romantically, male or female?"

Lorna stared at her, mentally. "Is it that obvious? I prefer female. But I would be driven out of the swarm if the others knew. They are very straight fliers. What gave me away?"

"Well, I *am* in your mind. But I was suspicious of the Demon professor's motive in putting me with the two of you at the same time."

"The two of us?"

"The other half of me is with a lesbian bug posing as a male."

Lorna made another mental stare. "Is she nice?"

"Yes, I think so. She has to play a role of being meanly masculine, but I think you'd like the real her if you got to know her."

"But we are in different swarms."

"I believe my mission is to get both swarms to the Queendom of Thanx, so the males can get together with the females and perpetuate your species."

"But I don't want to be with a male."

"I am thinking that you can be with Hayes—that's her name—and pretend she is male. Then you can be a couple, and no one will question it."

Lorna nodded mentally. "If we don't mate—and two females can't—we won't produce offspring and die. We will live on indefinitely."

"So the professor wasn't fooling about double measure. He must have done spot research when he came to understand your orientation and located Hayes. You will get love and life, as well as saving your swarm. It seems he does pay his debts."

"It seems he does," Lorna agreed. "Tell that other lesbian who I am."

Vinia switched to the other host. "My other host is lesbian. I told her about you. When your two swarms merge, go to her as a male, until you can get private. Then you can love each other as females and continue living. Maybe it will work out."

"Maybe it will," Hayes agreed thoughtfully.

"Now we need to arrange to take both swarms to Thanx, where you must defend your section from the human invaders. Can you do that?"

"Humans? Any males who sting any humans will make them hate each other, so they will fight. Any I sting will love whoever is closest, but in the melee no one should notice."

"And the lovebug swarm will be stinging freely. Except if the invaders are all male, what then?"

"Then they will love each other, which is apt to embarrass them. In any event they won't continue invading."

"Oh, this is fiendish," Vinia said. "Or rather, demonish."

"But how can you get our swarms to your Queendom?"

"I will signal the Demon professor, who will have a portal or two portals you can fly through. That should not be a problem."

"One caution. If the two swarms arrive together, they will dissolve into mating, and not sting any invaders."

"Oops. We'll have to keep them apart. I will tell Grossclout."

Vinia returned to Lorna and covered the situation with her. Then she spoke the name Grossclout to her ring.

"Yes," the professor said. "We will transport the lovebugs first, today, and the hatebugs tomorrow as the invasion starts. Both will encounter the invaders before each other."

"And you knew about their secret," Vinia said.

"Naturally. I knew you could handle it."

"One of these episodes, your confidence in me may turn out to be misplaced," Vinia said ruefully.

"No, I don't make that sort of mistake. Now get the two swarms organized for travel."

Vinia got to work, explaining to the hosts what was necessary. Both hosts went to the swarm chiefs, who quickly agreed to use the portals. They were after all in desperate situations, and this promised immediate reprieves.

Vinia signaled Grossclout again, and he set up the portal. The entire lovebug swarm passed through in single file, finding themselves in a delightful valley. They knew that in the morning the hatebugs would arrive. They were ecstatic.

And Vinia's sixfold mission was finally done. She flung her arms around the professor and kissed him on the cheek.

He frowned. "I would have avoided that, had you warned me."

"That's why I didn't warn you." But she knew that he was privately pleased.

Chapter 10

WAR

Vinia joined Ion in their room on the carpet, quite ready to collapse back into anonymity after her sixfold day. To sleep in his arms. But it was not to be.

Queen Demesne appeared. "The princesses and their consorts are concerned about the morrow," she said. "They want to be quite sure that our defenses are working. In fact, they want to actually see it happening."

Vinia knew this would be more effort on her part, because otherwise the queen would not have come here at this hour. But how could she say no? She was committed to do all she could to help the larger mission of establishing the queendom, and tomorrow was critical. The invasions had to be stopped. "What can I do?" she asked reluctantly.

"Oh, you won't have to do it alone. Grossy volunteered to help."

Grossy? Their relationship was evidently progressing by bounds and leaps. But that was of course the way with men and women. The men thought they were in charge, and the women encouraged that delusion. He had volunteered? In a pork's eye! He was doing Demesne's will. Still, Vinia was quite impressed with the professor's competence. She could work with him.

"What is the mission?"

"Merely to check on the six fronts and relay news to the assembled princesses. It seems that Grossy has a webcam you can use."

The webcam. Maybe she would find out what it did and how it worked. "I'll do it, of course."

"Thank you, dear. I knew you would help."

"But Vinia has had a hard day," Ion protested. "She has been fragmented and reassembled. She should rest tomorrow."

Demesne popped over, literally, and kissed him on the left ear. "What was that, dear?"

"Nothing," he said, plainly stunned. He was a Magician and a prince, but had become jelly.

"Then Vinia will see to it tomorrow. Sweet dreams." Demesne faded out.

Vinia only hoped she would be able to manage Ion like that when she turned adult. The power of a lovely adult woman over any male of any age was a miracle to behold.

Ion looked at her shrewdly, reading her unguarded expression. "You could already manage me like that, if you chose to."

Could she really? So she tried it. "Put your arms around me. Hold me close while I sleep."

He put his arms around her. He held her close. She dropped blissfully into slumber. "But that's not a valid test," he murmured as she fell. "I wanted to do that anyway."

Oh, well. At least she had made the effort.

In the morning Demon Grossclout was there, immediately after they had hastily eaten. "She Who Must Be Obeyed sent me." Just so. He thought he was joking.

In barely half a moment they were out at the fringe. "They will invade simultaneously," he said. "You will have to fission into six, again."

That meant another dose of the split personality elixir. "I am ready," Vinia said grimly.

"Not yet. First you must comprehend the use of the webcam."

Oh, yes. "I know virtually nothing about it."

"Precisely. You are typically ignorant. It is a type of camera that projects its images to the main receiver and large screen in the central chamber, where the princesses will be watching. Whatever you aim it at will appear there."

"But that's so pedestrian it's almost Mundane."

"It is borrowed technology from Mundania, yes. They use it in assorted places, such as their bedrooms."

"Bedrooms? But suppose they forget it's there and show more than they are supposed to?"

"That is exactly why it's there. Mundanes are gluttons for illicit images. They call it upskirting. They record the pictures and play them over again later."

They did it on purpose? Vinia made a mental note never to forget about any webcam in her vicinity, regardless whether she wore a skirt. "Whatever works, I guess."

"Exactly. We don't have time to assemble and adapt suitable magic mirrors, so must make do with that we have."

She would be wary of magic mirrors, too, especially small ones set on the floor. "Spell it out for me, please, so I don't foul it up."

Grossclout gave Vinia the cam, which she saw was indeed a kind of camera despite Lorna Lovebug's description. It had a lens and a handhold, and a few little buttons. "Point it at whatever seems interesting and press this button." He pointed to a red one. "A small screen on its side will show what it is sending. That's it."

"But that's so simple even I could do it," she said, surprised.

"Exactly. It is largely idiotproof."

Was he teasing her, or speaking literally? She decided not to challenge it. "Yes."

"When you have oriented it on a target, and the screen confirms that it is the correct picture, press this one." He indicated a green button.

"What does that do?"

"It locks the cam onto that target. It will continue filming it even if you turn away, correcting for shaky hands or whatever."

"That really *is* idiotproof!" she agreed admiringly.

"Yes. I amended it magically, to make up for likely deficiencies in student handlers."

"So someone would not accidentally film a dull foot instead of aiming excitingly upskirt?"

"Exactly."

She had thought she was joking. "I will try not to make that mistake."

"When you fission, so will it. You will be in your several hosts, but you will be able to handle this. Start when the action starts. Stop when the action stops. Speak my name if there is a specific problem."

"Got it," she agreed. Then, naughtily, "Grossy."

He laughed. "You will be delightfully dangerous when you are mature." He presented the vial of split personality elixir and opened it. Vapor issued forth in a faint cloud. She almost made out six parts to it.

Vinia sniffed the cloud and fragmented. Fortunately, she was now familiar with the procedure. She focused on a single fragment, tuning out the others. "Map," she said. It appeared. She touched the section of Thanx now marked SIRENS.

"Hello again, Vinia," Signal Siren said, feeling her presence.

"Hello, Signal."

"What brings you here? A sweet girl like you may not like seeing what we do when annoyed."

Drowning invaders who intended mayhem on the Queendom of Thanx? "I think I can handle it. Just so you don't do it to me."

Signal laughed. "Never to our friends. Besides, our music doesn't work well on girls."

Vinia thought of something. "What about lesbians?"

The mermaid paused to consider. "I don't know. We tune in on males who tune in on females. It might work at half strength."

"There are some lesbians on our side. But they won't be here, so maybe it will be all right."

"Let's hope so. But you never answered my question. Why are you here?"

"I have a, a webcam. It's a Mundane device that sends pictures to a screen in Dragoman's cave so the princesses can watch. They want to be sure the invasions are stopped."

"Oh, the ogres will be stopped," Signal said confidently. "I don't know about the other sectors."

"I understand that the images are recorded. Maybe we can play them again, when this is over, so you can see the other theaters."

"That would be nice. I understand one sector is to be defended by snails. I would like to see how they stop charging invaders."

"Yes." Vinia hoped that somehow the snails would succeed. Suppose they didn't?

"Here they come!" Signal licked her lips as she and the other sirens swing about in the water to face the intruders.

Vinia remembered to turn on her cam. She pressed the red button. A little picture appeared on its side, exactly as Grossclout had indicated. It showed huge hairy ogres appearing at the shore, where tree trunks were knotted and the ground was soaked in the juice of squeezed rocks, a sure sign of ogre presence. She remembered that ogres also taught young dragons the meaning of fear. And that an ogress could be so ugly that her smile could curdle milk. There was a story of an actress who emulated an ogress so well that her smile even curdled water. Nobody messed with an ogre!

"Mee see Shee!" an ogre cried. "Mee free Shee!" He looked to be the ugliest of the lot, which made him the leader. Vinia realized that she was hearing the voice via the cam: it was filming sound, too.

This was the right scene. She pressed the green button. Nothing changed. She experimented, shaking the webcam. The picture did not shake. She faced away. The picture remained focused on the ogre. This was an impressive device.

The other ogres halted in place. It seemed the first one had reserved the right to "free" the mermaid, whatever that meant in ogre terms. Maybe to make free with her.

"I believe that's us," Signal said, pleased. "We're closest to him."

So it seemed, though that did not thrill Vinia the way it did Signal. But she was just an observer. She kept the cam oriented and running, sending the picture. She hoped that she would not inadvertently find herself in anything forbidden by the Conspiracy. She might get goosed right out of her host and ruin the filming.

Meanwhile Signal faced the ogre squarely with her double circles up front. "Are you looking for me, big boy?" she called.

The ogre answered by splashing into the water, to his knees, thighs, belly, and chest. He was twice the height of a human man, so could handle deep water. But now he paused, because the depth ahead was beyond his height.

Whereupon Signal started singing. Her voice was strong and weird, sounding a bit like a charging Mundane machine, but it had a weird appeal. The ogre heard it and immediately plunged on toward her, his gaze fixed on her circles. He was making progress; it seemed that the tips of his hairy toes were able to just touch the bottom, propelling him forward with his nose just above the surface.

Signal smiled and flicked her tail, moving slowly backward, into deeper water. The ogre followed, now actually swimming, though it was clear that he didn't know how to swim: he just bashed the water with his limbs, bumbling forward. He almost reached the siren.

Then the first stir of the forming whirlpool caught them. Signal floated comfortably, twitching her tail just enough to maintain her position. But the ogre was caught by the current and carried away. In a moment he went under, leaving only the remnant of an unruly splash on the surface. He was gone, drowned.

The ogres at the shore were staring. They had seen what happened. Surely, they couldn't be stupid enough to go into that deep water themselves!

Then Vinia remembered: ogres were justifiably proud of their stupidity.

Signal swished her tail to heave her superstructure mostly clear of the water. "Who is next?" she called. "Any volunteers?"

They hesitated. Then she inhaled. They lumbered forward as one, plowing into the deeper water, their eyes reflecting swelling circles. But when they reached the limit that allowed them to breathe, they paused.

Several other sirens appeared, spaced in a line extending to either side of Signal. They all heaved their bodies up high and inhaled. The webcam's peripheral vision showed them, too.

The ogres stumbled forward. But the water rose to splash into their eyes so that they couldn't see well, and they thrashed in the water in place.

The sirens started singing. That did it: the ogres somehow made it to the deeper water, almost in reach. And the current caught them. They were gone.

More ogres appeared on the shore. This was after all an invading army. But now there was an ogress among them. "You idiots!" she called. "It's their song that mesmerizes you!" She was speaking normally; it seemed that ogres didn't *have* to speak in spot rhymes. "Stuff your ears with mud! So you can't hear them."

The ogres heeded her. Maybe she was somebody's mother. She was certainly ugly: it looked as if the water at her feet was trying to curdle. The males reached down by their feet and hauled up huge masses of mud and weeds. They jammed them into their flaring ears. Uh-oh. This would nullify the siren's main weapon.

Then the sirens sank down below the surface. The cam's picture remained focused, as if it were still above the water. This was an impressive device!

Signal stretched her tail out straight. Slowly it thinned in the center and divided, forming a tail-long split. She could make legs! She produced a pair of panties from somewhere, reached forward as she brought her half-tails up, and pulled the panties over her flukes, then up along the tails until they covered where her bottom should be. The parts of her tail were still touching each other, and they really were not great legs, but she did have the panties on.

She swam back up to the surface. The ogres were advancing. Signal waved at them to get the attention of the closest ones. Then she faced away, ducked her head and chest down under the water, and lifted her pantied bottom, flashing them. The other sirens were doing the same. Their legs might not be great, but their bottoms were. The webcam continued to focus.

The ogres freaked out. But that didn't do the job, because they just stood in place, unmoving. So the sirens looped about, swam across, and pushed the ogres into the deeper water. Soon they were gone.

More ogres appeared. The ogress faced them. "Turn around!" she cried. "Go home! This sector is impassable!"

The ogres obediently turned and departed. The ogress turned to face the sirens. "Well played, you fishtailed floozies. We didn't know you had backsides." Then she too departed.

The battle had been won. The ogres had been balked. They surely would not try it again. The ogresses wouldn't let them.

Vinia remembered to turn off the webcam. The picture ended. "I have to go," she told Signal. "But we'll meet again, maybe later today."

"I will be expecting you," the siren agreed. "Thanks for your help getting us here."

They exchanged air kisses. Then Vinia spoke to the ring. "Map."

It appeared. She touched the section marked NICKELPEDES.

Vinia instantly was back with Nimbus Nickelpede. "Hello again," she said.

"Hello, Vinia. Is it time?"

"Just about. The goblins are scheduled to charge."

"We are ready for them. We have nests of us scattered across this sector."

Vinia looked around. This was a pleasant valley, with a small deep river meandering casually in the center, as if not in a hurry to get anywhere. It hardly resembled a battlefield.

There was the sound of a horn. It had undertones of wind escaping an intestine. It was the signal for the goblin army to charge.

The goblins appeared in a solid line, running into the field. Vinia turned on the webcam. The picture appeared. She touched the green lock-on button.

"What is that?" Nimbus asked.

Vinia explained. Meanwhile the goblin wave was almost upon them. The goblin soldiers had nasty little clubs.

The nearest soldier rushed into Nimbus's section. She leaped onto his foot and gouged out a nickle-sized scoop. She tasted it, frowning. "I've had better!" she said, dumping it out. "He really ought to wash his feet before offering them to us."

"Owww!!" the goblin screamed, putting two whole exclamation points into it. He reached down to grab Nimbus off his foot. His fingers closed on her body. She bit one. "Owww!!!"

Then other nickelpedes jumped on, gouging at his feet, hands, and bottom. "Oooww!!!!"

In barely nine-tenths of a moment the goblin was scrambling back off the field of combat, shedding nickelpedes galore. The same was happening across the field. The goblins had been routed.

"Well, that was easy," Nimbus said with satisfaction.

Then more goblins appeared. They charged forward exactly as the others had. Hadn't the word spread?

Nimbus leaped on to the foot of the goblin who came her way. She started to gouge. "Yuck!!" she exclaimed, summoning her own second exclamation point.

"What's the matter?" Vinia asked.

"He's wearing nickelpede repellent. I can't handle that. Neither can the others."

Uh-oh. So the goblins had a backup plan and were protecting their second wave. Something had to be done in a hurry, or the goblins would get through.

Vinia spoke to the ring. "Grossclout."

The Demon professor appeared before them. "Problem?"

"The goblins are wearing repellent. Ion should have an elixir to nullify that. Can you check with him and bring it here?"

Grossclout didn't answer. He merely vanished.

"They're bashing us with their clubs, now that we can't scoop them,"

Nimbus said, scuttling aside as a club smashed down. "We can't hold out much longer."

Grossclout was back. "Prince Ion is temporarily short on nullifying elixir. He sent a substitute, but you may not want that."

"What could be worse than getting bashed?"

"It is essence of stink horn aroma. Goblins hate it as much as humans do."

"Oh, my!" Vinia tuned mentally to Nimbus. "Can you handle stink horn smell?"

"Oh, sure. We merely turn off our noses."

"Let it rip," Vinia told the demon.

The professor opened the vial. The dreadful stench poured out in putrid waves, soon suffusing the area.

"Ghaaa!" the closest goblin gagged. Soon others were gagging similarly. It seemed that they couldn't just turn off their noses. Too bad for them.

The goblins tried to use their clubs to fan away the odor, but it roiled up, blanketing them. They had to retreat, but the reek pursued them. They started jumping into the river to wash it off, but the moment their heads appeared above the surface, the stench dropped down to smother them. Finally, they fled back to their section of the field. Only then did the smell settle down for a rest.

It seemed the battle had been won after all. Vinia turned off the webcam.

Queen Nitro scuttled across to join them. "Did you summon that fetor?" she demanded, recognizing Vinia within Nimbus.

"I did," Vinia confessed, embarrassed.

"Good girl! It is sinking into the turf and will be there if the gobs ever return. Meanwhile we'll go out after them in hunting parties when we're hungry. What a turnabout!" Queen Nitro moved on.

So it was all right after all.

"We knew you would come through for us," Nimbus said.

"I-I was glad to help. Now I must move on to another sector. But we can visit after the war is done."

"Gladly," Nimbus agreed.

"Map," Vinia murmured. It appeared, and she touched SALAMAN-DERS.

* * *

Her venue changed. Vinia was aware that this sequence did not follow the nickelpede one, but was parallel to it, happening at about the same time. That was part of the marvel of multiple personality.

"Hello again, Vinia," her host Sali said, sensing her arrival. "We love it here. The grass grows up really fast and dry, just right for burning."

"That's good. I think the trolls are about to attack. I hope you are ready for them."

"We are always ready. We are spaced out across the field, ready to fire up. Bring on the trolls!"

But Vinia was concerned. The goblins had quickly adjusted to the defense and attacked again, prepared. "Do you have a backup plan; in case anything goes wrong?"

"We have Fiera Fire Cloud. She has turned out to be a lot of fun."

Vinia remembered. Fiera had been a key help in getting the salamanders here. "But her specialty is fire, the same as yours. Suppose the trolls bring, well, water bombs?"

Sali laughed. "Let them try."

Vinia looked at the field. The tall grass was waving in a gentle breeze blowing from left to right across the section. The land terminated in a rising cliff on the left, and a crevasse on the right that dropped to unknown depths, impassable except by birds or flying spells. Vinia would have been nervous about living here, lest she absentmindedly wander and step off the brink. But salamanders could cling to the vertical edge, so were not in danger.

There, at the brink, was Fiera in her sexy bare human form, dancing with abandon. Evidently, she was entertaining herself while waiting for the attack. She of course had nothing to fear from the gulf, because she was a cloud. Wasn't she concerned about the imminent invasion? She was supposed to be here to help the salamanders defend Thanx, not to disport herself alone.

"You'll see," Sali said, picking up on her thought.

There was a sound like a filthy breeze, not at all like the pleasant air current of the field. The trolls appeared, running in unlock step. They spilled out onto the field, resembling inferior ogres: shorter, thinner, weaker, less ugly, and not quite as stupid. That last might make them more dangerous. They carried not clubs, but lighter staffs and sticks. Still, they could be plenty of trouble, being larger than human folk and hungry for the taste of flesh, any flesh, no cooking necessary.

"Haaa!" one cried, spying Fiera. "A damsel in dis-dress." An accurate observation, to an extent.

Vinia turned on the webcam and locked it on the trolls.

The army advanced, bearing right. The creatures' ugly eyes were on the seemingly oblivious dancing maiden. Oh, did they have plans for her! This must seem to them like a side benefit to the conquest of territory.

When the charging line reached the center-right side of the field, the salamanders turned on them together, Sali and Vinia among them. They ran back and forth under the cover of the stems, trailing fire. The field blazed up right beside the trolls, the fire intensifying as it ignited the dry grass. It moved to the right, fanned by the breeze.

Which was where the trolls were, as they closed in on the fire maiden. "Oh, my!" Vinia said appreciatively. "Fiera assumed a form to attract the brutes to the side of the field where the fire would go."

"Yes. We can't control the wind, so we needed a lure. Fiera is perfect."

But the trap wasn't quite perfect. The trolls smelled the smoke and saw the fire coming. They scrambled back to get clear before it caught them. "Bleep!" Vinia swore.

Soon they were back, now wearing protective suits. They had evidently had some warning and come prepared. The suits might have been made from imported salamander fire ash so they would not burn. The trolls charged through the burning field to get at the bright damsel. The fire did not stop them.

Vinia knew that the fire spirit could readily escape them. But that would not stop them from charging on through the blazing field to reach Thanx proper. Bleep again.

"Keep watching," Sali said.

Fiera continued dancing as the trolls converged on her. But just as they were about to grab her, she jumped into the air above their heads and puffed into her natural cloud form. They halted, gazing up, maybe hoping to spy a skirt they could peer under. No such luck: she was all smoke and fog.

The trolls gave it up as a bad job. They turned toward the far side of the field and resumed their advance. This was surely mischief, just as Vinia feared, as the fire ploy had been nullified. Vinia tried desperately to think of something she could suggest to stop them, but her mind stalled.

"Don't be concerned," Sali said. "We have it covered." Her confidence seemed foolhardy. Maybe salamanders were blessed with permanent optimism, but that could get them squished in battle.

Then the burning cloud swooped down close to the leading troll, Fiera able to move contrary to the wind. A jag of lightning struck, just missing the creature's hideous head. The troll jumped back, alarmed. Another jag shot past his rear, almost singeing it. "Quit that, strumpet!" he yelled angrily.

That gibe must have annoyed Fiera. The third bolt struck the troll's right foot. The armor was no protection against this. "OoOoo!" he howled, staggering sideways.

Right off the cliff. "OoOoo!" sounded again, descending, as he fell.

It didn't pay to annoy the fire spirit. Vinia was happy that Fiera was on her side. Their friendship was paying off.

Fiera moved on to the next armored troll. They were unable to move rapidly because of their heavy fireproof suits and were vulnerable to the fiery lightning.

The remaining trolls got the message. They retreated in a clumsy mass as the grass fire completed its sweep to the cliff. They might have crossed the hot ashes but would still have been vulnerable to the cloud. Their invasion had ended.

This battle, too, had been won, thanks to Fiera. Vinia was glad to have recruited her.

"Great show," she told Sali. "But I have to move on now. See you when the war is over."

"Oh, yes," the salamander agreed.

Professor Grossclout appeared. "You succeeded here without my help."

"It wasn't my doing. The salamanders had it well organized, and Fiera Fire Cloud was wonderful."

"Your modesty becomes you."

Vinia didn't argue the case. "Map." It appeared. She touched the section marked GHOSTS.

* * *

She was now with Ghorgeous in the newly haunted house. "Oh, hello, Vinia! We have hardly gotten started here; it still looks almost habitable."

"That's all right. There are dragons to stop."

"Of course. We wouldn't want to miss our date with them. Let's get out there now." The ghost zoomed through a wall and out into the morning sky. Again, this was parallel to the other sectors, not following them. It felt a bit like traveling an hour back in time.

Vinia enjoyed seeing the landscape from this vantage. The ghost passed right through the foliage of a nearby tree without hesitating; solid things were immaterial to her. Vinia couldn't see the other ghosts, but suspected they were doing the same.

They were just in time. The dragons were already in the sky, having taken less time to arrive than the land-bound creatures. Air travel was faster. "I hope you have a plan," Vinia said worriedly. "Dragons are tough to stop, and you don't even have any solid substance. At least not enough to halt a hurtling creature."

"Firmed lips and bottoms won't be very effective on them," the ghost agreed. "But overnight we worked out what we feel should be a feasible plan of defense."

Vinia hoped they were right. The other sectors had been too chancy for her taste.

A formidable fire-breathing dragon came right at Ghorgeous, not even seeing her. She expanded to dragon size and shape and became fuzzily visible. It was illusion, but it seemed that was relatively easy to do. Vinia turned on the webcam, let it focus, and locked it on. This battle, like the others, was being filmed for posterity.

Ghorgeous concentrated, not taking any action. "What are you doing?" Vinia asked, concerned.

"I am reading what passes for his mind, now that he's in range. It affects my strategy."

The dragon's mind? Fire breathers weren't known for their smarts, because the heat of their breathing tended to fry their brains.

It seemed ironic that Thanx was made from the territory of a dragon yet was anathema to other dragons. The reason was its seeming threat to the masculine dominance of the kingdoms. Maybe they were afraid that their own females might start getting ideas of equality and independence and question the patriarchy.

Now Ghorgeous clarified her dragon image. It became female and older, formidable rather than beautiful, even in dragon terms. A matriarch?

The male dragon, coming torchingly close, spread his wings sideways, braking in air. "Mother!" he said, surprised. "But you died a decade ago!"

Vinia wondered how she could hear and understand the dragon's words. Then she realized that it was the webcam doing it; it had an audio translator. Marvelous device!

"My body died, but not my spirit," Ghorgeous replied in the dragon's fiery voice. "Now get out of here, you rascal, before I toast your tail to a crisp!"

Vinia understood that this was what the ghost had read in the dragon's mind. His formidable dead mother, who must have tanned his hide with fire when he misbehaved as a child. The memory of her remained like a hotly focused sunbeam.

"But this is our invasion. We're going to burn out the feminists."

The matriarch swelled a size larger. "You *what*?!"

"They can't be allowed to spread their poisonous ideas."

The dragoness seemed about to detonate. "Poisonous? My moldering scales! I never taught you that garbage. They are standing up for the civil rights of females. It's high time. You males have been ruining things for far too long."

"But—"

"I'm a female. Didn't you notice?"

"But this is different. These females think they're equal to males."

She huffed up another notch. "Equal? *Equal?* We're superior, in everything but size!"

Still he tried to argue, to the extent his shriveled brain permitted. "But size is all that matters to a dragon."

Vinia had to admit he had a point there.

The matriarch's horrendous face loomed so large it seemed about to chomp him in two. "GET OUT OF HERE, WRETCH, BEFORE I LOSE MY TEMPER!!" Indeed, her whole head was turning white hot.

The dragon turned tail and fled.

Vinia was impressed. It seemed that the dragon could not defy even the spirit of his mother. This was an effective strategy.

All around, the other dragons were retreating similarly. None of them could withstand the fury of the dragon ladies.

The ghosts did not let them go alone. They pursued; a host of spectral matriarchs bent on correcting errant offspring. Until they came to the dragon castle, where the females awaited the victorious return of their males.

The males flew right by them, afraid to stop lest their tails get toasted by the angry dragon spirits. But the matriarchs oriented, each on the proper young female, and contacted them mentally. "Hey, Drowsie!" Ghorgeous called.

The one addressed straightened up, startled, her tail switching nervously. "Who calls me?"

"Dropsie Dragoness, the spirit mother of your boyfriend. He tried to attack the neighboring queendom, to destroy feminism. I stopped him, because neighbors must live in peace. But the job is incomplete. You must assert your equality. You females are just as good as the males, in fact better in the ways that count, and it is past time for you to recognize it."

"But we never oppose our males," Drowsie protested.

"That's your problem. You must bring them into line so that we dragon spirits don't have to bestir ourselves again. Make them behave!"

Drowsie remained doubtful, but Ghorgeous kept after her, and gradually the dragoness saw the merit of her case. She would assert herself as an equal.

All around them, Vinia saw the other dragons in dialogue with their elders. The case was being made. The males would be tamed.

Finally, the ghosts departed. The job was done, maybe.

Vinia turned off the webcam. "Good show," she said. "You really figured it out."

"Well, we don't want rogue dragons toasting our house once we get it properly haunted. Fire is not good for haunts."

Ghorgeous was surely correct. "I must move on," Vinia said. "But we'll get together, maybe later in the day, maybe with all my contact friends. Physically."

"I am eager to meet them. But I will need a host if you want me to be physical."

"Welcome to use my body. You shared yours with me, after all."

"I will do that," the ghost agreed.

Grossclout appeared. "You did it again."

"They did it again. It was beautiful the way they handled those dragons."

"Just so." The Demon faded out.

Vinia braced herself. The next sector was the one she was most apprehensive about, because she just couldn't see how slow-moving snails could stop speedy gnomes, no matter how confident of success they might be. This was surely the weakest part of the defense perimeter. But she had to be there, to help if she could. Somehow. Even if it was only to call Grossclout to come rescue the situation.

"Map." The map appeared. Vinia touched the section marked SNAILS.

She was back with Snazzy Snail, she of the lovely shell. "Hello, Vinia!" Snazzy said.

"Hello, Snazzy. Are you ready for the attack?"

"More than ready. We've been working all night. Those gnasty gnomes will be sorry they ever tried."

There was that assurance, again. "That's good," Vinia agreed weakly.

The snail picked up on her doubt. "You lack confidence in us?"

She didn't want to lie, but the truth would not be nice. "I, uh, am sure you mean well."

"A nice evasion. But we really are prepared. You'll see."

Vinia hoped so. She gazed at the lovely field of florescent fennel. What a pity to have that trampled.

There was the sound of a bugle: a single gnotable gnote. The gnomes were about to attack. Vinia quailed inwardly, but she turned on the webcam. What would be, would be.

The gnomes appeared at the edge of the field, in formation, carrying their little swords. Each gnome was about one human foot tall, wearing a pointed cap, with a long white beard. They did not look impressive, but Vinia knew they could walk through deep rock, albeit slowly. Obviously, they felt no need of that here, so were traveling on the surface for the sake of convenience and speed. What was there to stop them?

They advanced about a quarter of the way into the field, half hidden by the fennel. Then they halted. This was evidently not intentional, because the ones behind the front row collided with them, and there was a jam, then a pileup. What was the matter?

"Stickum," Snazzy said.

Indeed, Vinia saw now that the gnomes' feet were stuck to the ground. They were struggling to lift them clear, but bands of glue pulled them back. The ones behind tried to circle around them, only to get their own feet similarly anchored. And as the ones farther behind tramped impatiently, their feet also got stuck.

"We set ourselves in a quadrant," Snazzy said. "We traversed each little square of it, making sure that there was no way to avoid it. Some is fast-acting stickum; some is slow. The ones in front encountered the fast acting; the ones behind, the slow acting. All are equally stuck. They got well into it before they realized."

"But can't they just walk down into and below the ground, escaping it?"

"They can walk into the ground, yes, but their feet will still be stuck where they are. They can't go far."

"Suppose they take off their boots?"

"And put their bare feet on the stickum? They know better than that."

Indeed, the gnomes were not stepping out of their boots. They had fallen into the trap but were not making it worse.

Snazzy and the other snails were ranged by the sides of the field, watching the proceedings. It seemed that their projecting antenna could pick up the sounds and images well enough.

Now the gnomides, the gnome females, appeared at the edge of the field. They were rather pretty little figures, with pointed feminine hats instead of masculine caps, and colorful dresses. They assessed the situation. Then one brought out a lasso, whirled it around her head, and hurled it at the nearest stuck gnome. The loop settled neatly around his torso, and he gripped it with his hands. Then the gnomide started to pull. She was stronger than she looked; the cord stretched tight. The gnome leaned but did not get free of the stickum. She enlisted friends, and several of them grabbed onto the rope and hauled.

Slowly the gnome's boots left the ground as he was pulled sideways. The elastic stickup elongated, stretching and thinning as the gnome was tediously hauled across the field, through the fennel, to the edge, where the gnomides grabbed hold of him. Now he was free to remove his boots.

He did so, and they snapped back to where they had been, standing by themselves.

So the gnomides had done it. They had in the course of half an hour freed the closest soldier. At this rate it would take them several days to free them all, and the last saved gnomes would get hungry and thirsty long before they were rescued.

"I think we have made our point," Snazzy said with satisfaction.

They had indeed. "But suppose they attack again, this time underground?"

"We buried some stickum too. They'll have trouble avoiding it. And of course, we'll be guarding the ground where they would be coming up again, slowly. We'll be ready to smear stickum all over them. I doubt they'll try it; it's not worth the effort."

Vinia doubted it too. This sector was secure. No gnomes had been killed, but they would not care to go through this battle again. She turned off the webcam.

"I was wrong to doubt you," Vinia said sincerely. "You really did have it figured out."

"Thank you. Now you'll be moving on to the next sector?"

"Yes. But we can get together again for a party, a physical one maybe this afternoon. With the friends I have made in the course of these contacts."

"You may have to come pick me up for that. I promise not to stickum you."

They both laughed. Then Vinia summoned the map and touched LOVE/HATE.

"Hello again," Lorna Lovebug said, feeling Vinia's arrival. "You're just in time. The humans are coming."

Indeed, they were showing at the far edge of the section, tramping across the slope toward Thanx. Vinia hastily turned the webcam on again and locked in the scene. "I am recording the action." Now she was hovering in a tiny bug, but the cam was with her in that size. Science magic was wonderful!

"Good. We lovebugs are on this side of the field, the hatebugs are arriving on the other side. We figure to close in as we eliminate the humans and encounter each other as we finish. Then Hayes and I will pretend to mate as we sneak off on our own."

Because they were actually two females. Vinia had lost track of that midst the other complications.

Now she looked more closely at the invaders. This was odd. The human soldiers appeared to be armored but unarmed. No swords clubs or guns, not that Mundane guns worked well in Xanth. They also did not look worried. Did they know something the bugs didn't?

"I don't trust this," Vinia said. "Humans are the most dangerous of enemies: Why are they walking blithely into trouble without weapons?"

"I don't know either," Lorna said. "Could they have found out about us?"

"If they did, wouldn't they be carrying nets or something to catch and nullify you without giving you a chance to touch them?"

"I would have thought so. Of course, we do have small cutting spells to slice through fine mesh."

"I think we'll just have to watch and see what happens," Vinia said uneasily.

"One question: you are human. Are you sure you shouldn't be on their side?"

Vinia laughed. "I support Thanx. Humans come in all manner of stripes, and adult male humans are not to be trusted by the likes of me."

"Especially not when a lovebug bites them."

"Especially," Vinia agreed grimly. She still didn't know what the Adult Conspiracy concealed but was pretty sure she didn't want to discover it that way.

"Fortunately, you are here only in spirit, so are in no danger."

"That's right. I was forgetting." But it wasn't much of a relief. Vinia suspected that this battle was going to get plenty ugly all too soon. She still might have to summon Demon Grossclout to bail them out.

The wave of human men didn't even notice the bugs as they forged on into the two swarms. They reached midfield. Then they started swatting themselves as they got bit, still not seeming to realize what was coming.

Lorna took her turn, diving in to sting the elbow of the man who passed her. He swatted, but she was already clear. He moved on, not seeming concerned.

"We can sting more than once but need time between to restore our supply of venom," Lorna said. "So this is rest time for me. It's the same with the hatebugs. Fortunately, there are enough of us in the swarms to take care of all the enemy soldiers."

Then the stung man paused, as others in the vicinity were doing. The venom was taking effect. Slowly he turned to the man next to him, just as the other was doing the same. They came together and kissed. They were in love!

"Let's see how the hatebugs are doing," Lorna said. She flitted on across the field to the other side.

There the men were starting to fight each other. Each one hated his neighbor. They were punching and kicking and swearing, no longer concerned about their mission. They were in hate.

"Good enough," Lorna said. "Now let's check the center."

"Is that different?" Vinia asked.

"When a lovebug stings one man, and a hatebug stings his neighbor, then it gets interesting." She approached two men. "There's a pair now."

They watched as one man approached his neighbor with a smile, while the other responded with a snarl. Suddenly they were clenching each other, one kissing, the other hitting. They fell to the ground, struggling.

"And look at this one," Lorna said zestfully. It was a single man who seemed to be fighting himself, flailing with arms and legs. "He got stung by one of each."

Vinia shuddered. "This is awful—for them." Then she thought of something else. "Suppose they send in couples? Men and women together."

"Hatebug stings would break up those couples in a hurry," Lorna said. "And lovebug stings would make them forgot about invading, in the interest of making love."

She was right. A couples invasion wouldn't work. Then Vinia realized something else: "This first wave must be a test case, to pinpoint the location of the bugs and verify their effect. These men were cynically sacrificed for information. The second wave will come better prepared."

"Smart strategy," Lorna agreed. "But we shall be ready."

Soon the second wave appeared. These men carried nets and wore special goggles to enable them to better spot the bugs. The moment any bugs approached they were swept up in the nets so they were helpless.

"And here's how we handle that," Lorna said. "We swamp them."

They joined the first swamp. Hundreds of bugs formed a cloud and flew at the men, who could catch only a few at a time in the nets. In moments they were stung and rendered helpless.

The third wave came bearing spray guns. Deadly mist spread out in clouds. Any bugs it caught dropped to the ground, dead.

"This is awful," Vinia said. "You are dying like, well, flies."

"But we have a way," Lorna said. "Our suicide squads will stop them."

"Suicide squads!" Vinia exclaimed, appalled. "How can that stop the dying?"

"They are coated in goo. They will jam the nozzles."

They watched from a safe distance as the cloud of suicide bombers flew right to and into the deadly mist, aiming directly for the sprayers. Most fell before they got there, but a few managed to splat directly on the nozzles. The bugs were dead, but the goo soon clogged the spouts, which stopped spraying. The men cursed as they tried to clean them, but the sprayers were hopelessly clogged.

The fourth wave was dressed in wet suits that completely sealed their bodies off from the outside, together with helmets, goggles, and masks that protected their faces. They did not try to attack the bugs; they merely forged on ahead, meaning to cross the section and enter Thanx proper with little delay.

"And, now, our hardened stingers," Lorna said. "They have been specially treated to be able to drill into just about anything."

Sure enough, the suited men were soon loving and hating, ruining their attack.

There was no fifth wave. The men had finally given up. This front, too, had held. And Vinia had it all recorded by the web. She turned it off, satisfied. "Now you can get together with Hayes."

"Yes, if I can find her." Lorna paused, steeling herself. "If she survives. We took a lot of losses."

Now Vinia froze. Hayes could indeed be lost. The two swarms were coming together, and the lovebugs and hatebugs were carefully joining. But was Hayes among them? "I can help," Vinia said. She fissioned into two and focused on her other self.

"Hello, Vinia."

"Oh, Hayes, I'm so relieved! I didn't think to tune in on you during the battle, and then we feared—never mind. Let me guide you to Lorna."

"I'm relieved too. I was concerned she could have perished in the melee."

"She's fine. This way." They flew toward the section where Lorna was. "There she is!"

The two bugs came together, clinging to each other. Then they flew away, linked, exactly like a normal couple. The other bugs paid them no attention, being busy with their own liaisons. *Thank you!* they thought together.

"You're welcome. Now I must organize the party. I will be back in touch soon." She reverted to her own body, merging the six or seven parts of it.

It was finally done. The war was won.

Chapter 11

VIRUS

Vinia approached Queen Demesne in Dragoman's lair. The dragon wasn't there: Vinia suspected that Chloe Centaur was occupying his attention in some private nook. Mature females had a way of doing that when they chose. If only immature females could do the same! "I want to have a party for the seven or eight creatures who really helped me organize the defense," she told the Demoness queen. "Is it all right if we gather here in the lair? It's the most convenient place, until the queendom has its own facilities." Those were still under construction.

"Of course, dear. You and they saved Thanx today. You are certainly entitled to some relaxation."

"I didn't want to disturb you, if you have something else going on."

"No, dear, I don't. I am about to retire for a while, as I seem to have caught a virus that has me feeling glum."

"But Demons don't get viruses!"

"That is part of what bothers me. Perhaps the strain of organizing the queendom has depleted me, and it will pass. I will tell the guards to admit your friends and will ask the princesses to cater your party."

"Oh, they don't need to do that! They have concerns of their own."

"Indeed, they do, and returning some token favor to you is their first priority. You must allow them to express their appreciation for your marvelous endeavors on behalf of their welfare."

Demesne had managed to phrase it in a way Vinia could not refute. "Thank you," she said as the Demoness faded out. What could make a Demoness feel as though she had a virus?

Hula Human appeared. "You performed phenomenally, Vinia. We watched on the screen as it happened. I will do a dance for your party, if you wish, though it will not be as entertaining for females as for males. I will also see to some decorations."

"Thank you. I really don't want to put you to any trouble."

"No trouble, dear. For you and your friends, we are glad to do anything." She walked away.

Cedar Centaur appeared, with tiny Elga Elf perched on his shoulder. Vinia remained privately amazed how they had become a couple. But with love and an accommodation spell anything was possible. "You will need tables, chairs, and a translator," Elga said briskly. She oversaw Maintenance, so naturally knew exactly what she was doing.

"Uh, I guess so," Vinia agreed. "Now that we're physical." These were details she somehow had not thought of before.

They got busy, with the elf directing and the centaur procuring and moving, and in barely three moments the necessary furniture had been set up, with the urn containing the universal translation spell in the center of the table. The two were done before Vinia could properly thank them.

Goblette Goblin and her partner Georgia appeared. "We'll make pastries and anything else your friends want to eat. Nothing is too good for you."

"Uh, thank you. But you really don't need to—" But the goblins were already gone.

Ah, well. Vinia turned her focus inward. The fragmentation effect of the elixir had not yet dissipated, so she was able to do it on her own. She tuned in on each of the six, no seven, no eight friends who had fought the invaders. "Hello all. This is Vinia. I am throwing a party in Dragoman's lair. Go there now, and the guards will let you in. There'll be entertainment and refreshments. Plus, I'll play the recording of your activities I made with the webcam, so that all of you can see what the others did."

"We'll be there," they chorused.

Then Vinia solidified in one place and another to pick up Snazzy Snail and Nimbus Nickelpede.

Ghorgeous Ghost joined her in her body. "Oh, it's so nice having a living host! I've been dead entirely too long. I have gravely missed the sheer physicality of the living state."

"Uh, yes." Yet as the ghost arrived, Vinia felt odd. Was something the matter with her? Like a virus?

"No, dear, not at all," Ghorgeous said, reading her thought. Vinia realized that she was unpracticed in hosting and didn't know how to keep her thoughts private. "Look in a mirror."

Vinia walked to the wall where there was a large mirror. There stood a lovely young woman who looked somehow familiar.

"Let me explain," Ghorgeous said. "I am a grown woman. Now that my spirit is in you, you have assumed the form you will be when you are my age. You are a grown woman, too. You are also familiar with the secrets of the dread Adult Conspiracy."

Vinia realized it was true. Suddenly she knew what it was all about! "Is that all?" she asked, disappointed.

"It is indeed," the ghost agreed. "Hardly worth tormenting children about, is it! Maybe one day they will abolish that foolish convention." She was Mundane, but it seemed that the Conspiracy was there, too.

"Hardly worth," Vinia agreed. It wasn't even all that interesting. But her body—it was beautiful!

"But when I depart your body, you will revert to your normal age and knowledge. Then you'll be frustrated all over again, physically and emotionally."

Vinia doubted that but didn't care to argue. She would surely remember and keep it to herself. If nothing else, she would remember that it wasn't worth obsessing about.

"Where would you like to be?" she asked Snazzy and Nimbus. "On a table or a wall? The other girls are larger than you are."

"I prefer to remain with you," Snazzy Snail answered. "You are bound to be the center of the action." The translation spell was operating nicely: it was just as if the snail were speaking vocally, when she had neither lungs nor verbal language. "I will stick to your right shoulder, if it is all right with you."

"That's fine," Vinia agreed, putting her there.

"I, too," Nimbus Nickelpede said, similarly vocal. "I will perch on your left shoulder."

"Okay." Vinia put her there. There was a faint smell of stink horn, but she remembered how it had foiled the goblins, and that made it almost pleasant.

Now the other girls arrived. First the two lovebugs flew in, and after brief discussion perched on Vinia's head. Then the salamander scrambled along the floor and perched on the back of a chair. Then Fiera Fire Cloud walked in, in her human girl form. Finally, the siren arrived, in a special wheeled tank so that her tail could soak in comfort.

It was time for introductions. "Hello, all," Vinia said. "I am Vinia, whom you have met astrally. I am looking older than I am, because I am hosting an adult spirit. Here in me is Ghorgeous Ghost."

She paused, and the ghost took control of her body. "I have to borrow Vinia as host, because I have no physical presence. I was murdered the night before my wedding and have been dead almost ten years. Vinia rescued us from being locked in the place we died. Now my girlfriends and I are haunting a house here in Thanx, and any and all of you are welcome to visit, as friends. We promise not to frighten you too badly."

"Hello, Ghorgeous," the others chorused, not at all frightened.

The ghost returned the body to Vinia. "This is Snazzy Snail," she said, nodding toward her right shoulder.

"Hello," Snazzy said.

"What a beautiful shell!" the mermaid said. The others chorused agreement. The ghost and the siren had met the snail before, but were glad to compliment her in public.

Snazzy blushed, turning her shell momentarily pink. "Thank you."

Snazzy did not tell how the snails had stopped the gnomes, so Vinia took the initiative. "Maybe she's too modest to describe their campaign against the gnomes, so I'll do it. They put stickum on the ground that caught the gnomes' feet, and they stuck tight and couldn't move. The gnomides are having to lasso them and haul them out one by one. They'll never mess with snails again. You'll see that happen when we play the webcam recording." The audience applauded. They liked the idea of sticking it to the invaders.

Vinia indicated the girl on her left shoulder. "This is Nimbus Nickelpede."

"Oh, my, you look good enough to eat," Nimbus said, to laughter. "It is good to meet you as friends. We nickelpedes don't have many friends."

Goblette and Georgia Goblin entered, carrying a tray of refreshments. "We tried to get delicacies for every taste," Goblette said. "But we're not sure what ghosts eat, or lovebugs, or fire spirits."

"About lovebugs," Vinia said. "You should meet Lorna and Hayes, both female. They're a couple. Just like you."

"Oh, my!" Goblette said. "We didn't know."

The two bugs flew up to perch on the two goblins' extended hands. "We couldn't come out until after the battle," Lorna said from Goblette's hand.

"We're so glad to meet you," Hayes said from Georgia's hand. "Openly. We've been in hiding."

"We know how that is," Georgia said. "Straights can be so cruel."

"You must visit again, after today," Goblette said. "We surely have notes to compare."

Vinia saw that new friendships were forming. She was pleased. "Why don't you two stay for the rest of the party," she suggested to the goblins, who remained with the bugs.

The introductions resumed. Sali Salamander, Fiera Cloud, and Signal Siren were acknowledged. Then Signal sipped the beverage. "This is the finest honey drink I've ever tasted. What is it?"

"Mead flavored with Heaven-Can-Wait honey," Goblette answered. "Our bee allies let us have a little."

"Let me try that," Fiera said. "In this compact form I can eat and drink, though I lose it when I revert to my natural form."

Signal held out the cup, and Fiera sipped. "Oh, you're right! Makes me wish I were mortal."

Then they watched the replay of the sixfold invasion and the defenses, applauding the several devices used to foil the soldiers. "What a lovely ploy, that dragon mother bit," Signal said.

"As was yours, with the panties," Ghorgeous returned.

"I hate to say it," Goblette said, "But I loved seeing those goblin troops get stunk!"

"And the way you snails stopped the gnomes was truly impressive," Fiera said. "I never much noticed snails before, but I'll make sure not to burn any hereafter."

The party dissolved into a happy confusion of spot dialogues. They were indeed becoming friends, despite being of widely different species.

Then Demon Grossclout appeared. "Oh, yes, you belong here too," Vinia said. "You made it all possible. You had the contacts."

The others applauded, agreeing. This was a girls' party, but they all appreciated the way the Demon had helped them, individually and collectively. Signal, Ghorgeous, and Fiera even went into flirting mode.

"Thank you," the professor said tightly. "But I am here on other business."

They sobered. "What is it?" Vinia asked.

"Something is wrong with Demesne. She has turned submissive."

Uh-oh. "She was feeling poorly an hour ago," Vinia said. "She didn't know whether it was overwork or a virus, so she was going to rest."

"Yes. I joined her there. She was completely amenable. Too amenable. She would not deny me anything. That's not like her. She is normally very much her own woman and will tell me exactly what is and is not acceptable. Now she has no limits of her own: I govern completely. That is not the creature I love. There is indeed a virus. I did spot research on it. It's a new one, with no known antidote in Magician Ion's collection. It causes a woman, any woman, to lose all ability to deny a man, any man, anything. It was surreptitiously introduced by the surrounding kingdoms, under the cover of the invasion. This is the real attack on the feminist queendom. I fear it is spreading. Therefore, I must ask you ladies to depart immediately, lest it catch you. We shall have to isolate any woman who catches it. Demesne is amenable to that, too, herself included."

"But who will defend the queendom?" Vinia asked, alarmed.

He made a humorless smile. "We males will have to defend it for the interim, until we discover the antidote. It is ironic, but we did not join the princesses merely for their beauty. We like their spirit, which is now being dissipated."

An unhappy look passed around and through the girls. None of them were submissive types. Then they bid hasty adieus and departed. Vinia helped those who needed it. The friendships remained, but the party had crashed.

Now Vinia and Grossclout were alone. "But I was talking with her right before the party," she said. "I was exposed. I should be catching it. But I don't feel submissive. How long does it take?"

"We don't yet know. But the chances are that you are immune to it, at least for the time being. Because you are juvenile. We have found no cases of underage girls catching it. And of course, no men or boys. It is highly selective. Mature females only, albeit of all types, Demonesses and ghosts included."

"But what about when I mature? I'm twelve; it could happen next year or sooner, regardless what the bleeping Adult Conspiracy claims." Vinia was back to her juvenile form, now that the ghost had departed. And realized that she had forgotten the adult secrets she had known moments before, to her consternation. She had come to some sort of conclusion about them, but that, too, had dissipated. The bleeping Conspiracy was still in ugly force.

"True. You are on the verge. Remember, the virus causes an emotional change, not a physical one. As long as you don't know the adult secrets, you should be safe."

Her juvenile frustration was now her prime defense? What irony! "Hilda will soon be vulnerable too. What should we do?"

"Vinia," he said seriously, addressing her as an equal. That would have thrilled her at any other time. "You have done so much for us! It seems unkind to ask you for yet more."

She laughed bitterly. "I have to save my independent attitude. I'm doing it for me, too, whatever it is."

"I do not know either. In any event I must stay with Demesne, to protect her from her own present nature, and help organize the defense against the second invasion that is sure to come once the kingdoms are satisfied that the feminists have been thoroughly submissioned. We need to take immediate action."

"*What* action?"

"You must go back to the Good Magician Humfrey. He is, after all, the Magician of Information. He will know."

Vinia nodded. "That does make sense. We'll go there. I'll tell the others."

"They already know and are preparing. I informed them before I came here."

"Then I am on my way." Vinia headed off to the carpet, as the Demon popped off to rejoin the Demoness.

The others were indeed ready. Vinia hopped on board and the carpet took off. Soon they were flying rapidly toward the Good Magician's Castle.

"It's good to be back together," Hilda said. "We missed you, Vinia."

"It was only an hour for the facets of the invasion, then the party." But Vinia was relieved too. She had been excruciatingly busy and needed to rest.

Hilda smiled. "It seemed like six times as long." They had of course been watching the webcam pictures.

"I don't want to ask anything of you, Vinia," Ion said. "Considering the threat of the virus."

"So I will ask it of you," Vinia said. "Lie down with me. Kiss my ear. Whisper sweet nothings. Be amenable."

He laughed. "I'm amenable!" He followed her orders precisely.

"Do likewise," Hilda ordered Benny. He fastened the steering stick in place and obeyed.

After an hour Vinia checked in with the queendom via the ring. "Demesne?"

"I am here," the Demoness answered. "We have set up a rotation so that the others can participate. Chloe is connecting the others telepathically, as she did before. We are all interested in your progress."

"Good enough. I will try to report regularly, as long as I have the ring." But she realized with sudden regret that she might not have it much longer, because she had to return it to Dara Demoness.

"You do that, dear."

If she could.

In due course they reached the castle. Benny returned to the control and guided it down to the ground. "Who tackles the Challenges this time?" he asked.

"We all do," Hilda said. "Vinia did it before, but now it's our turn. We have to leave our own magic behind: it's the rule." She set aside her needles and cloth and determinedly led the way forward, maybe demonstrating that she had not been caught by any virus. Benny set aside his thinking cap and followed, and then Ion without his bag of vials and Vinia walking together in lockstep, as was their wont. At least her telekinesis was still working, though she was pretty sure it wouldn't touch anything else.

A figure loomed before her. "Oh, no," she muttered. "I am not partial to zombies. I know they have their functions, such as guarding Castle Roogna, but I never much liked them."

Because the figure was a zombie in armor. It wore a plaque saying KNIGHT OF THE LIVING DEAD.

"That's the zombie king's champion," Ion said. "What's it doing here?"

"It must have had a Question for the Good Magician," Vinia said. "Now it is serving out its Service."

"What could a zombie want to know?" Benny asked. "Their minds are rotten."

"Maybe how to get the rot out," Hilda said impatiently. She stepped to one side, but the knight stepped that way too, blocking her. "Ugh," she muttered. "Its eyes are not rotten, though."

The truth was that nobody much liked zombies. Hilda was typical in that respect. That was part of what made them good guardians. But Hilda had a point: there was rot all over the knight's body, showing between the joints of its armor, but its eyes were sharp. In fact, it seemed to be looking with entirely too much interest at both Hilda and Vinia. Would it try to kiss one of them? UGH!

"There has to be a way to get around it," Ion said. "The Challenge is to find it."

"I know that," Hilda snapped. "But what?" She halted just before she collided with a large red can sitting beside the path.

"Uh-oh," Ion said. "That could be an innocent can, waiting for someone to come kick it, as in a game. But it might also be *The* Can."

"*The* Can?" Hilda asked, complete with capitals and italics.

"The one you kick when you want to end it all. It can lurk in unlikely places."

"Now what would *The* Can want with the Good Magician?" Hilda demanded. "It is not in the business of asking questions."

"Good point," Vinia said. "So maybe this is some other can."

"Well, it's in my way," Hilda said. She kicked it clear.

Only the can didn't fly. It fragmented into a dozen or so smaller cans, which in turn puffed into red smoke. Then the puffs formed into a line of quite shapely young women wearing short bright red cans in lieu of skirts. They were dancing. In a moment they kicked their legs high, flashing white panties.

"Oh, for sobbing out thunderously!" Hilda said. "They're Can-Can dancers!"

"Can-Can Cans," Vinia agreed.

The boys made no comment. Both girls glanced at them, as this was the sort of show the crude male gender preferred.

Both boys were frozen in place, Benny by himself, Ion supported by Vinia. They had freaked out. Theoretically they were too young, at least

Ion was, but the sheer number and quality of panties flashed at point-blank range had evidently overwhelmed them.

Vinia looked at the zombie knight. It too was frozen. Its eyes had functioned too well, and it had freaked out also.

Hilda, disgusted, raised her hand to snap her fingers, ending the trance. Vinia grabbed her hand. "Don't!" she hissed.

"What?"

"The knight is frozen too. Don't wake it until we are safely past it."

"Oh."

They carefully took hold of the boys, lowered them to the ground, and dragged them slowly past the statuelike knight. Vinia might have made Ion walk, but it seemed too complicated while he was unconscious. Only when they were all safely past did Hilda finally snap her fingers.

Ion and Benny woke. So did the zombie knight. All three looked confused.

"What happened?" Ion asked.

"The Can-Can Cans flashed you with their panties and you freaked out," Vinia explained. "But it got us past the zombie, whose eyes were too good for his welfare."

"Panties? Oh, let's see," Ion said, leaning forward. He could do that, because only his legs were crippled.

Vinia hauled him back. "No, you don't!" she said unsubmissively. "Lest you freak out again."

"But we're missing—"

"I've got panties too. Once we're grown, I'll freak you out all you want. You haven't missed anything except trouble."

"Oh." But he looked disappointed. Males were incorrigible.

"Same to you, goat boy," Hilda told Benny. "Now you lead the way; I took my turn." She pushed him to the head of their little line. They resumed their progress.

In only a few steps they came to something odd. It was a small creature with white fur and a bunny tail for a head, and whiskers on its rear side. It seemed harmless, but what was it? The four of them paused, staring.

"It's actually a reflection," Vinia said after a good moment and three-quarters. "See, there's a glass wall, and a normal rabbit beside the glass."

"So there is," Ion agreed. "But its reflection is strangely reversed, with the tail where the head should be."

"It's a tibbar," Hilda said. "Rabbit spelled backward."

"And look at our reflections," Benny said. "Weird!"

Now they looked into the glass at themselves. He was right. Vinia looked like a brown boy in a white dress; she was able to identify herself by pointing to her reflection, even though the reflection reacted by pointing away from her. Also, because she was right next to Ion: they were arm in arm. The others were similarly rearranged, with Ion sporting a pair of feet where his head should be, and Hilda's skirt on her head and her face on her bottom.

"So it's the glass," Benny said. "Do we need to get past it? That's not hard. He walked around the edge of the wall to its other side. "Not much of a Challenge."

"So it must be the answer to a Challenge," Vinia said. "Now we just need to find the Challenge."

Ion laughed. "So the glass reverses even that."

"The Challenge must be close," Benny said, "because the answer to it should be in range of it, if we can just recognize it."

"Maybe before it," Vinia said. "So we have to remember it was there."

They walked around the wall. There ahead was another oddity: it seemed to be a garden growing eyeballs. Some were huge, others dainty, many colors ranging from white to black with all shades between. They seemed to be of several species, including human. All were wide awake, staring at the visiting party disconcertingly as they waved on their stems. The path led right through the garden, but the eyes were leaning over it from either side, making passage difficult without brushing into them. Here must be the Challenge: to get past the garden without disturbing any plants. But what was hazardous about them? They looked weird but seemed harmless.

"Hey, this could be fun," Benny said. He reached out to pluck a deep brown one.

"Don't—" Vinia started warningly. But of course, she was too late. He was already touching the stem.

The eyeball was shaken loose from the stem, but it didn't fall. Instead it hovered in the air, eyeing Benny. "Oh, it stinks!" he exclaimed, backing away from it.

The eye followed him. Now the others smelled it. It wasn't as bad an odor as stink horn, but it was definitely bad news. Evidently the smell came when it came loose, because the other eyeballs didn't reek similarly.

"It's going to dirty me," Benny said, grabbing a leafy branch to brush the eye away. "It's a stink eye!"

That was it. The garden was filled with stink eyes, which could smirch a person merely by staring at him. If they had plowed into that garden, they would have been soiled all over.

"We've got to stop it," Hilda said, alarmed. "But how?"

That was the question. They had not blundered into the full garden, but the one stink eye was sickeningly oriented on Benny and would soon make him smell worse than a, well, billy goat. He was holding it off now, but it would soon get around his branch and tag him.

"There has to be an antidote," Ion said.

"The reverse glass!" Vinia said. "We almost forgot it despite knowing it was the answer to something."

They retreated to the glass wall, the stink eye following, keeping its glare on Benny. The leaves on his branch were curling up under the intensity of it: they would not shield him much longer.

Hilda gazed at it. "Now what?"

"Maybe it can reflect and reverse the eye," Vinia said.

"But it's here, and the eyes are there," Ion protested.

Benny made a gesture as of putting on his thinking cap, though he didn't have it at the moment. Nevertheless, he seemed to get an idea. It was as if ideas were all in the head, Vinia thought. "Maybe I can take a piece of it." He reached out and took hold of the edge of the wall, jiggling it. A section came loose.

"It's in sections!" Ion said. "It comes apart!"

Benny aimed the section at the stink eye. The reflection showed a much prettier and sweet-smelling eyeball. Vinia wasn't sure how she knew it was sweet: maybe it was the little heart-shaped rose leaves surrounding it.

The eye recoiled in horror. "Haa!" Benny said, pursuing it. "Can't take a nice smell, eh, stinker?"

The eyeball retreated toward the garden, with Benny following. The other three of them, acting as one, grabbed more sections of glass and followed Benny.

They formed a phalanx and advanced on the garden, holding their glasses menacingly before them. The eyeballs saw them coming and leaned desperately away from their own horrendously nice reflections. The path cleared.

The group of them marched on through, shielded on either side by their sections of reverse glass. Soon they were safely on the other side. The sections of glass dissipated into mist. So did the loose stink eye. They had navigated the second Challenge.

"That was a relief," Hilda said. "I would have hated to have you smell like a billy goat, Benny."

"Ha," he said, not completely amused by this reference to his alternate half. "Ha. Ha."

She kissed him. "Not yet, anyway. Wait till we're adults and have hormones."

Benny seemed mollified.

"My turn," Ion said bravely. He took the lead and walked down the path.

The path split. One fork led to a group of talkative women who looked like mothers at a gossip session. The other led to a seemingly ordinary man who was just standing there.

"Obviously the man is the better bet," Ion said. "Women can talk your ear off."

His sister opened her mouth to make a retort, but closed it again, appreciating the justice of his assessment. They didn't want their ears falling off, here where things just might be literal.

They approached the man. He certainly did not seem much like a Challenge. But he did block the path.

"Hello," Ion said. "I am Prince Ion, and these are my companions."

"I am a Were," the man replied, pronouncing it "where," but of course they heard the spelling.

"Where what?" Just in case that was the correct spelling.

"Were Big Foot."

The four exchange a puzzled glance. Did this make any sense? It did not seem to be a question or a direction. Maybe the man knew where Big Foot was.

"May we pass by you?" Ion asked politely.

"No," the man said, suddenly expanding into a huge hairy monster with monstrously giant hairy feet.

"Were Big Foot!" Vinia said, belatedly getting it. "Like werewolf."

"Oh, my," Ion said. "And if we try to proceed farther this way, we'll get stepped on."

"And squished," the Were Big Foot agreed, licking his lips. Evidently, he liked stepping on folk, when he got the chance. Vinia knew that some folk were like that.

They hastily retreated, and Big Foot contracted back into the ordinary man, who looked disappointed. He really had wanted to do some serious stomping. This was obviously the path, and the third Challenge.

"How do we stop him from stomping us?" Ion asked, frustrated.

"It must have to do with the garrulous women," Hilda said.

"I was afraid of that."

But they seemed to have no choice, so they took the other fork and approached the women. "Halt, intruders!" the nearest one called, spying them.

"Why?" Ion asked somewhat timorously, holding his hands near his ears as if to catch them if they fell off.

"You're not our kind. Your girls are too young to have much juicy gossip, and your boys are too young to be gossiped about. Go."

Ion began to get annoyed. "Why should our youth count against us? There are more things in Xanth than gossip."

She did not bother with further reasoning. "Because I said so."

They paused for another shared glance. "There has to be some sense here somewhere, doesn't there?" Hilda asked.

"If we can just figure it out," Vinia agreed. Then she got an idea. "That woman stopped us with an unanswerable reason. Is that the secret? Could we use it ourselves?"

Ion nodded. "Great idea! When we grow up, remind me to kiss you before you freak me out with your newly potent panties."

Vinia saw an opportunity. She grabbed it. "How long before?"

He looked puzzled. "Does it matter?"

"You didn't put a time limit on it. This is before. Maybe years before, but before. Kiss me now."

He remained confused. "Now? Why?"

"Because I said so."

Hilda laughed. "She got you, Ion. You're stuck for it."

"I'm stuck," he agreed. He turned to face Vinia and kissed her.

Vinia loved it, and she knew Ion did too. If flirting like this was this much fun now, what would it be like when they were grown?

They returned to the Were Big Foot. "Stand aside and let us pass, WBF," Ion said sternly.

The Were BF transformed, lifting a giant foot menacingly. "Why should I do that?" he demanded. "When it's so much easier to stomp you."

"Because I said so."

"Oh, bleep! You found the gossip gaggle." He stood aside, reverting to harmlessness.

They walked on past him. They were through the third Challenge.

Then Vinia paused, facing back. She had another idea. "You know, Were BF, some of those women are sort of pretty. You could ask one for a date. If she asks why, you can say . . ." She trailed off.

The Were brightened. "You're right! It should work on them too, at least while this set remains in play. They've been teasing me for hours. Some *are* pretty. Thanks."

"You're welcome." She turned to rejoin the others, mildly bemused by the fact that to a typical man, all that mattered in a woman was her appearance. She could have the mind of a cockroach and he wouldn't care. Fortunately Ion wasn't like that; he noticed appearance, but it was just window-shopping. She hoped.

"You'll be downright dangerous when you grow up," Ion murmured. "I am looking forward to it."

"So am I." They squeezed each other's waists.

The castle gate was ahead of them. They seemed to have bypassed the moat again. Too bad; Vinia would to have liked to see the moat monster.

A small side door opened as they approached the wall of the castle. A nondescript woman of indeterminate ago stood there. "Hello, all; I am Wira, the Good Magician's daughter-in-law. No need to introduce yourselves: I know who you are. Do come in."

They trooped into the castle, Ion and Vinia in their usual lockstep. Wira showed them into the same pleasant living room where Dara Demoness had been before. Vinia was disappointed not to see her there, but of course there might now be a different Designated Wife. "Take your seats," Wira said. "I will inform Magician Humfrey of your presence." She quietly departed.

Now Vinia said it as she sank into an easy chair beside Ion. "I'm sorry not to see Dara Demoness here. I liked her, and she really helped me. Helped us all, especially with the ring, which I must now return to her."

"That ring made all the difference," Hilda said. "I don't think we could have found all the princes for the princesses without it."

"And the good luck it brought was great," Benny said. "I really didn't get to know Dara personally, but she was a great hostess while we were here."

"There must be another Designated Wife here now," Vinia said. "But I'm glad it was Dara, last time."

"Thank you, all," Dara's voice came. "I remain here. It has been less than a month since you last visited."

They looked around. It seemed to be coming from the couch Ion and Vinia were sitting on. "Where are you, Dara?" Vinia asked.

Then she got goosed by the cushion. So did Ion. They jumped up together, laughing, propelled by her telekinesis. The Demoness had had her little joke.

The vacated couch dissolved into smoke, then formed into the Designated Wife. "It is good to see you again. I'm glad you made it through the Challenges in good order; Humfrey would not have let you in otherwise. He is of the old school; standard protocol must be followed." She grimaced cutely. "He was grumpy with me when I bypassed some of it with you before. It took some doing to degrump him." She made a little flirt of her hips as her skirt went translucent.

Vinia put her hand to the invisible ring as she and Ion took another seat together. "I must return this to you, now that it's done its job, though I am sad to part with it."

The Demoness shook her head. "Keep it, dear; your need for it is not yet over. It really was on loan to me, and now it is on loan to you."

"Yes, Demon Grossclout recognized it." Vinia was immensely relieved, as the ring had largely sustained her in the interim. Then she thought of something. "Would you like to talk to your friend Demesne? She is now the queen of the Queendom of Thanx."

"Why, that is very thoughtful of you, dear. Yes, please put her on."

"Demesne," Vinia said to the ring.

She answered immediately. "Hello, Vinia. Did you reach the Good Magician's Castle all right?"

"Yes. In fact I have Dara Demoness here. You can talk with her."

"Hello again, Demesne!" Dara said. "So much has changed since we were together."

"So much indeed ! Has Vinia told you of the virus?"

"She didn't need to. The Good Magician informed us when it struck. It's a mean one. How are you feeling?"

"Actually I feel normal. Except that I am now totally unable to say no to a male. Any male. It is the same with the other princesses. Our princes are defending us. They prefer us as we were, despite our complete submission to their desires. Grossy is protecting me."

"So you finally nabbed Grossy! I remember you had a crush on him."

"Still do. So I set about winning him."

"And when a Demoness sets about winning a man, any man, he's doomed." Dara formed into an excruciatingly sexy creature in filmy underwear.

"And the irony is, they don't mind it," Demesne agreed. They laughed together.

"Well, the children are here, getting ready to go after the virus antidote. Prince Ion will bring it back once they get it. Then things should get back to normal. You'll be able to tease your princes to distraction."

"Yes. As it is now, they know we can't ever say no to them, so teasing doesn't work. They seem to have mixed feelings about that."

"There's no understanding male reactions." They laughed again.

Ion, Hilda, and Benny had been completely silent, letting Vinia handle it. Vinia enjoyed having the two Demonesses act just like normal women.

Wira returned. "The Good Magician will see you now."

"Go," Dara told them. "Nice talking with you, Demesne."

"Yes. For a moment I could almost forget the virus." She faded out.

They followed Wira up a winding stairway to a small chamber almost filled by a giant tome. This, Vinia knew, was the Book of Answers. Behind it sat the gnomelike Good Magician.

"These are the querents," Wira told him.

"Thank you, dear." The Good Magician was reputed to be insufferably grumpy almost all the time, but there was no grumpiness when he addressed Wira. What was her secret? Then Vinia remembered: she was said to be the nicest person in Xanth. That must have had its impact, even here.

"Ask your Question," Wira told them.

"First we need to know the required Service," Hilda said. "In case it is prohibitive." She was still demonstrating that she had not been infected by any submission virus. She was a princess and a Sorceress in her own right, and not unduly awed by Humfrey.

Humfrey looked up with his sunken eyes. He was reputed to use youthening elixir to maintain his age at an even one hundred years, and he looked it. "Your Service is to accomplish your mission, which is of considerable importance in itself."

Oh. "If you already know about it, why do we have to ask you?" Ion asked.

"Protocol," Wira whispered.

Ion nodded. They had been warned. "How can we get the antidote to the submission virus?"

"That is a secret possessed only by the Lips tribe. They are attractive women with outsize lips. You must meet their leader, Queen Apoca, and persuade her to share the secret with you, or to provide you with a sample. The ring will enable you to get in touch with her, but there is danger. Their territory is a war zone. Proceed cautiously and indirectly, so as not to betray Apoca's location to the enemy."

"Enemy?" Hilda asked. "Who is it?"

"The Male Volents. Violent males who want to conquer and possess the Lips without being tamed by them. Any male a Lips kisses becomes her love slave. But if the males can catch Lips women without getting kissed, and infect them with the submission virus, they win. Neither side wants to kill the other, merely to master or mistress them as the case may be."

"This doesn't sound like a mission for children," Ion said.

"It is for children because they are immune to the adult hormones that are in play. But proceed carefully, because not all the Volents honor the Adult Conspiracy."

Vinia shuddered. She could not remember the detail she had known briefly when Ghorgeous Ghost joined her, but she knew it could be ugly when applied by force or to children.

The Good Magician's gaze returned to the tome. They had been dismissed.

Chapter 12

VOLENTS

They were on their way again, the carpet sailing over the landscape on the heading indicated by the Good Magician. Vinia spoke to the ring. "Thanx Officer of the Hour," she said as the others went silent. She was trusting that the ring would understand without having to have a specific name. The princesses had set up a rotation, so as to have one of them always on duty for this contact, day and night.

"Hello, Vinia!" Goblette's voice answered. "How are you doing? I ask not merely from politeness, but because we desperately need your success."

Surely so. "You sound all right," Vinia said.

"That's because I am talking to a young woman. The virus has spread despite our precautions, and infected us all, and we know that the moment a man comes, any man, we will be helpless to oppose his slightest whim. And of course his whim will be to take us to bed and do unspeakable things to us, and Georgia and I are lesbians! What utter horror." She was near tears, a signal of her submissive nature. In the old days she would have been angry and defiant.

Vinia assimilated that. Women who preferred women, being victimized by men. That did seem to make it worse. "I'm sorry."

"Not your fault, of course. But we pray you will return with the antidote elixir soon. No enemy men have intruded yet, but we know they will as soon as they are satisfied that the submission virus has done its awful job. The princes are on guard, but they can't stay awake around the clock. An enemy man might sneak in, and we couldn't even cry the alarm, if he told us not to. He could ravish us both without resistance, then go on to abuse the others." There was an audible shudder. "We hope you can return by nightfall."

So being submissive did not mean that they liked it, though they might have to pretend to like it if the man wanted it that way. He might even prefer to have them weeping, helpless in the face of his masculine dominance. Vinia knew there were men like that. Not the princes, but they were exceptions who actually preferred independent women.

"We are on our way to see one Queen Apoca, of the Lips tribe," Vinia said.

"The Lips? I don't recognize the name."

"They are new to us, too. I think it is a newly formed group. The Good Magician said that they have the secret of the cure for the virus, and she is the one to talk with."

"Oh, yes!"

"We are making good time on the carpet and should be there this afternoon."

"That is so good to hear!"

The contact ended. The others had heard. They knew how important this was. The virus had already taken over the queendom.

Vinia thought of something. "Does that virus infect other females, like the nickelpedes and ghosts?"

"We gather it does," Hilda said grimly. "We suspect that females all over Thanx are being exploited by their males."

Vinia winced. Poor Signal, Nimbus, Sali, Ghorgeous, Snafu, Lorna, and Hayes! Maybe even Fiera Fire Cloud.

"And by males of other species too," Ion said.

Worse yet. Vinia hoped the males did not have accommodation spells that would enable them to have at any females at all.

They were approaching the Lips zone, as marked on Hilda's new map. "Is it time to contact Apoca?" Vinia asked. "We are getting close, I think."

"Go ahead," Hilda said. "She's the one we have to talk with."

Vinia nerved herself and spoke the name to the ring. "Queen Apoca." She hoped she would get through, and that the queen would condescend to talk with her.

There was a moment of static. Then a voice answered. "Did someone say my name? I don't see anyone."

"Hello," Vinia said. "I am Vinia Human, a girl child from the Queendom of Thanx. I have a ring on loan from a Demoness that enables me to contact anyone. Good Magician Humfrey told us to contact you."

"Humfrey! I thought I had stayed off that gnome's radar."

Vinia chuckled, feeling more at home. "That's hard to do. He's the Magician of Information."

"I should have kissed him when I had the chance."

Now Vinia laughed. "And made him your love slave? His five and a half wives might have objected."

"So you do know something about me."

So Apoca had been testing her. "A little. He said you have the antidote for the dread submission virus that is infecting the princesses of Thanx. We need to get it from you."

"Unlikely."

"Please, their need is desperate. They are surrounded by brute patriarch kingdoms that want to destroy their feminist queendom. The virus is wiping them out. Without the antidote they can't even fight. We have got to get it from you. We'll offer a fair trade. What do you want?"

"It's more complicated than that. I can't help you."

"But please! It's our only chance. Name your price."

"Sorry." Apoca clicked off.

"That went well," Hilda said ironically. "She doesn't want to share, even to save the queendom."

"Maybe there's something else going on," Ion said thoughtfully. "She did say it was complicated."

"She did not sound unfriendly," Benny said. "Maybe she would help if she could, but she can't."

"Then we need to discover what is balking her, and fix it," Ion said.

"You boys just like the sound of her voice," Hilda said. "It's really sexy."

Neither Ion nor Benny argued the case. Vinia remembered that Ion already had male ambitions, and that Benny's goat half was considered mature, so could be affected by adult nuances.

"We are supposed to approach her indirectly," Vinia said. "So as not to give away her location to the enemy, those Volents."

"Maybe that's the complication," Benny said. "If the enemy is listening in, and she knows it, she could not be too encouraging."

"That seems reasonable to me," Ion agreed.

"So I will loop around and try to zero in on her from the far side." Benny sent the carpet into a wide turn. "Let me know where she is."

Vinia focused on the ring. "Location, Apoca," she murmured. A glint showed on one side. "To our left, a moderate distance."

They continued the slow turn, keeping the glint on the left. When they were halfway around the loop, meaning they had gotten beyond the queen, they turned back and headed directly in, keeping low, almost scraping the ground, to be, as Ion put it, below the radar.

And got caught in something. The carpet stalled, and the four of them were frozen in place. "Children!" a man's voice came, sounding disappointed. "No buxom babes."

"Dam," another said. Vinia wasn't sure how a barrier to hold back the water in a river related to children on a carpet.

"Well, we can change them, once we get the junk. Haul them off that floating rug. We don't need that."

Then four ugly men threw lassos over them, caught them, and yanked them off the carpet. They were quickly trussed up and carried into a building and into a cell, where they were unceremoniously dumped on the stone floor. A metal door was slammed shut as the men departed, and a plank dropped into place to bar it shut.

They were abruptly captive. By the enemy, by the look of it. Maybe it was a trap set to catch anyone who approached Queen Apoca's residence. How long would the four of them be left here before someone in authority arrived and the real mischief commenced?

"What did they mean by junk?" Hilda asked nervously.

"It's adult slang for magic drinks that change people," Benny said. "I think they mean to use them on us. We'd better get out of here before they do."

They were not completely helpless. Ion managed to get a hand into his bag of vials. He brought one out and worked it open with his thumb. Vapor emerged, surrounded him, and the ropes around him dissolved. Hilda got a sewing needle in her hand and used it to magically pry open a knot. Benny changed to goat form and stepped out of bindings that no longer snugly fit him.

Vinia made a mental note: their Volent captors evidently did not realize that they had caught a Magician, a Sorceress, and a crossbreed. Meanwhile Vinia used her telekinesis to carefully untie her own ropes, so that she was free about the same time as the others.

But they remained confined in a cell with a stout metal door. That might be more of a challenge.

But not a sufficient one. Vinia went to the door and used her telekinesis to lift the plank clear on the far side, then pushed it open. There was a hall, with another door at the far end.

"Let me check for a route," Benny said. He changed to buck form and charged down the hall. He reached the far door, changed back to human form, opened it, reverted to goat, and ran on, his hooves clicking on the stone.

"He's such a dear," Hilda said fondly.

"He's a goat, not a deer," Ion said, teasing her. She ignored that.

Vinia returned to Ion, and they stood and walked in the direction Benny had gone. Hilda walked beside them, looking around. There was nothing special to see: it was just a garden-variety dungeon passage.

There was the sound of an *Ooof!* farther ahead.

Benny returned and resumed man form. "There's a way out, I think. But the bad men are returning. I butted one in the gut, but the others avoided me. They're coming this way. Now they're on guard, knowing we're loose. I'm sorry."

"Not your fault, dear," Hilda said, kissing his cheek. "We'll handle them." She brought out needle and cloth and started sewing.

"We will," Ion agreed. He brought out a vial and held it unopened.

The men came toward them, clubs at the ready. "Now you tykes turn about and go back into your cell and you won't get hurt," one said.

"How the bleep did you get loose?" another demanded.

Hilda put on her best innocent-girl expression as she walked directly toward him, Vinia and Ion following closely. "Oh, sir, how glad we are to see you! Some mean men put us in a cell, but we managed to escape. Please help us get out of here before they return."

The men were taken aback. The children thought they were their rescuers? "Uh, well—"

Then they were close enough. Ion opened his vial. "Hold your breath," he whispered.

The other three obliged, knowing what was coming. Mist spread out from the vial, forming a cloud surrounding them and the men.

The men inhaled, not realizing. And sank to the floor, unconscious.

Benny hauled them by limp hands and feet, making a pile of them.

Hilda did some magically fast sewing, and soon had a thin cord that she wrapped around the fallen men. Vinia knew that when they woke, they would find themselves securely restrained, unable even to call for help. The pacification cord was like that. Like the submission virus, only inanimate.

They resumed breathing and walked on. They came to a closed door, but this one did not seem to have a bar in place. It had a lock, and they didn't have the key. Maybe one of the men had the key, but maybe they had been let in by someone else. Vinia's telekinesis was too crude to pick a lock.

"Let me try," Benny said. He changed back to buck form, drew away from the door, then charged it with his head down. He crashed into it at full force.

The door budged on its hinges but did not give way. Benny butted it again, and it budged a little more. The third time, the door crashed off the hinges and fell on the floor. "You did it!" Hilda said, patting his back.

They resumed travel and soon emerged from the building. It was late afternoon; their capture and escape had taken time.

"We need to get to the carpet before the Volents discover our escape," Ion said. "Do we even know where it is?"

Hilda smiled. "We can find it." She turned to Vinia. "Your map, if you please."

The map? Vinia dug it out of her pocket. She had quite forgotten it, once the physical invasion of Thanx had been repelled. But how would the map of Thanx help here? She offered it to Hilda.

"No, keep it. Just find the carpet on it."

The carpet? She looked. The map had changed. Now it showed their present environment, with the Lips territory marked, and the Volent territory halfway surrounding it. It looked bad for the Lips. Apoca was of course in the middle of the Lips.

There was a mountain range to the north, and a lake or sea to the south. Vinia looked up and spied the jagged peaks of the mountains. Now she knew where they were, roughly, in relation to the map.

And there was a spot marked CARPET, about halfway between warring sides, in contested territory. "That way," she said, pointing.

"Thank you," Hilda said, just as if she hadn't made another impressive demonstration of her Sorceress power. What a map! And it was only a tiny fraction of what Hilda could do.

But getting there was not straightforward. The terrain was rough, with sharp hills and vales, and bits of forest marked DANGER. They were no longer with the friendly tribes of nickelpedes, salamanders, ghosts, and whatnot. The ones here were strangers and would be deadly to the children.

But there was a protected path. Vinia knew, because it was marked on the map: PROTECTED PATH. Those paths traversed all Xanth and enabled people and creatures to travel freely to different parts of it without fear of being molested or eaten. They were commonly used to get to the Good Magician's Castle, or to Castle Roogna, or other key locations, but obviously they weren't limited to those. The path wound through the area and passed reasonably close to the carpet. Luck was with them. Maybe that was the continuing influence of the ring. But then why hadn't it enabled them to avoid the trap they had fallen into? Better not to depend on luck.

They made their way carefully to the path, got on it, and hiked with greater confidence. What a relief to be safe, at least for a while. Once they were back on the carpet, they would add a spell to repel the Volents and be back on their way to meet with Queen Apoca. Though persuading her to help might be another challenge. Still, their cause was just, and Apoca should appreciate it once she was more fully acquainted with it.

But Vinia had a nagging doubt. It seemed too easy. It wasn't easy at all, but somehow it didn't feel difficult enough. Was she missing something, yet again?

Ion reached into his bag and drew out a vial. She glanced at him inquiringly. "You're worrying," he murmured. "When you do that, there's apt to be trouble."

"I'm sorry. I don't mean to complicate things."

"Not trouble of your making. You have a special sense for it, and special ways of handling it. There may be hidden magic involved. You're not the naïf you think you are."

"Naïf?"

"A naïve or inexperienced person," Hilda said. She was holding her needle as if ready to sew.

Vinia hadn't realized that Hilda was listening. She was embarrassed. "I'm certainly not very knowledgeable or experienced. You know that."

"But you are modest and sweet natured," Ion said. "That's part of why I love you, but I think that's also why you're the protagonist, because you're likely to be in the center of things, through no fault of your own."

"I didn't ask to be the protagonist," Vinia protested.

"It is not a role anyone gets to choose for herself." He laughed uneasily. "I'm glad it's you and not me."

"And he's right," Hilda said. "When you worry, it's a signal of impending fate. We are likely headed into more trouble."

"Bleep," Vinia muttered, fearing they were right. She did seem to be a magnet for mischief. Maybe that came with the territory of protagonism.

They continued along the path, drawing closer to the carpet. There were four little dots marking their own positions on the map, moving as they moved.

Finally, they were as close as the path came to the downed carpet. They had to leave the enchanted way. That made Vinia nervous all over again. But what choice did they have? They needed that carpet.

They left the path and cut through the brush toward the carpet. Before long, it came into sight. It seemed to be in good order.

Ion opened his vial. "Anti-stasis elixir," he explained. "That spell may still be on it."

Oh. Of course. Now Vinia wondered: Why had the Volents left the carpet alone? Surely, they could have enjoyed playing with it, joyriding, or simply robbing it of its goodies. It was their stasis spell: they could have turned that off at any time. Why hadn't they? That didn't seem to make much sense.

They came close—and the trap sprang. Cages dropped over each of them as men closed in from hiding and grabbed their assets, such as Ion's bag and Hilda's needle, which were both dropped on the ground. The enemy had finally caught on to their nature. Maybe their escape from the cell and building had been its own kind of trap, to cause them to reveal their powers. Maybe they had underestimated the enemy.

Now they were caught without their main assets. Benny could change form, but it wouldn't help him in the cage. Hilda's needle and Ion's bag of vials were in plain sight but teasingly out of reach. Was that accidental, or intentional?

But there seemed to be one thing their captors had missed. They did not know about Vinea's telekinesis. *She* could reach the needle and bag. She couldn't open the cage doors, because they were padlocked, and locks were beyond her power to pick. But those tools of the trades she could recover.

She looked around. Hilda caught her eye and made a tiny no shake of her head. Hilda knew what Vinia could do; why was she against it? The twins were both smarter than Vinia; there had to be reason.

Vinia closed her eyes as if afraid to recognize her captivity and focused on that reason. And it came to her in the form of a question. Did the Volents know about her and were cruelly teasing her, too? Daring her to reach out telekinetically so they could grab the objects away and dump them just beyond her reach? Maybe they were testing her range, so they would know her limit. So she could not surprise them. They did seem to be waiting. Which meant that she didn't dare use her talent, at least not while they were watching.

Vinia opened her eyes. She left the needle and bag alone. Hilda now wore the trace of a smile. They were already fighting back, in their fashion. They were children; that did not mean they were stupid.

Vinia quietly examined her cage. It was round in cross section, rising to a closed peak above, with a stout ring that connected to a rope that rose up to a derrick boom. The three other cages were similar. Their operators had caught their victims, then jumped out to snatch away key items by reaching into the cages during the children's distraction with the capture. It had been a practiced operation, deftly performed.

The four of them had been alert for the wrong thing and thus been caught. The Volents had outsmarted them. This time.

"You've caught us," Ion said. "Again. What are you going to do with us?"

"Supe will answer," a Volent said, sounding a bit disappointed. Their waiting ploy hadn't worked; the children had not tried to escape. Score one for the home team, maybe.

"Soup?" Ion asked, playing stupid. "You're going to feed us?"

The Volent didn't answer. Instead he raised one hand in a signal.

Meanwhile Vinia continued to explore her cage. There was a large ring at ground level, with five stout spikes buried in the ground, securing it. The weight of the cage must have caused the points to strike deep. But this meant that it should be possible to dig out below, if they were left alone long enough. These were temporary, not permanent, prisons.

A fifth man approached. He had the look of a leader, with a fancy blue hat. "Hello, guests," he said. "I am Volney Volent, squad leader. My name means 'Most popular.' Do you care to identify yourselves?"

That would surely be mischief. The four children were silent.

"Then I will do it for you," Volney said, unperturbed. He looked at Ion. "You are Prince Ion, age eleven, a Magician who is immune to all elixirs."

All four children froze in horror. He *knew*!

"I know," Volney agreed. "I did some spot research while you were escaping the cell. We do have a competent library, with a knowledgeable magic mirror. You evidently were coming to the aid of Queen Apoca of the enemy Lips tribe. Naturally we could not afford that. Our King Vladimir means to make Apoca his submissive queen, and it just wouldn't do to have her escape our net when we are so close to success." He glanced at the bag on the ground. "Your collection of elixirs could wreak havoc on our troops, especially in her capable hands."

"Bleep," Ion muttered.

So the Volents did not know the real thrust of their mission. They got background on Ion without picking up his more recent connection to the Queendom of Thanx. Ion's childish curse implied that the Volent was completely correct. Maybe the man had hoped to provoke more significant information, but the twins were too smart for that. Vinia and Benny would of course follow their lead.

Volney turned to Hilda. "You are Princess Hilda, Ion's twin sister, and a Sorceress of sewing. I must say that your flying carpet is a most impressive indication of your skill." He smiled, and he was a handsome man. Charm might be part of the danger he represented. "You are a pretty girl who will in due course become a lovely woman. You will make some lucky man a wonderful wife, quite apart from your formidable magic."

Hilda tittered, plainly flattered. Which was an act, because she was not a natural titterer. She was playing along, fooling him with her cynical smartness.

"Maybe even mine," Vladimir said.

His wife? Hilda squeaked in horror. The man had punched right through her charade, making her react. He was no ignoramus himself. He might or might not have magic, but he knew how to handle people. That might be only part of the danger he represented.

The Volent faced Benny. "You are Benny Buck, a human-Caprine crossbreed, able to switch forms instantly. Your age in human terms is six, so you are technically a child while in human form. You serve the princess."

"Yeah," Benny agreed reluctantly, concealing his real role as Hilda's boyfriend.

And finally, Vinia. Volney's direct focus was disconcerting. There was something about him that commanded her reluctant attention. "You are Vinia Human, age twelve. You serve the prince by enabling him to walk with you, via your contact telekinesis. I suspect he likes you more than casually, for you also are pretty and will in due course become a supremely comely and obliging woman."

He was too close to the reality for her to try to deny it. "Yes, about helping him walk." But did he really think that her power was only via direct physical contact? If so, she too had part of a secret. Maybe the Volents were uncertain whether her ability could operate from a short distance, so had been trying to find out by leaving the needle and vial bag within tempting range. She hoped she had disappointed them.

Volney sighed. "I fear you four are still keeping some secrets. So now on to stage two. We shall encourage you to become more cooperative."

Vinia did not like the sound of that and knew that neither did her friends. All of them remained grimly silent.

"I am going to kiss you, Vinia," Volney said. "Perhaps do more than that, for you are surely a most appealing consort when you want to be." He paused, watching her.

He was trying to make her react, as he had with Hilda. Vinia was determined not to give him that satisfaction. Yet what did he mean by "when she wanted to be"? She did not want any contact with him, let alone the kind of friendliness implied by the word *consort*. Still, a naughty part of her was intrigued.

She needed to respond, without being helpful. "No."

"It depends on Prince Ion, who can stop my initiative at any time by agreeing to use his magic on our behalf. I should advise you that our Volent tribe does not practice what you may term the Adult Conspiracy. We have no secrets from children." He smiled again, and Vinia felt herself wanting to please him, foolishly. Maybe his smile was his magic. "A number of children from more traditional cultures have run away and joined us for that reason. This might interest you also."

Bleep! It did interest Vinia, who had long been frustrated by the Conspiracy. But this was treacherous. She could not afford to let this enemy man subvert her willpower. "No," she repeated.

"Ah, but it is not your prerogative to decline, precious girl. That decision belongs to Prince Ion."

This was getting rapidly worse. Ion did like Vinia; in fact, he loved her. Could he tolerate this rogue's abuse of her without capitulating?

Then she realized that to do anything with her, the man would have to take her out of the cage. She might be able to escape.

Volney produced a key. He put it to the lock on Vinia's door and opened it. Then he reached inside, caught Vinia by an arm, and drew her outside, maintaining a firm hold. He was strong; there was no way she could wrench free and escape. A part of her did not even want to.

Vinia knew he was testing her, maybe on several levels. To ascertain the extent of her resistance, and to force her to use her telekinesis so he could judge its power. And to make Ion capitulate, to save her. And maybe even to subvert her to his cause. He was making more progress than she dared acknowledge, even to herself.

What was her best course? Probably nonresistance, so that the man would be able to judge neither her physical nor her talent strength. She would have to submit to his kiss. What bothered her most was the fear that she would like it.

He turned her around to face him and slowly drew her in to him, as if she were his girlfriend. She yielded with only token resistance. He was doing it slowly in order to give her plenty of time to resist, one way or another. Also, to give Ion time to speak.

And in that slow-motion time she got an idea. They were standing right beside the needle. She marked its spot exactly so she could fix on it with her tele.

He put his face to hers and kissed her lips. She did not bite him or make them mush; she submitted to the pressure of it. In fact, she returned it slightly, as if involuntarily warming to his charm. That ruse was surprisingly easy to perform. She was a girl, not a woman, but she did know how to kiss, from her practice with Ion. She could feel his surprise; he had expected resistance or apathy, not cooperation. Maybe he liked it, too, though that plainly was not his purpose. Or was it?

And, during the Volent's momentary distraction, she lifted the needle telekinetically and stuck it in the inside of her skirt where it would not show. With luck the watching Volents were also distracted by the show and had not seen the slight movement of the needle.

Volney drew back and paused. "Now I know you're not flirting with me, servant girl, appealing as you are despite your age. What is in your mind?"

Vinia thought fast. "Sometimes my body reacts on its own," she said. "Despite my annoyance." Was she fooling him? The truth was that despite her suppressed outrage, she had enjoyed the kiss.

"You are verging on maturity. Let's try it again." He drew her in and kissed her again. This time he also put a hand on her bottom and squeezed.

She froze in shock. A man could kiss a child, but he never fondled her bottom. This really was Conspiracy stuff! How far was he going to go? Did he mean to force her to resist physically, or to break down and weep? Or to relax and enjoy it? Or to use her talent to try to foil him? Which alternative was the worst?

She decided to continue with nonresistance, to give him no satisfaction on any front. Or little satisfaction, anyway; he did seem to like what he was doing. He was not being rough with her at all. She held the kiss and let him squeeze. She hated to think how Ion was reacting, but she knew that he couldn't afford to give in. That would cost them everything.

Volney drew back again. "No apparent reaction from you or the prince. I am disappointed, despite my pleasure in the contact. I fear I am going to have to proceed to stage three."

He was not going to do further adult mischief with her? That was a relief. Not just because it could be a real problem to her innocence, but because she feared that she would continue to like it. She could not remember the details of what she had briefly known when Ghorgeous had made her adult, but the Volent would have made them clear. What was Ion thinking, seeing her getting kissed and squeezed like that? Was he good at suppressing his reaction, or was he not really jealous? That bothered her in another manner.

Whatever could the next stage be? Apparently Volney was not a molester of children, whatever he might imply. She gazed at him with unfaked apprehension. "Stage three?"

"Get back in the cage, girl. I think you knew I was not going to take you to the limit. You have admirable nerve. I think you are already more woman than child." He turned her loose.

Vinia did not try to bolt for the carpet, suspecting that he expected that. Instead she walked sedately to the cage, passing by Hilda's cage and teleporting the needle to the inside of Hilda's dress without looking, knowing that Hilda would be aware of its arrival. She reached her own cage, entered it, and pulled its door closed. A Volent came to lock it again.

Vinia had suffered some indignity but had accomplished something useful with the needle. And Ion had not cracked. This was not exactly a game, but so far, they had kept the score more or less even.

"Heed me, all," Volney said. "I am going to explain to you what is in store for the four of you if you do not cooperate. Then I will give you the night to consider."

They were silent, knowing that this was going to be ugly.

"As you may know, we have in our possession a virus that causes infected women to become completely submissive to the wishes of men. We are using it on the Lips women we capture, making them delightful girlfriends and wives. They retain their power to render men into love slaves but are careful never to use it, because they know the men do not wish it. Their kisses become normal. But it doesn't work on children, which protects you two girls, and of course not on boys. However, we also have an aging spell we can use to make children mature rapidly. If we use it on you girls, you will become women, subject to the virus. Do you understand?" He paused.

The four of them gazed at him with dismay. That combination was feasible and would destroy any resistance the girls had. He really did have a viable strategy, which their lack of cooperation could not prevent.

"However," he continued when the pause had been used up, "Two of you are boys. So we will utilize the gender-changing spell we also have to change you to girls. Then we will age you and infect you, and you will become obliging women for our troops. Your magic will be used on our behalf, because it will be your wish to do so when we ask. Do you understand?"

What was the use in pretending? "We understand," Ion said.

"Then I will leave you to your night of consideration," Volney said. He and three of the Volents departed for wherever their camp was, leaving one to guard the cages. That one sat down next to the bag of vials, picked it up, and gazed at it.

The four children circulated a glance. Vinia had had in mind hauling the bag telekinetically to Ion, who could then release a vial of metal softener to get him and the others out of the cages. But the Volent was accidentally messing that up.

Or was it accidental? This could be part of the enemy plan, to make Vinia show her power. She needed to use it, but not while the man was paying attention. Just as Hilda needed to use hers, and Ion his. They needed to distract the guard. Hilda or Vinia could have done it by flirting with him, but then they would not be able to focus on their efforts for escape.

Benny stepped into the breach. "Hello, Volent," he said.

"Shut up, goat boy," the man said irritably.

Benny laughed, taking no offense. "I once had a job entertaining tourists. I learned some things along the way. Such as the meanings of names. In Mundania they may be random, but here in Xanth they usually are descriptive. You can test me on this. What's your name?"

The Volent paused, considering. Then he answered "Vol."

"Now I doubt that's short for Volent," Benny said. "Members of a tribe tend to have alliterative names, so yours naturally begins with a V. So you must mean Vol as short for your larger name, which I am guessing is Volusian."

The man grimaced. "You're pretty smart, goat face," he said irritably.

"Not smart. Social. I know how to interest people."

"Well, you're boring me, goatee. So shut up."

Meanwhile Hilda had brought out thread from a hidden pocket and seemed to be sewing a cord. Vinia wasn't sure she would be able to use it on the guard, but at least it was something.

"Ah, but I haven't finished," Benny said smoothly. "Names have meanings. The magical powers that be surely had a reason for giving you that name. Do you want to know what your name means?"

"No, butt head," Vol snapped. But he was listening.

"It means 'bad-tempered.'"

"Oh, piss and conniption! You do know it."

"But you have reason. Who wants to be stuck with guarding four children, and you can't even touch the girls because you're not a squad leader, you're just a common grunt. It's a demeaning chore."

Vol mellowed. "You're pretty sharp. What's your name?"

"I am Benny. It's not short for Benedict or Benjamin or Benton, all of which are respectable. It's just Benny, meaning nothing in particular. I didn't rate a good name, because I'm a crossbreed, the lowest of the low."

Vinia was interested despite her focus on the bag. She had known and liked Benny for years, but it was true that there was a general prejudice against crossbreeds. He had found a way to relate solidly to Vol. He really was socially competent.

"Yeah," Vol agreed. "Me, too, on looking down on crossbreeds. Sorry about that. You seem like a good guy."

"I get along. Sometimes I look at the girls and wish they were nannies. A doe Caprine crossbreed can be sexy as Hades. In my goat form I can really appreciate that."

"Uh, I hate to say it, but you're scheduled to become a doe yourself."

"Oh, bleep! I forgot. I don't suppose I could talk you into letting me out of this cage so I can get away before they do?"

Vol shook his head. "Sorry, can't do. They'd replace you with me, and I don't want to be a slut any more than you do."

Their dialogue continued, but now Vol had forgotten the bag in his hands. Vinia tugged at it telekinetically, but the man's grip remained unconsciously tight. Bleep!

Vinia glanced at Ion. He made a little hand gesture as of opening something.

Okay. Vinia focused on working the bag ajar and wedging out the topmost vial, whatever it was. She pried it open. A thin vapor emerged, forming into a sticklike figure. Then it firmed into a brightly colored cane. What was it?

"Bleep," Ion muttered. "A co-cain."

Suddenly Vol became aware of it. "What's this?" he demanded, dropping the bag and grabbing it.

"A cane," Vinia said quickly. "Maybe it got blown in by the wind." There was no wind, but she couldn't think of anything better. "Probably better to leave it alone."

"The bleep I will! I caught it, and it's mine." He stood and put the cane to the ground, leaning on it. "Hey! This feels good! Almost like flying."

Then his feet left the ground. He *was* flying.

Alarmed, he dropped it. It floated away. He crashed back to the ground.

Meanwhile Vinia retrieved another vial from the bag and opened it, hoping it would be more effective in distracting the Volent from his duty as a guard. Ion could have selected effective vials, but these were random. Hilda now had a fair length of her cord.

Vapor issued from the second vial, forming into another cane. This one was numbingly dull. Vol saw it and grabbed it.

"Oh, it makes my hand numb," he said.

"Nova cain," Ion said. "Don't bang it, lest—"

Vol banged it into the ground. The cane exploded into a mighty burst of light and disappeared.

Vinia tried to move the bag away from Vol, but he saw it and grabbed it back. Another vial squeezed out, so Vinia opened that one. It formed into a third cane, with a spiral red-and-white pattern decorating it.

Vol caught the cane, dropping the bag again. This time Vinia snatched it away and flung it toward Ion. Fortunately Vol was focused on the cane. "This one looks good enough to eat." He put his tongue to it. "It *is* good enough to eat! It's a sugar cane!" He sat down again, biting into the cane with delight. He had quite forgotten the bag.

Now Ion had the bag of vials. He quickly opened one. Vapor emerged and clouded around the wires of the cage. They dissolved, and he was free.

Meanwhile Hilda had completed her cord and sent it snaking like a living thing to the connected derrick. It pulled a handle, and the cage heaved up on its rope, pulling free of the ground and freeing her.

The two of them came to the remaining cages. Hilda used her rope to pull the handle to Benny's derrick and lift his cage away, while Ion blew a bit of vapor on Vinia's wires and puffed them into smoke. The two couples hugged. Now they all were free.

Vol looked up from his candy cane. "Oh, no! I let you escape. They'll crucify me!"

"Not your fault," Benny said consolingly. "We're pretty slippery characters. All the same, they may not understand and could blame you. Maybe we should take you to some other Volent community where you can be anonymous."

"You'd do that?" he asked, amazed. "I'm one of the bad guys."

"But we're good guys," Vinia said, kissing him on the cheek. "We'll do it."

"Dam," he said, using that irrelevant river-blocking term. "I wish you were grown, girl, and liked me."

"We managed to escape that fate," she said. It was an evasion but would do. She did not really like him, but recognized that he was not a bad sort, for his kind.

They went to the carpet. Hilda checked it carefully before they boarded, just in case, but it seemed clean. It had been left untouched, as bait. "All the same," Hilda said, "I am going to sew a stasis trap detector, so we won't be caught that way again."

"You can do that?" Vol asked, amazed.

"She's a Sorceress," Benny said proudly. "She can do just about anything with her needle and thread."

They took off. Vol was amazed but appreciative. He directed them to another community where he thought he would be safe, and they dropped him off there. "Uh, if we ever meet again—" he started.

"We won't know each other at all," Vinia said.

Vol nodded. It was mutual protection. Neither side would approve of fraternizing with the enemy.

They ascended into the night sky. "Thanx Officer of the Hour," Vinia said to the ring.

In about one-seventh of a moment a buzzing sounded. "Turn on your translator, Beetrix," Benny called.

The buzzing became the bee. "Sorry," the bee princess buzzed. "How are you folk doing?"

"Well enough, considering," Vinia said. "We got caught by the Male Volents, twice, but managed to escape unharmed." She explained briefly about that.

"That's scary," Beetrix buzzed. "Grown and submissive, just like us."

"Our next stop should be with Apoca. If we can talk her into helping, you will be submissive no more."

"That would be nice." She disconnected.

"There's the rub," Ion said. "Apoca didn't sound very accommodating before."

"But face-to-face, maybe we can persuade her," Hilda said.

Could they? It just didn't seem promising, but none of them wanted to say that out loud. What would they do if it didn't work out? Vinia had no idea and feared that the others had even less.

It was time. Vinia nerved herself. "Apoca," she said to the ring. "Vinia here. We were caught by the Volents but escaped. May we come to you now?"

The queen was amazed. "You escaped them? Without getting transformed?"

"Without," Vinia agreed.

"Then you have more power or better fortune than I thought. Come on in."

A nod circulated. They were on their way. But an intangible cloud of doubt accompanied them. Could they really succeed? They had to, or all was lost. But *could* they?

Chapter 13

APOCA

"I see that cloud," Hilda said. "You're doubting again, Vinia."

Vinia could not deny it. "Suddenly it's too easy, again. She's not just going to let us come in without challenge. Not with enemies like Volney Volent."

"He kissed you," Hilda said shrewdly. "And you sort of liked it."

Vinia was unable to deny it. "I hated that I did."

Hilda nodded. "With Ion watching."

"I'm not jealous," Ion said. "He was using you to get to me, and you knew it, so you had to go along with it, playing the part. And you used his distraction to get the needle to Hilda, and later the bag of vials to me."

"That is true," Vinia agreed, relieved that they weren't blaming her. "But honesty compels me to say that despite all that, I did sort of like the kiss. I'm sorry."

"He's a handsome man," Hilda said. "With maybe some magic in his approach to women. That's probably his talent, to make them like it. I think I would have liked his kiss and squeeze, too, despite hating it."

Vinia saw Benny's hand on the till tighten. *He* was jealous. So probably Ion was too. That was perversely reassuring.

"But that doubt," Hilda said. "We all feel it, but maybe you can clarify it. What is it, specifically?"

Vinia focused, glad to have the subject change. "It's that Queen Apoca has to know about folk like Volney, and their King Vladimir is probably worse, and that he has his eye on her. She knows that the Volents captured us, and that we got away. She may think that they let us go on purpose, maybe after converting us to being submissive to their masculine will. She won't trust us, with good reason. How can we prove our good faith to her?"

Hilda nodded again. "I'd be suspicious. In fact, I'm suspicious now. Maybe they did let us go on purpose, letting us think we escaped. So we could subvert her."

"But what could we do to Apoca?" Vinia realized she was arguing the other case, but they needed to figure this out. Their escape did seem too easy, now that she thought about it. The way Volney had broken off the forced seduction and retired, after presenting them with a truly ugly threat, leaving only one guard who wasn't smart. It did smell like a setup.

"We could have the submission virus planted on us," Ion said. "To infect her, so she couldn't fight them anymore."

"The way the six or seven princesses of Thanx can't fight," Hilda agreed.

"We could," Vinia agreed with a shudder. The way Volney had handled her could have smeared virus elixir all over her, especially her face and her bottom. "It might not affect us, because we're children, but it could really mess up the Lips camp."

"The perfect infiltration," Hilda said. "Brought in unknowingly."

Ion smiled. "Fortunately, we can verify it, and nullify it." He brought out a vial and opened it. Vapor came out, forming a cloud that surrounded them.

Then Vinia was in the center of a burst of sparks. "What?" she cried, jumping up and slapping her bottom where they centered, zapping her. There was no burning, no pain, but it was alarming.

"The antivirus is eliminating the virus, combusting it into oblivion," Ion explained. "In a moment you'll be clean. We'll all be clean."

Vinia relaxed. Trust Ion to figure it out. She saw the sparks traveling out across the carpet, destroying the virus everywhere it had spread. "So we *were* trouble for the Lips."

"Not anymore," Ion said.

"But we can't blame them for not trusting us," Hilda said.

"They should have some protocol for verifying visitors," Ion said.

"We can tell them what happened," Vinia said. "How Volney pretended he was trying to make me react, when he was really planting the virus." She felt ashamed, now, for falling for it.

"He's good," Hilda agreed. "Too bad he's on the wrong side."

They flew on through the night toward Apoca. Soon they spied what looked like a wickerwork castle, with a clear lighted field around it. So the

Lips women were alert by night as well as by day. That was understand-
able. They glided in for a soft landing.

Two Lips soldiers strode toward them. Both were lovely mature
women, their beauty marred only by their outsize lips. One was shapely
in a green dress that matched her hair and eyes; the other, in blue armor
and helmet that matched her hair and eyes, stayed slightly back, holding
a club.

"Tarzana and Jane," Ion murmured, referring to an old Mundane leg-
end that had leaked into Xanth. It meant that one of them would be gruff
and tough, while the other seemed to take the side of the visitors, trying to
win their trust. Of the two, Jane was more dangerous to a real spy.

Jane smiled in a manner that reminded Vinia of Volney: charmingly
insincere. "Hello, visitors! What brings you nice children here at this late
hour? Did you get lost?"

"We are here to see Queen Apoca, who is expecting us," Ion said. "I
am Prince Ion of the Kingdom of Adamant. This is my sister, Princess
Hilda. These are our companions, Benny and Vinia. Please conduct us to
the queen."

"Not so fast, strangers," Tarzana said. "We have no idea who you
really are."

"But they told us," Jane said. "They're from Adamant."

"They could be lying."

"But they have the magic carpet."

"Which they could have stolen."

"But they're only children."

"They could be runaways."

The children let the skit play out. Then Ion glanced at Vinia. It was her
turn, again.

"Please," Vinia said, putting on her Uncertain Girl mode. "We are only
trying to do what is right. We're not runaways: we're on a special mission
for the Queendom of Thanx. We didn't steal the carpet: Hilda is a Sorceress of sewing, and she made it. We have been in touch with Queen Apoca
and she told us to come on in."

"A likely story," Tarzana scoffed. "Every visitor claims to know the queen."

"But it could be true," Jane said. "We have to give them a proper
chance."

"Why don't you ask Queen Apoca?" Vinia asked. "She should verify our contact."

Both Lips women laughed. "Dear, we don't bother the queen for every routine tourist visit," Jane explained. "We need to be sure of you before we let you into her residence."

Vinia got an idea. "Suppose Princess Hilda demonstrates her magic sewing ability? Then will you listen to us?"

"Do that, child," Tarzana said gruffly, obviously skeptical that she could.

Hilda got up and stepped off the carpet. She approached Jane, who stood still while Tarzana held her club ready, just in case. Hilda brought out her needle and a thread. She knelt before Jane and sewed the thread into the hem of her skirt, all the way around. Then she rose and stepped back.

The threaded hem lifted, showing nice legs. Then it showed nicer thighs. In fact, it hauled the skirt up until the woman's full green panties were exposed. Jane hastily pushed the skirt back down, but it continued to lift where her hands weren't holding it, delivering more thigh and panty flashes.

Ion and Benny seemed about to freak out. It wasn't just the panties, it was her extremely well-formed legs, her ample hips, and the general contours of her body. She was a stunningly shapely woman.

"I think she made her point," Tarzana said, her gruffness under siege by a threatening laugh. She was quite shapely, too, under her armor, in a heavier-set way.

"You made it," Jane agreed. "Now how do I get my modesty back?"

"This is a docile thread," Hilda said. "Simply tell it to relax. It's your thought that counts."

"Relax, thread!" Jane exclaimed desperately.

The hem subsided, returning to its natural place at the bottom of the skirt. Jane was modest again.

"But if you should ever want to, well, flash a man, or prove to a dubious woman that now your dress really is magic," Hilda said, "just say 'Thread, fly.'"

Jane couldn't resist trying it. "Thread, fly."

The hem rose up again, exposing her fine limbs.

"Thread relax," Jane said quickly. The skirt became sedate. Vinia suspected that the woman did not really mind showing off her assets, as it were.

"Okay, we believe you," Tarzana said, abandoning her gruffness.

"You're a Sorceress. But we still must check you out. We understand that your party was captured by the Volents. How did you escape?"

Vinia launched into the story. Both Lips women paid close attention. "Then when we were airborne, we realized that it could be a ruse. So Magician Ion used an elixir, and it burned out all the viruses Volney had planted on me. It really was a trap, but now we are clean."

"I believe you," Jane said. "But you must understand, we must verify that you are safe before we let you get close to the queen. The Volents can be extremely sneaky."

"We know," Vinia said. "I thought Volney was going to, well, do something naughty with me, though I am underage, when all the time he was just planting the virus."

"We are familiar with the name. He has a reputation. He does have a way with women. You are an attractive girl. Had you been of age, he would have been naughty with you *and* planted the virus."

"And you need to be sure there is not some other catch," Vinia agreed. She found herself liking these Lips women, as she got to know them. Maybe she just liked people. "How can we help you?"

"The primary threat is the virus. There could be some your antivenin didn't get. We'll run you through the submission test."

"We're not submissive," Hilda said.

"You're children. We need an adult woman. And a man."

Oh. "Whatever," Hilda agreed.

They brought a third woman, dark haired and eyed, together with a man, blond of hair, blue of eye. The woman was not a Lips; she lacked the lips and was not in uniform.

"These are Tony and Meg," Tarzana said. "They will touch each of you and tour your carpet. If anything is there, it will get on them. Then we'll see." She faced the pair. "Do it."

Tony turned to Meg. "Kiss me, floozy."

"Go take a flying fling at the moon," she retorted.

Tarzana nodded. "Parameters normal. Now explore."

The two shook hands with each of the children, then walked all around the carpet, exploring every detail. They stepped off. Tony faced Meg again. He opened his mouth. "Get lost," she snapped. "And take that erotic thought with you."

Tarzana smiled. "No virus," she reported.

"This way," Jane said as the test couple walked away.

They entered the castle. "This is very fine work," Hilda said. "You must have a Sorceress of Wicker."

"We do," Jane agreed. "We have been hard-pressed and have had to move frequently. She can make us a residence quickly."

They passed two men carrying boxes. Jane's skirt lifted almost too high as she passed. The men's eyes bulged, but they didn't freak. Jane smiled privately; she had already learned proper mental control.

Then they were ushered into the presence of Queen Apoca. She was the most curvaceous woman Vinia had ever seen. Her lips were bigger, too. But it was her hair that was her most remarkable feature. It looked gray but was translucent. It was not especially long but did nicely frame her face.

"Welcome, guests," she said, and her hair flashed pale green. "I'm sorry to have had to put you through that rigmarole, but we had to be sure."

"We understand," Hilda said. "Um, your hair—?"

"It is colorless, but conducts the color of my scalp, which glows with my mood. Green is welcome or agreement or positive; blue is disagreement or negative; red is frustration or anger; yellow is doubt or mystery; black is for the feeling of doom or approach of death. I normally wear a concealing cap when I go out, to have some privacy of feeling."

"This is remarkable," Ion said, openly impressed.

"Thank you." Her hair flashed dark green. "It is good to have a compliment from a Magician."

"And from a Sorceress," Hilda said. "I never even imagined hair like yours. It's marvelous! Is that your talent?"

"No. It is my nature. I was ridiculed for it as a child." Her hair turned blue.

"Children can be cruel. I am a child, but I hope not a cruel one."

"You clearly are not." Apoca reoriented, her hair turning yellow. "Now exactly what is it you want of me?"

"As we told you before," Vinia said, "we have to stop the virus before the Queendom of Thanx is destroyed. We need to make a deal for the antivirus."

Apoca's hair turned orange, which Vinia interpreted as a mood between doubt and frustration. "Ah, yes. But as I told you before, I can't help you. It is not that I am unsympathetic to your need, it is that I am unable. I fear you have come here for nothing."

"But we need the elixir to nullify it," Vinia said. "We were told that you have it."

Now the hair was dark blue. "Not exactly. Such an elixir may exist, but we do not possess it."

"But the Good Magician said—"

"Contrary to his reputation, the Good Magician does not know everything. He perhaps assumed." The hair was a cross between blue and red. "I am able to counter the virus, but there is no elixir."

Vinia looked at the others. Ion returned a gaze that suggested *Stall*. He was figuring it out but needed more time.

Vinia struggled to accommodate. "Please, Queen Apoca, we want to understand, but we know too little. If you have the time, could you tell us more about yourself, so that maybe we can better appreciate your perspective?"

Apoca considered, her hair shifting back to yellow. "Vinia, when you contacted me before, I was curious, so then I did a bit of spot research. Little is known of you, personally, but what there is is intriguing. You were an ordinary tourist with abundant allergies who met and somehow won the love of Prince Ion and have been with him ever since. Yet you are by the accounts an almost completely ordinary girl, though with a nice talent of telekinesis. Suppose we exchange more personal information?"

"Oh, I am of no importance," Vinia protested. "I'm just a nobody."

Apoca smiled, and her hair flashed a brilliant green. "You are modest to an extreme. Yet your three companions are in awe of you, despite the elevated stations of some of them, and they depend on you more than you may appreciate. I wonder whether you could have a second talent, a hidden one? That's very rare, but it does happen. Perhaps the other talent is an aspect of your personal state, as my hair and lips are mine. Yet it is surely the secret to your selection as the protagonist of this narrative. Please, I would very much like to get to know you better."

Vinia looked again at the others, confused. The Queen had done more than spot research on her! Yet this was not supposed to be about her, but about their mission. She was supposed to be a background character, not a foreground one. An observer, not a mover. She was really messing that up.

Three gazes bore on her. They all indicated *DO IT*.

What could she do, but yield in the manner of a true submissive? "As you wish, Queen Apoca."

The hair flashed yellow green. "Excellent." She turned to indicate a set of full-size mirrors, halfway facing each other. "Here is the protocol. These are matching magic mirrors of a special type I obtained when I did a special favor for a glassmaker. They are arranged to interact with each other, the reflection of one merging in a manner with the other. We will approach them carefully, delivering our reflections to one and thus to both, and merge in the common picture. Do you understand?"

"No," Vinia said. "I am not smart the way the twins are."

"No matter. You will pick it up soon enough. Also do not be concerned about your allergies; they will not occur here, because the ambiance of Ion now permeates this area. Come here."

Vinia went to her. She saw that Apoca was not a large woman: she was about the same height as Vinia, though her adult figure was infinitely superior. The queen took her by the elbows and aimed her at the right mirror. Vinia saw her reflection therein, a dull ordinary girl in a faint cloud of confusion. Then Apoca faced the left mirror, seeing her reflection. "Now walk slowly toward your image, until you reach the interaction."

Vinia obeyed, knowing that the others were watching them both. Apoca walked slightly away from her, toward her own mirror. They came at the same time to the spots right in front of the mirrors where the reflections managed to cross.

And then they were in a kind of neverland whose boundary seemed to be an endless series of reflections. Vinia saw herself from multiple perspectives, front, back, sides. When she moved a hand, all her hands moved, but in different directions. The same was true of Apoca.

"Take one more step," the queen said.

Vinia did. The myriad reflections disappeared, and the two of them were in some other kind of realm.

"We are of different ages, but here we can match," Apoca said. "Make yourself five years old."

Vinia obligingly pictured herself as she had been at that age. Her clothing remained the same, but her form changed within it, so that it still fit. Now she was a supremely ordinary little child.

"Hello."

Vinia turned to see Apoca, as another five-year-old girl. Now she lacked the adult shape, but her lips were big, and the cloud of hair remained translucent. It was definitely her.

"Uh, I'm Vinia."

"I'm Apoca. We are on the way to my Centaur School class."

They walked side by side along the faint path that showed before them. "I never had Centaur School," Vinia said. "I am a poor girl, having to learn things at home."

"You may be better off than I."

Several other children were on a converging path. "Oh, there's hair-brain Pocka with the big mouth," a boy said.

"Ignore him," Apoca told Vinia. "As teasing goes, this is not too bad. It's worse when they manage to embarrass me, and my hair turns blue red. At this age my mouth lacks its kissing power, so it is merely unsightly."

But Vinia, however obscure she might be in her larger life, had never been one to suffer insults in silence. "Your mouth is pretty big, too, buster!"

"Oh, yeah?" He cut across to them. "You take that back, snotnose, or else."

Vinia knew she should back off. But she did have her telekinesis if she needed it. "Or else what, fathead?"

"Or else this." He swung his fist at her face before she could dodge aside. She instinctively set up a telekinetic block just next to her head.

The fist passed right through her head without touching it. She was like a ghost in this realm.

"What?" he asked, confused.

"You get pretty poor aim, poop-face," she teased him.

Dismayed by what he did not understand, he backed off.

"Let him go," Apoca whispered. "We don't want to make an unscripted scene."

Vinia realized that manifesting as a ghost here could lead to complications. Most folk were spooked by ghosts. So she left off.

"I didn't realize that he couldn't touch me," she said as they walked on. "That was a surprise."

"You thought he could score on you, and you taunted him anyway?"

"I know I shouldn't have. I'm sorry. Maybe I need a dose of that submission virus."

"Sh. That's in the future, not now."

"That's right. We're only five years old. Almost half my life ago."

"A sixth of mine. But who's counting? Thanks for standing up for me. I like your spirit."

"My spirit gets me in trouble sometimes."

"Let's go see."

The scene shifted. Now they were walking in a park Vinia remembered from when she was eight years old, where she had been attacked and had to use her talent to ugly effect to get out of it. Her dawning prettiness was a liability. "Uh, this one's nasty. Maybe we shouldn't be here."

Apoca looked older. "You helped me. Now I'll help you."

Vinia wasn't sure about that but didn't argue. A bigger boy spied her. "Ha!" he cried. "Got you alone, tease bait! Now I'll have you."

Vinia tried to back away. It had been easier when boys merely tried to hit her, not hit on her. "We're children. We're not supposed to—"

He grabbed her. For this version, in her own memory, she was solid. He hauled her roughly in to him, making ready to forcibly kiss her, and maybe worse. She struggled but could not wrench herself away. She would have to use her talent.

"Hey, bully boy," Apoca said. "Turn her loose or else."

His head turned to face her. "Or else what, bigmouth?"

"Or else this." Apoca kissed him on the mouth.

He fell back, stunned. "Oh, bleep! I love you!"

"Then do what I say. Get lost!"

The bully backed away, then fled. "Now we're even," Apoca said, satisfied.

"But you shouldn't be real, in my frame," Vinia protested. "How could you kiss him?"

"I'm not physically here. I didn't touch him. But my power is not a physical thing. He never felt my physical kiss, he felt my submission kiss. That made him my love slave."

"Oh, my. You mean it's your kiss that does it? That cancels the virus?"

"Yes. When I use it on a man, it makes him my love slave. When I use it on a woman, it makes her fiercely independent. It is my kiss that cancels the virus. That how I protect the Lips women. They can kiss a man into oblivion, but only I can kiss a woman into recovery. That's why I'm queen."

"Now I understand. We'd have to bring the princesses to your territory to be kissed. That's really not feasible."

"As I said, I'd like to help you, but it is complicated."

Vinia thought of something. "Could you kiss me?"

"I could. But why? You're already independent, and you're a child."

"So I can get a better notion of it."

"Very well." They turned to face each other, and Apoca kissed Vinia on the mouth. She felt the weird magic power of it, but it didn't change her, because she was already independent in spirit. Unimportant, but independent.

"Let's go back," Vinia said. "I need to explain to the others."

"Not yet. We have another round to go."

"We do?"

"You need to know more of the background, and I still have not fathomed the underlying mystery of you."

"I'm just a largely ignorant girl."

Apoca smiled. "So you may think. But I believe that your presence here is not coincidence. Please, there may be more here than you believe."

Vinia shrugged. "I am trying not to waste your time. You're a talented queen, and I'm—"

Avoca stalled her with a hand on her arm. "Indulge me, please."

"Oh. Of course."

"Here is the sequence that brought me here." They walked forward, and the scene became—

"The Good Magician's Castle!" Vinia exclaimed, surprised.

"Yes. My power manifested at maturity. Then I could kiss bullies into oblivion. But it did not improve my lot. Now, instead of teasing or trying to rape me, they were afraid of me. Their folks did not want me among them, as they tacitly preferred defenseless girls. It was a problem. I was being ostracized. So I came here."

"I can imagine."

"I won't bore you with the Challenges I navigated. It's my interview and assignment that counts." Apoca was now a shapely young woman. Vinia remained a child, as she had no memories of maturity, apart from the fleeting time with the ghost.

Suddenly they were inside the castle, facing Wira. Wira was startled, seeing Vinia. "What are you doing here? You're out of context."

"Uh—" Vinia began uncertainly.

"It's a reprise visit via the mirrors," Apoca said, her hair blue green. "We are getting to know each other."

Wira nodded. "Now I understand. I hope you don't mind if I mostly ignore you, Vinia."

"Not at all," Vinia said. "I'll just stay out of things as much as I can." Which also meant that she might avoid embarrassing herself in this odd context. She was doubtful what was and was not real.

Wira conducted them to the comfortable room where another woman stood. Her face was thickly veiled, and her hair under her cap was distinctly strange; in fact, it seemed almost alive. "This is Apoca, and her ghostly friend." Then, to them: "This is the Gorgon, the Designated Wife of the Month. She is veiled so that her direct look won't stone you." She quirked a smile. "Originally she stoned only men, but as her power matured the effect extended to women and children, too."

"Oh, I have heard so much about you, Gorgon!" Apoca gushed, her hair now pure green. "I love your hair."

"And I love yours," the Gorgon responded as she removed her cap to reveal that hair. And it wasn't hair at all; it was a nest of little snakes! She glanced at Vinia, through the veil. "Don't be concerned, child; my vipers don't attack my visitors. They couldn't hurt you, anyway, since you're not really here."

"Uh, thank you," Vinia said awkwardly.

"I will inform Humfrey you are here," Wira said to Apoca. She departed.

"Our unusual hair is not the only thing we have in common, different as it is," the Gorgon said to Apoca. "We both can stun men, I with my eyes, you with your mouth."

"Stun? You stone them!" Vinia knew that what she meant was not intoxicating, but literally turning them to stone statues.

"Through the veil I can merely stun them, when I choose. When Humfrey gets too grumpy, I set him back somewhat." The little snakes seemed to be amused.

"Oh. Of course." Apoca laughed, her hair flashing yellow green for humor. "My talent wouldn't work at all through a veil."

"Oh, it might, when you want a partial effect. You might try it sometime."

The two women continued to chat amicably. Then Wira returned. "He will see you now."

They followed Wira up the winding stairway to the cramped office. The Magician looked up from the monstrous tome as they arrived.

"This is Apoca," Wira said.

"Ask."

"How can I make myself useful in Xanth, and get a boyfriend, considering that I can't really have a relationship that involves kissing?"

"You need training. Go to the School of Magic."

That was it? "About my Service—"

"That's it." The surly mouth cracked a token smirk. "You will find Demon Grossclout interesting."

Apoca's hair turned blue. "But how will I get into that class? I doubt I qualify as a future magical adept."

"Bribe him." The gaze dropped back to the tome. Apoca had been dismissed. Her hair flashed briefly red.

"But I have nothing to bribe him with," Apoca protested as they returned to the living room.

"Oh, you do, dear," the Gorgon said. "Put a gag on your mouth and take off your clothing. Grossclout does like the ladies, and you have a remarkable figure."

Apoca nodded, understanding. Vinia wished she did too.

Then they were with Demon Grossclout, and Apoca was removing her clothing. Her hair was yellow, signifying mystery, turning green as the mystery was teasingly uncovered.

"Nuh-uh," Grossclout said, though he was plainly interested. "Not with the child watching."

Oh. So Vinia went to join the assembling class.

There was Metria Demoness. "What are you doing here?" she asked Vinia, surprised.

"Just tagging along with Apoca's memory."

"Apoca. I remember her. She really prospered in class, maybe because she paid close attention. Maybe I'll try it sometime."

"How can you remember, when she hasn't started class yet?"

"I sneaked a peek at her future. I can play memory games too."

Did this make sense? Vinia decided not to challenge it.

Before long Apoca emerged from the Demon professor's study and joined the class. Her bribe had evidently been successful.

The following weeks were covered in passing fragments. Vinia saw Apoca learn how to control her kisses, so she could kiss without gutting a man's willpower, when she chose. Maybe the professor taught her that so he could kiss her himself. Then Apoca learned something significant: she could kiss women, too, enhancing their independence. This secret aspect was it seemed additional to her colorful hair. This class was really profiting her!

Finally, Apoca learned that she was not unique. She was a Lips, one of a special type of woman whose kiss could be devastating. There were other Lips, though their kisses affected only men. Grossclout told her where to find them.

"And so I came here to join the Lips," Apoca concluded as they returned to the present. "They were disorganized. I organized them, and made them into a tribe, and they voted me queen because of my ability to restore them when the Volents caught them and doped them with the virus. But the Volents did not like our new independence, and attacked."

"That's what happened to Thanx," Vinia said. "Men don't much seem to like independent women."

"So it seems. I never contacted the Good Magician again and trusted that he had forgotten me. Now you know all about me. Let's learn about you."

All about her? Hardly! But it was enough. "There's not much to tell."

"Start with why you traveled."

"It was just random. I got tired of staying home alone, so decided to try being a tourist. It was a crazy decision, because I'm highly allergic to just about everything. I can't think what got into me."

"I have a notion. Let's go there."

Before Vinia could protest, they were there at her home the day she made the decision. Her folks were about to go touristing, an activity they liked. Vinia had normally stayed home alone when they went, because only there could she clean out most of the allergens from her room, so she wasn't constantly sneezing. Spot medications for allergies existed, but they didn't seem to work on her. There was no magic doctor near, so she couldn't get a spell for it, and anyway she would have had to pay her way by doing messy chores. It might be even worse on other planets: she hadn't cared to gamble. But this time she decided to go with them, touristing. It seemed to be a crazy decision on her part, but her folks didn't argue. They were glad to take her along. It relieved them of worrying about her, and of the disapproval of neighbors when they left her home alone.

"But why did you decide to go touristing this time?" Apoca asked her.

"I don't know. It didn't seem to make much sense, considering my condition. Sometimes I do that, doing screwball things for no good reason."

"I am not at all sure of that. You had a reason."

Vinia shook her head. "I can see already that you are much smarter than I am. You pursue things that make sense. But if there was a sensible reason for my decision, I don't know what it was. I was just a nine-year-old girl with a talent of telekinesis that was useless against my sneezing."

"There has to be something, considering how well things turned out for you later on."

"You mean meeting Prince Ion? That was sheer phenomenal luck. Whatever I am now, it is because of him."

"Maybe. Maybe not." Apoca considered. "Let's freeze-frame right here, when you made the decision. Tell me again, why did you go touristing?"

This was getting tiring, but of course Vinia wasn't going to say that. She was even halfway flattered by the queen's interest, however misplaced. "I don't know. Maybe I was just tired of being home alone while everyone else had all the fun."

"The specific moment, please."

Vinia was beginning to wonder about the woman's smarts, but she focused. "I was in my room while they were packing." Now they were in the room, alone together. "And I thought about how lonely I was going to be, again. And—"

And now she saw what she had not, before. There on the floor of her room was a pattern, as of a path diverging before her. One fork was green, the other red. Like Apoca's hair. So maybe green was good, and red was bad?

"What are you seeing?" Apoca asked.

"A green path and a red path, right here in my room. Maybe I'm suffering eye strain."

"Did you follow one of them?"

"Yes, actually," Vinia said, surprised. "I didn't see them at the time, but now I see that I stepped onto the green one, because it somehow felt right.

It led to my parents as they packed. And that made me decide to go with them, this time."

"Which was the better long-term decision, as it turned out."

"I suppose. If I hadn't gone with them, I never would have met Ion. But that was sheer coincidence."

"Perhaps. Now the next crisis of decision. Just let yourself feel it."

Vinia let herself tune in on whatever it was. She was with her parents visiting the planet Animalia, populated by assorted crossbreeds. She was wearing a heavy face mask to protect her from the allergens of the local atmosphere. They were looking at the fine horses that the folk of Equine Castle maintained. They were such lovely animals that Vinia longed to ride one, but she knew she would get too much into it and dissolve into sneezing. All she could do was look longingly.

And there were the paths before her, one green, one red. She took the green one. "I want to stay here," she said in her memory.

Her mother smiled indulgently. "Dear, you know that would be futile. Your mask protects you for only an hour before it gets allergen-logged and you have to get back inside the protected vehicle."

Vinia knew that. Yet she persisted, following the green path she was not then aware of. "I'll stay," she said.

Now her father spoke. "You are a child, only nine years old, but you have to know that in a few years you will become a woman, a pretty one. Then one of these horsemen will want to marry you, because your children with him will be more than half human, so they can be recognized as human and have human rights and recognition, the way these present crossbreeds do not. They don't care about you personally, only that you are human. That's why they maintain the tourist facilities: to tempt full-blooded humans to visit and maybe to stay; it is their strategy for ultimate recognition."

"But they won't *make* me marry one of them," Vinia said. "I can choose to leave at any time."

"They can be very persuasive. You'll wind up marrying an animal."

Vinia knew he was probably correct. Yet her unseen path guided her this way. "I still want to stay."

"Then we are quit of you," her father said sternly. "We want no animals in our family line." Her mother did not disagree.

So it was that Vinia stayed in Equine Castle on planet Animalia, disowned by her family. She hated that, but somehow, she had done it. Was she insane?

"No," Apoca said. "Merely uncertain. Now the next nexus."

Vinia was in her room when she heard the news that Equine Castle was sponsoring a multicastle dance. Crossbreeds from across the planet would be visiting. She was of course welcome to attend, regardless of her age, and if she needed an escort, one would be provided.

The green path took her to attending and accepting the escort. He turned out to be a handsome young man, Benny Buck, with brown eyes, brown hair with a central white streak, and a goatee. He was a Caprine crossbreed but looked completely human. She explained to him about her young age, and her need to wear the mask, because of not daring to breathe the allergens, and he was gracious. "You are pretty, regardless. I will call you my secret lady."

"Thank you." She appreciated the way he was treating her, which was so much better than she had experienced at home.

"I understand you are telekinetic," he said.

"Yes." She demonstrated by lifting his tie out from his shirt without touching it physically. "Close range only."

"I am nevertheless impressed."

She felt unduly flattered. No one had praised her talent before.

They went to the dance, and it was glorious. Benny was a practiced dancer and made Vinia's faltering steps seem like refined nuances. He held her just so and showed her off as the secret lady, making her feel pride even though she knew it was make-believe. She was falling into a crush on him, deeper with each dance. He could have seduced her despite her youth, but he remained a perfect gentleman, taking no liberties whatever. He was truly treating her like a lady.

Then her mask gave out. She had not realized that an hour had passed. Suddenly she was sneezing uncontrollably. "Oh, bleep," she gasped. "I must go back to my room, right now."

"I apologize. I forgot about the time limit."

He took her back. Only when she was safe in her sterile chamber did the sneezing abate. "I'm so sorry for ruining it!" she sobbed.

He would not let her take any blame. "Not your fault. Had I been more alert you would not have had to suffer this mischief. I apologize again. You danced beautifully."

"Oh, Benny!" she exclaimed, overcome by gratitude and regret. Then she burst into tears.

He picked her up, carried her to the bed, and laid her down on it. Then he sat on the bed beside her and stroked her hair until she stopped crying and fell asleep.

Vinia did not see Benny again. He was of another residence, Caprine Castle. Slowly her crush subsided. There had not been any substance to it, anyway. She did not try to attend another dance, not wanting to risk another disaster. She entertained herself playing card games, using her talent to move the cards. It wasn't much of a life, but she knew it was her own folly that had gotten her into it. A year passed.

And now she was at the next nexus with Apoca. She was alone in her room when an equine crossbreed knocked on her door and informed her that she had visitors.

There were the paths before her, now apparent to her future self. The green one led her to a waiting chamber to meet her visitors. Benny was there. "Hello, Vinia," he said, as if they had parted only yesterday. "This is Ion, who as you can see is unable to walk, so—"

The green path led right to him. "Oh, Ion! I can help you stand and walk." She did so, using her telekinesis to power his legs.

"And that was it," Vinia concluded. "I didn't know Ion was a prince and a Magician. I didn't care anything about him, except that I could help him, and I wanted to, and I did."

"And the path had led you there," Apoca said. "That is your real talent, Vinia. Your telekinesis is your secondary talent, the way my man-melting kiss is mine. My real one is my woman-strengthening kiss."

Vinia realized that it must be true. "But why did it hide itself from me?"

"I remember a story about a man long ago whose talent was that he could not be harmed by magic. But if others knew it, they might harm him by physical means. So the talent hid itself, because if another person wanted to harm him, he would naturally try magic first, unless he knew that would not work, so would try something else. In that devious manner, his own talent might harm him, were it known. So it kept itself secret.

I think that's why it is best that others do not know my private talent; better to let them think I have an elixir."

"I'll never tell," Vinia said impulsively and saw a flash of green around her.

"Similarly, your talent might be fouled up if others knew. So it hides itself, letting folk think that telekinesis is all you have. Only here in the neverland were we able to discover it." She smiled. "I'll never tell, either."

"Oh, Apoca, I want to be your friend!"

"And I yours." They hugged each other, and the green was all around them, some from Apoca's hair, some from Vinia's path.

"But we still have a problem," Vinia said. "Thanx needs your help, but I see why you can't leave your Lips tribe, and I can't tell anyone else why."

Apoca's hair turned blue. "We have a problem too. The Volents are pressing us hard, and I fear that in time they will prevail, and the Lips realm will be no more. Were our situation less dire, I would visit Thanx and help you get rid of the virus."

"There must be an answer," Vinia said. "If only we could find it."

"Maybe we can." Apoca's hair became yellow green. "Surely there are paths. Your talent can show the right one."

"But my paths focus on me. I sympathize with you, maybe love you since you kissed me, but I see no paths before you."

"I wonder. We are friends now. We each want what is best for the other."

"True. But that's not enough."

"Unless my problem becomes your problem. Then you will be able to see paths for it."

Vinia remained perplexed. "How?"

"If the Volents overrun our redoubt, and I am reduced to be the submissive mistress of King Vladimir, how will you feel?"

"Awful! I don't think I could be your friend anymore."

"Would you feel as if a part of you has been lost?"

"Yes!" Vinia agreed, dismayed.

"Then let's try together." Apoca came to her and put her arm around her, drawing her close. "Picture my problem as your problem, too. I want to help Thanx; you want to help the Lips. Is there any way to do both?"

Vinia pictured the joint problem. How could they help each other?

Then the paths formed, in all colors, radiating away from the two of them. One was green. "This way," Vinia said. She stepped forward to the green path.

"I see it," Apoca said, stepping with her.

And there it was. "You and your tribe must come to Thanx, to stay," Vinia said. "There you will be safe, because we have friends defending us. And you will be able to privately kiss the princesses, driving the virus out. Our enemies won't even know you're there, but they won't be able to make any progress against us, because the princesses will be nervy again, and the Lips will kiss any men who get through our perimeter."

"I see it," Apoca agreed. "This will save us all. But how can we get there without being ambushed by the lurking Volents?"

"Our flying carpet is big, and Sorceress Hilda can sew it bigger. It can take all of you. The Volents won't be able to intercept it in the air."

"And the path is green," Apoca agreed, her hair matching that color.

They hugged again, pleased.

They walked back the way they had come and soon reached the place of multiple reflections. They walked through that and emerged before the two mirrors.

"You disappeared!" Ion exclaimed. "Where were you?"

Vinia smiled. "In neverland. It's complicated. But now I understand why Queen Apoca couldn't help us before. That has changed. We have worked it out. She can cure the Lips who get caught and dosed with the virus. She can do the same for our princesses."

"How?" Ion asked.

"Apoca and the Lips will return with us to Thanx," Vinia said. "Where Apoca will privately interview the princesses and enable them to fight off the virus with her secret technique. The Lips will become another portion of the queendom. Hilda can enlarge the carpet again, to carry them all, because we need to do this soon."

Ion and Hilda exchanged a glance. "Of course," Ion agreed, as if it had been obvious all along.

"We knew you could do it, Vinia," Hilda said.

Vinia laughed. "You had more confidence in me than I did."

"I will start sewing," Hilda said.

Chapter 14

HOME

"It will take me two days to sew the carpet amendment," Hilda said. "Fifty people is a lot to carry."

"Let's go sightseeing, Benny," Ion suggested.

"Sure," Benny agreed.

Hilda frowned, knowing they would be looking at the buxom Lips girls, whose clothing did not necessarily cover everything of interest, but she was not able to protest.

Vinia saw the green path. Now she could view it whenever she wanted to, and it gave her significantly increased confidence. "We can use the time to assemble the Lips tribe here."

"Yes!" Ion agreed a bit too readily.

She concealed her annoyance and turned to Apoca. "We need a private room for a very private conference."

"This way," Apoca said as her hair turned green. She led the way to the topmost chamber of the wicker castle. "I gather you have something special in mind."

"Yes. I am following the paths, now that I can see them, thanks to you. We may need an hour alone."

Tarzana and Jane were guarding it. "Protect this room from visitation," Apoca told them. "Spread word: all Lips to assemble here tomorrow with their belongings. We are about to move to a new location. But do not allow any but Lips to hear that. The Male Volents must not learn, lest they interfere." Which could be deadly.

The two nodded together. Then Jane departed, the hem of her skirt curling up naughtily, while Tarzana stood at parade rest facing the stairway below. No one would pass.

Alone in the chamber, Vinia explained. "I thought of alternative courses, and the paths led me to this. I will summon the Demons Grossclout and Demesne here. You can kiss Demesne and cure her of the virus. That way she will know that it is true and will arrange for the princesses and other infected females to be kissed. They will rely on her even if they don't yet know you."

Apoca's hair turned blue. "But I prefer to keep my secret. Demons can be mischief."

"And I prefer to keep mine. But these two can be trusted, and they have the authority to act. I am thinking that Prince Ion should have an elixir that prevents anyone from speaking the secrets elsewhere."

Apoca nodded, green again. "That would do it."

"My paths also indicate that they should bring a nonroyal friend to help you orient and meet the others. I was surprised by her identity, but I can't argue with the green, now that I can see it and know that it is not my wild guessing."

"A friend?"

"Nimbus. I got to know her during the one-day war. You can kiss her after you kiss Demesne."

"Nimbus? She must be a special woman."

"She is special, but she's not exactly a woman. She's a nickelpede."

"You mean she's excruciatingly nasty?" Apoca's hair was doubtful yellow. "Why would you choose her?"

Vinia laughed. "I mean a literal nickelpede. She's a nice girl when you get to know her. She won't gouge you but will gouge any person or critter who attacks you. We'll need a translation spell, and an accommodation spell for the kiss, but then it should be fine."

Apoca gazed at her, her hair light red. "You're not joking."

"I am not joking."

Apoca went to the chamber entrance, her hair now a neutral gray. "Ask Prince Ion to come here."

Tarzana give a directive. Soon Ion appeared. Vinia explained briefly, and he produced two vials. Vinia took them and pocketed them. "Thanks, Ion."

"Do I get a kiss?"

"Of course." She kissed him, flattered that he wanted one in public. Then he departed, satisfied.

"He loves you already," Apoca said wisely, her hair gray green.

"And I love him. We may still be children, but we know."

"Sometimes that is the case."

Vinia spoke to the ring. "Professor Grossclout, please."

In no more than two-thirds of a moment the Demon professor answered. "What are you up to now, wandering girl?"

"As you know, we plan to bring Queen Apoca to Thanx, along with the Lips tribe. But we need to make some arrangements. If you and Queen Demesne can come here to speak with Queen Apoca, we should be able to work it out."

"Demesne is unfortunately indisposed."

"By the virus," Vinia agreed. "Bring her here. Apoca will cure her. But the process is private."

"You *are* up to something, Vinia."

"Yes. And please bring Nimbus with you, if she cares to come."

He digested that. "We'll pop over in just over a moment."

"Thank you."

Right on time the Demon, Demoness, and the nickelpede appeared in the chamber. Vinia hastened to introduce them to each other. "Queen Apoca, these are Professor Grossclout, Queen Demesne, and Nimbus Nickelpede perching on Demesne's shoulder. Professor, Demesne, and Nimbus, this is Queen Apoca Lips."

"Evocative name," Grossclout remarked. "It smells of the destruction of a world."

Apoca smiled, her hair turning green with red curls. Vinia had not seen that before. But of course these two had known each other from the School of Magic. This might be a form of flirting. He had after all taught her how to use her kisses. "The end of patriarchies, perhaps."

The Demoness and nickelpede were meekly silent.

"What happens here must stay here," Vinia said. "If it got out and around, our enemies could use it to mess us up."

"Got it," Grossclout said, and the Demoness and nickelpede nodded obligingly.

"First I must explain that my mysterious good luck is actually a hidden talent that I prefer to keep hidden," Vinia said. "I can see the paths to the near future, and some are better than others. That's why I asked you three to come here; it is the most promising path."

"Ah, that explains a lot," Grossclout said.

"I have a vial of translation elixir," Vinia said, opening it. The vapor puffed out. "Hello, Nimbus."

The nickelpede clicked her pincers. "Hello, Vinia."

"And a vial of accommodation elixir," Vinia said, opening the second one. The vapor emerged and spread.

"Queen Apoca's kiss can render men her love slaves, as can that of any of the Lips tribe," Vinia said for the benefit of Demesne and Nimbus. "But she can also kiss women, and that is her hidden power. It renders them independent, curing the submission virus."

"Oho!" Grossclout said. "Not an elixir, but a kiss." This, too, was for the benefit of the others, masking his prior knowledge of it. He had kept the secret well.

"Yes," Vinia said. "Now, if you will, Queen Apoca, kiss Demesne and Nimbus."

Apoca went to Demesne, embraced her, and kissed her on the mouth.

"Oh, my!" the Demoness exclaimed. "It's gone! I can be assertive again."

"Yes," Vinia said. "But her secret must be kept."

Demesne turned to Grossclout. "And you will cease your flirting forthwith, you lecher. I don't care what your relationship with Hot Lips was before; you're mine now."

"Yes, dear," he said meekly. Then they all laughed.

Apoca leaned down to kiss the nickelpede on Demesne's shoulder. It was now feasible, thanks to the elixir. "Oh, thank you!" Nimbus said. "I am my vicious self again. With the virus I couldn't even gouge male prey."

"Please," Vinia said. "Join Queen Apoca, Nimbus, and stay with her so you can introduce her to the others of all species at Thanx."

"Gladly," Nimbus agreed. "If she doesn't mind having a nickelpede for company."

Apoca laughed, her hair green. "I kissed you, didn't I? Now that I understand you, and Vinia speaks for you, I can handle it." She extended her hand, and the nickelpede climbed onto it.

"I will protect you from any noxious vermin that appear," Nimbus said. "So that you may sleep securely in the wilderness."

"Including the human male kind?"

Nimbus laughed. "Their flesh tastes best."

"Then we should get along," Apoca agreed.

Vinia turned to Grossclout. "Are you satisfied about the nature of Queen Apoca's power, and her need for secrecy?"

"Oh, yes. I can feel the radiating independence of my beloved."

"That's good," Demesne said. "If you goose me in public, I will slap you."

"I know it and love it."

"And Queen Apoca will kiss all the submissive ladies of Thanx, in due course," Vinia said, "Then the queendom will be restored to its original vigor. That may take a while, as she can't do it in public, but soon it will be accomplished, and she will be there to counter any future virus infestations."

"Then I think we are done here," Vinia said.

"We are," Demesne agreed. She turned again to Grossclout. "Now I will show you how a truly nonsubmissive woman treats her man."

"I can't wait."

"You won't have to. We'll do it as we travel."

The two vanished, leaving a cloud of sulfurous smoke in a conformation that Vinia suspected would have freaked her out had she been old enough to understand what it was.

"Wow," Nimbus said. "That makes me eager to find a male of my own."

"Me too," Apoca agreed, her hair a mottled yellow. "And not a love slave. That relationship requires dominance in both parties."

Vinia couldn't wait until she grew up.

Then she got a peculiar green notion. She went to Tarzana, still on guard. "Do you have a man?"

"No. Men aren't interested in tough women like me, and I don't want a love slave."

"Would you like an independent one?"

The woman laughed. "Sure. Even a Volent, if he behaved. But what's the use? I'm a warrior, not a lover. Loving is for women like Jana. I can only dream."

Jana. Vinia's mental name of Jane was pretty close, coincidentally. Or was it coincidence? Had her path guided her even there?

Then Vinia got another idea, a wild one, but that path was green. She could hardly believe it, but she had to trust the color. "There might be one for you."

Tarzana laughed. "One who finds me sexy?"

"Yes."

"Bring him here. I'd play easy to get." She thought she was calling Vinia's bluff.

Vinia went to Hilda. "You still have the little carpet Ion uses when I am not with him?"

"I have two of them, so that when I need to repair one, he can use the other."

"May I borrow them?"

"What for? You're not lame."

"I want to go pick up Vol."

"Who?"

"The Volent guard we rescued from likely severe punishment."

Hilda stared at her. "This is green?" She had picked up quickly on the colored paths.

"Yes," Vinia said. "I find it hard to believe myself. But the green path is to pick him up and take him with us."

Hilda sighed. "I don't think I dare argue with the green. I have seen too much of your seemingly miraculous successes. Take the minicarpets. Take a vial of Ion's antivirus elixir, to be sure he's clean. Bring him back. I will clear it with Apoca."

"Thank you." Vinia took the carpets, rolling one up to carry and riding the other. It was controlled by her shifts of weight: she had practiced with it before, curious, and now she realized that there had been a reason she had not known at the time: to prepare her for this. How much of her life had been governed by the paths, before she became conscious of them? Maybe most of it. That was a bit eerie in retrospect.

Vinia went to Ion, who gave her the vial and a kiss.

She then flew the little carpet to the settlement where they had left Vol, using the ring to orient on him. "Vol!" she called when she approached it. The Volent women in that area stared submissively at her, but Vol heard her. "What?" he asked, confused.

"Remember me? Vinia? From the party of children who escaped you, then brought you here?"

"I remember. But you don't want to be here, girl. News of your appearance here is already spreading, and the men regard you as fair game despite your youth."

"Neither do you want to be here. You're not into submissive women." She unrolled the companion carpet. "Get on this and hang on to my hand. I am taking you to a better place."

He pondered most of a moment. Then he saw men converging on them. He jumped onto the carpet and took her hand. She flew up, towing him unsteadily. They barely cleared the heads of the men, who stared up open-mouthed at the flying carpets. Then they were high in the sky and away.

"If I hadn't been on your big carpet before, I'd never believe this." Vol glanced down. "Or dared to do it." He paused for a shaky breath. He was a soldier, but perching precariously on a miniature flying carpet was surely not his normal course. "Why?"

"I don't know," she confessed. "I . . . was told to do it. Do you think you could live with a Lips woman, if she did not make you a love slave?"

"Maybe. They're sexy as Hades. But why would she not enslave me? I'm an enemy man."

"I don't know. But I think they need an independent man."

"This is weird."

"Weird," she agreed. "How do you feel about a warrior woman?"

"If she's shaped like a Lips, I'd love to get my hands on her. I don't go for those virus-infected submissives, as you seem to know. I like a woman with fire."

That reminded her. "I need to disinfect you. This won't hurt you, just clean out any virus with you."

"Okay."

She opened the vial. The vapor surrounded them both. Little sparks flew. He had indeed been contaminated, but now he was clean. "Done," she said.

"I guess the virus would sort of mess up the point," he agreed.

They arrived back at the wicker castle. Tarzana was on guard. "Vinia! What is this? You took a prisoner?"

"Not exactly, Tara. Please, I want you to kiss this man without your power."

Both Tarzana and Vol stared at her.

"Please. It's important." Because the path was solidly green. Even for her accidental simplification of the name.

"The queen told me to do whatever you said." Tarzana approached

Vol, who was plainly of mixed sentiments: he was admiring her heroically female proportions, but afraid of her lips.

"Trust me, Vol," Vinia told him. "Kiss her."

The Vol and the Lips came together and kissed. Then he stepped back. "I'm not changed," he said in wonder.

"If you make peace with the Lips," Vinia said, "you can have one to be your girlfriend. She will not enslave you but will tell you what to do so you can be among them without trouble."

"How about her?" he asked, looking at Tara.

"If she is interested." Vinia knew she was. She had figured that these two could connect.

Tarzana looked at him. "You're a reasonably handsome man. Do you want me?"

"Your kiss did not enslave me, Tara, but it did tempt me. It made me wonder how it would be with you if you wanted to be with me, instead of just showing how you don't have to wipe me out. What would you give me if I agreed?"

"Everything." Tara was not socially subtle, being a warrior.

"Deal!"

"Deal," she agreed. Vinia could see that they were already quite interested in each other, he because he desired a shapely woman, she because she wanted the unforced desire of a man. Probably she had seen how men looked at Jane and envied it.

Vol's breathing had quickened. "When?"

She glanced sidelong at him, maybe a technique she had observed in Jane. "My shift ends in half an hour. Then I can get out of my armor. Maybe out of more."

He licked his lips. "I'll wait."

Vinia departed, following her green path away from them. She had two carpets to return to Hilda. Neither the man nor the women seemed to miss her.

Two days later they were all aboard the vastly expanded carpet: the four children, Apoca with Nimbus, and about fifty Lips women of all ages. All the grown Lips were buxom, and all had translucent hair amplifying the colors of their scalps, but they were limited to single colors: red, green, blue, yellow, black, gray, or combinations, which did not reflect their moods. It did make them easy to tell apart, because no two were identical. In fact Vinia found it easier to think of them by their colors rather than their given names.

Tara and Vol were there, too, holding hands. "Hello," Vinia said brightly, knowing they would not tell her what they had done together in the interim. "How is everything?"

Vol smiled. "She made a love slave of me."

The paths flashed black. "Oh, no! She wasn't supposed to do that."

Tara laughed. "Relax, child. I did it the old-fashioned way. I seduced him ten times in succession. It was fun."

Vol joined her laugh. "You didn't need to. You already had me locked in at nine, maybe eight."

"Maybe even seven or six," she agreed. Then, to Vinia: "The distinction between a kissed love slave and an earned one is that the first is the slave of any woman he encounters. It's like the virus, sapping all willpower. But the second orients on the one woman; he is not subject to any others."

That struck Vinia as a useful lesson. She lacked the power of the Lips kiss, but the earned attachment was better.

The full group stood on the front deck of the carpet as Apoca addressed them. "I regret being mysterious about our destination, before," she said, her hair flashing yellow. "But it was important that the Volents not know it, and there could be spies among the servants. Now it can be told. There is a new kingdom being established, actually a queendom, organized and run by militantly independent females of many species. Even the nickelpedes." She put a hand on her shoulder and lifted Nimbus up for all to see. "This is Nimbus, who as you can see is not gouging me. Neither will the ones in the queendom: you may safely befriend any you choose, and they will help you explore the premises. There is a truce between the species there." Nimbus waved a pincer as Apoca put her back on her shoulder. "The new nation is titled Thanx. There are males there, but they are not in charge, and they do prefer their females fiery. Any man who joins the Queendom of Thanx does so with the understanding that he has no political future there, and the woman he is with will be imperious." She smiled, her hair turning green yellow. "That said, an imperious woman can make a man quite satisfied to be with her, when she chooses."

The Lips women laughed. They knew exactly what she was talking about.

"Ain't that the truth," Vol murmured, covertly pinching Tara's bottom. She pinched his bottom back.

"When we arrive," Apoca continued, "I will be circulating among the females, doing my secret thing. Prince Ion has given me a vial of elixir that will lock the ones I meet into secrecy on that score: you already understand the need. You may go out to meet the men of the adjacent kingdoms, who are coming to respect the feminist state. We expect to reside there permanently, protecting it from the virus and invading males, and to establish families of our own. We will be safe there. We need fear no more Volent attacks."

There was a cheer. It was clear that the Lips woman were tired of being constantly besieged by men who wanted only one thing, which was not independence.

"When you meet the men," Apoca continued, as she beckoned Vol and Tara forward, "you will need to woo them without kissing them into slavery. Use the power kiss only when one attempts to abuse you. Now those interested will have a chance to rehearse. We have a man here, a Volent, a willing captive. You may kiss him and practice your wiles on him. But be warned: you are not to try to kiss him into slavery. If you do, you will have to deal with his woman." Tara, in full armor and armed, bared her teeth as if about to chomp off an arm or leg. She was a fearsome figure.

Then Vol and Tara embraced, and kissed, showing their relationship. They separated. "Jump," Tara ordered Vol. Instead he spanked her.

"As you can see, he has not been enslaved, at least not in the manner we do when we kiss for effect." Apoca said. "Each interview will terminate with that demonstration. You will not, I repeat NOT, kiss him for effect."

"Actually this is just practice," Apoca murmured to Vinia. "When a man is enslaved by true love, our kisses no longer have effect. But we need to have them amend their reflexes, so that other men don't get enslaved by accident."

They separated, and Vol took center stage. "One minute of flirting is all you get," Apoca told them. "Make the most of it. Perfect your technique."

An instant line formed. Tara sent the first woman, a red-haired vixen, on to interact with Vol. She smiled at him, then hugged and kissed him passionately. She put her hands on him in places she shouldn't, and he returned the favor. Then she ordered him to jump. Instead he spanked her bottom.

The group laughed. The demonstration had been made. He had not been kissed into slavery.

The next woman was green-haired Jana. Vinia was concerned, because she was significantly prettier than Tara, but the paths remained green. Jana kissed Vol and squeezed his bottom, and he squeezed hers. She drew his head down and pressed his face into her heaving bosom. Then she stepped back and let her skirt fly up to expose her marvelously full green panties. He looked and freaked out.

"Wake," she said, snapping her fingers as her skirt dropped back into place.

Vol recovered, seeming a bit bemused.

"Spank," Jana said.

Vol jumped.

The throng burst into laughter as Vol returned to Tara for a hug. It had been another little act, but three things were apparent: the man had not been enslaved, and he did belong to Tara, and he was very much enjoying this demonstration with the ladies, dangerous as they were. Tara, far from being jealous, was clearly proud to show him off. She had nailed her man, as she said, the old-fashioned way. Someday Vinia hoped she herself would be able to do the same with Ion. They loved each other already, but there was obviously more to learn.

There was more discussion and clarification, as other women took their turns, but that was the essence. Vinia and Ion retired to their cubby for some relaxation and kissing. That much, at least, they could do.

The flight continued, with frequent practice sessions, as it was manifest that all participants enjoyed them. Vinia herself even took a turn, kissing Vol and getting spanked by him. "You did me such an enormous favor, I don't think I can ever repay you," he told her. "You gave me my dream."

"Well, we needed a demonstration model."

He laughed. "I don't know what your secret is, but I can tell that you are the center of this narrative."

She shrugged. "Somebody had to be."

In due course they arrived at Thanx, where Queen Demesne welcomed them, clearly her old independent self. Then the Lips women went out to meet the men of the neighboring human kingdom, who had been advised of the occasion. It seemed that several of them were quite willing to swear fealty to the queendom, in exchange for shapely and accommodating Lips wives who were no longer enemies. Peace with the neighbors was already being established.

Meanwhile Apoca and Nimbus went quietly on their own errand, first to the princesses, then the allied females. The invading virus was being quietly eliminated.

In the evening there was a curious visit that occurred while Vinia, Apoca, and Nimbus were relaxing after a busy day. The queen of Hoo-Hah paid Demesne a visit, attended by the dancing girl Dulcie. Vinia remembered both from a certain complication with a potency elixir during the visit to WhoHe, the king of Hoo-Hah. This could be mischief. Yet the paths were generally green.

Demesne glanced at Vinia, who nodded affirmatively. There was something to be gained here.

Queen Wilda spotted Vinia immediately. "Introduce us," she snapped.

"Uh, this is Queen Wilda of Hoo-hah, with her servant Dulcie," Vinia said awkwardly. "Queen Demesne of Thanx, and Queen Apoca of the Lips tribe."

"Ah, the Lips," Wilda agreed. "That is what I am here for. I want a Lips woman as a mistress for my husband."

This set them back somewhat. "Are you aware of our nature?" Apoca inquired cautiously.

"Yes. If he mistreats her, she will kiss him into submission."

"But why would you want such a woman in your palace?" Demesne asked.

Wilda smiled glacially. "With her there, he is unlikely to seek any other mistresses. That will be a relief to the rest of us."

Apoca made a soundless whistle. "I note that you believe in candor."

Wilda glanced at Demesne and Vinia. "I believe you comprehend my husband's nature. A bit more self-discipline would be in order. Do you disagree?"

A smile struggled to escape Demesne's lips, and finally succeeded. "No."

"There are problems," Apoca said. "All my Lips subjects are required to remain resident here in Thanx. Going to the Kingdom of Hoo-Hah would not be in order. Also, the Lips woman would have to be amenable to such an assignment."

Wilda cracked a bit of a smile. "She would have what amount to royal prerogatives, with the very best in residence, food, and treatment." Now a frown appeared. "She would have to manage King WhoHe, but I suspect that a Lips woman would be capable."

"What do you offer for such a placement?" Demesne asked.

"Peace between our nations. Even cooperation."

Demesne nodded. Those were good offerings.

"Maybe if you set up an embassy," Vinia suggested, seeing a green path. "Wouldn't its premises be considered part of Thanx?"

"Excellent idea," Demesne agreed. "Would that satisfy you, Queen Apoca?"

"Their kingdom is adjacent to Thanx? I believe it would."

"Then perhaps you should query your remaining citizens." She glanced at Vinia. "To find an amenable one. I don't mind if it is an act, as long as she maintains it."

"I'll do it," Vinia agreed. Her paths would lead her to the right person.

She went to the section that had been set aside for the Lips. A man was constructing a large wicker framework. Of course; they had brought their architect along. There was a small crew of Lips women helping him, following his instructions, to make the work go faster. One of them stood close to him and kissed him occasionally. That, too, was obvious in retrospect: they had made him amenable by providing him with a friendly Lips woman, no slavery. Maybe she was more than a friend. It was surprising how eager these women seemed to be for nonslave men who were not demanding complete submission. It seemed that both genders preferred independence in the other, to a reasonable extent.

The green path led to one of the working women. This one was yellow of hair and eye, her dress matching, and her face was fair. "May I talk with you?" Vinia asked. "I'm Vinia, on an errand."

The woman looked at her. "Me? I know who you are; you're Prince Ion's consort. But I am Yasmine, supposedly a fragrant flower. In fact I am nobody."

"Didn't you go to check out the visiting men of Hoo-Hah?"

"No. I was busy here. I wouldn't have wanted any of them, anyway; I have delusions of grandeur. You know, fancy clothing, gourmet food, highbrow entertainment, lots of spare time. Those men couldn't provide it."

The path had been correct. "How would you like to be the mistress of the King of Hoo-Hah?"

Yasmine laughed. "I'd love it! It wouldn't matter how boorish he is; all men are like that. It is easy to satisfy their passion and put them to sleep. It's the royal life I crave. But now that we've had our little joke, why are you still talking with me?"

"Because Thanx is looking for an ambassador to Hoo-Hah, and we think you're the one for that."

"Ambassador! I'm a common girl. Isn't the joke wearing thin?"

"It's no joke. Come with me. You are about to realize your dream."

Yasmine shook her head doubtfully but did accompany Vinia to the dragon's cave.

Queen Wilda spied them as they entered. "She'll do," she said.

"But you haven't even met her yet," Demesne protested.

"She wouldn't be here if she weren't interested. I am judging by her appearance. She's got the goods; the king will like her. That's all that counts."

Demesne glanced at Vinia. "Green?"

"Yes." Then, belatedly, Vinia introduced them. "This is Yasmine Lips. This is Queen Wilda of Hoo-Hah."

Demesne looked at Yasmine. "You are now our ambassador to Hoo-Hah. You may spend your time with King WhoHe until we contact you."

"But I know nothing about politics!" Yasmine protested.

"Neither does the king," Wilda said. "I handle the routine things, like running the kingdom. He handles the important things, like grabbing girls. This way, dear."

Yasmine nodded, catching on. "I am up for grabs. You have gowns that will fit me?"

"Our tailor will custom-make them for you while you sample the royal cuisine. All you have to do is keep the king's attention while he's conscious."

Yasmine nodded appreciatively. This was indeed the kind of life she sought.

The two departed. "I think Hoo-Hah will not be invading us again," Demesne remarked, satisfied.

But Vinia had a qualm. "Uh-oh," Demesne said, seeing it hanging there. Qualms were uncomfortable things to have close by; no one really liked them. "You thought of something."

"Yes," Vinia said, regretfully. "The humans will not invade, but don't we need to make similar peace with the other kingdoms, to be sure none of them remain mad at us?"

"She is right," Grossclout said. "Thanx is not yet secure."

Demesne sighed. "But we can't expect the other kingdoms to resolve themselves the way this one did."

They looked at Vinia. "I'll follow the paths tomorrow," she agreed.

When Vinia woke in the morning, the paths were before her. She followed the greenest one. It led to the kitchen. Breakfast, of course. But it did not lead to the cafeteria section, but to head dietitian Goblette's office. What did it have in mind? Because sometimes the paths did seem to have wills of their own, as she became more familiar with them.

"I know why you're here," Goblette said.

"You do?"

"Demesne mentioned it last night. Relations with the neighboring kingdoms, so they won't try to invade us again."

"Oh. Yes."

"And we know how typical goblins feel about our kind."

About gay and lesbian goblins. "Uh, yes."

"So Georgia and I will go see the king and offer to quietly employ any goblins who want to come here. Those will be the gays. They'll be happy here, and the kingdom will be free of them. No one will say anything, and we will keep their secret." She glanced at grapevines on her desk. "The grapevine says that the king's niece Godeleva, Godel for short, is the shame of his family. We know exactly how that is. She should make a nice addition to our staff and can serve as liaison when there is need."

She had it all figured out, to Vinia's relief. "I think you have it covered."

"We do. Have a nice breakfast."

Vinia did. Then she followed the next green path. This led to the Communications Office, where Chloe Centaur worked. Dragoman snoozed in the background.

"Ah yes," Chloe said, her telepathy advising her before Vinia spoke. "Get on my back. We'll go see the ogres."

Vinia climbed on. "Be back shortly, dear," the centaur called. The dragon flicked an eyelid. He looked pleasantly worn out. This was a queendom, but its consorts were well satisfied.

They trotted off. "I love your paths," Chloe said as they got outside and headed for the ogre kingdom. She was seeing them through Vinia's mind.

"Uh, yes," Vinia said. "They do help."

Chloe spread her wings and took off. Now the green path was in the air before them. Soon they came to the ogre king's castle, a brutish mass of twisted tree trunks and traumatized stones.

An ogre soldier was on guard. "Who you?" he demanded belligerently.

"I am Princess Chloe of the Queendom of Thanx. I have come to see King Ogden, who is free at the moment."

The guard tried to think of a suitable denial but was unable. Ogres were justifiably proud of their stupidity, and he was proud. Chloe trotted past him and entered the king's chamber.

King Ogden was an ugly brute, which was probably his main qualification for his status. "Who you?" he demanded, in much the manner of the guard.

"I am Chloe Centaur, in charge of communications at the Queendom of Thanx. I am telepathic, so I know your secrets. You have a shameful minority element in your kingdom you need to clear out."

Ogden started stupidly at her.

"You are unable to get rid of them," Chloe continued. "Because they turn up in the best and worst families. They are not mean-spirited, but there's always that risk of embarrassing exposure. You try to hide or ignore them, but it is a continuing problem."

Vinia was uneasy. Did the ogres have the same problem the goblins did? This could be awkward. Yet Chloe stood directly on the green path.

"You know what I'm talking about," Chloe said. "You need to be quietly free of them."

The king grunted affirmatively.

"Thanx offers you a way to do that. We are opening a facility where ogres of this persuasion, male and female, will be welcome. Especially the females, as we are a feminist state. All you have to do is let them join us."

"Who?" the king demanded.

"For example, your daughter, Ottie. She's a secret reader." Her gaze slanted off to the side, where a young ogress sat. "She's way too smart for your court."

The ogress looked guiltily up from the book she had been furtively reading.

So that was the ogre's shame! Some of them were unconscionably smart. What an embarrassment to have one in the king's family.

"We need a librarian at Thanx," Chloe said. "Ottie can be it. Any others who want to join are welcome to come help her, and if they sneak in a little reading, no one else need know. We will never advertise their true nature."

The king capitulated. "Go," he told the girl.

Ottie got up and joined them. Soon they were on their way back to Thanx. Another kingdom was now at peace with Thanx.

"I can read all I want?" Ottie asked as they flew.

"All you want," Chloe agreed. "In fact you will be in charge of fetching in new books, to fill out the library."

The girl gave a sigh of pure delight.

The green had scored again.

The next path led Vinia to the salamander field, where they had held off the trolls. There was Fiera Fire Cloud, in her human manifestation. Vinia approached her. "I need to talk with the troll king, and I hesitate to go alone."

"They do have a taste for young girls," Fiera agreed. Vinia wasn't sure whether that was figurative or literal. Maybe both. "I will protect you."

They went to the king, Truant Troll. He was eyeing Fiera, half wary of her fire capability, half admiring her form. "You here for fun or fury, hot wench?"

"Neither," Fiera said.

Then Vinia got an idea, and it flashed green. "The trolls maintain the trollway that crisscrosses Xanth. But there is no stop here. We need to set one up."

"They wouldn't come here. We're way in the hinterlands."

"But suppose this stop was run by young, fair lady trolls? That would make it appealing for traveling trolls and others of similar persuasion. They could maintain it just inside the Thanx border so that nontroll travelers would not be concerned, but the personnel would be yours. Neat jobs, nice contacts."

Truant focused on her. "You interest me, girl." Fiera fired up warningly. "I mean your idea. Thanx would support it?"

Vinia spoke to her ring. "Demesne."

"I heard," the Demoness said. "Yes, we would approve it, in the interest of harmony between nations."

Truant nodded. "You clear it with the trollway authorities. We'll recruit the girls."

Thus readily was it accomplished.

The next was the gnome kingdom, the one that had been balked by the snails. Grossclout clued Vinia in on a key aspect, and she went to see Elga Elf, who was the princess in charge of Maintenance. Then Vinia and Elga went to see Snazzy Snail, who was readily identifiable by her lovely shell, who took them to Queen Snafu. "Our survey indicates petrol power crystals buried beneath your territory," Elga said. "They could free the robots from burning polluting coal and wood. There will surely be a market that will make this territory important. We can't mine them, but the gnomes could."

"I have heard of those crystals," Snafu said. "They radiate energy that makes nearby males impotent. That's why they have not been seriously mined before."

"You are well informed," Elga said. "However, there is no such effect on females. The gnomides could do it, especially here in the feminist queendom."

Snafu's feelers wiggled appreciatively. "In that case, let the lady gnomes in."

Vinia realized that they hadn't even yet approached the gnomes, but the deal was as good as done.

Finally Vinia went to see her friend Ghorgeous Ghost, still following the green path. "You ghosts stopped the dragons admirably. Now do you think you could work with them to make them friendly to Thanx instead of antagonistic?"

"We are already well on the way," the ghost replied. "We are working with their ladies to animate revered ancestors. They know they're not real, but they very much like the appearance."

"So the dragons will not be invading Thanx again?"

"That's right. We're pretty much friends now."

"That's a relief." Vinia had had a long day and was glad to see it end.

"Things seem to be in order, here," Grossclout said. "The queendom is established and secured. Tomorrow you children can fly home."

That seemed good to Vinia, especially since green surrounded him.

The four of them packed up the carpet, now separated from the huge addition that had transported the Lips tribe and made ready to depart. Vinia was feeling a little sad and knew the others felt much the same. It had been such a marvelous adventure, for all its problems, and now it was over. "I'm almost sorry to leave Thanx," Vinia said. That was an understatement; all her new friends were here as citizens.

"Me too," Ben said. "And not just because of the Lips girls." He glanced at Hilda, but she was wise to him and refused to be baited.

"Still, we need to check out—" Ion began, before Vinia's look threatened to chop off his knees. "With Demesne," he finished. "She mentioned it." Then they both smiled. It was a kind of game between them, her supposed jealousy of his nascent interest in other girls.

They walked to the main cave. Queen Demesne was there, in front of a broad curtain that closed off the rest of the cave. "What is it, dears?" she inquired, looking up from her desk of papers.

Ion glanced at Vinia. She took the hint. "It is time for us to go home. We're just here to clear it with you."

Demesne smiled. "That's fine, dear. Oh, one detail: Apoca will accompany you. She wants to meet your folks and establish formal relations between Adamant and Thanx. I have deputized her for that."

Now Vinia saw Apoca and Nimbus standing behind Demesne. "Oh, of course, if she wants. We have room on the carpet." She loved the idea of her closest new friend coming along. Apoca was the most recent, but she was special, and not just because she had enabled Vinia to discover her hidden second talent. The two of them just seemed to relate very well.

"Thank you," Apoca said. "I am taking temporary leave from kissing women, to rest my lips, though I shall return soon to resume."

Yet Vinia was strangely reluctant to end it. There were so many new friends here in Thanx! But that was the way of it. She belonged with Ion.

"One other detail," Demesne said. She put a hand to the curtain and drew it aside.

There beyond it were all the other princesses, together with their consorts, and all Vinia's friends from the invasion. "Surprise!" they chorused.

"It's a farewell party," Hilda said, surprised.

Then they were all clustered around the four children. "We owe everything to you," Hula Human said.

"Everything!" Goblette Goblin agreed, with Georgia nodding behind her.

"And more," Elga Elf said.

"You made it all possible, when we were crystallized," Chloe Centaur said, with Dragoman Dragon behind her.

"And we can never truly repay you," Beetrix Bee buzzed.

"But we will always honor you as the true creators of Thanx," Demesne Demoness said, with Grossclout behind her.

The other friends Vinia had made were there, too: Signal Siren in a bucket of water, Sali Salamander, Ghorgeous Ghost, Snazzy Snail, and Lorna Lovebug. Even Fiera Fire Cloud was present, in her human form. Nimbus Nickelpede was with Apoca.

It was a lovely send-off. Vinia felt tears in her eyes and knew the other children were sharing her mood. They had managed to rescue the six crystallized princesses!

"More than that," Chloe murmured, reading her mind. "You have been marvelous. You have enabled a new nation in Xanth. You will be remembered."

It was quite a party, with all the trimmings, the four children at the center.

Then they were on the carpet and flying toward Adamant. It was routine, except for the feelings. Vinia and Hilda cried openly with mixed joy and grief, while the boys suffered in silence.

In due course they arrived at Adamant. Now Ion and Hilda had tearful reunions with their parents Hilarion and Ida, while Vinia waited to introduce Apoca and Nimbus to them more formally.

"A nickelpede!" Queen Ida said, surprised.

"She was my host when I enlisted the help of the nickelpedes to save Thanx," Vinia explained. "She's a nice person." And before long Ida was holding Nimbus on her hand, amazed and appreciative. Any friend of her child was a friend of hers.

But the main new interest was Apoca. Vinia told how she had become friends with Apoca, having common interests, which she did not specify.

"And do you have a consort, Apoca?" Ida asked.

"None as yet," the Lips queen answered. "But I am not yet old. There should be time." Vinia saw a flash of green as she spoke. There should indeed be time.

There was a sumptuous welcoming banquet. Then, full and tired, the children retired to their chambers, and Apoca and Nimbus joined them. They settled down to sleep.

But something was bothering Vinia. She focused and realized it was the colors around her. They had been generally green throughout, but now were a tangled blue, red, and yellow. The paths were wrong!

"Tell," Ion murmured.

"It's not right for us to be here anymore," Vinia said. "I don't understand it, but that's what the paths indicate."

"Conference," he said, catching on immediately. He raised his voice. "Hilda. Benny, Apoca. Nimbus. We need to talk."

The others joined them in their assorted nightclothes. "The paths are troubled," Apoca said, her hair yellow, reflecting her own doubt. "Am I correct?"

"Yes," Vinia said sadly. "Something is wrong."

"We feel it too," Hilda said. "Somehow this no longer feels like home. That's weird, because it *is* home."

"Where is the green?" Ion asked.

Vinia searched. Finally she found a green sliver. She oriented on it and it broadened, pointing to somewhere. Then she recognized it. "Thanx."

"You four are children only chronologically," Apoca said, and Nimbus on her shoulder nodded: the nickelpede was adult. "In experience you are now well into adult status. You can no longer be satisfied to be obedient members of your childhood context. You need a new venue, where you can be accepted for what you are now and will become in the near future. I believe the Queendom of Thanx is that venue. That is where your real friends are, and where you want to grow up."

A four-way look circulated. Then they nodded together. The green was all around them. "My true home is wherever you are, Vinia," Ion said.

"And mine is with you," Hilda told Benny.

"I believe Thanx can use a Magician, a Sorceress, a crossbreed, and a seer of paths," Apoca concluded. "Apart from valuing your friendship. I saw that they were as sorry to see you depart as you were to go. Now you can return."

"We're going home," Vinia said, relieved. "Even if it isn't where we thought."

Then they hugged together, the six of them, and the green brightened.

Author's Note

Yes, I am setting up Apoca for the next Xanth novel, #47, *Apoca Lips*. I just couldn't resist that pun. She may or may not be the protagonist (that is the viewpoint character). Sometimes that changes at the last moment. It did for the present novel: I had planned on Prince Ion, but then realized that Vinia would be better, as she observed him, and she came through splendidly. Sometimes a minor character watching the action does better than the main one. Sometimes the minor one becomes major herself. Writing has its own rules that the writers don't always properly understand. Um, no, I'm not sure that Nimbus Nickelpede observing Apoca would make a good protagonist. Yes, I can tell you the man who comes to claim Apoca. He is Prince Nolan Naga, the son of Nalda Naga and Mela Merwoman. Remember, Mela is the one who accidentally freed Princess Ida from the crystal, which really started this story, way back when. Nolan is fascinated with the color plaid, because his mother's plaid panties contributed to his genesis, and he has plaid hair. Apoca's hair can be plaid when she has mixed emotions, so naturally they are meant for each other. I trust you appreciate the fine logic that goes into the genesis of a Xanth novel. Critics don't, for some reason.

Now into more serious material. My wife was declining in 2019, and I needed some distraction. I considered writing more stories, or a novelette, or novella, and I had ideas for them, but my mood just wasn't in them. So I thought why not try a chapter or three of the next Xanth novel? I had scheduled it for writing after the turn of the year, beginning 2020, but I could do a bit of it early. So on AwGhost 8, 2019 (remember, I use the Ogre Months here: they are more descriptive), I set up the directory or folder for *Crystal* with my working files. Next day it disappeared, as the computer had swallowed it, and I had to make up a new one. Then the first one reappeared. This is the kind of magic computers like to perform, just because they can. On the tenth I started writing.

I have received many fan letters telling me how important Xanth is in giving readers a refuge when their mundane lives are fouled up. Guess what: that works for me, too. When I'm in Xanth, I am not worrying so much about a troubled home life. The novel moved well. One chapter, two chapters, three. I loved the princesses' splash party on Cloud Nine. AwGhost passed, and SapTimber, the way ahead opening before me as I traveled it.

When I was about halfway through it, when Vinia was getting to know Ghorgeous Ghost, my wife took a turn for the worse. In fact just after midnight OctOgre 3 she died. She was eighty-two. Now it was my own grief that I needed to cope with. So I took a month off to read the six books on handling grief that our daughter bought me, I attended the local hospice bereavement meetings, and I wrote a novelette-length history of our marriage titled "My Rose with Thorns." Piers and Cam, from her maiden initials Carol Ann Marble, together for a bit over sixty-three years. It wasn't a perfect marriage, but then what real marriage is, outside of fantasy? It was good enough, and if I could have waved a magic wand and saved her, I would have. But this is drear Mundania; no such magic here. She had supported me in my wild dream to become a published writer, and she even went to work to earn our living so that I could stay home and write full time. That was when, after eight years of trying, I finally did make my first sale. For all of $20. But it was proof that I could do it, thanks to Cam. Chances are that you would not be reading this book now if it had not been for her. You may, if you wish, remember her by the Xanth title she suggested, *Fire Sail*. So she is in Xanth in her fashion. After that month off, I returned here to Xanth, and it continued sustaining me, and I completed the novel in DisMember 2019, the month before I had meant to start it. Probably after the turn of the year I'll start writing the next.

How is life otherwise? Not bad. Cam had managed our accounts, and we did not waste the money earned during my bestselling days of yore, so we lived on the little tree farm that we own, with no debts and a secure situation. Our daughter, Cheryl, is here to take care of the myriad details death in the family generates, and that really helps me cope. I can't say I am happy, but I am looking toward the future and trust that things will improve as I learn to handle life without Cam.

Now a note on the credits. I try to use puns and ideas from new suggestors before using more from prior suggestors, and try to credit all that I use. But in this time of personal grief I find myself making errors and omissions. I am coping as well as I can. I hope I haven't missed any but can't be sure. So if your suggestion is used here, and you aren't credited, please let me know and I will give you the credit in whatever the next novel is, inadequate as that may be.

Credits:

Rescuing the crystallized princesses—Alex Ewida

Baby changing table; chick magnet; girl tattoo on dragon; Knight of the Living Dead; reflection mental as well as physical—Richard Van Fossan

Email; Were Big Foot; because I said so—Crystal Farmer

Magic marker—Douglas Brown

Spring of Forbidden Love—Clayton Overstreet

Paradox; webcam—Misty Zaebst

Looking daggers; stink eye—Mary Rashford

Sin-seer—Richard Davenport

Weird mare—Cleta Darnell

Badge-hers, Badge-hims—Ann Marie Mohrmann

Fire Cloud; the Can-Can Can—Bill Seeley

Reverse glass—Nicole Valicia Thompson-Andrews

Mnemonic plague—Jeremie Maehr

Cleaning a dirty construction pencil—Jason D. Shepherd

Bedbug—David D'Champ

Pasteurize; Lettuce as "Let us"—Dale Davis

Talent of omission—Stephanie Florin

O'Clock setting local time—John Knoderer

Promise Ring—Emilio Ross

Thank Q; energy crystals for gnomes to mine—Timothy Bruening

Lie briery with briers—Scott Latini

Tony—Tony Massey

And credit to my proofreaders, Scott M. Ryan, John Knoderer, and Doug Harter. If you want to know more of me, you can check my website at www.HiPiers.com, where I do a monthly blog-type column, have news of my new projects, express my ongoing opinionations, and maintain an ongoing survey of electronic publishers for the benefit of aspiring writers.

Until next time . . .

About the Author

Piers Anthony is one of the world's most popular fantasy writers, and a *New York Times*-bestselling author twenty-one times over. His Xanth novels have been read and loved by millions of readers around the world, and he daily receives hundreds of letters from his devoted fans. In addition to the Xanth series, Anthony is the author of many other bestselling works. He lives in Inverness, Florida.

THE XANTH NOVELS

FROM OPEN ROAD MEDIA

OPEN ROAD

INTEGRATED MEDIA

OPEN ROAD

INTEGRATED MEDIA

Find a full list of our authors and
titles at www.openroadmedia.com

FOLLOW US
@OpenRoadMedia